W9-CCK-962

DISCARDED

TO THE MOON AND BACK

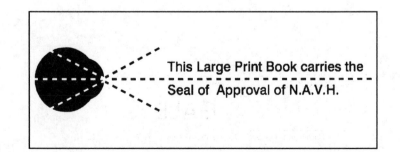

This Large Print Book carries the
Seal of Approval of N.A.V.H.

THE BAXTER FAMILY

To the Moon and Back

Karen Kingsbury

WHEELER PUBLISHING
A part of Gale, a Cengage Company

GALE
A Cengage Company

Farmington Hills, Mich • San Francisco • New York • Waterville, Maine
Meriden, Conn • Mason, Ohio • Chicago

Copyright © 2018 by Karen Kingsbury.
Scripture quotations are taken from the Holy Bible, New International Version®, NIV®. Copyright © 1973, 1978, 1984, 2011 by Biblica, Inc®. Used by permission of Zondervan. All rights reserved worldwide. www.zondervan.com. The "NIV" and "New International Version" are trademarks registered in the United States Patent and Trademark Office by Biblica, Inc®.
Wheeler Publishing, a part of Gale, a Cengage Company.

ALL RIGHTS RESERVED
This book is a work of fiction. Any references to historical events, real people, or real places are used fictitiously. Other names, characters, places, and events are products of the author's imagination, and any resemblance to actual events or places or persons, living or dead, is entirely coincidental.
Wheeler Publishing Large Print Hardcover.
The text of this Large Print edition is unabridged.
Other aspects of the book may vary from the original edition.
Set in 16 pt. Plantin.

LIBRARY OF CONGRESS CIP DATA ON FILE.
CATALOGUING IN PUBLICATION FOR THIS BOOK
IS AVAILABLE FROM THE LIBRARY OF CONGRESS

ISBN-13: 978-1-4328-5265-8 (hardcover)

Published in 2018 by arrangement with Howard Books, an imprint of Simon & Schuster, Inc.

Printed in the United States of America
1 2 3 4 5 6 7 22 21 20 19 18

To Donald:

Well . . . we are ending our second year as empty nesters. I never liked that term. And I can tell you now with all my heart that there's been nothing empty about the last few years. They've been full of beautiful walks and meaningful talks, nights when we randomly jump into the car and spend an evening with Kelsey and Kyle, little Hudson, and now our newest grandbaby. We play tennis and Ping-Pong and hang out with our wonderful friends. And yes, we miss having our family all together every day. But when they come home the celebrating never ends. What I mean is, I've loved raising our kids with you, and now I love this season, too. God has brought us through so many pages in our story. The Baxter family came to life while we were raising our kids. When they told stories around the family dinner table, we were doing the same. And when their kids auditioned for Christian theater, our kids were singing the same songs. Our family is — and always will be — inexorably linked with the Baxter family. So thank you for creating a world where our love and life and family and faith were so beautiful I could do nothing but write about it. So that some far-off day when we're old and the voices of our many grandchildren fill the house, we can pull out books like this one and remember. Every single beautiful moment. I love you.

To Kyle:

You will always be the young man we prayed for, the one we believed God for when it came to our precious only daughter. You love Kelsey so well, and you are such a great daddy to Hudson and your newest little one. I literally thank God every day for you and for the friendship all of us share. Thank you for bringing us constant joy. We pray and believe that all the world will one day be changed for the better because of your music, your love and your life.

To Kelsey:

What an amazing season this has been,

watching as you went from being the best mommy ever for Hudson, and now as you've welcomed your second precious baby. Little Hudson is so happy, and I know that Baby Nolan is, too. Your home is full of love and joy, peace and patience and God's Holy Spirit. Because you and Kyle have intentionally welcomed the Lord into your home. What a beautiful time for all of us! Hudson is strong and kind and joyful, with a depth that tells all of us that some way, somehow, God is going to use him. I can't wait to see all the ways God pours His gifts into your newest little angel, also. I believe God will continue to use your precious family as a very bright light . . . and I know that one day all the world will look to you and Kyle as an example of how to love well. Love you with all my heart, honey.

To Tyler:

I remember that long-ago day when you were a ten-year-old and you said, "Mom, someday I'm going to write music and make movies. But I think I'm also going to write books in my spare time. Like you do!" And now, my talented son, that's exactly what you're doing. How amazing is it that we have the privilege of writing together?

Already we've had one screenplay — *Maggie's Miracle* — show up on the Hallmark Channel, and now a series of books about the Baxter children. I always knew God had gifted you with great talent. But I never would've imagined the ways God would work it all together. You're still songwriting, still writing original screenplays and dreaming of making movies. But now you're writing books in your spare time, too. I love it! God has great things ahead, and as always I am most thankful for this front-row seat. Oh, and for the occasional evening when you stop by for dinner and finish the night playing the piano. You are a very great blessing, Ty. Love you always.

To Sean:

Later this year you will finish your time at Liberty University, earning a degree and growing in your faith and strength as a man. You have listened to God, Sean. You have taken the difficult moments of your earlier years and turned them into strengths, and for that your dad and I are so proud of you! From the first day we held you, we knew your spirit was bright. You love God and people with a passion and joy that defied your first five years. Yet we agreed with you that it was time to take your faith to another level. I am convinced God has amazing plans ahead for you, Son. I love you forever.

To Josh:

You are out on your own, finding your way. What a blessing to know that wherever you go, you take us with you . . . and Jesus with you. Always remember that having a relationship with Him is the most important gift you will ever give your family. You belong to Him, Josh. You always have. As you lead your family in the years to come, as you walk out your faith together, walk humbly. And just know how much we love you. We are here for you, always.

To EJ:

What a tremendous time this is for you, EJ. You are doing so well at Liberty University, so excited about the career in film-making you have chosen. Isn't it something how God knew — even all those years ago when you first entered our family — that you would need to be with people who loved God and loved each other . . . but also people who loved the power of storytelling. I'm so excited about the future, and the ways God will use your gifts to intersect with the gifts of so many others in our family. Maybe we should start our own studio — making movies that will change the world for God. Whatever the future holds, remember that your most powerful hour of the day is the one you give to Jesus. Stay in His word. Pray always. I love you.

To Austin:

I'm so grateful I can see you when I travel to Liberty University to teach. You are tall and strong and a godly presence on that campus. But not only that. You are a loyal friend with a very deep heart. During breaks we will continue to have many happy times together. But I still miss you in the everydayness, Austin. You have been such a light in our home, our miracle boy. Our overcomer. You are my youngest, and no question the hardest to let go. At times the quiet here is so . . . quiet. Even with your dad's jokes and two little grand-children in our lives. So . . . while you're at Liberty, on nights when you lie awake in your dorm, just know that we have cher-ished every moment of raising you. And we are still here. We always will be. Love you forever, Aus.

And to God Almighty,
the Author of Life, who has — for now —
blessed me with these.

THE BAXTER FAMILY

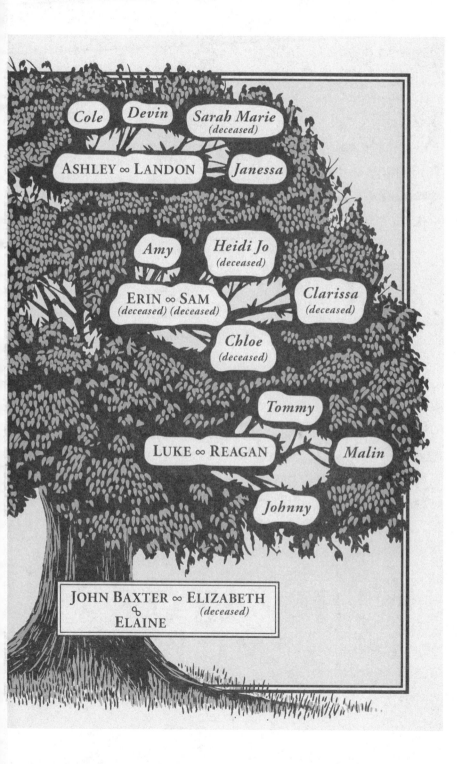

THE BAXTER FAMILY

This book is part of the Baxter family collection, but it can be read as a stand-alone novel. Find out more about the Baxter family at the back of this book. Whether you've loved the Baxters for a decade, or you're finding them for the first time — *To the Moon and Back* is for you.

1

The roots of the tree had taken residence in Amy Hogan's heart, where they wouldn't let go. She could see it in her mind, feel the rough bark against her fingertips. The way its branches spread out like the hands of God. Amy had never seen the tree, but she would soon.

The Survivor Tree.

A hundred-year-old American elm growing out of what used to be a parking lot in front of the Alfred P. Murrah Federal Building in the heart of Oklahoma City. Now its boughs shaded the highest part of the memorial site. The place where an evil man parked a moving truck loaded with fertilizer and blew the federal building to bits.

Amy was only twelve. She wasn't alive when the Oklahoma City bombing happened way back in 1995.

She had no idea what it was like to be part of the terrible morning when the truck bomb ripped through the building that April 19. She didn't know the specific aftermath of twisted metal and broken bricks and battered men, women and children that made up the imagery of that horrific day when 168 people died.

But she could imagine the screaming and anguish; she could almost feel the glass in her skin, the blood on her body. She could picture the looks on the faces of the survivors.

Because Amy was a survivor, too.

And that's why the tree meant so much to her, why she could hardly wait for spring break to begin. When her family would take a road trip to a dozen different destinations. But one of them would be the Oklahoma City National Memorial.

It all started with a photo Amy had found.

She lived with her Aunt Ashley and Uncle Landon, and their kids. Her cousins, Cole, Devin and Janessa. In every possible way this family had taken her in as one of their own. Sometimes she even thought of her Aunt Ashley as her mom. Because her aunt loved her that much.

One of the ways Aunt Ashley proved it was how she had set up Amy's room. In the corner was a chair that faced the window. So Amy could sit and talk to God about her family in heaven — any time she wanted. Next to the chair, against the wall, was a bookcase full of everything that reminded Amy of her childhood.

A teddy bear her daddy gave her when they went to the fair the year before the car accident. A small treasure chest full of notes her mom had written while Amy was growing up. Notes just for her. Because taking time to put her feelings on paper was important to her mother. That's what Aunt Ashley said.

Amy took a break from packing for the trip. She sat on the bench at the end of her bed and stared at the bookcase. There were also a dozen framed photographs scattered on the different shelves. Photos of Amy and her mom, Amy and her dad. One of both her parents and her all snuggled up on the couch on an ordinary day.

Back when they thought they had forever.

And then there was Amy's favorite photo. The one of her whole family. Her parents and three sisters and her. They had been getting pictures taken for their Christmas card and the photographer had already snapped a million shots. Amy stared at the image across the room and let it fill the broken places in her heart one more time.

She could still hear her mother telling

their story. How her mommy and daddy had been praying for a child when a social worker told them about Amy. Of course, Amy was just a little baby back then. But her birth mother had been a drug addict, and at the last minute the woman decided to keep Amy. That's when God brought Heidi Jo along. The littlest olive-skinned sister in the group. But as soon as her parents adopted Heidi Jo, they got a call from the social worker. The woman was on drugs again and she had been arrested. Which meant not only Amy but also her two older sisters were available for adoption.

Her parents were thrilled and pretty much overnight they went from having no children to raising four little girls. Clarissa, Chloe, Amy and Heidi Jo. The first three all tan with pale blond hair. They were the closest four sisters anyone ever knew.

Until the accident.

Amy stood and walked to the bookcase. A layer of dust dimmed the black frame. Amy hated dust. She picked up the photo and lightly brushed the edges clean, then she looked again at the people she missed so much. Her mom and dad were on either side of Amy and her sisters. The girls had their arms around each other and they were laughing. Laughing so hard that this picture had turned out to be the best that day.

For a few seconds Amy closed her eyes. The sound of her family still filled her heart. Still made her smile on days when she wasn't sure she'd survive the missing and hurting. The terrible losing. She blinked and her eyes focused on Clarissa. It was Clarissa, her oldest sister, who had said something funny that day. Something about her mouth feeling frozen or how she was glad she wasn't a model because of all the smiling.

The details weren't as clear as they used to be.

Whatever Clarissa had said, the day instantly became one of their favorites ever. Amy touched the glass over her sister's face. It was good to have these memories. That was something Aunt Ashley talked about a lot. Memories were God's way of saying something had actually happened. And it mattered a great deal.

Amy returned the frame to its spot in the bookcase. Then she stooped down. The bottom shelf was filled with eight photo albums. All the ones Amy's parents had ever put together. When everything from Amy's old home in Texas was gone through and sorted, after the furniture and the house had been sold, her Aunt Ashley had collected a few boxes of things for Amy.

She would always be grateful to her aunt for saving them. Every item and picture mattered. They were all she had left of her old life. Before the car accident that took everyone else in her family home to heaven. Everyone but her.

Yes, she understood what it meant to be a survivor.

Amy pulled the fourth book from the bottom shelf and took it to her chair by the window. She flipped to the back page and looked for the photo that had started her interest in the Oklahoma City bombing.

Before they'd adopted Amy and her sisters, her parents had taken a trip to Oklahoma. Amy's daddy had cousins in Oklahoma, and one of them had hosted a family reunion.

The album told the story. There were pictures of Amy's parents with people Amy didn't know or couldn't remember ever meeting. Most of them had reached out when the accident happened. A few of them had written letters since then. Her daddy's parents were dead, but his great-aunt had started a scholarship account for Amy. So she would always know how much they cared about her. They came to visit every summer for a few days.

Amy scanned the images. There were photos of sunsets and scenery, her mom and dad happy and in love. But the picture that caught hold of Amy's heart was one of her mama. While they were on their trip, her parents had gone to the Oklahoma City National Memorial. In the photo her mother was standing at the base of the Survivor Tree, her hands on its thick trunk, eyes lifted up to its beautiful branches.

Amy read her mother's words, written next to the photo: *"Me at the survivor tree. With God, there is always a way to survive. I love this living reminder."*

Amy ran her fingers over the image and then lightly over her mother's words. Her mama was tender. That's what Aunt Ashley said. She had a heart deeper than the ocean. No wonder she and Amy's daddy went to the memorial site while they were in Oklahoma.

Amy hadn't heard of national memorials until last fall, when her history class was studying them. But the idea filled her heart. Places of recognition and honor for very great losses suffered by Americans.

A few weeks after that lesson in class, Amy was looking through her photo albums when she saw the picture of her mother at the Survivor Tree. She Googled what had happened that day.

That's when she found the history of the Oklahoma City bombing. And the tree.

Amy looked out the window at the storm clouds drifting closer. The tree had been there before anyone thought about putting a federal building on the site. When it came time to pave a parking lot, someone must've decided the tree was too pretty to cut down.

So they built around it.

And that's how the tree stayed for lots and lots of years. Decades, really. Right up until the bomb went off. The bomb was so big it had something called shock waves. It meant that cars parked nearby exploded and the tree caught fire. Pieces of glass and metal from the blast shot out and struck the old elm's base. Most of its branches were cut off by flying debris. When the dust settled, all that was left was a smoldering, blackened, barren trunk.

In the weeks that followed, the people cleaning up after the bomb intended to cut the old tree down. The elm was dead, they figured. Of course it was dead. But they left it standing because of the glass and metal lodged in its bark. The way the pieces were positioned told investigators what they needed to know about the location of the bomb.

So since the tree trunk was evidence, it stayed.

Then something beautiful happened. On the one-year anniversary, survivors of the bombing and family members of the victims, as well as firefighters and police officers, all gathered at the old parking lot to remember.

That's when a police officer noticed something amazing about the tree. Sprigs of green were coming from the bark. The tree was alive! Horticulture experts were called in to tend to the tree and help nurse it back to health. The glass and metal were removed from the trunk and the tree was fed good nutrition. One year led to another and its branches began to grow again.

Today it was one of the biggest, most beautiful trees in Oklahoma City. Each spring workers at the memorial swept up seeds from the boughs. The seeds were grown into saplings, and every year those little baby trees were given out to people who wanted them.

People who had survived something.

People like Amy.

It was just as her mama had said all those years ago. The Oklahoma City tree was proof that with God, there was always a way to survive.

So Amy had gotten an idea, and a few months ago she shared it with her aunt. Maybe they could go to the memorial site for spring break, and maybe Amy could get one of the saplings.

She could plant it out back near her Grandma Elizabeth's flower garden, and it would grow and give shade and comfort and a reminder of the family she'd lost. Then Amy would have her own Survivor Tree.

For spring break, they had been planning to visit Branson, Missouri, and Silver Dollar City and spend time on a houseboat on Table Rock Lake. But her Aunt Ashley and Uncle Landon talked about it and decided, yes, they would go a little further and visit the Oklahoma City National Memorial, too.

They were going with Amy's Aunt Kari and Uncle Ryan and their family. Two cars, caravan-style. Aunt Ashley said that on the day they'd visit the memorial it would just be the two aunts and the older kids. The younger kids would go with the uncles to Frontier City for rides and stuff.

The memorial would be too sad for them.

But it wouldn't be too sad for Amy. She wanted to be there, wanted to see the empty chairs and tall gates that had been built in honor of the victims. She could hardly wait to stand next to the tree and feel its trunk against her hands.

The way her mama had felt it.

Because the tree's roots really had taken hold of her. And somehow, she knew that God was letting her go there, not only to see the tree. But to learn something from Him.

Something about surviving.

2

The guys made the decision to leave at six in the morning that Saturday. Ashley Baxter Blake wasn't thrilled with the idea, but by the time they were on the road the sense of adventure had gripped them all. Even her.

The older kids had agreed to turn off their cell phones until after dinner each day. So they used walkie-talkies to keep up with their cousins in the other car. The old-fashioned way, as the kids had said earlier.

"We're stopping for gas at the next exit, right, Dad?" Cole shifted forward and looked at Landon.

"Yes, sir! Next exit!" Landon grinned.

Ashley could only admire him. Landon had always loved road trips with the family. These were his favorite vacations. He'd told Ashley that a thousand times.

Cole sat in the seat directly behind Ashley. He grabbed the walkie-talkie from the cup holder and held it to his mouth. "Stop-

28

ping for gas at the next exit." Cole loved the handheld device. "Roger?"

A static sound came from the speaker. Then RJ's voice. "Roger! Over."

"Over and out." Cole leaned in to the space between the two front seats. He looked at Ashley. "This thing is amazing. I can't believe you talked like this in the olden days."

Ashley looked at Landon. *"Olden days?"* She mouthed the question.

"Hey now!" Landon shook his head. "We're not that old, Cole."

"I know." Cole patted both of their shoulders. "Just teasing."

They'd already been on the road for two hours. Ashley watched Landon pull off at the next exit. Her husband was more handsome than ever. He wore a white T-shirt and dark jeans, his arms and face tanned from his daily jog, his dark hair short to his head. The muscles in his shoulders were as defined as they were back when the two of them got married.

Ashley flipped the visor down and used the mirror to check on the kids. Devin was in the seat next to Cole, and Amy and Janessa were in the back row. Last night when they were loading up the car, Ashley had pulled Amy aside and taken her to a quiet bench in the backyard. Ashley was glad for the moment. She had been meaning to ask her niece if she felt nervous about the trip.

After all, it was on a road trip from Texas to Bloomington that Amy's family was rear-ended by a semi truck. For weeks now Amy had seemed excited about the adventure ahead — especially seeing the Oklahoma memorial site. But Ashley thought she should hear from her niece on the subject. Just in case.

"Are you worried?" They had settled in on the bench and Ashley had taken hold of Amy's hand. "About the drive?"

Amy hesitated for a minute. "Sometimes." Her voice was quiet. "When I really think about it." She looked across the field toward the stream that ran behind the old Baxter house. Then she turned to Ashley. "The Bible says to live is Christ. To die is gain." Her smile didn't quite fill her face. "I believe that."

"Me, too." The Scripture had helped Ashley learn to live in such a way that she didn't feel heartbroken for Amy every time she saw her. All of them had learned to live normal lives again. Almost. Ashley felt tears well in her eyes. "Just look how many people we have in heaven. Right?"

"Yes." Amy's expression softened. She

lifted her eyes to the starry sky. "When I think about that, I have nothing to worry about."

Her wisdom was breathtaking.

Ashley watched Amy now, curled up with her pillow in the third row. She and Janessa had been sleeping for the past hour. Before that they were playing I Spy and giggling over things they'd spotted along the drive.

Ashley flipped the visor up and exhaled. She shifted so she could see Landon better. "Amy's come so far."

"She has." Landon smiled. He kept his voice low. "Thanks to God . . . and you."

"And you." Ashley reached for his hand. They had all helped with Amy's healing. "You're wonderful to her."

Landon squeezed her hand as he turned in to the gas station. Ashley's sister Kari and her husband, Ryan Taylor, and their three children had followed them the whole morning. Ryan towed a pair of Jet Skis behind his truck, and he pulled the entire rig up to the pump across the way. It was supposed to be unseasonably warm this week. But they had brought wetsuits just in case.

Fifteen minutes later they were on the road again. During the next stretch, Cole chose the music and everyone sang along.

There was Colton Dixon's "Through All of It" and Danny Gokey's latest hit, along with songs from Francesca Battistelli, Newsboys, Natalie Grant, MercyMe, and Matthew West.

At one point they were all singing at the top of their lungs. "Hello, my name is . . . Child of the One True King. I've been saved, I've been changed, I have been set free!"

Ashley grinned at Landon. Most of them weren't the greatest singers. Amy probably had the best voice in the family. But the sound was joyful all the same and it made the final leg of the trip fly by.

They reached Branson just after three o'clock and checked into their hotel. Then both families climbed back into the cars and drove the short distance to the beach. They laid out their blankets not far from the boat launch.

Half an hour later the Jet Skis were flying across the lake. Landon and Ryan took the first round while the kids cheered them on from the shore. Ashley and Kari settled into chairs near the blankets.

"What a great day." Kari looked at her and took a deep breath. "Easier than when the kids were little."

"Right?" Ashley laughed. "Diaper changes

at gas stations. I don't miss that."

Kari stared at the kids still jumping around on the sand. "So true. But still . . . I sometimes long for those days." She blinked a few times, like she was just seeing their kids for the first time in awhile. "When did they get so old?"

Usually Ashley tried not to think about that fact. This was Cole's junior year, and already he was talking about colleges. Liberty University was at the top of his list. He had heard about it from Connor Flanigan, the son of their good friends. Every time she thought about Cole moving away, Ashley's eyes filled with tears.

"Live in the moment, appreciate every day." Ashley watched Cole pick up Janessa and run toward the water as she shrieked with delight. A smile filled Ashley's words. "God gives us only so many days with our families. As long as we know that, we can live without regret."

"Agreed." Kari stared toward the water. "Even when it seems they're growing up right before our eyes."

Ashley appreciated the time with Kari. Sure they saw each other at family dinners and holidays, at Clear Creek Community Church each Sunday and on the occasional day at the nail salon. But there was something very special about having a week to-gether.

Kari stretched her legs. "I wish the others could've come. I really thought Brooke might."

"It should be a law — all spring breaks must be on the same week." Ashley uttered a light laugh. "I guess that's not very likely."

Kari shaded her eyes and nodded toward the kids. "They love playing together."

"If they don't kill themselves!" Ashley laughed. Devin and RJ were running up and down the shore, trying to push each other into the water. Just at that moment they both wound up in the lake, splashing and dunking each other. Ashley sighed. "At least it's all in fun."

Kari laughed. "Boys." They were quiet for a moment. "What's the story with the new movie for Dayne?"

The setting sun was warm against Ashley's shoulders. Perfect after the chilly start to spring. She filled her lungs with the fresh lakeside air. "Dayne said he'll produce it, and he and Katy will star in it."

"Really?" Kari looked surprised. "They haven't done that in years."

"They miss it." Ashley smiled at her sister. "They think this one will be big. Not just at the box office. Dayne said the message is just what our country needs. It's called *Shades of Blue*. About healing after abortion."

"Wow." Kari faced the water again. "Powerful. I'm glad they're working together."

Ashley was happy for Dayne and Katy, too. "I only hope they don't stay in L.A. too long. Their kids love Indiana."

"True. They're crazy about their cousins." Kari grinned.

Ashley stood and stretched. "Come on. Let's join the kids."

"I was just thinking that." Kari smiled.

The sand felt warm on Ashley's toes. Everything about Table Rock Lake reminded her of Lake Monroe back home and the dozens of beautiful times their family had shared there. She glanced at Kari. "One of these days we'll get all five of us and our families together for a family vacation. Somewhere at the beach. Florida, maybe." She paused. "Even if we need to plan it a year in advance."

"I agree." Kari smiled. They were almost to the shoreline. "Can you imagine? So fun!"

Cole was the first to run to them, a football in his hands. "I'm next on the Jet Skis. Jessie, too." He tossed the ball to Ashley. "You and Aunt Kari should play catch."

Kari laughed. "Last time I caught a football I jammed my finger." She shook her head. "It's Frisbee for me."

Devin must've heard the conversation. He was Cole's Mini-Me, an almost exact, younger, blond replica of his older brother. His eyes lit up. "I'll play with you, Mom!"

Ashley wasn't very good at throwing a ball, but for Devin she would try. They found a spot a few yards from the others and Ashley gave it her best effort.

"Mom!" Devin snagged the ball from the air. "Look how good you are! You've been practicing!"

Everyone laughed, and Jessie and Annie high-fived. "Yay for Aunt Ashley!" Jessie jumped around, her hands in the air. "You should play for the Colts!" She skipped closer and fist-bumped Ashley. "I'll be the cheerleader!"

This was what Ashley loved about vacations together. No clocks. No reason to leave the beach. Just fun and family and laughter. And on this occasion, even a little football.

Ryan and Landon pulled up on the Jet Skis and turned the machines over to Cole and Jessie. Landon came up the beach and watched Ashley. The sun glistened on his bare arms as he brushed the water from his shorts.

Ashley could feel his admiration without looking at him. She caught the ball, repositioned her fingers on the laces and threw it back to Devin.

"See, Dad?" Devin grinned. "Mom's crazy good at this!"

Landon closed the gap between them and kissed her cheek. He winked at Devin. "I taught her everything I know."

Amy was building a sand castle with RJ. She yelled out her approval, too. "You taught her good, Uncle Landon! Just watch her!"

Ashley held on to the moment. The sun almost to the horizon, the sky still warm and clear and blue. Diamonds of light dancing on the lake and her family gathered around her. Everyone whole and healthy and happy.

Even Amy.

An hour later they were done for the day. The sky was nearly dark as they loaded the Jet Skis onto Kari and Ryan's trailer.

When they were back in their SUV and the kids were buckled in behind them, Landon smiled at her. "You really were impressive with that football."

She could feel the sparkle in her eyes, the

way she felt it so often around Landon. "I did know a little before I met you." She stifled a laugh. "Truth be told."

He chuckled and fixed his eyes on the road ahead. "Whatever happened to the idea of your dad and Elaine joining us?"

"They talked about it." Ashley would've loved that. There were only so many chances for her dad and his wife to join them for a spring break like this. She turned to see Landon better. "Dad had a conference at the hospital." She thought about how healthy her father was, how committed to the field of medicine, to helping people. "He might be retired, but that doesn't stop him. The younger doctors need someone to teach them, you know."

Landon smiled and gave a slight shake of his head. "I want to be like him when I grow up."

"Mmm." Ashley rested her head against the seat. "Me, too."

Back at the hotel, they got ready and met in the lobby for dinner. After they ate, everyone gathered in the hotel's private theater, adjacent to the restaurant. That night both families filled the place and Amy sat next to Ashley as they watched Disney's *Tangled.*

Ashley took a mental snapshot of the evening.

If today were a painting, the most obvious setting would be the scene from earlier, her family playing at the beach. But Ashley felt more drawn to paint the one here, inside the theater. Not the movie screen or the seats or the entire group of them. But just Amy and her, and the fact that even at twelve years old, Amy still felt comfortable to hold Ashley's hand.

That simple gesture was proof that Ashley had become more mom than aunt to the girl. Even if Ashley would never replace the mother her sister Erin had been. Still, Amy's hand in her own assured Ashley that however much healing was still ahead, they were on the right path.

And God, in all His mercy, was with them.

They spent the first four days of the trip in Branson, playing on the beach and letting the kids take turns on the Jet Skis. A couple times, Ashley and Kari even took the little ones, Janessa and Annie, for a slow ride along the shore. Then in the late afternoons they'd head into town.

Each day was a different adventure. They played mini golf and rode go-karts and toured the Ripley's Believe It or Not! museum. All the kids loved the room with the slanted floors and the mirrors that made

Cole look two feet taller than Landon.

"You wish." Devin laughed.

Landon raised his brow. "It's not too far-fetched." He put his arm around Cole's shoulders. "Cole's about to pass me up. Any day now."

By the end of the four days, Ashley had already taken hundreds of pictures — some with her camera, some with her heart — memories to hold close years from now.

When the kids were grown and gone.

As for the pictures on her camera, once they were back home she would make an album of their fun times this week. Each of the kids would get a copy. Photo books were among Ashley's favorite ways to create proof of the years gone by.

Wednesday afternoon they packed up their vehicles and headed to Oklahoma City. Tomorrow was the anniversary of the bombing. The day Amy wanted to be at the memorial. The day they gave out saplings from the Survivor Tree. After they checked into their hotel rooms and once the kids were tucked in and asleep, Landon hit the lights.

In the darkness, Landon reached for her hand and rolled onto his side. He spoke close to her face. "I love you, Ashley. Everything about you."

"Thanks." She slid closer and kissed him on his lips, quiet so they wouldn't wake the kids, sleeping in the bed beside them. "I love you, too."

Landon paused, and even in the stillness Ashley could tell something was weighing on him.

"What are you thinking?" She kept her voice quiet.

"About Amy's sapling." He put his hand on Ashley's cheek. "I've been praying she gets one. There's no guarantee."

"I know." She thought for a minute. Then she whispered, "We'll get there right when it opens. That should help."

Landon kissed her again and another time. Then he settled in on his side of the bed. "You'll have to tell me all about it."

"I will. Good night, love."

"Good night."

Ashley rolled onto her back and stared toward the window. Their new hotel was in the heart of Oklahoma City, not far from the memorial. Her eyes were adjusting to the dark, and now she could see lights from adjacent hotels and buildings.

God, please . . . let Amy get a sapling. I have no idea how we'll care for it on vacation, but we'll figure it out. It's just . . . it matters so much to her.

Ashley lay there, silent. Waiting. Sometimes when she prayed she heard from God. A Scripture or something He had been laying on her heart. But not tonight. Tonight there was just the soft breathing of the kids sleeping and the nearness of Landon. She closed her eyes. God would come through on this. Ashley was sure.

Because if anyone deserved their own Survivor Tree, it was Amy.

3

Thomas "Brady" Bradshaw had been counting down the days for a month. The way he always did when springtime rolled around. For the past few weeks, his work as a firefighter for Oklahoma City had taken second seat to his memories and heartache, his confusion and anger. And all of it led to this one day. This one morning.

The anniversary of the Oklahoma City bombing.

Brady had the day off. He pulled his motorcycle into a spot near the back of the memorial parking lot and killed the engine. For a long time he just sat there, helmet and sunglasses still in place.

He was twenty-eight now. Twenty-three years removed from the little boy he had been when the bomb went off. The sky overhead was clear today. Some years it rained. A few years had seen storms and even a tornado warning or two. Brady could see today's events as clearly as if they'd already happened.

It was the same every anniversary.

People would stream through the front gates, quiet and somber. Some of them tourists, curious people passing through, remembering for the first time in years the terrible terrorist attack that had happened here. In America's heartland. They would walk the grounds and take pictures. Look at the exhibits in the museum and stop by the gift shop. A mug and a postcard later and they'd be on their way. Off to explore the nearest park or Frontier City.

Brady released his grip on the handlebars and stared at the memorial. The people here today wouldn't all be tourists. Some would be connected to the bombing. They might've lost a friend or a family member. Or they may have survived the attack from inside the building. For those people — like Brady — the anniversary of the bombing was reverent. A day they would never forget.

But only a small number were really anything like him. For Brady, the Oklahoma City bombing was personal.

He shoved up the sleeves on his navy sweatshirt and stared at his forearms. When people looked at him they didn't see the scars. They saw the guy who had done a

season on the *Survivor* show. A guy modeling agencies once fought over.

Brady never wanted any part of it.

He didn't do *Survivor* to become famous.
Battling fires in Oklahoma City was his passion, not standing in front of a camera. He
only did *Survivor* because he was one. And
if anyone could prove it, he could. Never
mind that he lost in the second round. The
show couldn't hold a candle to real survival.

The way it felt twenty-three years ago,
when he was buried in the rubble of the
Alfred P. Murrah Federal Building.

A quick look at his arms and he could see
them. Jagged scars that crisscrossed his
forearms. Sure, they had faded, but they
were still there. He ran his hands over the
marks and looked up again. Yes, today
would be the same as every anniversary that
had come before it.

He would go through the gate with the
others and make his way to the outdoor
area. In utter silence he would find the chair
with his mother's name and he would leave
her a single long-stemmed rose. Then he
would place his hand on the trunk of the
Survivor Tree and he would try to separate
his memories from the long-ago news accounts of the day. The ones still up on
YouTube.

Brady took a deep breath and removed his helmet. He set it in the compartment at the back of his bike and pulled the paper bag with the rose from the same spot. Then he headed for the front gate.

Of course, there was one more reason he came every year. At least for the last eleven years. The reason was simple. The chance that he might see her. Brady clenched his jaw and stood a little straighter.

Her name was Jenna.

He didn't know her last name. She was a girl he'd met only once, here at the memorial site on the twelfth anniversary of the bombing. Back when they were both only seventeen. Back then she'd been a wisp of a girl with forever long legs and the face of actress Emma Stone. At least that's how he remembered her.

And Brady remembered her every day.

Jenna. The only girl in the world who would ever fully understand him.

Brady paid his admission and thought the same thing he did every year: Survivors should get in free. He shoved his free hand into the pocket of his black jeans and made his way out back to the field of chairs.

Like every anniversary there were more people here than usual. The noise wasn't soft and reflective, but more an intentional somberness. As if people knew they should be quiet. Respectful. But it was forced. Because they didn't have a million memories clawing and fighting their way to the surface.

The way Brady did.

His sunglasses were still on, where they would stay. No one ever saw Brady Bradshaw cry. He would make sure about that. Also because he didn't want to be noticed. The *Survivor* show had highlighted his history, his connection to the Oklahoma City bombing. Since then occasionally he'd responded to a call and someone would identify him. Dark hair. Tall. Built like a professional quarterback. At least that's how they described him on television.

Whatever. People recognized him. That was fine. Brady liked the people of Oklahoma. They were the family he didn't have. He enjoyed talking to them. Signing the occasional autograph, taking the handful of selfies in a month's time.

Not today.

Her chair was in the third row, somewhere near the middle. Brady moved past the people taking pictures and whispering. Beyond the handful of visitors carrying saplings from the Survivor Tree. No one seemed to notice him as he made his way.

He was as familiar with this walk as if he lived here. And in some ways maybe he did.

Always would.

Three chairs down, and then —

There it was. Her chair. The one with her name etched into it. Proof once again that she had died here on that terrible day. Brady felt the first sting of tears. The routine was the same every year. He set the rose in the vase. Every chair had a vase attached to the side of it.

But not every chair had a rose.

With both hands Brady gripped the edges of the seat. He closed his eyes. There it was. The familiar feeling that came over him, the same one that hit him every anniversary. An aching, desperate, deep sense of protection. As if Brady Bradshaw, strong, tall, broad shoulders, could certainly do something to keep his mother safe.

The way she had done for him that horrible day.

"Mom. I'm here." He choked on the words. Then he ran his fingers over the plate with her name.

Sandra Bradshaw.

Two tears trickled down his cheeks, but Brady ignored them. Almost didn't notice. This was his time to remember. He wasn't in a hurry.

A few photographs of Brady's mother had been collected from their apartment after her death. Brady kept them in a small flip-book in a drawer near his bed.

That was it. Six pictures. The only evidence that his mother had ever existed. Brady thought about the photographs. One was his mom in her first year of college. The year she got pregnant with him. She had blond hair past her shoulders and a graceful, athletic build. She had gone to school on a tennis scholarship.

But that had ended when she found out she was having a baby. Brady had no idea who his father was or why he had abandoned his pretty mom. From what Brady could piece together, his mother hadn't been close with her parents. She had moved in with a few girls and gotten a job waiting tables.

The second picture was of her with two friends, all of them in their restaurant uniforms. In both photos, his mom's eyes were bright and happy. Young and full of life. The rest of the images grew less carefree. Deeper. But whatever the details of her story, Brady could see his mother had loved being a mom. She had loved her boy. Brady was everything to her.

The next four pictures were of the two of

them. Her and him. One when he was hours old, lying in her arms, still in the hospital. Another when he was maybe two. He wore overalls and sat on his mother's hip, him grinning up at her. The next must've been taken at Christmastime when he was maybe four, and the last one was from his fifth birthday. In that photo, his mom stood beside him, her arm around his shoulders while he blew out the candles on what was the last birthday cake she'd ever make.

Yes, Sandra Bradshaw had loved being his mom.

The only other keepsake Brady had was an old weathered children's book. The one his mom had read to him every night at bedtime.

To the Moon and Back.

Brady gripped her chair and let the memories come. There were so few, he had to concentrate. Even then he wasn't sure if they were real or something he imagined. One moment he recalled was of his mom at nighttime. Maybe a few weeks before the bombing.

In the memory, Brady was wearing green race car pajamas. He could see himself, running into his room and hopping on his bed, his mom behind him. It was the clearest real-life picture Brady had. The one he held

50

in his heart. His mother's blond hair wind-blown. Beautiful. Happy. Her eyes bright with laughter.

No hint of the tragedy to come.

"Brady boy, it's time for your story." Her singsong voice had called to him then. It called to him still.

And she was sitting on the bed beside him and opening their favorite book and reading every line, every page. "I love you to the moon and back, Brady. I always will."

He had giggled and laughed and yawned through the story. And she was turning off the light and lowering her voice. "Let's pray to Jesus."

"Yes, Mommy." In his memory it was always *Yes, Mommy.*

And she was praying for God to put His angels around Brady and their little apartment and for God to show him the good plans He had. "You're going to do great things when you grow up, Brady. Very great things."

Her smile had lit up his heart and then she was leaning close and kissing his cheek and tucking him in. Her hands soft against his arms. "I love you, Mommy."

"I love you, too, Brady."

Brady blinked and two more tears slid past his sunglasses and onto her memorial chair.

There were only a handful of other memories. Mainly ones from the building that day. He and his mom had done errands together. Brady hadn't felt good. He'd had a cough, so he'd stayed home from preschool.

They had gone to the bank to pay bills. At least he thought that was why. And then they went to the Murrah Building to see about getting help. That's what his mom had told him. Brady had long since understood that the help must've been financial aid. Housing assistance or food stamps. Something to ease the burden of being a single mom and living with very little income.

Whatever the reason, they were in the building that morning. Brady felt his heart rate speed up. The way it always did at this point in the flashback. They were in line and Brady was playing with the stanchion.

The gray weathered filthy stanchion.

And his mom was saying, "Don't touch that, Brady boy. You'll get germs." And she was looking right into his eyes and he was staring into hers. Her sweet blue eyes. She smelled like minty toothpaste and flowers. The way she always smelled. She smiled at him. The warmest, most wonderful smile. Her blond hair spilling over her shoulders, framing her face. And she had touched his cheek. "We're almost done here."

Those were her last words before the bomb exploded.

We're almost done here.

Brady's next memory was cold and frightening and painful.

Even still.

The next thing he knew, he was lying in a hospital bed with tubes attached to his arms. His mom's friend was there. He couldn't remember her name, but she had dark hair and she was crying. Crying hard. She had her hands over her face.

Brady tried to talk and she must've heard him because she jumped up and came to the side of his bed. "Brady . . . can you hear me?"

The room was spinning a little. Brady could still feel the dizziness every April 19 when he allowed himself to go back. He looked at the woman, stared at her and tried to feel steady and strong and brave. "Wh . . . where's my mommy?"

And the woman cried harder. Tears streamed down her cheeks. Or maybe those were the tears sliding down Brady's face now. The memory was old and grainy and fainter every year.

That's when the woman put her hand on his little arm. She smelled like pizza. Nothing like his mother. "Brady . . . I'm so sorry, honey."

Whatever was she sorry for? Brady couldn't understand. And why was she crying? Those were the thoughts in his little five-year-old mind. But before he could spend any real time wondering, the woman told him.

His mother was dead.

She rambled on, doing her best to explain what she thought he wanted to know. How a bad guy had parked a big truck near the building and blew it up, and how there had been flying glass and metal and concrete. Which was why his arms had bandages all around them. Brady was almost certain he could remember the woman saying all that.

But the part he was absolutely sure about was what she said next. She told him the reason he didn't have any cuts on his face or his head was because the very last thing his mother did before she died was cover him.

She protected her little boy. Guarded him at the expense of her own life.

When the bomb hit that Wednesday morning, it ripped the front off the building, leaving a gaping hole and exposing every floor. Brady and his mom hadn't fallen to the ground along with the mountain of people and debris that collapsed that day. Instead, they were buried under rubble on the fifth floor. Later Brady learned from the paperwork in his mother's things that a chunk of steel had hit his mom in the head while she lay over Brady.

That was how she died.

The rest of the details were a mix of Brady's memories and news accounts he'd studied. For years after the bombing he had been obsessed with details about survivors and the monster who did the deed.

At least until five years ago. At that point he'd had enough of the true accounts. He still visited the memorial each year, but otherwise he lived his life. Brady let the memory fade into the cool wind around him. With no family to take him in, his mother's friend had kept him at her house. But only until the state found his first foster home.

After that, his childhood was more like a court dossier as he was passed from one foster home and social worker to the next, shifting between three elementary schools, one middle school and two high schools until he graduated.

His sophomore year, on the anniversary of the bombing, Brady connected with a couple who had lost their baby in the attack. The little boy was one of nineteen children killed in the daycare center on the second floor of the building. From their first meeting, the woman and her husband had embraced Brady. They would've done anything for him. But Brady struggled with one thing.

The husband and wife were Christians.

Brady didn't hold that against them, exactly. Faith was a personal thing. He just didn't want to be around it. If God was for him, then why did the bombing happen? What about the good plans God was supposed to have for him? And how come evil was so much a part of this world? None of it made sense. So while he still stayed in touch with the couple, he mostly kept to himself.

When he turned eighteen he started volunteer work with the Oklahoma City Fire Department. Two years later they hired him. Ever since then he'd been doing something for strangers that no one had been able to do for his mother.

Helping people survive tragedies.

Brady used the fabric of his sweatshirt to dust the top of his mother's memorial chair. The S in Sandra looked grimy. A little spit on his sleeve and he used it to work the dirt free. He stood straight again and studied her name. Yes. That was better.

He ran his hand over the letters one more time. "Next year, Mom. I'll be here."

The tears welled up again. He blinked them back, his sunglasses firmly in place. Then he turned and walked away. He knew where to go next. He moved across the open space to the reflection pond.

He took a seat on an empty bench and stared at the two bronze walls on the other side of the water. They stood four stories high. Engraved at the top of one was a simple time stamp: *9:01*. The other was engraved with a different one: *9:03*.

The first one represented the minute before the bomb went off. That morning at 9:01, when life was still whole and innocent and beautiful. Not just for Brady and his mother, but for everyone in the building.

Right up until the explosion.

Brady closed his eyes. The dirty gray stanchion. The smell of the musty government office. The people in line ahead of them. *We're almost done here. Almost done.*

He squinted and shifted his gaze to the second one. *9:03.* The minute after the bomb went off. People in Oklahoma City liked to say that time stamp represented the first minute of whatever would come next. The beginning of life after the bomb. The start of recovery. The numbers were meant to give victims and their families and all who loved the city a belief in one important idea:

Healing was possible.

Brady worked the muscles in his jaw. Never mind any of that. For him it would always be 9:02. The minute the bomb went off. There was no fancy wall memorializing that moment. An ache filled his chest and pushed down on his soul. *Breathe, Brady. Take it in.* He lifted his gaze to the sky. The explosion ripped through his life every morning, keeping him from something that came easily for most people:

Love. All kinds of love.

Letting someone in would mean the possibility of losing that person. Brady hadn't figured out how to do that, so he hadn't found healing. And he was almost certain he never would. Every now and then his buddies at the firehouse tried to set him up with one of their sisters or friends. Brady would last one or two dates. Once in a while he would spend a couple weeks or a month interested in a girl. But always things fell apart. Brady was never surprised. Not only did he have trouble loving, but the reverse was true, also.

He wasn't easy to love.

Girls didn't understand him. One date put it succinctly: "You're gorgeous on the outside, Brady. But you're a haunted house on the inside. I don't want to get caught in the cobwebs."

Brady thought of it another way. His heart was like the Murrah Building. Still in pieces from the aftermath of the bombing. The way it had been since he was that five-year-old little boy, waking up in the hospital.

Since high school, Brady lived alone, no roommates. He liked it that way. Besides, he was hardly ever home. When he wasn't working, he volunteered with several city service groups. The work gave him purpose. If God wasn't going to help the people of Oklahoma City, then Brady would step in. It was what he lived for. Helping other people. That and one other thing.

The hope that someday, somehow he might find Jenna.

Brady stood and walked around the pond to the hundred-foot section of chain-link fence. Here was where he would spend most of his time this morning. Looking at the letters and pictures and hand-drawn cards people would leave today.

Eleven years ago, Brady had met Jenna here at this very spot. But that was another story. Something he wouldn't think about until later. Depending on how he felt. Right now he only wanted to find a spot in the fence for the letter and wait. In case she showed up the way she had that day.

Brady took the letter from his pocket. It was a copy. Every year he wrote her a letter and always he kept the original. That way if he ever found her, she could have the whole collection. One for every year.

Proof that Brady had never forgotten her.

He took a deep breath and read this year's letter once more. He'd written it last night. Usually that was when the words came to him — the day before the anniversary. From his other pocket he pulled a piece of blue ribbon. He rolled the letter like a scroll and tucked it into the chain link. Just above a large red paper heart with the words *We miss you, Papa* scribbled in crayon across the front. Next to a faded copy of an older photo. A husband and wife on their wedding day. Four words were handwritten across the top: *I miss you still.*

Sorrow rushed at him like a tsunami. Brady tried to steel himself against it, but then he moved closer to the fence. Closer to the heartache. He grabbed the chain link and squeezed his eyes shut. Why? Why would someone fill a truck with fertilizer and blow it up in front of the federal building?

How could anyone hate that much?

Brady felt his tears become sobs. Deep. Quiet. Relentless. He fought them with everything in his being. It was time to move on, time to get past this. If only he could. Because for all the people he had ever rescued, the one person he couldn't save faced him in the mirror every morning.

For a long moment Brady didn't let go of the chain-link. Couldn't let go. So much pain. So much hurt and loss. Generations changed forever. Brady clenched his teeth and finally . . . finally he found control again. He sniffed and willed his tears to stop. He wanted only one thing. The same thing he always wanted.

9:01.

We're almost done here . . . almost . . .

Brady stepped back from the fence. A woman was watching him. She was beautiful. Older than he was, but still very pretty. *Probably remembers me from* Survivor, he thought. But she wasn't Jenna, and Brady didn't feel like talking.

He started to walk away. There was still the tree and the museum to visit. He needed to look through it all, every detail. Every memento and remembrance, like he did every year. Before he left he would take a piece of chalk and write something on the children's patio. Visitors were encouraged to do that. It was another part of Brady's routine.

And the whole time he would keep his eye on the fence. Checking it. Looking back at the spot where his letter remained. Just in case he might see her. Maybe walking the fence the way she'd done all those anniversaries ago. Just in case this was the year.

The year Jenna actually showed up.

4

The bad news came when Ashley and Kari and three of their older kids had been standing in line for thirty minutes. No more saplings. Apparently, there were more people wanting a piece of the Survivor Tree this year. There were still dozens of people ahead of them when a man with a megaphone stood on a picnic table at the front of the line and made the announcement.

"Sorry, folks! We're all out!" He wore a park ranger shirt and a sympathetic expression. "Try again next year. We do this every anniversary."

Amy didn't seem to grasp the information at first. She looked up at Ashley. "Wait. Is he serious?" Alarm filled her eyes and her cheeks looked suddenly pale. "Does he mean . . . I can't get a sapling? Even though we got in line so early?"

Ashley felt terrible. "Yes." She put her hands on her niece's shoulders. "They might find more. We can ask someone inside." Ashley glanced at Kari. Maybe her sister would have something more to offer. But Kari managed only a sad shake of her head.

Defeat seemed to come over Amy all at once. "I can't believe it."

Ashley looked into her niece's eyes. "I'm sorry, honey." Next to Amy, Cole and Jessie stood, silent. All of them helpless.

For a few seconds Amy said nothing. Then she nodded, her eyes dry. "That's fine. I just . . . I really hoped . . ." She hesitated and looked off. "It's okay. Can we see the tree now?"

"Of course." Ashley's mind raced. How could she still get a sapling today? Her niece wouldn't cry or make a scene or even complain. The poor girl had lost her whole family, after all. At twelve, she was used to disappointment. But there had to be a way.

Ashley ached for her precious niece. The baby tree was a big part of the reason they were here. And now . . .

Ashley felt like she was responsible. Like she'd let Amy down. She hung back with Kari while Amy, Jessie and Cole walked ahead. Cole must've said something kind, because Ashley saw Amy give him a slight smile.

"I really blew that." Ashley linked arms with her sister for a few seconds. "We should've gotten here at six. Clearly."

"You didn't know." Kari patted Ashley's hand. "It'll be okay. She can get a sapling another year."

But they both knew what the little tree would've meant to Amy. They were quiet as they followed the kids. Ashley crossed her arms and looked around. The feeling of the memorial was one of complete serenity. Ashley had expected something more hopeless.

Instead somehow the place felt inviting. As if many people who had walked these grounds had made peace with the past. A quick glance around told her that most of the people here today were likely tourists. Patriotic types. Oklahoma natives. Visitors from out of the state and even out of the country.

Ashley wondered if the families of victims and survivors visited anymore. There would be fewer now, twenty-three years later. People might have moved or passed away.

Following Amy's lead, their group walked into the museum. She didn't stop to look at any of the exhibits. That would most likely come later, Ashley figured. Instead Amy was moving more quickly now, her cousins working to keep up. Like she had a single-minded mission, and nothing could distract her until she'd carried it out.

Amy walked through the back doors of the building and there on the landing she stopped, her attention locked on one thing. Ashley and Kari were close enough behind her that they could see it, too.

The Survivor Tree.

It stood much larger and grander than Ashley had imagined. The five of them continued outside and up a few flights of stairs. And there they were. In the shadow of the big old tree.

Ashley and Amy had searched online for photos of other American elms. None of them looked so grand. This one had a trunk thick and proud, if somewhat slanted. The branches spread out like a canopy.

A hundred people could've sought cover under its shade.

With quiet steps, Ashley moved next to Amy. After a while, Amy looked at her and smiled. Not with her mouth, but with her eyes. "It's beautiful."

"Yes." Ashley gazed at the tree. There was definitely something special about the tree. "No wonder your mama loved it."

The others came closer. "It's the prettiest I've ever seen." Jessie leaned against Kari.

"Right, Mom? Don't you think so?"

"I do." Kari nodded, her eyes on the old elm.

Cole stood on the other side of Ashley. "It's almost a hundred years old. I can't believe it's still here."

Amy didn't stop staring at the tree. "I saw pictures of it after the bombing. It looks like a totally different tree now."

"I know. I Googled it." Cole nodded. "It was basically just a burned-up tree trunk, all black and shredded from the bomb and the cars that caught fire around it."

Amy's eyes grew noticeably soft, her attention still on the elm. Her voice grew quiet. "But God let it survive."

Disappointment came over Ashley again. She lifted her eyes to the blue overhead. *We should've gotten that sapling for her. Please, Father, help us get one. No one deserves one more than Amy.* They had already researched how the little tree would look when it was grown and Amy had even found a place to plant it. Ashley let the thought go.

There were two other groups of people nearer to the tree. When they were gone, Amy walked to the trunk. At one point she stopped and looked straight up through the branches. "I can't believe it's so tall."

The others didn't say anything. This was

Amy's time and Ashley wasn't going to miss the moment. She pulled her phone from her jacket and as soon as Amy put her hand on the trunk, Ashley captured it.

For a long while, Amy closed her eyes. When she opened them she turned to Ashley and then Kari and her cousins. "I asked God to let my mama and daddy see me here. So they'd know the truth about me."

They all watched her, like they were waiting for more explanation. Amy looked at the tree and then back at the rest. "You know. That I'm a survivor. Just like the elm."

Cole joined Amy at the tree, and put his hand on the bark. "God really can get us through anything." He turned to Ashley. "I think that's why He let it survive."

"I think so, too." Ashley walked to the trunk and touched it. Pressed her hand against the rough bark. Suddenly she knew what she was going to do. She was going to paint the tree. She could see it in her heart already. A bright blue sky, two or three puffy white clouds. And there in the middle, in all its glorious splendor, the Survivor Tree. At the base, a blond girl. Amy. Sitting against the trunk, her hands raised toward heaven.

Yes, she would paint it for her niece. Ashley smiled. She would start as soon as they got home.

Kari and Jessie joined them, too. "Amy . . ." Kari took a step closer, her words gentle. "Your mom always loved trees."

"She did?" Amy leaned against the trunk.

Ashley loved the privacy of the moment. There were no other tourists on the patio near them. They could take their time. She slipped her arm around Cole and listened as Kari explained.

"Yes. They were some of her favorite things." Kari linked arms with Jessie, her attention on Amy. "She once told me she felt closest to God when she looked at a tree. She liked to say we could learn a lot from them."

Tears filled Ashley's eyes. Dear Erin. The revelation was sweet and poignant. Something Ashley had never known about her youngest sister. She looked at Kari. "I love this. How long ago did she tell you?"

"We were at church camp one summer. Taking a walk." Kari gazed into the distance, clearly remembering. "Ash, you and Brooke were back at camp for some reason."

"Probably cleaning our cabin." Ashley uttered a light laugh. "I was always in trouble. Too much talking. Not paying attention."

Kari grinned. "Probably." She turned to Amy again. "Anyway, your mom said that trees raised their arms to praise God, no matter the season. Even in the dead of winter, when no sign of life existed. When its leaves might never come again, the tree's branches were still lifted high toward heaven."

"Really?" Amy's eyes brightened. "I love that. I never knew."

All of them seemed caught up in the story. Ashley looked to the beautiful elm, grasping the imagery as deeply as Erin once had.

"She said something else." Kari's voice was soft, gentle in the breeze around them. She had a way of bringing a memory to life. This was one of those times.

"The reason a tree can survive the storms of any season is because its branches bend in the wind. Otherwise it would blow over and die." Kari gave Amy a slight smile. "Your mother said she wanted to be that way, too. Whenever God's Spirit might talk to her or lead her in a certain direction, whatever He whispered for her to do or not to do . . . she wanted to be sensitive."

"That's beautiful." Amy kept her eyes on Kari.

"She said the Holy Spirit was like the wind." Kari patted Jessie's arm and separated herself so she could go to Amy. In the most tender way, Kari took hold of both

Amy's hands. "I want you to know something." She looked into the girl's eyes. "Your mom *was* like the trees she loved so much. She moved easily to the sound of God's voice in her heart."

A few tears slid down Ashley's cheeks as she listened. She wiped them and put her free hand on Amy's shoulder. "It's true. Your mom's faith was everything to her."

"Wow." Cole took a deep breath. "That's powerful. The tree in the wind analogy."

Amy hugged Kari and then Ashley. "Thank you." She kissed each of her aunts' cheeks. Kari put her hand alongside Amy's face. "I'll remember that about your mom as long as I live. Every time I look at a tree."

Ashley's heart ached. The story was indeed one of the most precious she had heard about Erin. She had been at the camp that summer, too. And somehow she had missed that moment. The way she had missed so much about Erin while she was alive. The two of them had often been at odds. Erin, close to their mother. Ashley, more rebellious, independent.

She blinked back another few tears. At least she had stories like this. And she had Amy. One day in heaven she would have forever to get to know her little sister in ways she never did here on earth.

Several tourists were headed their way. God had given them private space here at the Survivor Tree. Now it was time to move on. Ashley took another few photos, including one of Amy and Kari. A reminder of the story that had come to life today.

"Can we see the fence next?" Amy was at Ashley's side again. "Do you know about the fence?"

"I don't." Ashley put her arm around Amy's shoulders as their group started to walk toward the steps.

"None of us do." Cole looked at Jessie and then Kari. "Tell us about it."

Amy had done her research on the memorial site and while they walked, she told them what she knew. The site had opened in 2000, on the fifth anniversary of the bombing. It sat on three acres in the heart of Oklahoma City and included the museum and the open space behind it.

"See those?" She pointed to a nearby field with rows of chairs made of bronze and what looked like blown glass. Amy stopped. "There's one for each of the people who died that day."

"How come some of the chairs are smaller?" Jessie shaded her eyes.

Amy was quiet for a moment. "Those represent the children. Nineteen little kids were killed. Most of them were in the day-care on the second floor."

Again Ashley's heart felt the weight of the tragedy. The realness of it. Good thing the guys had taken the younger ones to Frontier City today. The sadness here would be more than they could understand.

They were passing a large rectangular pond. Amy motioned toward it. "That's the reflecting pool. Come on." She stepped away from Ashley and headed toward a low stone wall. "Look into the water."

Everyone followed her lead. The only thing Ashley could see was her own reflec-tion — almost as clearly as if she were look-ing into a mirror.

"I see myself." Cole looked from the water to his cousin.

"Exactly." Amy smiled, but her eyes held a deeper sorrow. "It's meant to show you the face of someone harmed by the bomb-ing. Someone changed by it." Amy looked at the others. "Because when terrorism hits, we are all affected. Always."

Ashley could hardly believe her niece's depth and insight. She had definitely studied the memorial. The reason for the pond was spot-on. Of course every American had been harmed by what had happened that sad day. Ashley had been in high school.

The feeling then was the same now: only God could heal America. For this bombing and for 9-11 and so many other ways the people of the United States had turned against Him.

Amy sat down on the stone bench and the rest of them did the same. "See those tall thick walls?"

They were impossible to miss. Covered in bronze and at least a hundred feet high, each of them glistened in the morning sun. Amy explained that the walls were called gates, and that the times engraved at the tops of them represented the minute before the bomb went off and the minute after.

"The bronze is so that people would see more sunshine than memorial. The promise of life outside of the disaster site."

"Wow." Cole patted her shoulder. "You did your homework."

Amy looked more relaxed. She smiled. "My history teacher said I could do an extra-credit report on it."

"So what about the fence?" Jessie turned and looked over her shoulder at the long stretch of chain link at the far end of the grounds. "It has things all over it."

"Right." Amy stood and looked that way. "Come on. I'll show you."

As they walked, Ashley kept her eyes on

74

Amy. *I couldn't be more proud of her.* Amy's composed way of sharing the details about the memorial. The way she carried herself, head high. Smile ready. Even surrounded by reminders of her own loss.

Amy wasn't a victim. No matter what had happened to her because of the car accident. Even though the rest of her family was in heaven, Amy was whole. Of course she had moments of feeling sad and missing her parents and sisters. But she was determined to live life.

Coming here to see the Survivor Tree was further proof.

Her cousins walked on either side of Amy as she talked about the fence. "The original bombing site was fenced so people wouldn't disturb it. But crowds still came to see the area, to remember. Some of them because they'd lost a person they loved here." Amy pointed to the fence, now just ahead of them. "People began to leave things tucked in the chain link. Letters and cards, photos and teddy bears. Whatever reminded them of the husbands and wives, daughters and sons they had lost."

"This part of the fence." Cole pointed down the length of it. "Is that what they kept when they opened the memorial?"

Amy nodded. "Exactly." She motioned to

75

a pink teddy bear. "Every day people leave things here. And every day the memorial site workers collect everything and put it in storage."

"All of it?" Kari sounded as amazed as Ashley felt.

Amy thought for a few seconds. "I guess. I'm not sure."

They reached the fence and for a few minutes Ashley looked at the items. A faded baseball cap with the words *Hey buddy . . . still think about you every day* written across the bill. A birthday card tied to the fence so the inside could easily be seen. Ashley stooped low to read it.

"Every birthday. Every Christmas. Every time I see a sunset. I still miss you, Son. Love forever, Dad."

Ashley felt her tears again. She wanted to spend an hour here. Reading the notes and messages. Imagining the heartache behind them. But they didn't have that much time, which was just as well. The sense of grief and loss was bound to be overwhelming.

Kari walked up, dabbing at the corner of her own eyes. "It's beyond sad. I mean . . . the emotions here. Just heartbreaking."

"So much pain." Ashley looked at the birthday card again, then at her sister. The three kids were a few yards away, still studying other items on the fence. "Are they ready to move on?"

"Actually, Jessie and Amy and I are headed to the restroom. Cole, too." Kari took a step toward the kids.

"Okay." Ashley hesitated. "You go ahead. I'll stay here." She glanced at the fence and then back at her sister. "Come find me when you're done."

"Okay." Kari smiled. "This has been so special."

"For me, too." Ashley searched her sister's eyes. "I feel closer to Erin because of the story you told."

For a quick second Kari reached out and squeezed Ashley's hand, then she turned and met up with the kids who were a few yards away, and the group headed toward the museum.

Ashley faced the fence once more. As she did, she noticed she wasn't alone. A few feet away stood a guy who looked like he could be Landon's brother. Tall, dark hair. Strong and fit. Maybe in his late twenties. He wore sunglasses and held what looked like a rolled-up letter. Ashley took a few steps back and watched him.

The guy was clearly caught up in his own world. He took a blue ribbon from the pocket of his jeans and tied it around the rolled-up paper. Then he slipped it into the fence. Ashley narrowed her eyes. Who was the letter for? And how was the man connected to the bombing?

Something about him looked familiar, but Ashley didn't think she'd ever really seen him before. Maybe just that he resembled Landon. The guy turned and caught her staring. She managed a weak smile and a quick nod before she focused her attention again on the fence. In her peripheral vision she saw the man shove his hands deep into his navy blue sweatshirt pockets and walk the other direction. He definitely didn't want to talk to a stranger.

Ashley watched him go. *What's his story, God? He looks so hurt.* The man seemed isolated and distant. Like whatever his connection to the bombing site it was deeply personal. Maybe even devastating. She stared at the white paper and the blue ribbon. Why was the man here today? Ashley wished she could've asked him. But more than that she wanted to know something else.

What was in the note?

5

Somehow, Amy felt closer to her family here at the memorial site. As they met up with Aunt Ashley and headed toward the field of empty chairs, she breathed in the quiet air. Maybe it was the other people who had come here today. Some of them were probably tourists.

But she had a feeling lots of them were survivors like her.

Long ago when she was little, her mother had read her a story about an ugly duckling. The little duckling was different from his siblings. Everywhere they went, he felt set apart. He imagined the other ducks whispering about him, feeling sorry for him.

Then one day the ugly duckling came upon a family of swans. And suddenly he realized he wasn't different or ugly after all! He was a swan.

That's how Amy felt today. Her aunt and uncle loved her as much as they loved their own kids. Amy knew that. Her cousins treated her like she was a sibling. No one was mean to her and she'd never seen them whispering about her.

But they felt sorry for her. Of course they did. Her entire family was dead. Amy understood that, and she was thankful for her home and the way she had been accepted and loved by her aunt and uncle. Still, no matter how much they cared for her, no matter how much they still hurt over their own losses, none of them could ever really understand how it felt to have your whole family die.

Here, though, it was different. At the memorial — especially on the anniversary of the bombing — there had to be at least some people walking around who knew what it was like to be so young and to lose a parent in a sudden moment. Amy was sure of it. They were here because they were still healing. Here because they wanted to remember the person they'd lost.

Amy and the rest of them reached the chairs, and quietly they walked the rows. That was Amy's idea. Because each person should be remembered in some special way, she told the others. They didn't stop and read every name, but they paid their respects.

That's what Aunt Ashley called it.

Amy could picture her parents walking these very rows, noticing each of these exact chairs. Of course they had. Her mom had loved visiting here, she definitely would have taken time to see the chairs.

They were almost done. Today's time would end in the museum, where they would read about the events of that April 19.

Amy wished she could meet everyone here who was just like her. The family of swans. The survivors. People still stuck somewhere between 9:01 and 9:03 that Wednesday morning. But since that couldn't happen, she let herself believe that everyone she could see, everyone they passed by knew her pain. She smiled at a few of them and nodded at others.

Her aunts and uncles and cousins were her family and she loved them with all her heart.

But these were her people.

The guy kept returning to the fence. Checking on the letter. Looking one way and then the other, like he was waiting for someone. Ashley noticed him the whole time they visited the chairs and afterward as they left for the museum.

Amy was doing well. She hadn't brought up the sapling again, and she seemed at peace having spent time here. But through it all, Ashley kept an eye on the fence. Whoever the guy was waiting for, the person apparently hadn't shown up.

As they neared the museum, Ashley watched the man leave the fence again. He seemed on a mission now. He actually passed by them, apparently unaware of Ashley's surveillance. Only Kari noticed. "Who was that?"

"Who?" Ashley blinked and turned to her sister.

"The guy." Kari laughed quietly. "Ash . . . you've been staring at him for ten minutes. He was standing by the fence, right?"

"He was." Ashley drew a quick breath. "I don't know. There's just . . . something about him."

"Yeah." Kari raised her brow. The two of them were walking a few feet behind the kids. "Every girl here today noticed something about him."

"It isn't that." Ashley felt embarrassed. "Come on. You know me better." Ashley watched as the guy entered the building. "He looks like Landon. Maybe that's it."

"Yeah." Kari nodded. She seemed content with that explanation. "He kind of does. I can see that."

"Plus, did you see the pain on his face? The guy's hurting for sure." Ashley pointed back at the fence. "He left something. A note. Tucked into the fence." She turned to her sister again. "I saw him leave it. When you were in the restroom."

"Got it." Kari's tone grew more serious. "You think he lost someone here?"

Ashley paused. "Absolutely. I wanted to say something. Offer to pray for him." She shrugged. "He just looked so . . . like he needed help."

They reached the museum and walked up the steps to the double glass doors. "You didn't say anything, right?"

"Definitely not." Ashley scanned the building as soon as they stepped inside. She didn't see the guy anywhere. "He looked like he wanted to be left alone."

"Mmm." Kari appeared to understand. "Probably a lot of people like him here today."

"Probably."

They moved from one exhibit to another. Amy had done much of the research about the bombing, but the rest of them had not. Kari and Ashley were old enough to remember it, of course. But details of that day were hazy. So they read every display.

Ashley was trying to pay attention. She was. This truly interested her. It was a part of history, after all. But she couldn't stop thinking about the letter back in the fence. If the person never came, if he or she never found it, then what would happen to it? What if no one ever read it? The staff would collect it and throw it in storage and the message would be lost forever.

Which would be another kind of tragedy.

The letter could be written to someone who had died here. In which case it was never actually meant to be read. But then why had the guy kept searching, looking one way and then the other? He must've been waiting for someone. A living person.

Finally she tapped Kari on the shoulder and whispered, "I'll be right back."

"What?" Kari walked with her a distance from the kids. She seemed slightly alarmed. "Don't tell me you're looking for that guy again?"

"No!" Ashley gave a hurried shake of her head. "Of course not. He's gone, anyway. I saw him leave."

"Ashley." Kari studied her. "You're freaking me out a little here. He's a stranger."

"I know. But what if he needs help?" Ashley kept her voice low. "I'll be right back."

"Where are you going?"

"To the fence." She was already moving toward the exit. "I won't be more than a few minutes."

"What am I supposed to tell the kids?" Kari looked exasperated. She folded her arms in front of her. "This is crazy, Ash."

"Tell them I'll be right back." She blew Kari a kiss, turned and opened the door. Before she stepped outside she looked back. Amy and Cole and Jessie were completely caught up in a lengthy survivor account posted on the far wall. They'd never know she was gone.

Out in the sunshine again, Ashley flew down the steps. She jogged toward the fence as fast as she could without drawing attention. The mood was still somber, reflective. Calm. She couldn't break into an all-out sprint. But she didn't want to leave without at least looking at the letter.

The urgency that filled her heart reminded her of other times in her life when she couldn't walk away from someone else's heartache. Like years ago when she worked at Sunset Hills Adult Care Home. She spent her off-hours studying the elderly residents. Learning their stories so she could find reasons for their behavior. One Alzheimer's patient at the home screamed when she used the bathroom. Every single time. Ashley's research showed that six decades earlier the woman had been a beauty queen. No wonder the mirror terrified her. Ashley's investigation paid off. She put a sheet over the mirror and the woman never screamed again.

Now her feet moved a little faster. Maybe it was her creative nature, or the fact that she was drawn to hurting people. Either way she couldn't stop herself.

After having watched the guy return to the exact spot along the fence, Ashley knew right where to go. The rolled-up scroll with the blue ribbon was next to a big red heart. Ashley stopped right in front of it and stared, breathless. There were two words written across the front in blue ink. The writing was too faint to see from far away. But from here Ashley could make out the message clearly.

For Jenna

That was all. Just "For Jenna." As if whoever Jenna was, if she came here today she would know the note was for her and she would take it from the fence without hesitation. Ashley blinked a few times. Or maybe not. Maybe Jenna was the guy's family member. Someone he had lost in the bombing. The note might just be his form of therapy. Maybe he did this every year. Wrote a letter to the person he'd lost so that somehow this Jenna would know from heaven how much the mysterious, hurting guy still missed her.

Ashley tapped her foot.

What if the guy came back? He might be watching her now, wondering why she'd been stalking him, waiting to prevent Ashley from touching the note. She looked to the right for a long while and then to the left. The man wasn't anywhere near the fence.

She must be losing her mind.

Of course the man wasn't here. Ashley had seen him leave. She spun around and searched the grounds. No, he definitely wasn't here. But what about Jenna? If she was alive, then there was still a chance she'd come by today. A chance she could be walking by this very spot even now, looking for her letter.

Be discreet, Ashley, she told herself. *Don't look like a crazy person.* She studied the people on either side of her. There were no single women of any age. No one moving along the fence searching for a letter. At least it didn't look that way.

No one seemed to notice Ashley.

She really should leave. The letter was for Jenna. That's all she needed to know. It was the reason she'd come back to the fence. Just so she'd know. Ashley stared at the scroll again. Wrong. *Be honest with yourself, Ash. You came back to read it.*

Fine. Ashley took a deep breath. Her heartbeat picked up speed. If she was going to do this she needed to get it over with. Fast. Before someone accused her of stealing notes from the memorial fence.

Which would almost certainly be a crime of some sort.

With shaking fingers she removed the letter from the fence and untied the ribbon that held the scroll in place. Then she unrolled it and there, inside, was a full-on letter. Ashley held her breath. She had gone too far to stop herself. She let her eyes race to the top of the page and she began to read.

Dear Jenna,

Like I do every year, I wrote you a letter. In case you come to the memorial today. In case you want to find me as much as I want to find you. Every year I —

"Excuse me." A woman tapped her on the shoulder.

Ashley gasped. She dropped the letter and the ribbon and then immediately bent to pick them up. "I'm sorry, I didn't . . ." This was it. They were going to arrest her right here and then Kari and the kids would come out in time to see her handcuffed and hauled away and —

"Oh, my." The woman took a step back. "Sorry. I . . . didn't mean to startle you." She looked around. "I was hoping you might know where the restrooms are."

Only then did Ashley realize that the person talking to her wasn't alone. There were others in her group and all of them seemed to be waiting for Ashley's reply.

"Oh. Right." Ashley grabbed a breath. "They're . . . back at the building. Where the museum is."

The woman nodded. "Sorry again." She pointed to the note. "I didn't mean to disturb you."

"It's fine." Ashley forced a light laugh. "I just . . . I didn't see you walk up." She was rambling now. Already the group was turning away, toward the museum. Ashley waved and then looked back at the paper. Her breathing was fast and jagged. She had no idea if it was a crime to take a letter off the fence and read it. But she needed to get back to Kari and the others.

No way could she stand here and read the whole thing. She skimmed over it and then an idea hit her. Holding the paper in one hand, she pulled out her phone and tapped her camera app. Carefully she opened the note enough so she could see all the words.

Then she took a picture.

If reading other people's letters was a crime, surely taking photos of them must be, too. Ashley didn't know. But she had to get out of here. She rolled up the paper, tied it with the blue ribbon and slipped it into the fence again.

She positioned it so the words were clear once more. For Jenna.

Then she took another picture.

Without hesitating she returned to the museum as fast as she could. Kari and the kids were only a few exhibits down from where they'd been when she left. Cole spotted her as she walked up.

"Mom, where were you?" He didn't look worried. But clearly he wanted an answer.

"Hi." Ashley smiled. Her heart was still racing, shooting adrenaline through her veins. "I . . . uh, I wanted to see something at the fence. I didn't get a good look before."

Cole hesitated, but only for a couple seconds. "Okay." He took her hand and led her toward the wall where Kari and Jessie and Amy were still reading. "You have to see this. You won't believe how God saved this one guy."

Not until Ashley reached the exhibit and Cole had resumed his place between Amy and Jessie did Kari finally notice she was back. Her sister turned and looked at her. Then she mouthed, "Did you steal it?"

"Of course not." Ashley straightened her jacket and focused her attention on the display. "Cole . . . you mean this one?" She could feel Kari watching her.

"Yes." Cole and his cousins were already on to the next display. "You've gotta read the whole thing."

Ashley fought the guilt rising inside her. She would tell Kari later about what had happened, how she'd thought she was going to be arrested and how she'd taken a picture of the letter. She and Kari could read it together. Ashley tried to focus on the exhibit, but she couldn't. Her heart was still pounding.

Maybe God wanted her to see the man today. Or maybe not. Sure, the timing could've been a coincidence. But what if the Lord had lined up the two of them so that Ashley would be intrigued? So she'd come back and take a picture of the letter and maybe even help the guy somehow?

It was possible, right?

Whatever the reason Ashley couldn't forget him. Not because he was attractive. But because of the hurt on his face. There was something familiar about him. Beyond the fact that he looked like Landon.

Stop, Ashley. This was ridiculous. She would put the whole thing out of her mind. He was a stranger. What could she possibly do to help? She moved on to join the others. *Put it out of your head,* she told herself. *Enough.*

On the way out of the museum, Amy led them to a patio with chalk drawings. A man who worked there stood nearby, supervising. Beside him, on a small table, was a bucket of chalk. Amy looked from Kari to Ashley. "So many kids were killed that day, they decided to make this chalk yard, with squares for drawing and writing. That way children and parents . . . whoever wants, can leave something behind."

The patio was a good distraction. Ashley watched as Amy sorted through the chalk. This was why they were here. For Amy. And if this was the last thing she wanted to do before they left the memorial, then they would all take part.

Ashley studied the childish illustrations and simple words written across the concrete. There were still many open squares. Each of the kids took chalk from the bucket. Then she and Kari followed suit. As they walked together, Kari whispered, "Ashley. What did you do?" She shot her a doubtful look. "You have to tell me."

"Later." Ashley sounded urgent. Friendly, but urgent. She didn't want the kids hearing them. She returned the whisper. "Everything's fine."

They spent another ten minutes on the chalk yard. Amy drew the Survivor Tree. Beside it she wrote, *Dear God, help me be like this tree. Amen.*

Ashley studied Amy's artwork. "It's beautiful." She put her hand on her niece's shoulder and worked to control her emotions. What had she been thinking? Concerned with a stranger? This day was about Amy, not helping some guy she didn't know.

"I really liked the story about my mom. How she loved trees." A softness filled Amy's eyes. More peace than pain. "Today was perfect." She smiled. "Thanks for bringing me."

Ashley worked to keep her emotions in check. "I'm glad we came."

"Are you gonna draw something?" Amy laughed. "You almost have to. Professional artist and all."

Ashley breathed deep and steadied herself. "Yes. That's exactly what I'm going to do." She stared at a blank square. How would it feel to be Amy today? Or the dark-haired young man? Or all the others who had suffered such loss?

And what about Jenna? Whoever she was.

Ashley bent down and began to write. *Beauty from ashes. Please, God.* The words came easily. When her letters looked swirly and artsy, she surrounded them with a wreath of springtime flowers.

"Not fair." Cole was standing over her. "Mom, you're so good."

Ashley stood up and dusted off her hands. "Not at basketball."

Cole laughed. "True."

"God gives us different gifts." Kari joined them. She smiled at Ashley's drawing. "He just happened to saturate your mother with the gift of creating art. Even from chalk."

Jessie walked up and added her voice to the others'. Kari pointed at Amy's drawing. "I think we have another artist in the family." She kissed the top of Amy's head.

"Really?" Amy's eyes shone.

"You have a gift. I've been telling you." Ashley put her arm around Amy. "How about we get some basic supplies next week when we're home."

"Okay." Amy grinned. "Thanks."

When they were finished, they washed their hands and headed for the car. As Ashley drove to the hotel, Kari shot her another look. She hadn't forgotten about the letter.

Ashley definitely didn't want to talk about it now. She kept her phone in her pocket on the short drive. As soon as she had a minute alone, she would read the letter. And of course she'd share it with Kari and later with Landon. They could all brainstorm how to help the guy. Which actually might not be possible. Ashley had gotten only one detail in the brief time she'd had the note open. Something she couldn't stop thinking about. It was the guy's name. The guy who clearly had a broken heart.

Brady Bradshaw.

6

Brady gripped the handlebars and leaned his motorcycle into the curve ahead of him. He took the ramp onto the freeway faster than he should've, the wind rushing at him like it was alive, washing over him. He lowered his head to cut the draft and picked up speed.

Jenna hadn't come.

Eleven years in a row and still she hadn't been back. At least not that he'd ever seen. And she'd never found his letters. Otherwise she would've at least contacted him. Because you don't just have the best day of your life with someone and not reach out if you get the chance.

That's what Brady figured.

Back in the beginning, on the second and third years after the two of them met, Brady assured himself that his feelings for her would grow less over time. If he never saw her again, eventually he would forget they'd ever met. He might even stop going to the memorial.

But it was more than a decade later and Brady hadn't forgotten her. Not at all. Her image in his mind had grown stronger, clearer. His determination to find her had never been more consuming. He exited the freeway and slowed for a stoplight. What was it about her?

Brady knew the answer. He had convinced himself that she was the only girl on the planet who could understand him. Or was it something deeper? Maybe having feelings for a figment of his imagination was easier than falling for someone right in front of him. One of the girls he'd met over the years.

The light turned green. Brady clenched his jaw as he sped through the intersection. Whatever it was, the girl had hold of his heart. That much had never changed. He lowered his head again, the wind pushing at him. If only it were tomorrow already. Then he would've survived another anniversary.

He wove in and out of traffic until he saw Jefferson Street. A quick right and he picked up speed again. Images from earlier filled his mind. The people along the fence, the way none of them were Jenna. And who was the pretty brunette who kept staring at him?

For a few minutes back at the memorial he'd even wondered if she maybe knew Jenna. Maybe the girl Brady dreamed about had sent this woman to see if he'd be there.

The idea was crazy. Whoever the brunette was, Brady didn't know her. It had to be she recognized him from *Survivor,* or maybe from some news show about the bombing. He leaned hard into a left turn. Speed like this wasn't his usual style. Only once a year, when he wanted to outrun the brokenness inside him. Most days he drove his pickup truck. He'd been at the scene of too many motorcycle accidents. He knew better than to drive like this.

But the anniversary had its own rules.

A right turn at the next light and another right. Two lefts and there it was. The house where he had first learned he might actually survive all this. The home of Cheryl and Rodney Fisher. The couple he'd met at the memorial when he was still in high school.

Brady cut the engine, parked his bike and locked up his helmet. He removed his sunglasses and set them in the small compartment next to his helmet. He wouldn't be here long. Just enough to let the couple know he remembered them.

He still appreciated them.

Cheryl opened the door before he reached

the front walkway. She stepped onto the porch and smiled. Not the typical smile of a person expecting company. Not the smile Cheryl would've had before April 19, 1995. But the smile of someone wounded. The closer Brady got the more he could see she'd been crying.

And of course.

This day was a nightmare for them, same as it was for him. The day all of them wanted to rewrite. That they might be anywhere but the Alfred P. Murrah Federal Building that fateful Wednesday. The Fishers had lost their two-year-old son, Jimmy, in the bombing. He wasn't actually in the day-care center. His nineteen-year-old aunt — Cheryl's sister — had just entered the building, intent on signing Jimmy in at the facility.

They were ten yards away from the front desk when the bomb hit.

Cheryl's sister had died, too.

Brady reached the top of the stairs and immediately Cheryl's arms were around him. He was never sure, but Brady had a feeling that in some ways he took the place of Jimmy. Never mind that Jimmy was black and Brady was white. Brady felt like Jimmy was his sibling. The boy would've been a few years younger than Brady. Like a little brother. Or maybe a best friend. Jimmy had been the Fishers' only child. They never had another baby after the bombing. Their doctor said sometimes high levels of stress could make a woman infertile.

Collateral damage after the bombing.

"Brady." Cheryl pulled back from the hug and found his eyes. "Thanks for stopping by." She kept her arm around his waist as they headed into the house. "Rodney's waiting for you." Brady followed her inside and there was Rodney, sitting at the kitchen table, newspaper spread out before him. One of the last of a generation who still read one.

Brady took a step forward. "Mr. Fisher."

"Brady." He closed the paper and stood, stretching out his arms. "Come here."

This was their way. The Fishers saw Brady as family. One of their own. They had moved past handshakes and formalities years ago. Rodney hugged Brady the way parents hug their kids when they return from war. The older man drew back and studied him. "You look good. Still doing that workout?"

"CrossFit? Yes, sir." He chuckled. "Gotta be ready for the next big fire."

Cheryl patted his hand. "You'll be ready." Her tone told him she was proud of him.

"No one's more ready than you, Brady." She motioned to the living room. "Let's sit down. I put out coffee and snacks."

Of course she did. Sweet Cheryl Fisher was one of the kindest people Brady had ever met. On the table between the two sofas Cheryl had set a pot of coffee and a plate of chocolate chip cookies. Brady didn't typically do either. But he would fake it today. He could at least do that for Cheryl and Rodney.

Brady sat next to Rodney while Cheryl poured the coffee. "Still no cream?"

"No cream. Thank you, though. You're too nice." He looked from Cheryl to her husband and back again. "You don't need to do this."

"Brady, don't you know?" Cheryl handed him the coffee. Fresh tears filled her eyes. "We look forward all year to this visit with you."

Guilt thudded Brady in his chest. He lived seven miles away, but he made this trip just once every twelve months. On the anniversary. He glanced at the nearest bookcase. Had to be six Bibles on the various shelves, and on the wall was a framed print. It read: *With God all things are possible.*

Brady narrowed his gaze. Try telling that to his mother. Or to Jenna.

There you go again. Thinking mean and cynical. Trapped in hate and unforgiveness. Brady forced the slightest smile and turned back to the couple. He knew about God, of course. He just didn't believe in Him. That's why he didn't come more often. Brady set the coffee down. "You gonna tell me about Jimmy?"

They did this every year. A smile lit up Cheryl's eyes as she took her seat at the table. The first real smile since he'd gotten here. She looked at her husband. "Rodney, should we tell him?"

"Let's do." Rodney put his arm around her. He nodded at his wife. "You start."

"Jimmy, Jimmy." Cheryl shook her head and sighed. "Sweet little baby boy. Biggest brown eyes you ever saw." She looked long toward the front window. Like she was seeing all the way back to 1995. "Oh, how that boy loved life. Right straight out of the womb."

"True." Rodney poked his finger into the air as if to highlight the fact. "Other babies cry when they're born. Not Jimmy."

"No, not Jimmy." Cheryl glanced at her husband, and then at Brady. "Doctors thought something was wrong with him. How come he wasn't wailing like a baby's supposed to do?"

She stood and found a photo album on the nearby coffee table in the next room. When she was back at the table, she opened it. The same photo album they looked through every anniversary. "Here he is." She pointed to the photo of a newborn Jimmy. His eyes shining with possibility. "Look at that. Grinning right straight from heaven into our arms."

"That boy was always happy." Rodney leaned close, studying the picture.

Cheryl turned the page and raised the book every so often to show Brady. "On his first birthday he put his whole fist in the cake." She looked at Rodney. "Remember that? He learned how to say 'Uh-oh' that day!"

"Couldn't forget it." Rodney shook his head and turned to Brady. "Except he didn't eat it like other babies. He held it out to me and his mama. 'Dada?' That little voice of his. 'Dada?' "

Cheryl closed her eyes for a moment and opened them again. "I can still hear him, still see the way he looked at me that day. Just like it was happening all over again." Cheryl turned the next page.

Brady knew the stories. He knew the pictures. He'd been sixteen when he met the Fishers on the anniversary of the bombing. The couple had bought him lunch that day and listened to his story. Before they parted ways, Cheryl had given Brady a phone number and an address. "Join us for dinner next Sunday. Four sharp." And Brady did. That was the first time he'd heard the story of Jimmy.

In the early years after that dinner, Cheryl and Rodney had been there for Brady when he wasn't sure he had the will to live. When he felt alone and when he couldn't find Jenna. But then the Christian thing kept coming up. Cheryl would invite him to church or Rodney would want to open the Bible. Eventually Brady visited less often and in the last few years just on the anniversary. The least he could do was sit here and listen to them talk about Jimmy. Who else would care about their loss this many years removed from the bombing? Who else would care about his?

Cheryl continued through the photo album. She talked about the exact day Jimmy started walking and the day he threw a ball for the first time.

"He was gonna be the next Michael Jordan." Rodney chuckled at his wife. "Isn't that so?"

"Sure could shoot a basketball." Cheryl touched a photo of Jimmy in a red Michael

Jordan T-shirt, number 23, holding a small orange ball and smiling like it was the best day of his life. Cheryl grew quiet. "Played with that mini hoop all day, every day."

Brady knew each detail of the story that followed. Jimmy was running by the time he turned two. Racing through the house, laughing and talking. He loved Bible stories and playing with blocks and Winnie-the-Pooh. He thought he was Christopher Robin. So much so that on his second birthday, Cheryl and Rodney threw him a party with a theme Jimmy had loved: the Hundred Acre Wood.

Two weeks later Jimmy was dead. Christopher Robin never got a chance to grow up.

The story slowed down as it neared the end. Tears spilled from Cheryl's eyes. Rodney's, too. Quiet tears. Stoic. Tears of regret and loss and what might've been. Especially that. Cheryl took a napkin from the table and dabbed her eyes. "We watched *Winnie-the-Pooh* one more time. Before . . ." Her voice trailed off.

Rodney covered her hand with his.

Cheryl closed the photo album. "That was him. Little Jimmy."

"He's with Jesus now. We know that." Rodney looked straight at Brady. "We'll see him again. Our Jimmy. Closer every day."

Tears clouded Brady's vision. He blinked them back. Struggled for composure. This was always the awkward part. How could he just get up, climb on his bike and ride away? Listen to them tell Jimmy's story and then leave? Rather than be a friend to this kind couple all year long? Brady had no answers for himself.

He clasped his hands and stared at the floor. Until he could hear Cheryl's crying slow some. "Jimmy and I . . ." Brady lifted his eyes to Cheryl's, then to Rodney's. "We would've been friends. Somehow . . . we would've found each other."

The couple nodded. This was what they held on to. The possibility that Jimmy might've been Brady's friend. And in that case, somehow seeing Brady was almost like seeing Jimmy. Grown up and happy and whole. That was the gift Brady gave them whenever he came around.

Even if only once every April.

He stood. "I have to go."

"Brady." Rodney stayed seated. "Let us pray for you. At least that."

This hadn't happened last year or the year before. He'd told the Fishers long ago that he wasn't a praying man. Didn't want to talk about God or open the Scriptures. They respected his wishes, but today . . . well, today, there was an urgency in Rodney's voice.

Brady stifled a sigh. "Yes, sir." He sat back in his chair and clasped his hands again.

"You and God still on the outs?" Rodney narrowed his eyes, like he was trying to see through Brady's soul.

"Yes, sir. I guess you could say that." Brady looked at the man. "But thank you for praying. I know it matters to you and Mrs. Fisher."

They were both quiet. Cheryl spoke first. "It does matter, Brady. It matters to God."

Brady couldn't take much more of this. Not on the anniversary. He bowed his head. The signal was clear, the discussion finished. Across from him Rodney led the prayer. Something about healing a little more every year and asking God to watch over Jimmy and Cheryl's sister and, of course, Brady's mama.

Then at the end the man prayed something he hadn't before.

"Whatever it takes, God. Please. Get Brady's attention. So that when You do, he'll know it was You. Because only God could have done it. Whatever that might be." When Rodney finished, they shared their usual goodbyes and Brady made his annual promises to come around more often. Before he left, Cheryl stood in front of him and took hold of his hands. Hers were gentle, but firm.

The way his mother might've held him.

"Brady." She searched his face. "Nothing good ever came from being on the outs with God." Her eyes were damp again, imploring him to see her. Hear her. "Let this be the year. Please."

He stared at the ground and gritted his teeth. A slight nod and he looked at her again. "Yes, ma'am." He kissed her cheek. "Thanks for the coffee."

"We love you." Rodney hugged him next.

Brady couldn't say a word. His throat was too tight, his heart too broken. He turned and walked to the front door. A look back at each of them, a quick wave and Brady was gone.

On the ride back to the freeway, he couldn't stop reliving Rodney's prayer. He wanted to forget the words but he couldn't shake them. Rodney had asked for a sign from God, and that He would look out for Jimmy and Cheryl's sister and Brady's mama. In heaven. Which left Brady with just one question.

Why hadn't God done that before? While they were still on earth.

Ashley hadn't looked at the letter. The kids wanted lunch, so the five of them ate at the hotel restaurant. Landon had texted her: They were still a few hours from leaving Frontier City.

Not until they were headed back to the room after eating did Cole come up with a plan. "A cousin plan," he called it. The three cousins would meet in Cole's room and watch a movie. They were worn out from the day.

"Something happy." Amy made the suggestion.

"I love it." Ashley nodded. "You're right, Amy. A little laughter would be perfect right about now."

Fifteen minutes later the kids were settled, and Ashley met up with Kari in her room. As soon as Ashley shut the door, her sister was on her feet. "Okay, what happened? Tell me everything."

"It's no big deal. I took a picture." Ashley pulled out her phone and called up the photo. "I haven't read it." She dropped on the bed opposite Kari. "It's a little blurry."

Kari sat cross-legged, facing her. "I still can't believe you took the guy's letter off the fence." She hesitated. "Or that you took a photo of it."

"Maybe I can help him." Ashley felt completely justified. The stranger could've picked any section of the fence to leave his letter. But he chose that spot. Right next to Ashley. She squinted at the photo and made it larger with her finger and thumb. "There it is. I can read it now."

"You don't feel guilty?" Kari's mouth hung slightly open. Like she was incredulous.

"Not at all." Ashley looked at her sister for a second or two. Kari was the cautious one. Following orders. Coloring inside the lines. Ashley was the risk taker. It was what had gotten her in trouble when she went to Paris after school. But this wasn't like that. Ashley drew a quick breath. "I didn't *take* the letter."

"Okay . . . read it." Kari still sounded concerned. She hesitated. "I'm dying over here."

Ashley found the beginning and started.

"Okay . . . here it is: 'Dear Jenna, Like I do every year, I wrote you a letter. In case you come to the memorial today. In case you want to find me as much as I want to find you. Every year I do this, I leave you a note in case. Anyway, here I am again, eleventh year in a row.' " Ashley paused, taking it in. " 'Eleven times I've come to this fence and looked for you. Eleven times I've written you a letter and left it here. Hoping you'd find it.' "

Kari gasped under her breath. "Eleven times!" She motioned to Ashley. "Keep reading."

"I'm trying." Ashley raised her brow slightly and smiled.

"Sorry. Go on. Really."

Ashley found her place. " 'Every year things wind up the same way. You don't come to the memorial. You don't walk the fence. You don't find my letter.' " Ashley adjusted the photo again. The picture was still blurry. " 'Don't you remember, Jenna? What it was like having that one day together?

" 'We met here and I thought . . . I don't know, I thought it would be easy to find you. I had your name and number in my pocket when I left that day. It was sitting on my dresser for three days. I know it. But then . . . something happened. Someone moved it or took it or threw it away. I'll never know, but it was gone.' "

"Gone?" Kari covered her mouth. "That's terrible."

"So sad." Ashley picked up where she left

off. " 'And now — even after all this time — I still think about you. I guess at first I hoped you would call me, since I didn't call you. The truth is, I don't think about anyone but you. I'm a firefighter in Oklahoma City. It gives me purpose. But I'm alone. I'm always alone.' "

Ashley stopped for a minute and lowered her phone. "He's a firefighter." She said the words more to herself than to Kari. Was that why he had seemed so familiar? The way he stood and moved and walked? She glanced at her sister. "No wonder he looked like Landon."

Kari sat forward. "Ash. Be careful." She waited, watching Ashley. "You don't know him."

Her sister was right. But still.

Ashley lifted her phone again. "I'm almost done." She tapped the photo and made the image even bigger. She took a deep breath. " 'That day, the day we had together eleven years ago, we were only seventeen.

" 'But I knew I'd never meet anyone who shared my story the way you did. I lost my mom and you lost both your parents in the building that horrible Wednesday. There's never been anyone who could understand that. Not until you, Jenna.' " Ashley closed her eyes for a brief moment. The guy's letter was killing her. She blinked away the tears welling in her eyes.

When she could see clearly, Ashley continued. " 'Please find this letter. Look for me. Call me. My number's at the bottom.' "

"Wow." Kari was clearly captivated. "All these years."

"I know." Ashley looked at the letter again and kept reading. " 'I'll be waiting for you. And if I don't hear from you, if you don't find this, then I'll be back at the memorial again next year. On the anniversary. And the year after that, and the next one.

" 'And one of these days, Jenna . . . one of these days you'll be here. I'll find you. I have to believe that. Remember what you said? Our hearts are the same. And so they are. Always. Brady Bradshaw.' "

Ashley put down her phone and looked at Kari. She felt like she'd been kicked in the stomach. "The guy won't make it another few years."

"I know." Kari wiped at a single tear. "So sad."

The image of Brady at the fence consumed Ashley. Her mind raced. "I have to help him. I can find Jenna. I know I can."

"Ashley." Gentle disapproval colored Kari's tone. "It isn't your place. You're a married woman."

"Yes!" Ashley felt her own frustration rise up. "And I'm more in love with Landon every day." She forced herself to calm down. *Patience, Ashley. Patience.* She exhaled. "This has nothing to do with the guy. How he looks, or whatever you're thinking."

"I'm sorry." Kari's eyes grew soft. "That was out of line."

"It's okay. I get it." Ashley felt the fight leave her. She took her time, sorting through her thoughts. "It's just . . . what if God put him next to me for a reason? What if there's more to the story and I'm supposed to . . ." She looked around the room trying to find the words. Finally she lifted her hands and let them fall to her lap again. Her eyes locked with her sister's. "I don't know, maybe it's up to me to help them find each other."

Kari nodded. "Okay." Her expression was more sympathetic. "I hear you." She hesitated, her voice soft. "But, Ash . . . you don't even know her last name. Just Jenna."

Kari had a point. Ashley tapped her fingers on her knee and studied the bedspread for a few heartbeats. "I could find Brady on Facebook. Somewhere. Maybe even reach out to him." She turned to Kari. "Just to tell him I want to help."

"Or maybe Landon could contact him."

114

Kari wasn't pushing. Ashley could tell. Her sister just wanted to guide Ashley in the right direction.

"Good idea." Ashley smiled. Kari was right. Landon was a firefighter. Maybe he could talk to the guy. Surely, Landon would be in favor of the idea.

There was a sound at the door. A key sliding through the lock. Kari jumped up. "They're back!"

Ashley stood, too. The timing was perfect. She could hardly wait to tell Landon about their day. About the Survivor Tree and the memorial and the chalk patio. And the heartbroken firefighter she'd met at the fence. And her idea.

That somehow the two of them could help him.

7

The heartache that lived in the deepest places of Jenna Davis was a private one.

She didn't tell many people about her past. Her co-workers knew her story, but only the basic details. Her loss that dark April day wasn't something she talked about, the feelings hers alone. And without a close friend in her life, Jenna had no one to share her pain with. No one who remembered what happened to her twenty-three years ago at the Alfred P. Murrah Federal Building.

If she were still in Oklahoma, maybe.

But Jenna lived in Columbus, Ohio, and the tragedy of that far-off April 19 was the last thing on anyone's mind. Even today. Sure the late night news might make mention of the bombing. If more pressing stories didn't fill up the hour. But it wasn't likely.

Jenna smoothed the wrinkles from her black wool pencil skirt and checked her look in the mirror of the staff restroom. Martin Luther King Junior Elementary School had one of the nicest newly renovated facilities in the city. Jenna was blessed to work here. She had the best second-grade class in all of Ohio and her colleagues were some of the finest teachers in the state.

She added another layer of lipstick and fixed her hair. Her eyes looked greener in this light. Same eyes as her mother. That's what her grandma used to tell her. Jenna studied herself. Last night at the science fair one of the parents had told her the same thing Jenna had heard a hundred times.

"You look like Emma Stone." The woman had smiled at her. "Anyone ever told you that?"

"Yes, ma'am." Jenna had thanked the woman and moved on.

She loved the compliment, but not for the obvious reasons. She loved it because that's what Brady had told her. Back then Emma Stone had done her debut film — some teenage comedy. At that point no one really knew the actress.

They had both seen the commercial for the movie, and neither of them liked it.

Something else they had in common.

Jenna took a deep breath. *Where are you today, Brady? Whatever happened to you?*

She hesitated, waiting. But there would be no answer. Not from the bathroom mirror and not from God. She had asked enough times to know that. She slipped her lipstick back into her purse, walked to her second-grade classroom, and shut the door behind her. The kids were still at lunch, still running around the playground, laughing and carefree.

Unaware of the anniversary, or the sadness in their teacher's heart.

Music. That's what she needed. She used her phone to start her favorite playlist, something she liked to do before the kids returned to their desks. There were speakers on either side of the room. The set started with Kyle Kupecky's song "Come Home."

As the music played, Jenna couldn't help but sing along.

My life's a different story, than I thought it would be . . . I've collected a few memories, never thought I would see. I've traveled far . . . far away from home.

Jenna leaned against her chair and closed her eyes. She could've written the song herself. She drew a breath and blinked. Ten minutes and the students would be back in their seats. A pile of papers with the afternoon's reading assignment sat on her desk. One for each of the boys and girls.

She took the stack and distributed it while the music played on.

But You tell me You love me . . . and You say to me it's never too late. Wherever you are, no matter how far . . . you can still come home.

They were God's words to her. Jenna knew that. She had lived them, after all. Somewhere along the journey of years since her last visit to the Oklahoma City memorial she had indeed found her way home.

Back to God.

The classroom door opened and a stream of twenty-three children ran inside and took their seats. Other teachers had a rule against running. Not Jenna. Life was too short. Olivia, the smallest child in the class, rushed up to her. "Miss Jenna, Edward hit me with the ball at recess!"

The girl had a red welt on her cheek. Jenna shifted her gaze to Edward. The child's head was practically bald — the result of an outbreak of lice last week. Before that Edward's hair had gone down to his shoulders. Didn't seem to matter, long or short. Edward's eyes sparkled with the possibility of mischief, though he gave her his best impression of an angel.

Something else the boy was good at.

"Edward." Jenna raised her brow. "Come

119

here, please."

The other students were still getting situated, looking at the papers on their desks. Edward did as he was asked. When he reached Jenna, his eyes grew large. Innocence personified. "Yes, Miss Jenna?"

She looked at Olivia's red cheek and back to Edward. "Did you hit Olivia with the ball during recess?"

"Not really." Edward blinked a few times. "I was playing dodgeball." He smiled at Olivia. "Hits happen in dodgeball."

"No!" Olivia's eyes welled up. She rubbed the mark on her face. "We weren't playing dodgeball, Miss Jenna. We were playing kickball. And kickball means you don't throw the ball at someone's face just because they got a good kick."

"You're right." Jenna looked at Edward again. "It's only dodgeball if everyone agrees. Do you understand?"

Edward lowered his chin nearly to his chest. He crossed his arms with a huff. "I was tired of kickball."

"Edward." Her tone was more serious now. "Tell Olivia you're sorry."

"Yeah, tell me." Olivia was small, but feisty. She wasn't having any of this from Edward.

He looked like he was in actual pain. An

apology was clearly the last thing Edward wanted to do.

"Fine." He looked at Olivia, his eyes more squinty than before. "Sorry you didn't want to play dodgeball."

"No." Jenna needed to get the afternoon started. She stood and looked down at Edward. "That's not an apology. Say it now. Unless you'd like to spend the afternoon in the principal's office."

"Okay." The boy's expression softened. His tone followed. "Sorry for hitting you, Olivia."

The girl touched her red face again. "I forgive you. I guess."

"Listen." Jenna looked from Edward to Olivia and back. "What's the number one rule in our class?"

Both kids looked at Jenna. Olivia spoke first. "Always love each other . . ."

Edward nodded and finished the statement. "Because second grade doesn't have that many days."

"That's it." Jenna gave the two what she hoped was an encouraging look. "Now go sit down."

Olivia hesitated. She smiled up at Jenna. "You're pretty."

"Thank you, Olivia." Jenna loved teaching kids this age. They said whatever they were thinking. No shame. "You're pretty, too."

The girl should've gone to her desk, but she was fixated on Jenna's necklace. "Why do you wear a key around your neck?"

Jenna fiddled with it. The key was dark bronze on a chain the same color. She'd had it for three years today. A gift she'd bought herself for the anniversary. The year her husband left without looking back. Jenna stooped down. *Focus on the child,* she told herself. "It's called a Giving Key."

"The key's giving something?" Olivia reached up and touched Jenna's necklace. "Seems like a regular key."

"It is." Jenna smiled. "Kind of."

The rest of the class was settling in. They had two minutes until the bell. Olivia lifted her blue eyes to Jenna. "Why's it called 'giving'?"

"Because one day I'm supposed to find the right person to give it to. With a Giving Key necklace, you look for a reason to give it away."

Olivia nodded, but she still appeared confused. "Why'd you get it?"

"Because." Jenna felt the beginning of tears, but she refused them. "It reminds me of my mommy and daddy."

"Oh." The answer seemed to do the trick. Olivia grinned. "Bye!" She skipped back to her chair.

Jenna held the key and ran her thumb along the surface. She wore it as often as she could. Some of the teachers and several of the kids had noticed over the last few years. For Jenna it was a reminder. She'd had it custom-made, with just one thing engraved on the front and back.

She drew a deep breath and stuffed her emotions to the basement of her heart. Thoughts about the anniversary could come later. A smile lifted the corners of her lips. "Who remembers what book we're reading?"

Hands shot up around the room, but several children yelled out the answer before she could choose one of them. *"Noah's Ark! Noah's Ark!"*

Just hearing them say the name of the Old Testament Bible story brought a rush of joy. None of the other teachers had thought she could do it. Get the principal to approve *Noah's Ark* for the reading project this month. But Jenna had done her homework.

The story of Noah and the Ark was listed as approved literature in the Ohio State Board of Education guidelines. Jenna assumed it was an oversight, but nevertheless, the title remained among other classics. Jenna was thrilled for the chance to tell kids the story, to introduce them to the truth. Because even children didn't have all the time in the world.

As Jenna knew all too well.

So when she sought permission to share the story with her class there wasn't really any discussion. Reluctantly, her principal agreed. A few of the parents had expressed shock that they were studying *Noah's Ark* in a public school. Most of them were thrilled but a few seemed on the fence about the idea. One or two were even upset. Jenna had just smiled and shrugged. "It's classic literature according to the state."

Jenna had used her own money to purchase every student a copy of the children's version of the story. Each afternoon they would read a section of the book out loud, and answer the questions on the handout.

They had already talked about the people being wicked, and how God had asked Noah to build an ark even before it started to rain. Today they were reading about the animals coming two by two.

From the beginning the kids' questions were hysterical.

"Miss Jenna, why didn't Noah just leave the spiders and ants behind?"

"Do you think the bear was the scariest animal on the ark?"

124

"Was there an indoor play yard for the animals to run around?"

Jenna did her best to answer. Spiders and ants must've been part of God's plan. The bear was probably tied with the lion for most scary. And an indoor track would've been a good idea. "I'll bet they had one," she told the child who asked. "They needed some way to get their exercise."

Today's discussion was good. Especially the last question of the day. One little girl raised her hand. "Miss Jenna, do you think the story of Noah and the Ark is real?"

"Absolutely." Jenna smiled and sat on the edge of her desk. "I believe God created the world, and I believe He sent the flood. Because people had turned against Him."

"And only God could do something like that, right?" The child grinned.

"Exactly." Jenna checked the clock on the wall. "Okay, boys and girls. That's it for today!"

Jenna could hardly wait to talk about the rainbow tomorrow. She walked her students outside to the front of the school and waited as every child boarded a bus or was picked up by a parent.

Andy Collins was last to leave. His grandparents had custody of him and most days his grandpa was late. Jenna didn't mind waiting. Andy struggled more than all the kids in her class. His parents were convicted drug dealers, so the hurt from that spilled into his time at school.

"How was your day, Andy?" Jenna often had this conversation with the boy while they waited for his grandfather.

Andy shrugged and looked away. "Not good."

Jenna studied him. "I'm sorry." She put her hand on his shoulder. "What happened?"

For half a minute Andy didn't say anything. Finally the boy looked at her again. "It was those same ones. The boys who always pick on me."

"Oh, no." Jenna knew the kids. They were mean to lots of the younger students. Andy was quiet and shy, often standing off by himself during lunch and recess, which didn't help.

Andy looked at her. "They pushed me down and kicked me. A lot of times."

"What?" Anger shot adrenaline through Jenna's body. "That's terrible." She worked to keep her cool. "I'm sorry, Andy. That never should've happened. I'll talk to the principal. We'll figure this out."

Andy pressed the heel of his shoe against a crack in the sidewalk. He looked at her, hope in his eyes for the first time that afternoon. "Really?"

A quiet sigh drifted up from her aching heart. "You know why they pick on you, right?" Jenna took both his hands in hers, still at eye level with him.

"Because they're mean." Andy looked so little. He was still so young, like all her students. They needed much love and care.

"Yes." Jenna waited for Andy to find her eyes again. "But the reason is because they're unhappy. Very unhappy."

Andy tilted his head, like he hadn't actually considered that. He managed the slightest smile. "It's okay, Miss Jenna." Andy let go of her hands and stood a little taller. "I have you. That's all I need."

"Okay, then." She smiled. *God, don't let him see my broken heart.* Andy didn't need sympathy. He needed people to believe in him. She kept her tone upbeat. "Tomorrow we'll read my favorite book."

Andy's eyes lit up just a bit. *"To the Moon and Back?"*

"Yes!" She straightened and pushed his bangs out of his eyes. "Because that's how much I love you."

"And that's how much I love you, too." He found his laugh again just as his grandpa pulled up.

127

Jenna stood and watched him go. A deep satisfaction came over her. This was why she was a teacher. The kids who otherwise might fall through the cracks were the exact boys and girls God put in her path. And one day, if He was willing, she would have her own children. Until then, Jenna had Andy and another twenty-two kids to call her own.

At least until summer.

Andy's words stayed with her as she reported the incident to her principal and later as she drove home to her town house and ate dinner from her Crock-Pot. The principal had promised to deal with the students responsible. Even so, Jenna would do a better job looking out for Andy. His words played in her heart again. *And that's how much I love you, too.*

Sweet boy.

Music made Jenna's beef stew and butternut squash dinner less lonely. Tonight it was Colton Dixon's latest album. She could've eaten with someone else. A group of her teacher friends, maybe. Three of them were single like she was. Sometimes they shared meals together, planning for the school week and swapping stories about their students. But tonight Jenna wanted to be alone. Finally, after dinner, it was time to do what she'd wanted to do all day. What she'd planned to do.

Find a quiet place and remember.

The second floor of her home had a back deck. Not very big. Just a couple chairs and a small table. But from there Jenna had a view better than any place in Columbus.

Trees grew behind her condo. Over them, the sky stretched on to eternity, and tonight the stars were brighter than usual. "That's so like You, God," she whispered. "Giving me a sky like this. Just when I need it."

She sat in one of the chairs and looked at the moon. It was only a sliver, the reason the stars were so clear. She stayed still for a moment, taking in the view. Her mother had loved the stars, so the backdrop was perfect for remembering. Which was something she did often. But it was different on the anniversary.

More intentional.

Jenna wasn't in the Alfred P. Murrah Building when the bomb went off. She was at her grandmother's house. The way she always was on Wednesday mornings.

Both her parents worked in the building, on separate floors. Jenna wasn't sure if it was her imagination or an actual memory, but she could picture her mom talking to

129

her grandma about watching Jenna before and after school.

"If she can be with you, that'll always be better." Her mom had stood beside Jenna just inside the front door of her grandmother's house. "She loves you so much, Mama."

In the memory, Jenna was five. Not in kindergarten yet. So little. The images took shape. Her mom was dropping her off before heading to work, and Jenna could see herself, reddish-blond pigtails, pink bows at the end of each, grinning at her grandmother. "I love Grammy's house."

So the decision had always been an easy one, apparently. Jenna would stay with her grandmother while her parents were at work. At the end of the day, her mom would pick her up and the two of them would run errands or stop by the library. They'd go home and read or finger-paint or color. And then Jenna would help her mother make dinner.

The whole time — through every wonderful activity — her mom would talk to her about Jesus. "The reason we're here, Jenna, is because God loves us so much."

"That's why He sent Jesus, right, Mommy?"

"Right, baby girl."

Jenna had another favorite memory. It wasn't clear like it used to be, but the important details were there, safe in the most sacred room of her soul. It was almost bedtime and her mom was reading to her. And she could see her mommy's green eyes, see the smile on her face and hear her voice. "I love you to the moon and back, precious daughter." Her mother's face was forever etched in Jenna's mind. Then and now, Jenna thought the same thing: Her mom was the prettiest woman in the world.

Later, Jenna's grandma would tell her that she looked like her mama. Jenna believed it. The picture in her heart was a lot like the one she saw in the mirror each morning.

Another memory came into view. They were making meatloaf, and Jenna was using her clean hands to work in the bread crumbs. Her mom said something about having meat fingers and suddenly both of them were laughing. Just Jenna and her mom, working in the kitchen side by side, laughing about their meat fingers.

Jenna had a new nightgown that night. A gift from her grandmother. And Jenna's mom was helping take off the tags and slipping it over Jenna's head, kissing her forehead. "Sweetheart, look at you! You're more beautiful than any princess who ever lived!"

And in that moment, Jenna could do nothing but believe her. "Princess Jenna, Mommy." She twirled around in the kitchen. "That's me."

Just then, her daddy came into the room. He was tall and blond and handsome. Her mom used to say he looked like Captain America. Sometimes Jenna liked to pretend that was her daddy's real job. Captain America. But by day he worked as a supervisor in the social services department of the government. There were times the accounting kept him late at work. Nights like this one, preserved forever in Jenna's heart.

Her dad dropped his briefcase and his mouth fell open. "Princess Jenna!" He bowed. "I had no idea I was stepping into the presence of royalty!" Her dad had an imagination bigger than the state of Oklahoma. "Your Highness, I request the honor of giving you a piggyback ride!"

Giggles overcame Jenna and she twirled over to her daddy's arms. He swept her up and onto his shoulders. Then he galloped her around the living room and kitchen until she was laughing too hard to breathe. He was her royal stallion, and she was princess of all the land.

She could never know if that was the night before the bombing or not. But it was close.

Sometime during their last week. Jenna knew because they had gone to the zoo that weekend. Her grandma always told her the story. How her dad had Saturday work to do, but he said it could wait. The weather was nice and he wanted to take Jenna to the zoo.

Jenna's grandma had gone, too. She took pictures. The ones Jenna kept in a book by her bed. Proof that she'd had the most wonderful parents and that they had spent their last weekend on earth with her. Watching lions and tigers and laughing at the long-necked giraffes.

Like always, at 8:30 the morning of April 19, Jenna's mom dropped her off at her grandmother's house, just a few blocks away. And like every morning, Jenna's mom got down on her level and kissed her cheek. Then she put her hands on both sides of Jenna's face and they rubbed noses.

"How much do I love you?" Her mom's eyes had sparkled that day. At least that's the way Jenna recalled them.

"To the moon and back." Jenna remembered smiling. Remembered thinking that her mommy must be queen of the whole building where she worked.

Half an hour later Jenna was still at her grandma's when something happened. A call came in and when her grandma answered it, she suddenly let out the loudest cry. Like someone had kicked her leg. That's what Jenna thought at the time. She could still see her grandma's face, the look of raw terror.

Jenna got up from the couch and backed as far away as she could, until her feet bumped into the wall. Her grandmother rushed to the TV and turned it on. And the news filled the screen, fire and smoke and people crying out.

Then in an instant, her grandma seemed to remember Jenna. She gasped and turned off the television. "Jenna!" And suddenly Jenna was in her grandma's arms. "I'm sorry, Jenna . . . I'm sorry. We need to pray, baby."

We need to pray.

They were the words Jenna remembered most from that morning. Her next memories were a blur. All except the funeral. Two caskets. And more tears than any princess should ever have to cry.

That day Princess Jenna died.

In her place was a little girl whose mommy would never hold her again, whose daddy would never give her a piggyback ride. She was just Jenna after that.

The memories faded. A cool breeze

seemed to heighten the bright stars, making the night feel special. Which it was. The anniversary always felt different. Like God was meeting her in this place. The memories weren't too sad or painful. They were beautiful. All she had of the parents she loved so much.

Jenna narrowed her eyes and tried again to see back to that time. Her parents had been on different floors, but they had gone home to heaven together that morning. And Jenna had moved in with her grandmother, where she stayed until she left for college. Jenna's grandpa had been dead for a decade by then. And in Jenna's sophomore year, her grandma passed, too.

No matter how distant Jenna grew from God after her parents died, she never told her grandmother. Through middle school and high school Jenna went with her grandma to church and together they read the Bible every Sunday afternoon.

Jenna knew the answer to every Christian question. But the whole time she didn't want anything to do with God. He could've spared her parents, but He didn't. Didn't He know? Jenna needed her parents far more than He did. Her parents were praying people, people who believed in Him. So why hadn't He answered them?

For Jenna, the answer was obvious: God didn't love her.

That's what she told herself, anyway. It wasn't until college that Jenna attended church with a friend. The message that day was about why bad things happen to good people. Jenna would always remember the pastor's words. "God isn't the reason bad things happen. He's the rescue."

God was the rescue.

It was something Jenna hadn't considered. After that, something changed in her heart. She began to see things differently. Her heart softened and she realized the pastor was right. God wasn't the cause of her loss. He was the solution. Because of Him, Jenna would see her parents again one day.

She moved to Columbus after graduation, where the teaching job at Martin Luther King Junior Elementary was her first. By then she was even closer to God, so when her church hosted a financial planning meeting, Jenna attended. That's when she met Dan Davis. International businessman. Financial entrepreneur. They had their first date that Friday. Six months later they were married.

In the beginning they attended church together, and Dan seemed to believe in God the way she did. She made an assumption that would haunt her later. She figured since she'd met Dan at church, he must be a Christian. He must want to live his life according to the Bible. Looking back, she could see that every conversation they ever had about faith was started by her.

They celebrated their first anniversary with news that she was pregnant. She was ten weeks along when she miscarried. In the months after that loss, Jenna would spend hours reading her Bible, memorizing Scripture. She would cry out to God and He would remind her of His promises.

Come to me, all you who are weary and burdened, and I will give you rest. . . . Do not be anxious about anything, but in every situation, by prayer and petition, with thanksgiving, present your requests to God. And the peace of God, which transcends all understanding, will guard your hearts and your minds in Christ Jesus.

And so many others.

Dan said something to her during that time that should've alerted her to what was coming. He walked into their bedroom and found her in the rocking chair reading the Bible. He stopped and lowered his brow. "Really, Jenna? The Bible? Again?" He laughed, but the sound was mean. "You need more books."

She looked at him, trying to figure out if he was kidding. "Dan . . . I couldn't get through this if I didn't read the Bible."

"Sure, but you've read it." He laughed again. "Three times, right?"

Concern came over her even before she knew what was coming. "It's not like that . . . With the Bible, it's different. It's like God's talking to me." She paused. Dan should've understood that. "It's alive and real."

He looked at her for a long few seconds, and then he shrugged. "Suit yourself."

That was it. *Suit yourself.* He didn't ask what she was struggling with. He didn't tell her he was sorry about the miscarriage, and he didn't ask why the Bible spoke to her so deeply. Just *Suit yourself.*

Sometimes she would try to talk to Dan about her miscarriage and even about losing her parents. Especially when the losses built and grew in her heart until she could barely breathe. Dan would usually change the subject. Death and loss made him uncomfortable. When Jenna felt like crying, Dan always found other places to be.

Eventually those places involved other women.

A week before their second anniversary, Dan announced that he was moving to

138

London. A better job, he told her. But the next week he expanded on that. He didn't want to be married anymore. Didn't want the possibility of more babies. Didn't want to be a father. Jenna nearly suffocated from the shock, but she couldn't fall apart completely.

She had her job and her students. She had the strength of God.

Dan left three days later and Jenna never heard from him again. Once he was gone, she drove to Lake Michigan for a weekend. To clear her head and her heart. And there, on a beach chair overlooking the water, Jenna made a promise to God. Never again would she marry a man who didn't share her faith.

The promise was as much for her as it was for God. She would rather be single than raise a family with a man who couldn't understand why she read her Bible. She wanted a man who would read the Bible *with* her.

Period.

But a year passed and then two more, and she remained single. Guys would cross her path, but none of them shared her faith. When she'd find out that they had no interest in going to church, she would move on.

Because she absolutely would not consider

breaking her promise to God.

And so she had figured a way to make a life for herself alone. With a small inheritance from her grandmother and her teaching salary she got along just fine. She was even ready to visit the memorial again — something she hadn't done since the year she met Brady.

This summer she would make the drive to Oklahoma City. That was the plan.

She had a reason. Each victim of the bombing had a glass box for mementos in a designated room at the memorial museum. A worker at the memorial had told Jenna that her parents' boxes currently had only their black-and-white photos from the news accounts that day. Nothing more. Jenna wanted to do something about that. So she had gathered copies of several of her parents' photos and letters. Items she could laminate and take to the memorial.

Besides, Jenna had avoided the memorial long enough. This coming summer it would be time. Proof that Jenna was moving forward. Getting on with her life. Ready to distance herself from all things Oklahoma City Bombing. That's how she felt. Or at least it was how she usually felt. Every day except today, when all she wanted to do was find the one person on earth who truly understood her.

Brady.

Only then could she see if he had made peace with God, the way she had. A month ago when she finalized her plans to drive to Oklahoma City, she began to pray for Brady, asking God to let their paths cross. Even for one more day. So she could see if he was okay. If he believed again.

It was the reason she had bought the Giving Key. The reason she had it engraved with the numbers that represented her life. Her journey of faith. She wasn't stuck at the moment of the bombing. She had moved on. Tragedy and loss didn't define her. Her personalized key was a constant reminder of her healing.

Her life after the tragedy.

It was a key she would give Brady, if she ever saw him again. Whether he was still running away from God or not. The key could at least remind Brady that God wanted his return. Because Brady was the only other person in her world who would understand the numbers on the key, and the healing they represented. Jenna ran her thumb over the etching. It was the only thing she could've engraved on the key.

9:03.

8

Ashley mustn't have explained the situation right, because Landon wanted nothing to do with contacting Brady Bradshaw. Even if the stranger was a firefighter.

When Landon and Ryan had come back to the hotel, they'd dropped the younger kids off with the older cousins. Then both men had listened to Ashley talk about what had happened. How the stranger at the fence had seemed so upset.

Like he could barely breathe for the weight of his losses. Whatever they were.

"I thought you might want to reach out to him." Ashley had finished the story and taken Landon's hand. "Maybe we could help him find the girl. Jenna."

Landon had stared at her for a long moment, like he was waiting for the punch line in a not-very-funny joke. "You're not serious, Ash."

Across the room, Kari had shrugged in

Ashley's direction. "I tried to tell you."

Ryan had seemed completely confused. "You want Landon to reach out to some guy he doesn't know and offer to help him find a girl none of us has ever met?"

When he put it that way, Ashley felt ridiculous. "Never mind." She'd let the idea go for then. "You're right."

There was no point debating it. But no matter how hard she tried, she couldn't get the image of Brady out of her mind. What if they *could* do something to help? A couple times that evening Kari and Landon had asked her if she was okay. She'd told them she was. But later that night, Landon had pulled her close and apologized. "You were serious about that Brady guy." He searched her eyes. "Weren't you?"

Ashley had nodded. "Of course." She smiled, feeling the hurt in her expression. "I wouldn't joke about that."

"Hey." He hugged her and ran his hand along her back. "I'm sorry. Really, Ash." After a minute he'd looked at her again. "Let's pray for the guy. Then you can let it go."

Ashley had agreed, and together they prayed for Brady. That he'd find God and peace and yes, one day, that he'd find Jenna. Whoever she was.

The next morning, though, Landon had looked at her with the slightest bit of humor in his eyes. "I can't believe you took his letter off the fence." He shook his head. "And took a picture of it." He came to her and kissed her cheek. "That's my wife." His smile had been genuine. "One in a million, baby. No one like you."

He'd meant the words as a compliment. Ashley knew that. He always said he admired her courage. How she could have a tough conversation with anyone or help a complete stranger. But this time his attitude frustrated her. He'd seemed to be making light of the whole thing.

What if she wasn't supposed to dismiss the situation so easily? She had thought about asking Landon if he minded if she looked up the stranger. If she at least tried to help the guy. But she didn't ask. Mostly because she didn't want his disapproval.

Now it was Saturday morning and they were out on their rented houseboat, the culmination of the spring break trip. Landon and Ryan took turns driving the boat around the lake and then they headed for the quiet side of the shore, so the kids could swim. Everyone wore life jackets — even the adults. Landon's suggestion. So they'd set a good example for the children.

For now, the cousins were on the top deck with the men, in the observation area. And Kari was on a phone call with Ryan's mother, getting caught up with his side of the family. Ashley assessed the situation.

There couldn't be a better time.

She pulled her laptop from her bag and found a table near the back of the boat. They'd been so busy having fun she hadn't opened her phone, let alone her laptop. All she had was maybe ten minutes. And since the boat had Wi-Fi, it couldn't hurt to look. Guilt rattled her heart as she signed on to Facebook and typed in his name. There were several Brady Bradshaws but only one of them who could've been the man at the fence. She opened his page and saw she had the right one.

Firefighter. Oklahoma City.

A little snooping and she realized he'd been on the show *Survivor.* No wonder he looked familiar. He was also the June photo in a calendar of firefighters. Ashley looked at the image for a few seconds. There had to be a clue here somewhere. Then just as quickly she moved on. Never mind that. She searched his friends, typing in the girl's name: Jenna.

Nothing.

Of course nothing. She sighed. If Jenna was

his Facebook friend, Brady wouldn't be looking for her at the memorial. She thought for a moment. It took no time to realize Landon was right. She had no leads, no last name. No possible way to find the girl.

Not unless she contacted Brady for more information.

She opened her photos and called up the picture of the letter again. His phone number was right there. All the information she might need was a mere text away. Then she could at least help the guy. Ashley stared at the number, and as she did she felt a hand on her shoulder.

A quick turn and her regret was immediate. "Landon!"

He looked from the laptop and phone to Ashley. Confusion clouded his face. "Didn't you hear me cut the engine?"

"No." She forced a laugh. "I was just . . . checking Facebook."

"Okay." Landon wasn't one to doubt her. Not ever. Their marriage was something other couples dreamed about. But as he stared intently at her computer screen, the slightest hurt filled his eyes. "Brady Bradshaw?"

Ashley closed her laptop and clicked off her phone. She stood and faced her husband. "I'm sorry. I should've told you." She felt terrible. Landon didn't deserve this. "It's just . . . Honey, I want to help him." She took hold of his hands. "Is that crazy?"

For a while, Landon just looked at her. He seemed slightly irritated. "I don't know if it's crazy, Ash." He leaned in and gave her a quick kiss. As if he wanted to show her how much he trusted her. Like he was determined not to be angry. "How about you come swim with the kids?"

"Okay." She felt her muscles tense. Good thing they were alone. They didn't need an audience for this. "I might just reach out to him first."

"Now?" He still wasn't mad, but his patience was clearly unraveling. "The kids are swimming. We're on vacation."

"Exactly." Ashley tried to smile.

"I guess my question is why? Why look him up?" Landon worked the muscle in his jaw. "I thought we agreed to pray for him. Leave it at that."

"I know. But the more I think about it . . . Landon, listen." Ashley shifted so she could see him better. "If I can do something to help him, I should do it. Now."

"No." Landon let go of her fingers and took a step back. "Look, the guy's not exactly unattractive. That's kind of obvious." No question he was trying to stay

147

calm. But frustration sounded in his tone. "You reach out to him, and . . ."

"And what?" Heat coursed through her body and her heart pounded. "What, Landon?" She uttered a single laugh, but there was nothing funny about it. "You can't be serious." Her anger took root. "You think I'm *hitting* on him?"

"Of course not." He lowered his voice. "But . . . those things start somewhere."

"Those things?" Now *she* was upset. "Really, Landon, that's ridiculous."

Suddenly she heard herself. What was happening? Why was she doing this? Fighting with the guy she loved more than her next breath? *Father, calm me. Please.* She closed her eyes for a brief moment and exhaled. "I'm sorry." She stared down at her chair, and then back at Landon. "That was rude."

He looked at her, like he wasn't sure what to say. The hurt in his eyes told her he was still struggling. "I'll let it go. I shouldn't have made a big deal out of it."

She still wanted to help the guy, but why right now? "It can wait. Or I can just drop it."

Landon drew a slow breath. He closed the distance between them and reached his hands out. "You don't even know him. If you contacted him, I guess you might find out more about the girl. But . . . I don't see how that would help."

"True." She gently wove her fingers between his. "I really am sorry." Something bothered her. She had no choice but to voice it. "You . . . trust me, right?"

"Baby." They were only a few inches apart. "Of course I trust you." He took his time as he leaned in and kissed her. More tentatively this time. When he looked into her eyes he found her heart. "I'm sorry, too." The corners of his mouth lifted into a slight smile. "Let's go swim."

"Okay." She hugged him, brushing the side of her face gently against his. The situation wasn't worth talking about now. "I'm sorry again. I love you, Landon."

"I love you, too." He ran his thumb lightly along her fingers.

Ashley savored the feel of her hands in his, his cheek against hers. No one could ever understand her or love her, the way Landon did. "You're the best husband in all the world. Have I told you that lately?"

"Mmmm." He kissed her again. His words were a whisper, close to her neck. "You have the most beautiful hair. Has anyone ever told you that?"

Ashley felt her heart melt. Those words

mattered only between the two of them. Words spoken long ago by dear Irvel, one of the Alzheimer's patients where Ashley worked when she and Landon fell in love. When all the world spun around the two of them.

The way it still did.

Ashley kissed him again. "Swim, right? Wasn't that it?"

"Yes." He hugged her and spoke in a whisper. "Until tonight."

She grinned. The private moment with her husband had turned everything for the better. The fact that even after getting frustrated with each other, they could still come together and be okay. The reality that Landon trusted her. He wasn't angry.

And later if she still felt compelled to help Brady, she would. Because this wasn't only about following God's lead in helping a guy find the girl he longed for. Brady might need a lot more than a girl named Jenna.

He might need God, Himself.

Ashley and Landon met up with the kids one deck down.

They had climbed out of the water and now all of them were sitting at the long table adjacent to the galley, eating sandwiches. Ashley saw the red cheeks on a few of the

150

kids. "Let's do another round of sunscreen."

Janessa came running up. "Cole tried, but I need your help, Mommy."

Across the deck Cole shrugged. "I think she's good." He grinned. "But moms do a better job. That's what she said."

Moms do a better job. Ashley shot a quick look at Amy. Cole didn't mean any harm by his comment, but still it must hurt. Hearing something like that.

Ashley grabbed the sunscreen and rubbed it onto Janessa's shoulders and cheeks. Then she called Amy over. "Aunts do a better job, too." She smiled at her niece. "Right?"

For a moment, Amy stood there. As if she wasn't sure she wanted anyone but her mom to help her. But very quickly a smile lifted her lips. "You're right. No one's better than you, Aunt Ashley!"

Tears stung at Ashley's eyes, but she refused them. Ashley had a feeling her niece's recent growth had a lot to do with her fascination with the Survivor Tree. Like the tree, Amy was determined to live. The thought of that warmed Ashley more than the sunshine.

After lunch the kids swam and paddled around in the rafts. Cole and Devin and RJ learned how to do flips off the back of the boat. They each had a floating ring and for a while they used those to play a slow version of water tag until they were laughing too hard to keep going. They returned the boat just before sunset, and after dinner the group headed back to the hotel.

But as they turned in that night, after Landon was asleep, Ashley couldn't settle her thoughts. What if she really could find this Jenna? Research was Ashley's specialty, right? Wasn't that something she'd known about herself for a decade?

And maybe if she connected with Brady, she could find out what he'd done to try to locate Jenna. Maybe Brady and Jenna were meant to be together, and maybe Ashley was supposed to help. Couldn't that be the reason she had gotten the chance to take a photo of his heartbreaking words?

Her thoughts kept her awake far too late.

Lord, is this from You? Is this something I should take on? She didn't exactly hear a clear answer, but she felt a sense all the same. As if God had arranged for Brady to be there at that exact moment. So Ashley could help him.

The next morning they set out early for home, and all the while Ashley found herself thinking about the firefighter. At one of the stops, while Landon was getting gas, Ashley went to the photos on her phone and read his letter once more. What could it hurt to reach out to him?

Whoever Jenna was, the guy had only shared his story with her. No one else understood him. No one else had the same heart as him. At least that was what Brady thought. By the sounds of it, Brady and Jenna were both survivors of the Oklahoma City bombing. But in what way? Had they been in the building, too, when their parents were killed?

Ashley closed her photo app as they hit the road again. She looked at Landon, his familiar profile and the joy in his eyes. Should she tell him she was thinking again about the letter, about helping Brady?

Landon must've caught her looking, because he met her gaze and smiled. "Perfect day for a road trip."

"Definitely." Her smile was quick. "It's been a great spring break."

"It has." He kept one hand on the wheel, and reached for hers with the other. "I love these years. While the kids are still young."

Her heart lurched. Probably best not to tell him now. Why ruin the mood with something harmless? She could tell him later, when they were home. Instead they talked about his job as the marketing director for the fire department. He was second in command now, but the understanding was that when the fire chief retired in a few years, the job belonged to Landon.

He'd come so far since the days when he had a constant cough, back when it looked like Landon might have a lung disease because of the months he'd spent in New York City at Ground Zero. Now his breathing was great. He still went in for an X-ray every year, but last time the doctor had told Landon his health had never been better.

Ashley was grateful to God. She had resisted Landon in her earlier years, back when she had rebelled against everyone who loved her. Now she only prayed for a long, healthy life with her husband. That they could be a source of faith and hope for their family and friends.

And maybe even for the stranger from the memorial.

They'd been home two days when Ashley couldn't stand waiting another minute. She had to reach out to Brady. The idea of telling Landon first crossed her mind, but her husband was already in bed. He had an early breakfast meeting tomorrow. Once the kids were down for the night, Ashley settled into the living room sofa and stared at her phone.

Once more, she called up the photo of Brady's letter.

It was only nine o'clock in Oklahoma City. He would probably still be awake, so should she text him? She tapped her finger on the phone and thought for a minute. Of course she should text him. How else could she help the guy? Why wait?

Ashley dismissed the subtle feelings of guilt. No reason to feel sneaky or awkward. She would tell Landon tomorrow, once she'd made contact with Brady. Ashley didn't want anything weird here. Didn't want Brady thinking she had any motives other than to help him. So she wrote her text very carefully. Then she read it back to herself.

Hi, Brady. You don't know me. My name's Ashley Baxter Blake, and I saw you at the Oklahoma City National Memorial on the anniversary. I watched you leave a note on the fence for someone named Jenna. I know this is strange, but I know you're trying to find her. Don't be angry, but I read the letter you left for her. I actually think there's a reason I saw you. I think God is telling me I'm supposed to help you.

Ashley smiled. Yes, that was the right way

to word this. She kept reading.

If you could tell me Jenna's last name, I'll
see what I can do. I'm not sure why I feel
compelled to reach out. But I'm very good
at research and I have time to help you. I
have a feeling I'll find her.

She thought about Irvel and Sunset Hills
Adult Care Home. Also, the situation last
year when Devin's teacher had mentioned
she'd been trying to find her birth parents.
The woman had tried everything. It wasn't
until Ashley stepped in and helped that she
finally located them. She still had photos
from the teacher of that happy moment.

Time and again she was drawn into the
lives of other people to make a difference.
Helping people was her specialty.

She stared at her phone. The text needed
just a bit more explanation.

Anyway, if I can help at all, let me know.
Just give me her last name and I'll see
what I can find. And if there's anything else
I can do, let me know. Until then, I'm praying for you.

The text was perfect. Exactly what Ashley
wanted to say. When Landon came home
tomorrow she'd let him read it. She already

knew how it would go. He would smile at her and give a slight shake of his head. "You're an interesting one, Ashley," he would say.

Then he would pour himself a glass of water and watch her from across the kitchen. He would say something kind and understanding. Something like "I believe you're right, Ashley. Maybe God is using this situation for His good."

And if he didn't . . . well, if not then she would let the whole thing go.

She hesitated a moment longer, then she hit send. For the next hour while she washed the kitchen sink and counters and got ready for bed, she kept an eye on her phone. With every passing minute, she felt more foolish. What had made her think Brady would reply to her? Why would the guy trust a complete stranger?

By the time she climbed into bed she was sure of one thing: Landon had been right from the beginning. The guy didn't want her help.

Well, she told herself. *That's that. He isn't going to answer.*

Even still she would tell Landon about the text tomorrow, maybe while they watched the Reds game on TV.

She'd laugh it off with Landon and tell

him he was right. "The poor guy probably thinks I'm a lunatic." She would utter a sad chuckle and she'd look straight at Landon. "Do you think I'm a little crazy?"

And Landon would give her an understanding smile and he would tease. "Ashley," he would say, "I married you because you're a little crazy. I like you that way."

Yes, that was how it would go. The whole thing would be over and she could get back to life without obsessing over a stranger's problems.

Ashley had barely finished writing the imaginary script for how tomorrow would play out, and had just turned off the lights when her phone dinged. She stared at it for a moment, plugged in by her bed. Then she picked it up. One new message. She pressed her thumb on the screen, and there it was.

A text from Brady Bradshaw.

Ashley's heart quickened as she opened it, but at the same time her hopes fell. His reply held no clue as to what he thought about her message, no words as to whether he believed Ashley could be of any help. His text said just this:

I don't know her last name.

9

The anniversary of the bombing had a greater hold on Jenna this April. She wasn't sure why, it just did. So on Friday after school when all her students were picked up and she'd finished her lesson plans for the next week, Jenna drove to Schiller Park.

The place had been one of her favorites since she'd moved to Columbus. Nicely kept with dozens of trees, all hundreds of years old. A path wound a little more than a mile around the perimeter, perfect for a walk. And today Jenna wanted nothing more.

She started near the statue of Friedrich von Schiller, the German poet. Clouds had gathered overhead, the air chilly for late April. She slipped her hands into the pockets of her rain jacket and stared straight ahead. Why was it so hard to move on? So hard to let go of what happened to her parents?

The answer was obvious. Healing was difficult. For nations and cities. But especially for people. She kept her eyes open, but gradually the images in front of her changed until she was no longer seeing trees and stretches of grass and park benches.

Rather she was seeing the Alfred P. Murrah Federal Building. After the bombing. Of course, Jenna didn't remember firsthand what it had looked like. Neither her grandmother nor she had ever driven by the ruins of what remained that spring. Her grandmother had been busy planning two funerals, and no one would've considered taking Jenna by the place where the building once stood.

It didn't matter.

On the fourth anniversary, Jenna's teacher presented a slide show of the devastation. Jenna must've seen pictures before then. But the photos that day were the first time she understood the scope of horror involved in the explosion. Watching the images, Jenna had started to cry, and when she couldn't stand to see another, she had gotten up and run from the room. After that, her grandmother never sent her to school on the anniversary again.

Staying home kept her safe from having to see reminders of the terrible reality of that day. It assured she wouldn't be sitting in class when a photo of her parents buried under rubble might randomly appear as part of a classroom discussion. But staying home left her with no one to talk to about that day. No one except her grandmother. And since her grandma had lost her daughter and son-in-law, the dear woman had no desire to speak about the tragedy.

Not with Jenna. Not with anyone.

Out of sight, out of mind. That was her grandmother's way of thinking. Which was why — when Jenna was seventeen — her heart had been nearly exploding for the chance to talk to someone about the bombings. The year she met Brady.

Jenna kept walking, slower now. She didn't think about Brady all the time anymore. Only around the anniversary. Sometimes not even then. There were years recently when she'd been so busy processing her miscarriage and then her divorce that she'd barely made time to find a quiet place to remember the anniversary at all.

The clouds overhead grew darker and the wind picked up. Jenna didn't care. She needed this time too much to worry about the weather. Besides, her coat kept her warm enough. She lifted her eyes to the sky as she walked.

The day with Brady had happened a month after Jenna's birthday. At first her plan had been to sleep in, get up around noon and get ahead on her homework.

But school had always come easily for Jenna, and she wasn't one to sleep late. She woke around seven that morning, took a shower and got dressed. By eight-thirty she knew where she wanted to go. The place she hadn't been to since her parents were killed.

The Oklahoma City National Memorial.

Once in a while she'd think about going there, heading through the gates and seeing the place dedicated to those killed. But Jenna had never seen any reason why she should go. Better to remember her parents as they were. Happy and in love, sitting with her at the end of her bed, reading to her. *Love you to the moon and back, Jenna.*

As she headed out, her grandma had stopped her. "Honey? You okay?"

Jenna's answer was the same as always. "I'm fine." Then she hugged her grandmother and looked into her eyes. "What about you?"

And her grandma's tears had come. Just enough to wet her eyelashes. She shook her head, and her lips quivered. She put her hands alongside Jenna's cheeks. Her words took time to come. "I miss them. That's all, I just miss them."

Jenna used to feel jealous of her grand-mother for that reason alone. She had more memories of Jenna's parents. For Jenna the memories were so distant, so dim that she was denied even that. The chance to miss them.

That day as she drove, Jenna hadn't even been sure how to get to the memorial. She got lost a few times, but finally she found the place. For thirty minutes she sat in her car and just stared at the entrance. She wasn't sure what she'd expected it to look like.

Certainly not like a park. Yet that was how it looked. Trees and grass, open and invit-ing. Jenna hadn't known where to start. She wasn't sure she would do more than sit in her car and look at the place from a dis-tance. But something about it drew her inside.

Jenna paused the memory. She was still walking, but now she stared up through the leaves of the trees overhead, and suddenly she remembered another detail. In those first few minutes at the memorial, she had been struck by something deeply profound. What had happened to her parents didn't happen to her alone. It happened to the whole country. To everyone old enough to remember April 19, 1995. Of course, that had always been the case. But Jenna hadn't registered the fact until the moment she saw the scope of the memorial.

The significance of it.

She kept walking along the Schiller Park path, still slower than before. And as she did she gave herself over to everything about that distant memory. How the air had smelled of sweet jasmine planted near the pathway. The way the bronze walls stood, reaching to the sky with their time stamps.

9:01. That was the one Jenna could see from the parking lot. The minute before the bomb went off. The last minute her parents were still alive. With every step she took, every breath, the memory of her long ago visit came to life a little more.

Until finally she wasn't walking in Schiller Park at all. Rather, she was getting out of her car and crossing the memorial grounds. The sky had been cloudy that day, too, so Jenna wore a lightweight navy raincoat and a white knit beanie. She paid the admission fee and slipped through the gates unnoticed. The museum had displays with enormous photos of the horror.

Jenna didn't want to see any of them. That wasn't why she had come. She could go online anytime and see images of the bombing. No, she was here for one reason. To honor the memory of her parents. To stand where they stood in their final moments on earth.

The empty chairs called to her first. They were each lit, translucent almost, one for every person killed in the attack. But almost at the same time she was drawn to another part of the site. The spot where most people milled about.

A stretch of fence that bordered one side of the grounds.

Jenna wandered that way and only then did she understand why so many people were there. The chain link was covered with cards and letters, photos and flowers. Things left in honor of those who died.

The entire stretch was quiet and reflective. Here, the memories were a living, breathing thing. Until that instant Jenna hadn't known the fence existed. That she could've brought letters or cards there in her parents' memory. Or that she maybe should've been visiting the site every year.

Jenna stepped back and took it all in, just watched the people around her. Some of them stood in one place and didn't move, not a step to the right or to the left, their gaze fixated on some object or photo, something written. Others walked slowly, reading the messages, caught up in the offerings.

Most people seemed to be by themselves. On pilgrimages of their own.

It was then, a few minutes after she'd found a spot near the fence, that Jenna saw him. She thought he was older, twenty, maybe. Twenty-one. He was tall, tan with dark hair and muscled shoulders.

What's he doing here? she thought. Even now she remembered catching her breath as he walked closer. His attention was on the fence, as if he were looking for something. Or reading the letters left by other people.

Just as he was about to pass by, their eyes met.

Jenna wanted to look away. She'd been caught staring at him, after all, but she couldn't. She couldn't break contact with the stranger if her life depended on it. He slowed and then sauntered toward her.

"You're new."

She pointed to herself. "Me?"

"Yeah." He smiled, but it never reached his eyes. "You're new. I'm here every year. I've never seen you."

She shifted, captivated by him. "You mean . . . you know these people?" Her glance moved along the fence. The visitors were a mix of different ages. "Are you all . . . like from a club or something?"

He looked more intently at her. "You could say that."

Jenna wasn't sure what he meant, so she held out her hand. "I'm Jenna."

"Brady." His fingers felt warm against hers. He crossed his arms. "If you're here . . . today . . . something tells me you're in the club."

She looked at the fence. "What is it? The club?"

For a long time he said nothing. He slid his hands into his pockets and stared at the people around them. Like he was studying them. When he turned to her again the walls in his light brown eyes were down. Just a little. "Why are you here, Jenna?"

"I've never been." Her answer was quick. She didn't just tell people her story. Not so soon.

He nodded slowly. "That's it? You've never been?"

"Right." She tilted her chin and looked at him straight-on. "Why are you here?"

That's when he pushed up the sleeves of his cream-colored sweater. He held out his arms. "Look."

She took a step closer. At first she didn't see anything unusual. His forearms were as nice as his shoulders. Then she looked more carefully and there they were. Small lines etched into his skin.

"Touch them." His voice soothed the raw edges of her heart.

This was crazy. Jenna wouldn't typically touch strangers. But something about him drew her in. She ran her fingers lightly over the marks. Only then did she know the truth. They were scars. Her eyes lifted to his. "You . . . were hurt."

The dots connected all at once. She turned and looked at the place where the federal building had stood and then back to him. "You . . . you were in the building?"

He pulled his sleeves down and took a long breath. "Walk with me, Jenna."

She'd never met the guy. Never seen him before. But somehow he felt like a friend. Like she'd known him all her life. She walked beside him, both of them quiet. He led her up a set of stairs to a bench not far from a large tree. The image of the tree was familiar, its trunk and outstretched branches something she had seen before.

They sat on the bench and Brady sighed. "Me and the tree. We're the same." He turned and faced her. "We both survived that day."

Jenna felt the connection between them

grow. "What happened?"

"You first." His eyes were kinder now. "Why are you here?"

From where they were sitting Jenna could see the field of empty chairs. She stared in that direction and took her time. If Brady had been here that day, if he'd been in the building when the explosion went off, then he would understand.

If anyone would.

She looked at him again. "My parents worked in the building. Different floors." Her eyes welled up. She hadn't expected to cry in front of him. "I . . . I lost them both."

Slowly, deliberately, Brady reached for her hand. He didn't say a word. He didn't have to. For a long time they stayed like that. His warm fingers around hers, his thumb soft against her skin. "Where were you?"

With her free hand, Jenna caught the first tear as it fell down her cheek. "With my grandma. I stayed with her while my parents were at work." She tried to smile, but it did nothing to stop her crying. "I was five."

That last part seemed to hit Brady harder than the rest of her story. "Five." He squinted toward the sky, then back at her. "I was five, too." His hand was still safe around hers. "I was here with my mom when . . ."

His voice trailed off. There was nothing rushed about their conversation. The silence was easy between them. Comfortable and achingly sad all at the same time.

Jenna waited. Brady's story would come eventually.

And after a minute it did.

10

Jenna had watched Brady, studying him. He was quiet for a long time, as if the train that held his memories only came by every so often.

He looked at the stormy sky again, or maybe to some far-off place he clearly didn't want to visit. He filled his lungs. "My mom and I were in line at one of the federal offices." He shifted his attention to her. "I was playing with this gray stanchion, this thick dirty cord that kept us in line, and my mom was telling me not to touch it. I'd get germs." He paused. "And then . . ." His eyes glistened, the memory alive again. "She came down to my level and smiled at me. Straight at me."

Jenna could picture it. Like a movie playing out in the space between them.

"She told me we were almost done." He sniffed and looked to the sky once more. "That's all I remember." He was still holding her hand, but he held up his other arm. "I woke up in the hospital with these cuts. That's it. My mom . . . she protected me from everything else."

He didn't have to say his mother didn't make it. Jenna already knew.

Brady pointed at the tree. "You know the story about that?"

"Not really." For the first time, Jenna wanted to know more about what happened that April 19. "I've . . . stayed away."

The empathy in Brady's tone was a connection Jenna had never felt before. Kind and understanding. The same hurt as her own. "I get that. Staying away." He searched her face. "You're still in the club. Whether you come here or not."

She nodded. The club. "The people along the fence. They all . . . they all lost someone?"

"That's what I tell myself." He looked over his shoulder back to where the people still stood. Some of them gripping the chain link. "I see lots of them every year." He turned to her again. "Why else would they be here?"

Jenna could think of a few reasons, but she liked Brady's explanation better. Wanderers, broken people. All of them survivors, one way or another. She motioned to the tree. "Tell me about it."

"The Survivor Tree?" Brady stood and helped her gently to her feet. Maybe because of the weather, there was no one else on the patio near the elm that day. Just the two of them, making their way to the tree trunk.

He still had hold of her hand. When they reached the tree, Brady put the palm of his other hand against the bark. "Every bit of this tree was ripped to shreds. Glass and metal. Who knows what else." He paused. "Its branches were sheared off." Brady glanced at her. "It even caught fire."

"It did?" Jenna pressed her free hand against the trunk, too. "You could never tell. It's so . . . strong." That was what surprised her most. The tree was easily the biggest and most beautiful at the memorial.

"Which is why I love this place." Brady pulled back and Jenna did the same. They faced each other. "If the old elm can be strong again . . . so can we."

"Yes." It was something Jenna desperately wanted to believe. But for that moment it was enough to be here with Brady.

For a second he looked like he might kiss her. But then he gave her the slightest smile. "Is it weird? That I'm holding your hand?"

"No." It wasn't just that he was the cutest boy she'd ever seen. Somehow holding hands here at the memorial with someone else who had lost his mom seemed perfectly normal. Better than normal. She felt the corners of her lips lift a little. "It's nice."

"Good." They walked down the stairs to the pond and found a low-slung stone wall. He released her hand as they sat side by side, facing the water. Close enough that his arm brushed against hers. He waited a minute. "I can't believe you haven't been here."

His tone didn't hold any judgment. Just surprise. If she'd known she might meet him here, she would've come sooner.

She glanced at him. "I can't believe you come every year."

"It's my way . . . I don't know." He breathed in, deep and slow, and leaned toward the pond, elbows on his knees. "My way of keeping her with me."

"Mmm." Jenna let that settle for a minute. "I don't think about this place." She hesitated. "When I think of my parents, I guess I think about heaven. They . . . went there together." Jenna smiled at Brady through fresh tears. "That makes me feel better."

"I get that." Brady looked past her eyes to her heart. "If they were anything like you . . . I wish I could've known them."

"Me, too." Jenna lifted her eyes to the sky.

"Sometimes . . . I'm not sure what I remember is even real." She shifted her gaze and let herself get lost in his eyes. "Tell me about your mom."

Brady sat up straighter and took her hand again. "She was beautiful." He was in no hurry. "Her smile was like the sun."

Jenna kept watching him. It was sinking in, the fact that she and Brady had both lost their parents when they were five. Right here. On the same day. "Do you remember her?"

"Not like I want to." Brady sighed. "Maybe that's why I come every anniversary. I don't want to lose her. The part of her I can still see and hear."

They got up and walked to another bench, one near a grove of trees at the other side of the memorial. The clouds were darker still, and a cool breeze had picked up. They sat facing each other this time. He didn't reach for her hand, but it didn't matter. Their hearts were still connected. Jenna searched his face. "What about your dad?"

"I never knew him." The hesitation in Brady's eyes was gone now. Completely. "After my mom died, I lived with a friend of hers. Then the state moved me to foster care and I stayed in the system. One house to the next."

Jenna leaned forward. This time she took his hand in hers. "Even now?"

"Yeah." He looked at where their fingers touched. "It's fine. I'm gonna be a firefighter. I'll be on my own soon."

Her heart broke for him. She figured she knew the answer, but she had to ask anyway. "A firefighter? Because . . ."

"Yeah." He managed a quick smile. "Definitely." He saw all the way to her soul. "So some other little kid doesn't have to go through what I went through."

They talked about growing up in Oklahoma City and how every April 19 they felt alone. Like no one could understand what they were facing. "The bombing didn't just happen to the city." Brady removed his hand from hers and laced his fingers behind his head. He stared across the grounds of the memorial. "It was our tragedy." He glanced at her. "It's personal for you and me. It happened to us."

Us. Jenna loved how he said that. She took a quick breath. He might as well know the rest of her story. "I grew up with my grandma." She told him about the time her teacher had showed images from the bombing and how upset she'd gotten. "My grandma never made me go to school on April nineteenth again."

"But you never came here." Brady shifted so he could see her better.

"I think . . . somewhere in my childhood I allowed myself to believe a fantasy. That my parents were still alive. Living overseas somewhere like London or Rome. And one day they'd come back and we'd all be together again."

"So being here —"

"Yes." She had the feeling he knew exactly what she meant. What she was feeling. "Being here makes it real."

The breeze gusted now. Brady looked at the sky and back at her. "Storm's coming."

"Fitting." She tightened her jacket around her. "I used to fall asleep asking God just one thing. That in the morning I'd wake up and come downstairs and my parents would be there. Sitting at the kitchen table, sharing coffee."

Tears filled her eyes again. "They'd see me and we'd run to each other and I'd be in their arms. They'd kiss my head and tell me how much they missed me and every-thing . . . everything would be okay." She hesitated. "I prayed that till I was in middle school."

Brady let her story hang there for a min-ute. Blowing in the wind between them. Then he sat a little straighter. "We prayed the same thing, Jenna. I remember . . . I was six or seven . . . eight. Nine. Lying in bed, begging God that before I fell asleep my mom would walk into the room and sit on the edge of my bed. And just one more time she'd say, 'Love you to the moon and back, Brady. Love you to the moon and back.' "

A chill ran down Jenna's arms and legs. "Your mother used to say that?"

"Every night."

It was one more connection. "Mine, too." She paused, her tears spilling onto her cheeks. "After bedtime prayers. It was our special thing."

"They probably would've been friends, our moms." Brady seemed to think for a long moment, and gradually the hurt returned to his eyes. And something else. Anger or bitterness, maybe. "I remember the night I stopped praying. I told God if He didn't bring my mom back, then I was done talking to Him." He paused and for a moment his eyes grew harder. "I kept my promise."

"Me, too." The sad picture of the little boy he must've been was suddenly etched in Jenna's heart. "I don't pray anymore." The sameness of their stories was more than Jenna could take in. "I mean, I still go to church with my grandma. It would hurt her if I stayed home. But I guess I'm just . . . I don't know, frustrated with God." She looked straight at Brady. "Like why did He have to take *my* mom and dad?"

"And my mom." Brady took a deep breath and stood. The pain eased from his expression again. "Let's get coffee."

At that point, Jenna would've gone anywhere with him. No one had ever understood her feelings the way Brady did. They started walking. "So you don't go to church?"

"No." He made a sound more laugh than cry. "Hardly. The state says foster parents can't force us to do anything. Especially where religion is concerned."

"Makes sense."

Again Brady took her hand. This time he worked his fingers gently between hers. "Have you seen the commercials for that movie *Superbad*?"

"I think so . . . It looks, I don't know, not that great." She laughed, and he did, too.

"That's what I thought."

They left the memorial grounds and made their way down the street. The wind played with her hair. "Why did you ask? About that movie?"

"Because." He slowed his pace and

stopped, facing her. With his thumb, he brushed her bangs out of her eyes. "You look like the actress in it."

She angled her head. "Thanks." Her smile came easily now. "I think. Right?"

"Definitely." He looked down, and then back at her. His cheeks grew slightly red. "You're very pretty, Jenna."

His words sent a rush through her. It wasn't the sort of thing she heard often. Not from guys who looked like Brady, anyway. Jenna tried to focus. "My grandma tells me I look just like my mom." She smiled again. More shy this time. "Dark red hair and green eyes like her. So I guess that's a good thing."

"Very good." Brady studied her for a few seconds before they started walking again. They got coffee from a small café and took the trip back to the memorial more slowly. Brady talked about the first year he came here. He was ten and one of his foster parents brought him. "That day I could really feel my mom with me again. Right beside me." Brady cast her a quick look. "After that I always asked someone to bring me here. My foster parents or my Little League coach. Whoever."

"Which is why you started recognizing people at the fence."

"Exactly." They stopped at a bench and sat down. For several minutes, neither of them said anything. They just sipped their coffee and listened to the wind from the coming storm. Jenna felt like she'd slipped into some other world. For the first time someone knew exactly what the hurt felt like.

Then the rain hit. Not the slow sort of rain that starts with a few drops and builds to a downpour. This one came over them all at once. Brady grabbed her hand and they ran with their coffees down the street and into the museum. By then they were drenched, and there — inside the building — they had nowhere to go, no way to avoid the photos mounted on the wall.

Brady let go of her hand and walked slowly to the first picture. A shot of the Alfred P. Murrah Building a few days before the bombing. Brady stood as close as he could, his eyes locked on the image. Jenna came up beside him. She blinked the rain from her lashes. At the same time they both seemed to notice something about the building.

The windows were lit.

Which meant her parents were somewhere in there. Walking around. Working. Putting in their time until they could come home and be with her. Princess Jenna. She narrowed her eyes and found the third and fifth floors. The places where their offices used to be.

"My parents . . . they would've been there that day." A chill came over her. Jenna wasn't sure whether it was from the rain or the reality of what she was taking in. "I can almost see them. Through the windows."

"Think about that, Jenna." He moved closer to her, the heat of his arm warm against hers. "How beautiful. It's like . . . they're still alive. At least in that picture."

She hadn't thought of it that way. More just the reality that if they could've gone back, if they would've known how little time they had . . . then maybe they wouldn't have gone to work that day . . . and maybe things would've turned out differently.

"What about you?" She leaned into his arm a little, her eyes still on the photo. "What do you see?"

"I guess I see what might've been." He examined the image. "That could've been us. Inside the building *that* day. Running errands on the sixteenth or seventeenth. But never on April nineteenth."

The possibility sank deep inside Jenna's heart. Her parents hadn't known they had so little time. Nothing had warned them that if only they had taken that Wednesday off everything would still be okay. Their family would still be together. Same for Brady. There was no way for his mother and him to go back and do their errand another day.

So they'd be anywhere but the federal building that fateful morning.

Jenna drew a deep breath. "I have to go." Her grandmother would worry about her if she was gone longer than this. Rain still poured outside, so they were stuck in the museum. And Jenna couldn't bear the thought of studying the rest of the photos.

The destruction.

Brady nodded. He finished his coffee, tossed his empty cup and hers in a nearby trash can and shoved his hands in his pockets. The intimacy that had been between them earlier seemed to fade. They were strangers, after all. Two kids who had grown up with the same heartache, the same sad story.

But that was it.

He hesitated for a minute. "Hold on." A quick jog to the information desk a few yards away and he returned with paper and a pen. "Here." He wrote something on the sheet and handed it to her.

Brady. And beneath that, his number.

"You're in the club." He smiled, but his eyes were deep with sadness. "Call me. We'll come here together next year."

She nodded. The idea sounded good. Brady and her, the two of them here. Their heartache against the world. A smile tugged at her lips. "Okay."

Brady hesitated. "This is where you give me *your* number." He chuckled lightly. "So I don't have to wait a year to see you."

Her own laugh caught her off guard. "A year is a long time."

"A week's a long time." His eyes landed on hers and held.

She felt like she'd known him all her life. "Here." She ripped off a part of the paper and followed suit: *Jenna.* And beneath that, her number.

"Thanks." He looked at it and slipped it into his pocket. "I'll call you soon." His expression faded. "I will."

"Okay." She liked him. Everything about him. "Call me."

The museum was crowded, people trying to get out of the rain. Even so, Jenna felt like they were the only two people in the building. They were still facing each other. Jenna had a feeling their hearts would be connected, long after they said goodbye.

He took a step closer, his voice quieter

than before. "I want to kiss you, Jenna."

She wanted that, too. But she couldn't say so. Instead she felt her grin warm her face. "I think we should wait."

"Yeah." He was teasing her now. Flirting with her. "Come here."

They were only inches apart. Jenna did as he asked and for a second she thought he might kiss her anyway. Instead he pulled her into his arms. Not a lovers' embrace. But something more tender, deeper. Protective. Without any words, being held by him told her that after today she would never be alone in her missing, never be by herself in her sadness. She had Brady now.

She was part of the club.

Rain finally broke through the clouds and began falling over Schiller Park. As if God Himself were crying because of the memory she had just relived.

Brady hadn't written his last name on the slip of paper and Jenna hadn't noticed until she got home. She'd expected him to call her that day or sometime in the next week.

But he never did.

A week later she took his paper from the top drawer in the nightstand next to her bed and realized the rain had blurred the numbers. She could only make out a few of them. She threw the paper away and tried not to feel hurt. Their day together almost didn't seem real, anyway. He probably has a girlfriend, she told herself. Or he'd gotten away from the memorial and wondered why he'd given his number to a complete stranger.

Months passed and Jenna eventually put him out of her mind. Until the following April, anyway, when the anniversary came back around. But that year Jenna was sick on April 19. Too sick to get out of bed. She figured he had her number, and that maybe because of the anniversary he'd finally call.

But he never made contact.

Whatever the reason, Jenna clearly wasn't going to hear from Brady. And as time passed she told herself she was crazy to still think about him. She didn't even know his last name. The detail hadn't seemed important back then. He was going to call her that week. They had forever to figure out last names and logistics.

Instead, they missed whatever might have been. Though Jenna would always remember the magic of that single day.

The next four April 19 anniversaries, Jenna was in college at a small private university in Texas, so she never made it back to the memorial. She did, though, make her way back to Jesus.

Yes, God had a plan for her. She still believed that. A plan that included her teaching job in Columbus. But clearly it did not involve a dark-haired stranger from a lifetime ago. A guy she only knew by his smile and handsome face, his deep eyes and a name she would never forget as long as she lived.

Brady.

11

They'd been back from spring break for a week and this Saturday was one Ashley and the entire Baxter family had been looking forward to for a month. In a few hours, all of them were meeting at the Christian Kids Theater for a matinee performance of *Peter Pan*. Annie and Janessa and Amy were in the show. Amy was playing Wendy — her biggest role yet.

After the show, everyone was coming back to Landon and Ashley's house for dinner. Ashley checked the time on the microwave. Just after noon. She'd already dropped the girls off at the theater and three pot roasts with vegetables were cooking in her Crock-Pots — all lined up on the counter.

The show didn't start for another two hours.

Landon and the boys were fishing at Lake Monroe, so Ashley had something she didn't often have: time.

She still hadn't found Jenna, though she'd searched every way she knew how. No bombing survivors or grieving children by that name. Nothing in the Internet archives. None of the survivor registries listed her name. Which meant she must not have been in the building when the bomb went off.

Bottom line, Ashley needed more information. Sure she had Brady's cell number. But maybe if she revisited his Facebook page. Or found something on social media. Maybe then she'd know more about him and his story. Like why he'd been so short with her in his response last week.

Ashley grabbed her laptop and sat out on the back porch. The day was mild and breezy, the blue sky dotted with white puffy clouds. Spring had filled in green where bare branches were just a few weeks ago.

She turned on her computer and brought up Facebook. She'd seen his page before, that day on the boat, but only briefly. She still hadn't found the right time to tell Landon about her text to Brady. But it didn't matter. She hadn't texted Brady again.

Maybe Brady's social media would tell Ashley something new. Something about Jenna or the reason Brady felt so alone. He didn't have many posts on his page from

189

what she remembered. But maybe she'd missed something. Ashley typed his name in the Facebook search bar: "Brady Bradshaw."

She closed her eyes. *Lord, why is this guy on my heart? If You want me to drop the whole thing, I will.* She took a slow breath and opened her eyes. She clicked enter and . . . there he was. Same as before. Brady Bradshaw. Firefighter. Oklahoma City. Dark hair and chiseled face. He didn't have sunglasses the way he had at the memorial. But it was him. No question. She scanned the page. Still not much here.

Okay, Ashley. Go slow. Look for clues.

She read the most recent post. It was from the anniversary. The picture was the fence, and there at the center of the image was his letter tucked into the chain link. *For Jenna.* Ashley could only read the girl's name because she knew what it said. Otherwise it would've been easy to miss. Just an artsy photo from the memorial.

But Ashley knew better.

It was a sign, of course. If Jenna were to look for Brady, and if somehow she were to find his Facebook page, then just maybe she would know. That every year since they met, Brady had come back to the site for her.

All for her.

The status wasn't long. Ashley read it.
Some years I wait a little longer at the fence.
Just in case this is the year you join me.

Chills ran down Ashley's arms. The guy was obsessed. Whatever had happened between him and Jenna, he wanted to find her more than he wanted his next breath. Or at least it seemed that way.

"Okay," she whispered. "So who are you, Brady?" She scrolled down the page. The older posts were about a fund-raiser the fire department was hosting. A little more reading and she figured it out. A firefighter had died working a fire a year earlier. The benefit was to raise money for his family.

She checked his photos. In case there might be something else, something from the memorial. Maybe a snapshot of the two of them eleven years ago. He didn't have many pictures. A few of the firehouse, and his rig. One of him with a couple fellow firefighters.

Another scroll down and there was the calendar image of him. He was August in the Oklahoma City Firefighters Calendar. This time Ashley studied the look on his face. He was smiling, but his eyes looked dead. Closed off. Whatever his story, it colored everything about his life. Even when he was supposed to be having fun.

Another page of pictures and there were a few of him much thinner, wearing only a scrappy pair of shorts. Super tan. From when he'd been a contestant on the TV show *Survivor.* Didn't make it more than a few weeks, by the look of it.

Ashley read every caption and post. There was no mention of faith or gratitude or the blessings of life. No signs of a deep friendship or close family members or a girlfriend. "He meant what he said in the letter," Ashley muttered. "He really is alone."

After half an hour on his page, Ashley understood him a bit better. Brady seemed dedicated to his job but otherwise without anyone important in his life. Not even God. She sighed, closed out of Facebook and took her laptop into the house. She set it on the kitchen table and looked at the pantry. Time to get the sweet potatoes in the oven. She was doing that when the boys got home.

They left their muddy boots by the back door and came in like a rush of sunshine, talking all at once and laughing about something. As they entered the kitchen, Ashley saw they were all three drenched.

"Dad did it." Cole shook his head. He was still laughing so hard he had tears in his eyes. "We were in the canoe, almost back to the shore."

"And Dad sees an eagle." Devin leaned against the counter, catching his breath. "You know how Dad always thinks he can talk to animals?"

"His talent works with Toby." Ashley felt the afternoon get so much lighter. At the sound of his name, their one-year-old Labrador puppy came trotting into the kitchen. His paws were muddy, his coat as wet as the boys. Ashley took a step back and grinned at Landon. "So what happened?"

"I was calling the eagle." Landon shrugged.

"You know, Mom. 'Ca-CAW . . . ca-CAW!' " Devin slapped his knee. "Only Toby thought Dad was calling him."

"So the eagle flies off and Toby jumps to that side of the canoe and —"

Cole made a splashing sound and threw his hands in the air. "The canoe flips and we're all in the water. Just like that."

"Don't worry." Devin grinned. "We all had life jackets. Dad said that part would make you happy."

"So there we were. All your boys in the water." Cole patted Landon on the back. "At least we were close to the shore."

"Yes." Landon raised his brow at Ashley. "Guilty as charged." He winked at the boys. "I still say the eagle would've come closer if it wasn't for Toby."

"I wanna hear more about it. But maybe go shower up first." Ashley laughed. "Another adventure for the books."

"Definitely." Landon leaned close enough to kiss her, all while keeping his distance so she didn't get wet. "I'll be back."

After he left she stared for a minute at her computer. She needed to tell him about texting Brady and looking him up again. She really meant to. But there never seemed to be the right time. Besides, Landon would understand. Ashley was sure.

She stood and followed him to their bathroom. While he showered she did her hair and makeup.

Thirty minutes later she was ready for the show, sitting at the kitchen table when Landon returned. The kids were still upstairs and they had time before they needed to leave. Landon grinned at her. "You look gorgeous." He walked over to her.

She stood. "You, too." Ashley hesitated. Her nerves were struggling. Everything was so good about this day. Why ruin it by — Before she could finish the thought, he came to her and kissed her again. This time with his body against hers.

"Mmmm." She loved moments like this. "I wish I could've seen the canoe flip." A giggle crossed her lips. "You're such a good dad, Landon." She brushed her cheek against his. "Did you catch any fish?"

"Four." He laughed. "Lost them all when the boat tipped."

Ashley winced. "A memory for sure." She put her hands on either side of his face. "At least we weren't counting on fish for dinner."

"Whatever's cooking smells a whole lot better." Landon put his hand gently against her cheek and searched her eyes. "What did you do? Besides miss us?" He pointed to her computer. "Email?"

"No." She hesitated. "Right. I was just going to tell you." Ashley took a step back and folded her arms. "I went to Brady Bradshaw's Facebook page again. Just, you know, looking for clues." She paused, gauging his reaction. "In case there was something more about Jenna."

"Oh." Landon's smile fell. He blinked, his expression frozen for several seconds. Then he slid his hands in the pockets of his black jeans. "I guess I thought you were past that." He leaned against the kitchen counter and searched her eyes.

"I was." She looked at the floor and then at him. "I mean, I was before. But I just . . . What if I can help him?"

"And why is that your job?" His eyes clouded. "The guy's a complete stranger, Ash."

"I know, but . . ." Frustration colored her tone. "Someone has to help him. I keep thinking maybe God wants me to do this. Have you thought about that?"

"No." Landon gave a single laugh. "God doesn't ask married women to befriend single men."

"I'm not *befriending* him." She shook her head and dropped to the chair nearest her laptop. "I can't believe you're mad."

His expression was a mix of hurt and anger. "So what'd you learn? That you didn't learn last time."

"I was looking for clues." Her answer was quick. Just short of snappy.

Landon nodded at the computer. "Open it up. Let's see the clues."

Ashley couldn't believe this. "You're really angry." Her disbelief came out as a solitary laugh. "Are you saying you don't trust me?"

"No." He took a few steps closer. "I want to see the clues."

"That's ridiculous, Landon." She thought about Brady's calendar photos. "I'm not going back to his page."

"Then tell me." His voice sounded harder now. "What did you find?"

Ashley hated this. She should've kept it to herself. Looking up Brady Bradshaw meant nothing. There was no reason for Landon to be upset. She released a pent-up breath. "Fine." She shifted in her chair so she was facing Landon. "He doesn't seem to have faith in God. No family or girlfriend. He's mostly about his job at the firehouse. Some firefighter calendar he was in and pictures of his time on the show *Survivor.*"

"Calendar pictures?" Landon's eyes grew darker. "Do you hear how that sounds?"

"Okay, so I found nothing." This was getting worse. "I was actually going to tell you I'm glad you never did the Bloomington firefighter calendar." Ashley stood and took a step back. The closeness between them a few minutes ago was gone. "It wouldn't have been fair to the other guys." She tried to smile. "You would've gotten the cover every time."

Landon didn't smile. "This isn't funny, Ashley." His tone was more hurt than mad. "I asked you to stop looking up the guy, but it's become . . . I don't know, an obsession."

"Landon!" She felt her own anger rising. "Because I want to help somebody, suddenly I'm obsessed?"

"You're not helping." Landon shook his head. "You're stalking. Or meddling. Something . . . but there's no point to it."

She felt her heart sink. Did he really think that? "Wow." She shrugged. "I don't know what to say."

Landon walked to the cupboard and grabbed a glass. He filled it with water and drank it, his eyes on Ashley the whole time. When he stopped for air he angled his head. "That's easy." His tone was more controlled now. "Tell me you'll let it go. You don't know him, Ash. There's nothing you can do to help him." He hesitated. "Let the guy figure out his own life."

"Let it go?" Determination gradually replaced the hurt. "I haven't found Jenna. I know you're mad but . . . I'd like to at least try."

"Are you serious?" He set his glass down. "How will you find her, Ash? Do you have special Internet powers?" He clenched his jaw. "This Brady guy's been looking for her every year for more than a decade."

"What if . . . what if I text him?" She couldn't tell him that she already had. "Maybe he could point me in the right direction. Maybe there's something he's missed." She took a quick breath. *Let Landon hear my heart, God. Please.* "This isn't about Brady. It's about . . . doing what's right."

This time disbelief flashed in Landon's eyes. "Doing what's right, Ash? The right thing is to forget all about it."

From upstairs the sound of the kids interrupted the discussion. They were headed down, ready for the show. Ashley felt like running out the back door and finding her favorite spot. The rock by the stream at the far side of their property.

The last thing she wanted was to spend the afternoon with Landon. Not when he was so mad at her. What had she even done? She lowered her voice. "I want to be honest here, Landon. I'm sorry. I'm not . . . trying to hurt you."

He studied her, clearly still upset. "We can talk about it later." A quick turn and he left, headed toward the stairs. "Let's go." He switched to a pleasant tone as he called for the kids. "We need to leave."

Ashley stared at the floor. How did this happen? They should still have been standing here laughing about the incident with the canoe. Kissing and teasing and flirting. The way they were before.

Instead they were in the saddest, most rare place. Stuck in the middle of a fight. And the craziest thing was even now, even still, Ashley wanted only to do one thing. The thing she absolutely couldn't do. Not until

she and Landon were on the same page.
Contact Brady Bradshaw.

Ashley's stomach hurt. The distance between Landon and her as their family arrived to the play still weighed on her.
Landon had all his attention on the kids.
He and Ashley hadn't even made eye contact since they left the house.

Once they found their seats Ashley spotted Bailey Flanigan Paul talking to another
theater parent in the main aisle, several rows
away. She needed a diversion so she got up.
"Excuse me."

Landon stood and let her pass. But he
didn't say a word.

A sigh worked its way through Ashley's
troubled heart. She walked up the aisle and
waited for Bailey to be free.

"Ashley!" Bailey hugged her. "I can't
believe it's opening night!"

"And this auditorium." Ashley looked
around. Bailey and her husband owned the
theater and the entire city block. "The place
is amazing. And the buildings around it.
Better than ever."

"It's our dream." Bailey looked toward
the front of the lobby. Her husband was
holding Hannah, their little girl. She was
ten months old now. Bailey nodded in their

direction. "Brandon's the best dad."

"Makes life pretty amazing, doesn't it?" Ashley smiled. Landon was a wonderful father, too. She glanced back at the row where Landon was still sitting. She hated that they were fighting. They needed to figure this out when they got home. Ashley turned to Bailey again and tried to focus. "So Hannah's almost one."

"Time keeps flying." Bailey's eyes were soft. "Being a mom is the best." Moments like this Ashley wondered where the years had gone. It seemed just yesterday Bailey was a teenager, back when the Baxters and the Flanigans first became friends. Of course, in reality that was many years ago. Ashley had painted sets for CKT and Bailey had been one of the young actors. The Flanigans and Baxters were practically family, and Ashley couldn't be more proud of Bailey.

"Hey, guess who's pregnant?" Bailey's eyes lit up. She didn't wait for an answer. "Andi! She and Cody have tickets for today's show. They're in town to see her family."

The news warmed Ashley's heart. All through high school and college, Cody had been in love with Bailey. But the two were never meant to be. Meanwhile Bailey's best friend, Andi, had been secretly in love with Cody. Years of missed chances later, Cody and Andi were finally married. Beyond happy. "That's wonderful. They've been married almost a year, too. Right?"

"Exactly." Bailey's eyes lit up with her smile. Anyone could see that her happiness for her friends was as genuine as her beautiful heart. "They got married the same day Hannah was born. I'm thrilled for them."

Bailey caught Ashley up on the rest of her family. Her brothers were playing sports at Clear Creek High, where Shawn and Justin were both on the basketball team. Bailey's oldest brother, Connor, was still at Liberty University. "You probably know about Connor and Maddie." Bailey did a slight shrug. "On again, off again."

Ashley had heard. Maddie was her niece, Brooke's daughter. She'd been struggling with direction lately. Ashley wanted to get back to her seat, back to Landon. In case they could find at least a little breakthrough before the show started. For now, she kept her focus on Bailey. "Brooke says Maddie's at that age. Doesn't know what she wants."

Bailey smiled. "I think Connor knows. But he's being patient. He has some new girl at Liberty. Just friends, he says." She shook her head. "I keep praying for him."

"Brooke's doing the same for Maddie." Ashley hugged Bailey. "Again, just so proud of what you've done here. Your theater, the whole city block. It's the talk of Bloomington."

"Thanks." Bailey turned as Brandon walked up with their baby girl.

"Little Hannah!" Ashley touched the child's cheek. "She's beautiful."

"Thanks." A deep joy shone in Brandon's eyes. Like he couldn't have been more thrilled with life. "Good to see you, Ashley. Your whole family's here today."

"Of course. It's Amy's big night." Ashley remembered the main reason they were here. The other kids were in this show, but Amy was a lead. Tonight was her niece's debut as Wendy in *Peter Pan.* Ashley glanced at the stage. "I hope she's not nervous."

"A little. But she'll be fine." Brandon smiled and put his free arm around Bailey. "She's a natural. The perfect Wendy."

Bailey leaned into her husband, her eyes still on Ashley. "Amy's wonderful. You'll love the show."

"Can't wait to see it." Just then the house-lights flashed. Ashley pointed to where her family was. "I better get going. We'll talk after."

She returned to her row and again Landon stood to let her pass by. Nothing more.

In front of them Ashley watched the Flanigans and their boys take their seats. Jenny and Jim waved and Landon lit up and returned the gesture. Ashley did the same, but as soon as the Flanigans were settled, Ashley watched the smile fall off Landon's face.

From the beginning, the show was even better than Ashley had hoped. Bailey was right. Amy was the perfect Wendy. Still, it was hard for Ashley to focus. Not once did Landon reach for her hand, even when the lights went down. But after a few scenes, Ashley stopped thinking about Landon and directed her full attention to the play.

When Wendy asked Peter Pan if he didn't miss having a mother and a father, Ashley got tears in her eyes. She wanted to lean her head on Landon's shoulder. This was a time when he would normally give her hand a soft squeeze. Instead the distance remained.

Ashley kept her eyes on Amy. What other little girl in the theater group could so personally understand the weight of missing her parents?

When the show ended, Landon walked over to the Flanigans. Ashley didn't join him. Pretending to be fine was exhausting. Instead she started slowly for the doors at the back of the theater. Cole and Devin stayed with her. As they went, Ashley saw Cody and Andi talking with Brandon and Bailey.

Despite her own sadness, Ashley smiled to herself. God was so good, allowing the four of them their own beautiful happily-ever-afters. Not what they had pictured once upon a yesterday. But more perfect than they could've imagined.

As they made their way to the parking lot, Ashley remembered dinner. Everyone was coming over to celebrate Annie and Janessa and Amy and the show. Even Dayne and Katy were in town with their little ones. Again on the way home Ashley and Landon barely talked.

It's going to be a long night, she thought. She kept her eyes on the side window most of the ride home.

The dinner was more fun than Ashley had expected. The joy of having her entire family around helped her forget for a while the trouble with Landon. The kids ran out back along the stream and looked for tadpoles in the pond. Ashley's dad and Landon stayed outside with them until it was nearly dark.

Ashley watched out the kitchen window

and Kari and Brooke joined her. "Wasn't that just us?" Ashley looked at her sisters. "Running through that magical backyard. Pretending we were on some crazy adventure every afternoon?"

"Have you ever showed your kids the rock?" Brooke's tone was wistful as she stared at the kids. "The one with our handprints?"

Ashley grinned. "A few times." The rock sat along the stream at the edge of their property.

Now Ashley used it as a place to talk to God.

"I still love that spot." She looked at her sisters. "We used to hang out there all the time when we were little."

"Whenever life got hard." Brooke paused. "Remember?"

Ashley had taken her own children to the area years ago, but she wanted to show them again. Ashley sighed. "We definitely need to bring all the kids there. Maybe next time."

As they were sitting down to dinner, everyone complimented Amy on her work as Wendy. If anyone else noticed the similarities between Amy's character and her real life without actual parents, they didn't say so. There was also much praise for Janessa and Annie, both of whom were Tiger Lily's sidekicks.

The cousins sat at the kids' table a few feet away, and halfway through dinner Dayne and Katy updated everyone on their new movie. They were both starring in it, and though the film was slated for a limited theatrical release, Dayne still thought it would do well at the box office. "We're making it for under a million."

"The message is powerful." Katy glanced at Luke. "Right to life . . . and then it looks like our next movie will deal with religious freedom."

"Speaking of which." Ashley looked at her younger brother. "What's happening with Wendell Quinn, the principal of Hamilton High?"

It was a case Luke had taken on, one that thrust him into the national spotlight for a time. Luke set his napkin on the table. "Wendell is engaged to Alicia — remember her?"

"I do." Ashley grinned at Luke and then at Landon. "We figured that was going to happen. And he's still leading the voluntary Bible study for the students?"

"He is." Satisfaction shone in Luke's eyes. "God won that case, for sure."

"Yes." Reagan smiled at the others. "And Luke's home more. Only forty hours a week at the office." She put her arm around Luke's shoulders and kissed his cheek. "So life is good."

"Definitely." Luke kissed her on the lips and looked around the table.

Ashley was grateful for the things Luke and Reagan had figured out. Luke had let his dedication to law get the best of him last year. Too much time at work. Ashley could tell from her younger brother's eyes that he was doing much better.

The one thing Luke and Reagan didn't talk about was the fact that they'd run into Andi at the performance. Some time ago, during one of Andi's rough seasons, she had given birth to little Johnny. The father wasn't in the picture at all, and Andi knew she couldn't raise her son alone. Through a series of miracles, Luke and Reagan had adopted him.

Little Johnny knew he was adopted, but not necessarily that Andi was his birth mother. Apparently, all of them had agreed that Andi would only be a close friend whenever they all met up. Andi wanted it that way.

Less confusing for Johnny.

Before the show, Ashley had watched Andi drop down to Johnny's level to talk to him. After that, Andi and Reagan had spoken.

Ashley could see they were smiling, but the moment didn't last long. Ashley would have to ask Reagan about it later.

During dessert Kari and Ryan updated everyone on Jessie's search for the right university. She and Cole were both looking at Liberty in Virginia. Ashley thought about how soon those changes were coming.

For now, though, there was just tonight and their time together.

When everyone was gone, Landon and the boys moved to the garage to clean the canoe and the fishing gear. Janessa and Amy were already asleep and Ashley was dying to talk to Landon. But in the meantime, she wanted to work on her sketch. She found her book and sat down at the kitchen table.

Ashley was lost in the drawing when Amy tiptoed downstairs in her nightgown. Her niece held a hand-painted picture. "I couldn't sleep." She set the picture down in front of Ashley. "I drew this. I thought you'd like it." She looped her arm around Ashley's neck and stared at her own artwork. "I think maybe I draw like you."

"Wow. That's beautiful, Amy." Ashley stared at the girl's drawing. She could hardly believe it. "Look what I was working on." She slid her sketchbook over so it was side by side with Amy's artwork. "When were you working on this?"

"The last few days." She looked at Ashley's illustration and then her own. "After we came back from spring break."

They'd been working on the exact same thing: the Survivor Tree.

Amy looked at her. "Are you going to paint yours?"

"I think so. People here don't really know about the tree. I think God let it live to symbolize what's possible. With Him."

"That's what I think, too." Amy gazed at her picture. "I'm glad you like it."

Amy was talented, for sure. What a privilege to help her niece discover gifts like this one. Ashley could only hope that somewhere in heaven, Erin and Sam were watching. "We'll have to frame it. Then you can hang it on the wall in your room."

"Near the bookcase."

"Yes, sweetheart. That would be perfect." She put her hands on Amy's shoulders. "You were very good today as Wendy."

"Thanks." Amy's face filled with tenderness. She kept her eyes on Ashley's. "I understand Wendy. All she wants is to go home to her mom and dad."

"Even though she's happy with Peter in Neverland."

Amy hesitated. "Yes." The hint of a smile

lifted her lips. "Exactly."

Ashley hugged her close for a long while. "When you get to heaven one day, they'll be there."

"I know." Amy leaned back and looked at Ashley, her expression both innocent and sincere. "Until then, I do like it here. In Neverland."

Tears filled Ashley's eyes. She hugged Amy close again. "Sweet girl. I'll never be your mom. I'll never be good enough." She ran her hand along Amy's long blond hair. "But thanks for letting me try."

"Actually" — Amy shifted back and grinned at her — "you're very good at it."

Ashley put her hand alongside Amy's cheek. "Thanks, honey. I love you."

"Love you, too." Amy yawned. "I'm glad you like my painting."

"It's perfect." Ashley kissed the girl's forehead. "Just like you."

Amy left for bed, and Ashley stared at her computer a few feet away on the kitchen table. She closed her sketchbook. Brady Bradshaw was the only person she knew who could get a Survivor Tree sapling for Amy. Ashley hesitated, but just for a few seconds.

She could at least reach out to him one more time. For Amy. The sound of the boys' voices outside caught her attention. Maybe she should ask Landon first. Just get his opinion on the matter. But she couldn't do that. Things were already terrible between them. She needed to prove to Landon that she was only trying to help. She couldn't do that if she didn't do some good first.

Then Landon would understand.

The sapling gave Ashley the perfect reason to contact Brady. Once they talked about that, she could ask Brady about Jenna. She turned to her laptop and brought up his Facebook page again. A private message couldn't hurt anything.

Dear Brady, thank you for responding to me earlier. I can see why you've struggled to find Jenna if you don't know her last name. I haven't found her yet. Is there anything else you could tell me? What high school she went to, or what university? What year did you meet her? Anyway, I know the chances are slim. But I'm praying that I find her. I still think there was a reason I saw you that day at the memorial.

Ashley read over what she'd written. Then she typed a few more lines.

Also, on a personal note, how would I go about getting a Survivor Tree sapling for my 12-year-old niece? It's a long story, but the sapling is something she wants very much. They were gone by the time we got there that day. I'll wait to hear from you. Blessings, Ashley Baxter Blake.

A quick glance over what she'd written and she hit send.

She would tell Landon about it later.

12

The firehouse was active that day. An electrical fire in an old home on the edge of the city. A sweet widow whose cat was stuck in a tree. And a teenager with a shoe caught in a moving escalator.

All three calls had happy endings.

Brady sank into the sofa in the station's living room. He grabbed his laptop from his backpack and opened it. Now that things were slow, maybe he could catch up on Facebook. Like on most weekends, he needed to do another search for Jenna. In case she finally showed up on social media.

Where she hadn't been since he first started looking.

A sigh slipped from his lungs. The anniversary had been more than a week ago, but this year it had stayed with him. Like a bad cold he couldn't quite shake. He opened Facebook and immediately spotted the notification.

Someone had written to him.

Not too strange. People would find him from his time on *Survivor* or because of the calendar. There were the occasional offers on his page. Modeling agencies. Casting directors. Girls. Most of them weren't legit. Especially not the women. Did they really think he'd strike up a relationship with them? Because of a private Facebook message?

Since meeting Jenna, Brady had dated a dozen girls. At least that many. He only remembered the names of a few of them. They were pretty or funny or interesting. But as soon as they learned about his mom, as soon as they discovered he'd been raised in foster care, something changed.

It wasn't their fault.

The blame was Brady's. He had an aversion to pity. When girls realized the details of his childhood, they looked at him differently. Like he was a project or a charity case. Whatever it was, Brady hated it. He didn't want sympathy.

He wanted empathy.

Sympathy felt sorry from the outside looking in. It knew nothing of a person's pain or experience.

Empathy lived it. The sorry feeling came from the inside looking out.

Which was why things never worked with the women he dated. Sure they were sad about his past. But they didn't understand it. And in the end it left a chasm too great to cross. A divide no bridge could span.

It was fine. Brady didn't need love. If he couldn't find Jenna, he would go on the way he had every year for more than a decade. Fighting fires. Serving the people of Oklahoma City. Working out at the local CrossFit gym. Maybe it wasn't the life he had hoped for. Not the life his mom would've wanted for him. But it was enough.

Brady opened the message and scanned to the bottom.

Ashley Baxter Blake.

Brady sat up straighter and stared at the screen. *Ashley?* She was the brunette from the memorial. The one who had randomly texted him a few days ago. She said she'd read the letter he'd written for Jenna. How she wanted to help. It had seemed harmless at the time, so he had texted back. He didn't know Jenna's last name, so what could the lady do to help? He had figured that would be the end of it.

So what was her deal? Why was she writing to him again? So bizarre. The woman was a complete stranger. So what was her interest?

He started at the top of the note.

Dear Brady, thank you for responding to me earlier. I can see why you've struggled to find Jenna if you don't know her last name. I haven't found her yet.

He hesitated. Did she really think she could find Jenna? When he had been looking all these years? He kept reading. The woman wanted to know Jenna's high school or college and when Brady had met her. As if that would help.

Brady read the last few lines.

He felt his heart soften. Ashley wanted a sapling for her niece. Maybe that was what this was really about. He stared at the message. What had happened to the young girl that she wanted a piece of the Survivor Tree? Writing back made no real sense. But the part about the niece caught him by surprise. If he could help the child, he would.

"Okay, Ashley." He uttered the words under his breath as he hit the reply button. He kept his response brief.

I don't have the information you asked for. We met in 2007, that's about it.

He hesitated, picturing Jenna the way she

had looked back then. He could tell Ashley about that. The information couldn't hurt. He positioned his fingers on the keyboard again.

> Here's something. Eleven years ago Jenna looked like Emma Stone. Not sure if that helps. Also, I would like to help you find a Survivor Tree sapling for your niece. Are you coming back to the memorial next April? That's usually the only time they're given out. Was your niece related to someone who died in the bombing?

He looked at what he'd written and gradually felt his heart engage. Ashley didn't have to reach out. She didn't seem to have an ulterior motive. Just some sense about the situation. How had she said it? There was a reason. That was it. A reason she had seen him at the fence. Brady finished his note.

> Anyway, thanks for taking time to write. I don't think you'll find Jenna. But you mean well, and I appreciate that. Take care. Brady.

There. He hit the send button. It was still odd, a complete stranger trying to help him find Jenna. But he was touched by her kindness.

He searched through a few local websites. The downtown mission was hosting a fund-raiser next month. He sent a quick email to the organizer. Like last year he wanted to attend. Brady would act as a table host and get the word out about ticket sales.

Next he checked his email. A thank-you letter from the children's hospital, where he was also a regular volunteer. Brady didn't have his own family. So helping people gave him purpose. A way to do for children what no one had been able to do for him at that age.

Give them a reason to smile.

He read to the bottom of the letter. Would he be interested in coming in every week instead of every month? Brady felt the ache deep in his heart. Yes, he would be interested. Sick kids needed as much love as they could get.

Brady wasn't finished writing his response when the sirens went off. It took only seconds to know that the call was a big one.

"The structure is fully involved," the voice crackled over the radio. Then came other details.

The address was a warehouse on the east side of the city. The building sat adjacent to a retirement home, which according to the call was also ablaze. Trucks were being sent from every station in the area.

Brady was immediately on high alert. Fully involved was never good.

He'd been trained for moments like this. Trained to go from zero to a hundred in a few heartbeats. All around him firefighters were slipping into their gear, racing to get to the truck as fast as they could. Eric Munez, thirty-year-old father of three, jumped into the cab beside him. "Biggest fire of the month." Eric raised his brow. He and Brady had been working together for a long time.

"Biggest of the year." Brady was behind the wheel. He slammed the truck door shut. "Let's roll. We got this."

Wind whipped through the city. Brady felt it gust against the side of the rig. No wonder the fire was spreading. If they didn't get it out quickly, other buildings would ignite. The fire was in an area where structures sat almost on top of each other.

They reached the scene at the same time as four other trucks, from the lower east and central stations. All of them first responders. Even before they parked, Captain Jerry Cranston took charge over the radio.

"Checking the retirement home." Cranston ran up to a man who looked like the manager of the place. A dozen elderly residents milled about. Some leaning on nurses. Several in wheelchairs.

Cranston barked out orders for two trucks to get water on the residential building. The other three were to start on the warehouse. Brady and Eric's team was part of the latter group. The wind was fierce now, and already several other buildings were in imminent danger.

Even as Cranston shouted the instructions, Brady could see the threat. The warehouse was the tallest in the district. Four stories, easily. They could spray water from the ground, but they wouldn't gain control over the blaze unless they got on the roof.

The sound and heat from the fire were like something from hell. Brady squinted at Eric through the smoke, but before he could speak, Cranston gave the order.

"Munez, Bradshaw, get on the roof." He rattled off another four names. "All of you. Hurry. We need to take the life out of this thing."

Brady grabbed a hose from the truck and led the way as the six men scrambled up the ladder to the flaming roof. The most dangerous spot was the middle. Warehouse roofs were generally weaker and less supported than roofs on other buildings. Collapsed warehouse roofs killed more firefighters than almost anything.

The headsets inside their masks were all connected. Brady shouted over the line. "I've got middle." No way was he going to let Eric join him out there. He had a wife and kids at home.

Brady had no one.

Cranston must've agreed with the decision. "Munez, the rest of you, take the perimeter. Bradshaw, be careful. Don't go too far."

"Yes, sir." Brady trudged across the surface with the hose. Flames were whipping up and over the edges, lapping at the structures on the north side of the warehouse.

"Unit Three, hurry up. Those people don't have time!" Cranston sounded frantic.

Brady kept his eyes straight ahead. There was no time to look down at the ground, no time to see if the other team — Unit Three — had rescued the residents or not. Brady focused. Get the hose to the middle of the roof and he'd take out the heart of the blaze. He dragged the line further, toward the center.

"Bradshaw, that's far enough." Munez hung back near the roof's edge.

"A little more," Brady shouted over the roar of the fire. He could feel the spray from two additional hoses behind him. Munez had his back for sure. His friend wouldn't let him get caught too far out. He'd be okay.

His hose shook in his hands, the force of the water at its maximum level. Brady doused the flames but as he did he took another few steps toward the core of the fire.

The cracking sound was exactly what he didn't want to hear. It pierced the roaring blaze and wind and shook the building. Brady lost his footing and fell to his knees. The roof was collapsing! "No!" he shouted, desperately trying to reverse, to find his way to a safer spot.

Someone was pulling on his fire hose, dragging him back. Eric Munez. His friend had him. Everything was going to be okay. The last thing he heard was Eric's voice, telling him he was almost safe. Just a few more steps and then —

The roof gave way and Brady was tumbling down, forever down. Steel beams and sheet metal and flames engulfed him even before he hit the ground. This was it. Firefighters didn't survive these situations.

Something shot at his gut and a metal rod smacked against his head. Brady fought for oxygen, for a way to keep his face above the blazing debris. Smoke and searing air.

That's what killed firemen who fell through burning warehouse roofs.

Stay awake, Brady. They'll come for you. He ordered himself to survive, to fight. Keep his head up. But as his body landed he was buried alive. The heat from earlier wasn't hell.

This was.

He clawed at the rubble, at the wreckage pushing him down. "Get me out! I can't breathe!" Panic pressed in on him, the weight of the roof more than he could bear. Why couldn't he draw a breath? Brady pushed hard at whatever was crushing him. There was no room for air. Just heat and flames and smoke.

Several thoughts hit him at once. First, he flashed back to the bombing. *This is what it was like for my mother. Her final moments.* She had gone from these terrifying seconds into paradise.

That wasn't all. He would never see Cheryl and Rodney Fisher again. Why hadn't he gone by their house more often? Taken them up on the offer of an occasional dinner.

I'm sorry. I should've cared more for them. How could I miss that? Regret burned hotter than the flames. *Give me another chance. Please . . .* He didn't know who he was talking to, who could possibly help him now. He tried to inhale, but nothing came. He was dying. This was it. *Please, get me out!*

His final thought was her.

Jenna.

Was it possible Ashley Baxter Blake had been at the memorial for a reason? Maybe Ashley really would find Jenna. As his heart felt ready to burst inside him, as the weight of the burning roof settled in around him and Brady lost consciousness, he realized the worst part of all. He had lost his only chance, even if Ashley found Jenna.

Because after today, he would never know.

13

The painting was developing beautifully, better than Ashley had hoped. Landon was at work and the kids were at school, but the hours were flying by. Ashley had set her easel up outside on the front porch. The sky was blue, the air warm.

No better day to paint.

Her pieces were still being sold at the gallery in downtown Bloomington. The shop owner had asked for more of her work. Lately, people from all over the country stopped in asking about Ashley's art. Her paintings were going for five times the price she'd originally set. Enough to put aside money for the kids' college tuitions. Since those days were fast approaching.

Ashley stared at the canvas. The Survivor Tree looked lifelike, its branches spread out over the patio. She was using a photo she'd taken at the memorial. Not everyone who saw it would know what it was. But some would. And for those people this image would be everything. To Amy it would.

Especially if she didn't hear back from Brady about the sapling.

Her heart drifted to Landon. The day after Amy's play she had told him about her text and Facebook message to Brady.

He had come in from the porch, looking to talk to her. When he walked through the door Ashley met him in the foyer. He looked physically sick. The slow way he walked, his resigned expression, the hurt and discouragement in his eyes.

Without saying a word she had come to him and slipped her arms around his neck. For a long time they stood there, clinging to each other. No words needed.

He leaned back enough to look at her. "I can't think or work." He'd searched her eyes. "I'm sorry, Ash." He paused. "Yesterday . . . I was wrong."

"I'm sorry, too. I just . . . I didn't see the problem." She had known even then that she had crossed the line. "A few days ago . . . I texted him. I didn't tell you, Landon. I'm so sorry." A quick breath. "And then . . . last night while you were cleaning out the canoe I private-messaged him on Facebook." She hadn't waited for his reaction. "That was wrong. I should've talked to you first."

The news had seemed to hit Landon like a round of pellets. Like hearing it wasn't comfortable. But he could take it. He swallowed and after a while he nodded. "You can do this, Ash. I won't stand in your way."

She had felt her heart melt. "Not if it's going to come between us."

"It's not, Ashley." He looked almost desperate. "Nothing could come between us." He placed his hands on the sides of her face and his words had gone easily to the deepest place of her heart. "Nothing. Not ever."

After that, Landon had listened patiently while she explained what she'd written to Brady and how she hoped he could help get a sapling for Amy.

Then Landon had taken hold of her hands, the two of them still standing just inside the front door. "I may never get this, Ash." He smiled and shook his head. "But I get you. The girl I married. Wanting to help someone, whatever the cost."

"Exactly." Tears had filled her eyes.

He kissed her and his lips lingered for a minute or more. The two of them finding their way back to north. "Help the guy find Jenna." He crooked his finger and put it gently beneath her chin. "If anyone can do it, you can."

"Thank you." She dabbed at a single tear. "I needed to hear that."

"But . . ." He had run his fingers lightly through her hair. "If this doesn't work out. If you don't find her in the next few days . . ." He paused, his eyes locked on hers. "Please, Ash, in that case let it go. Otherwise . . ."

"Otherwise?" Even now Ashley could hear the conversation playing in her mind. "Otherwise what?"

"Well." He had kissed her cheek and then her lips once more. "You're a very beautiful woman, Ash. You don't want to give him the wrong idea."

Ashley had smiled. "Deal." Landon was right. The last thing Ashley needed was a young firefighter pen pal.

So the two of them had come up with a reasonable plan. Three days. Then she'd check to see if he'd written back.

Today was the third day.

A car pulled into her driveway and slowed as it came closer. Ashley stood. Her father! She loved afternoons like this when her dad stopped by unannounced. It was one of the joys of his retirement. Or at least his semi-retirement. He still taught classes and gave lectures at the hospital.

But he had freedom for times like this.

Her dad parked and walked up the path. He carried a flat of bright red strawberries. "Hi there!"

"Hi!" Ashley met him at the top of the porch steps. "What a surprise!"

He hugged her and held out the berries. "Farmers' market got an early crop."

"All this warm weather." Ashley took the fruit. "Wanna come in?"

"Let's sit out here." Her dad tilted his face to the sun, already making its way toward the horizon. "No place like this old porch."

Ashley smiled. "I've thought that since I was a little girl." She ran the strawberries inside and returned with two glasses of lemon water. "Here." She handed him one and they took the rocking chairs, side by side a few feet from her easel.

He glanced at her painting as he sat down. "Beautiful." He paused, really studying the piece. "You're so talented."

"Thanks, Dad."

His eyes were still on her work. "That tree. It looks familiar." He narrowed his brow. "An American elm, right?"

"It is." Ashley looked from the painting back to her dad. "It's called the Survivor Tree."

Slowly, he nodded. "Ahh, yes." He paused.

"The Oklahoma City bombing."

"Right." Ashley took a sip of water and stared at the yard. The open fields and red oaks that dotted their property. She wasn't sure, but it seemed her dad was more interested than what might be normal. A quick glance his way. "We went there for spring break."

"Yes." Her father's tone said there was definitely something on his mind. "I talked to Kari yesterday. She told me about the young man. The firefighter you saw at the memorial."

Ashley braced herself. She resisted the urge to say anything biting. Really? Kari had talked to their dad about this? What was with everyone? Her days as the black sheep were a lifetime ago. That didn't mean she'd make a mess of things now.

Ashley took a slow breath. "Did she tell you about the letter?"

"Yes." Her dad searched her eyes. "I'm not worried, Ash. If that's what you're thinking."

She was quiet.

"That's not why I stopped by." He smiled and patted her hand. "Your faith in God . . . your love for Landon. Clearly you only want to help."

Relief spilled from her head to her heart.

"Thank you."

"I do think you need to be careful." His expression was still warm. "You don't know this young man."

Ashley nodded. "I get that. I've told Landon all about it." She paused, searching his eyes. "Dad. It's fine."

"Okay." He leaned back in the rocker. "So you're trying to find the girl this young man is looking for?"

"Yes. Jenna. I don't have a last name." Ashley felt the weight of discouragement. "It really seemed God put me next to the guy for a reason. Like I was supposed to help." She shook her head. "But I haven't found her."

Her dad drank half the water in his glass. Then he set it down on the porch railing and stood. "Have you tried looking up her parents?" He turned and leaned against the railing.

Ashley was struck by his kindness. He really was only trying to help. Finding a reason to bring by some berries and talk a bit. "Her parents?" She settled into the chair. His question was interesting.

"They were both killed in the bombing. That's what Kari said." Her dad looked at her. "There were only so many couples in the building. I keep thinking maybe if you

232

search that, maybe you'll find that one of them had a daughter named Jenna."

"Hmm." Ashley hadn't thought about that. She'd read the list of victims, of course. When she'd first Googled Jenna's name in relation to the Oklahoma City bombing. But she'd never thought to check the husband and wife pairs killed in the bombing, and then look up their children. "You're thinking someone might have written about them?"

"Maybe." Her dad angled his head. His face was tan from his daily walks with Elaine. He continued. "The twenty-year anniversary was a few years ago. Everyone was doing stories on what happened. It's possible someone did a follow-up on the deaths of people with the same last name. The children orphaned."

"You're right." Ashley felt a surge of hope. "Why didn't I think of that?"

"You have a lot on your plate." Her father laughed. "Like four kids to feed and help with homework." He shrugged. "If I'd known her last name, I would've already looked myself."

"See?" Ashley laughed, too. "Now you know where I get it!"

"True." He paced to the spot in front of her easel.

Ashley appreciated her father's heart, his time. More than he would ever know. "I think there's a spiritual side to all this, too."

"For the guy?" Her dad turned to her.

"For both of them, maybe." Ashley stood and looked at her dad for a minute. "I guess we won't know until we find her."

"Until *you* find her." He chuckled. "I have a paper to write for the hospital administration. I'm presenting it next week."

"So here we are" — she smiled — "two fairly busy people. And we can't stop thinking about how to help a stranger." Ashley paused. "God's up to something. I have to believe it."

"Well." He breathed deep and glanced at her easel once more. "I'll let you get back to your painting." He grinned at her. "Just thought it'd be better to talk about this in person."

Ashley understood what he meant. If he had texted or called, she might've misunderstood him. She could've assumed he was doubtful about her intentions. But that wasn't the case at all.

He only wanted to help.

The way he always did.

She hugged him and kissed his cheek. "Tell Elaine I said hi." She stepped back and smiled. "And thanks for the berries.

The kids will love them."

"Elaine's making shortcake back at home." He shook his head, his eyes sparkling. "She made enough for the neighborhood."

"I have an idea!" Ashley laughed. "Why don't you and Elaine join us for dinner? Landon's grilling, and Elaine can bring the shortcake."

Her dad nodded. "Sounds like a perfect night. I'll talk to Elaine." He paused at the bottom of the stairs. "I love this, Ash. Being so close. Having time with you and your siblings."

"We love it, too." She waved and watched him leave, waited as his car moved along their paved drive to the road.

As soon as he was out of sight she went inside, found her laptop and brought it back out to the front porch. Why hadn't she thought about looking up Jenna's parents? Like her dad said, there were only so many couples killed in the bombing. She Googled the list of victims.

She went through a full search of the surviving family members of couples killed in the tragedy. Then she came to Bill and Betsy Phillips. "Bill and Betsy Phillips." Ashley whispered their names as she typed them into the search line. Then she typed "survivors."

Suddenly she was looking at a headline.

WHERE ARE THEY NOW? CHILDREN OR-
PHANED BY THE OKLAHOMA CITY BOMB-
ING.

Ashley felt her heart skip a beat. Could
Bill and Betsy be Jenna's parents? The
article was in *The Oklahoman,* still online
after a decade. She opened it and began to
read. The first part of the article led to a
section titled "Life After the Bombing —
Bill and Betsy Phillips." Beneath that was a
list of their surviving family members,
including a daughter named Elizabeth Jenna
Phillips.

Elizabeth *Jenna* Phillips?

Ashley felt the porch begin to spin. Her
heart pounded as she read this part of the
story.

Elizabeth Jenna Phillips was just five years
old when her parents went to work that
April 19 and never came home. She lived
with her grandmother for the rest of her
school years.

Ashley kept reading. The article was
heartbreaking, detailing the jobs the little
girl's parents had held, and how long they'd
worked at the Alfred P. Murrah Building.
But nothing more about the child.

In a rush, Ashley switched to Facebook.

"Elizabeth Jenna Phillips," she typed. Four matches came up, but none were younger than forty. She searched again with just "Jenna Phillips," but again, nothing.

She was so close. Ashley tapped her fingers on the table. "Come on." There had to be something. *Please, God, lead me to her.* Ashley took a deep breath and tried again. This time she Googled "Elizabeth Jenna Phillips" and "Oklahoma City Bombing."

The results that came back were slightly different.

Top of the list was an article titled OR-PHANS OF OKLAHOMA CITY — TWENTY YEARS LATER.

Ashley couldn't read the story fast enough. The opening paragraph explained that in honor of the twenty-year anniversary the paper was doing a series of profiles on the victims and their surviving family members. How life had changed when the bomb exploded through the Alfred P. Murrah Federal Building.

"Dear God, thank You," Ashley whispered. Her hands trembled as she scanned the article for the names Bill and Betsy Phillips. The two weren't quite thirty years old when they reported for work at the federal building in downtown Oklahoma City that April

19, 1995. Betsy on the third floor, and Bill on the fifth.

Ashley could picture the couple saying goodbye to their little girl, heading off to work. Parking across the street and climbing out of the same car, headed to their separate jobs. They couldn't have known it would be the last time.

Ashley kept reading. Both Bill and Betsy were killed when the bomb went off, but their only daughter, five-year-old Elizabeth Jenna, had survived. Safe at home with her grandmother, who had moved to Oklahoma City a year before the bombing. Otherwise she might've been in the daycare when the attack happened.

Apparently the child went by the name Jenna. Her grandmother once said even though her daughter and son-in-law had missed seeing Jenna grow up, they would've been grateful she survived. Grateful that she had been raised by her grandmother. The girl had eventually finished school and married.

Married? Ashley closed her eyes. Brady was going to be heartbroken. She couldn't imagine being the one to tell him the news. That is, if this was her. And Ashley believed it was.

She opened her eyes and kept reading.

This part of the feature finished with *Elizabeth Jenna Phillips — now Davis — graduated from college in Texas and is currently a teacher in Columbus, Ohio.*

That was all there was. The article ended with a section on the memorial, the husband-and-wife team who designed it and how many visitors came through each year.

Ashley's head was spinning.

She stared at the screen.

She couldn't believe it! This was the best and worst news. She'd found Brady's girl, but she was married. She was Jenna Davis now. A teacher in Columbus. At least it seemed that way. Ashley wasn't sure what to do next. She started to set the laptop down, to head inside the house, but then she stopped herself.

Where was she going? She couldn't call Brady out of the blue. Besides, she hadn't actually found Jenna. But she'd most likely found more information than Brady had discovered in all these years.

All because of her father's suggestion.

Her hands were shaking so hard she could barely type. Facebook. She needed to look there first. In case Jenna Davis wasn't the one Brady was looking for. She entered "Jenna Davis" in the search line and several names appeared. One of them lived in Columbus.

She clicked it. "God, You're amazing." She whispered the words, her eyes glued to the young woman's profile page as it came up. Jenna Davis. Teacher at Martin Luther King Junior Elementary School. Ashley enlarged her profile picture as big as she could make it.

The photo was of Jenna surrounded by twenty children. Ashley hesitated. If this was Brady's Jenna, married and living in Columbus, at least he'd have closure. Maybe that's what she was supposed to bring to the situation. A reason for Brady to let go. She scrolled down Jenna's page.

Ashley kept reading until she saw something that stopped her cold. It was a status she'd posted on Christmas Eve.

A status that changed everything.

Beneath a Christmas photo of the front door of what must've been Jenna's house she had written this: *Thankful that with God, I'm not alone this Christmas. I never will be.*

Alone? Ashley blinked a few times, trying to understand. Another five minutes of searching her time line and Ashley was sure. Jenna was divorced. Whatever had happened, the young woman seemed to have faith and hope. At least according to her Christmas post.

Ashley hurt for Jenna, for everything the girl had been through. Losing her parents when she was so little, and then losing her husband. Whatever the situation. Yet, she appeared to be making it on her own. She seemed to enjoy teaching.

Assuming this was the same girl Ashley had been looking for, what did Jenna think about Brady?

Did he ever cross her mind? Or had she forgotten him after their one day together? Ashley looked more closely at Jenna's face. The sweet girl-next-door look. But even still the hurt was there in her pretty green eyes.

Ashley took a deep breath. What to do next? Suddenly she remembered her message to Brady. All this time she'd been on Facebook studying Jenna's profile and she hadn't thought to check her in-box. She glanced at the icon on her screen and sure enough, there was a message.

She opened it and immediately she saw who it was from.

Brady Bradshaw.

And something else. The letter was longer than two words. She started at the beginning. He said he didn't have much information except the year they met. She closed her eyes, picturing Brady finally deciding to trust her, to open up. Even a little. She blinked and kept reading. He described Jenna as looking like Emma Stone. And yes, he said he would try to help find a sapling Survivor Tree.

A few clicks and Ashley had Jenna's picture back up. This had to be the same girl Brady had met that day. No question Jenna looked like the famous actress.

Ashley wanted to shout for joy. She'd done it. She had actually found Jenna. She went back to Brady's letter and felt her heart melt a little. The tough guy had a soft side. Clearly. Otherwise he wouldn't have been touched by Amy's request. She found her place and finished reading. He closed by thanking her but he added that he didn't think she'd have much luck finding Jenna.

How surprised would he be when she reached out to tell him that she had actually found the girl? And yes, she still looked like Emma Stone. Ashley tapped the keyboard, and then absently she pulled up Brady's profile. In case he'd included something else about Jenna.

Instead, it took her a few seconds to grasp what she was seeing.

Someone had posted a link to a Go Fund Me page: "Help with Expenses for Brady Bradshaw." "What?" Ashley leaned forward. Her heart was pounding again. What had happened?

She clicked the link and struggled to catch her breath. Brady Bradshaw was in intensive care in an Oklahoma City hospital after falling through the roof of a warehouse during a huge fire two days ago.

Two days ago? Ashley checked the time and date on the private message he'd sent her. Then she Googled his name and details about the fire. He must've gotten hurt just after sending her note.

And now . . .

She found the most updated article on the Web. It had been posted a few hours ago. DOCTORS LOSING HOPE FOR OK CITY FIREFIGHTER IN ICU.

"No!" The word came out as a cry. How could this be happening? *Dear God, please let him live.*

Suddenly Ashley knew what she had to do. Columbus was less than four hours away. She needed to pray for Brady Bradshaw and she needed to find her way to Martin Luther King Junior Elementary School. The only way to have this conversation with Jenna was in person. When she helped someone, she gave it everything she had. No Facebook message. Not this time. Driving to see Jenna was the right thing to do. Ashley was convinced. She would tell

Landon when he got home.

Then first thing in the morning she would set out for Columbus.

14

Minutes into lunch, one of the other teachers gave Jenna a message. Someone was waiting for her in the main office. A woman. The teacher shrugged one shoulder. "Might be a parent, but I've never seen her before."

"Thanks." Jenna hadn't been very hungry. She wrapped up the rest of her sandwich and slipped it back into the staff refrigerator. Then she made her way through the hall to the office.

Before she opened the door she saw that her coworker was right. The woman waiting wasn't someone she'd ever seen before. Jenna stepped inside and approached her. "I'm Jenna Davis." She smiled. "Are you looking for me?"

The strange woman's eyes filled with tears. "Yes." She held out her hand. "I'm Ashley Blake." She looked around. Like she didn't want to say too much here, with the staff in earshot. "Can we . . . go outside?"

Jenna felt her stomach drop. Who was this Ashley woman and how come she was here? Had something happened to Dan in London? If so, this was no time to tell her. He'd been out of her life too long for anything about him to be urgent.

Or maybe she was a lawyer. Maybe someone was suing her. For reading *Noah's Ark*, perhaps. But then why would the woman have tears in her eyes? None of it made sense.

Jenna stuffed the possibilities into the corner of her mind and led the woman outside. There was a bench in front of the school. The clouds overhead meant they could talk without wearing sunglasses.

Jenna sat first and Ashley took the spot next to her. Jenna shook her head. "I'm sorry . . ." She tried to sound confident. "What's this about?"

With kind, concerned eyes, the woman looked straight at her. "Are you Elizabeth Jenna Phillips? Was that your maiden name?"

Jenna felt the blood leave her face. "Yes. That's me."

"That's what I thought." Ashley seemed relieved. "I had to come talk to you in person. It's about Brady Bradshaw. From Oklahoma City."

246

Brady Bradshaw? Jenna's heart skipped a beat. Could this be . . . was Bradshaw his last name, after all these years? Jenna's breathing was suddenly jagged and her heart pounded in her throat. What in the world? "How . . . how do you know Brady?"

"I don't know him." The woman seemed flustered. "It's a long story. I'll try to make it quick." Ashley glanced at the building. "I know you have to get back to class."

"Yes." Jenna felt like she might pass out. What did the woman know? And what was so important that she needed to come here in person? "Please tell me."

The story was as unbelievable as meeting this strange woman. So unbelievable it had a ring of truth to it. Ashley had been at the Oklahoma City memorial on the anniversary of the bombing. She'd stood at the fence next to a random stranger, a guy with dark hair and a world of hurt on his face.

"He left a note in the fence. For you." Ashley pulled her phone from her purse. "I took pictures."

"You did?"

"Yes." Ashley hesitated. "I don't know if you believe in God, Jenna. But I do. My family does. And in that moment . . . in that moment when I saw the letter in the fence . . . I felt like God put me there to help. However I could."

Jenna's heart was still pounding. "Yes. I believe in God. Very much so." She leaned closer. "Can I see the picture? The letter?"

Ashley pulled up the first photo. "This is how it looked on the fence. When Brady left it there."

Jenna tried to focus. Was she dreaming? Could this really be happening? Someone had found Brady after all this time? She squinted at the photo, then used her fingers to make the image larger.

Sure enough, there it was. Written across the front of a scrolled-up letter. *"For Jenna."* She brought her hand to her mouth and stared at the screen. "He left that there? For me?" Jenna looked at Ashley. "Just a few weeks ago?"

"Yes. My family was visiting for spring break." Ashley shook her head. "Look at the next photo. Please, Jenna."

She scrolled to the right and there it was. A photo of the letter, opened. And at the bottom, his name and number. Brady Brad-shaw. Jenna couldn't catch her breath. She exhaled. *Relax. You have to relax.* In twenty minutes she needed to be back in the classroom. She couldn't fall apart.

Ashley handed over the phone, and again Jenna made the image larger. As she did, she read every line of the letter.

Dear Jenna,
   Like I do every year, I wrote you a letter. In case you come to the memorial
today. In case you want to find me as
much as I want to find you. Every year I
do this, I leave you a note in case.
Anyway, here I am again, eleventh year
in a row.

Jenna closed her eyes for a few seconds.
Eleven years in a row? He'd been there
every year, looking for her? She found her
place and kept reading. He said that again
he had come to find her, because every year
wound up the same. No response to his letter. Next he had a question for her. One
that hit a place in her heart she had ignored
for so long.

Don't you remember, Jenna? What it was
like having that one day together?

"Yes," Jenna whispered. "I still remember." She was so lost in the letter she forgot
she was sitting next to the stranger. She kept
reading.
   His letter said that he'd lost her number,
but he'd thought it would be easy to find
her. And how after all this time he still

thinks about her.

The truth is, I don't think about anyone but you. I'm a firefighter in Oklahoma City. It gives me purpose. But I'm alone. I'm always alone.

Tears filled Jenna's eyes and spilled onto her cheeks. She looked up at the sky, warding off the sobs building in her heart. *Brady, I'm so sorry. How could I have missed this?* All these years. She steeled herself against the heartache and read the rest of the note.

It was the hardest part. He wrote how he was waiting for her and he'd be back again next year. On the anniversary.

And one of these days, Jenna . . . one of these days you'll be here. I'll find you. I have to believe that. Remember what you said? Our hearts are the same. And so they are. Always. Brady Bradshaw.

Jenna was shivering, but it had nothing to do with the cool afternoon. She handed the phone back to Ashley. "I . . . I can't believe this."

"I looked you up on Facebook. I . . . don't know your situation. You're divorced? . . . Your last name is different. But I figured it might be you. And if it was . . ." Ashley hesitated. "I thought you'd want to know."

Jenna felt the familiar sinking feeling. "I'm not married. My husband, he left me a few years ago. He's . . . moved on."

A genuine look of sadness filled Ashley's eyes. "I'm sorry. Really."

"Me, too. But I'm not alone. I have my faith." A supernatural strength resonated within her. The way it did whenever she remembered her situation. "That's what matters."

Ashley's face grew serious. "There's more, Jenna." The color seemed to drain from her cheeks. "Brady . . . he's hurt. He's in ICU at a hospital in Oklahoma City."

"What?" Jenna stood and paced away from the bench. Her legs shook. How could any of this be happening? "How did he get hurt?"

"In a fire a few days ago." Ashley slid to the edge of the bench. "He's fighting for his life." She hesitated, as if she wasn't sure what to say next. "I knew the only way to tell you any of this was in person."

Jenna hadn't even asked the woman where she was from. "How far did you drive?"

"I live in Bloomington. My husband is a firefighter. Maybe that's why . . ." Ashley's voice trailed off. "I don't know. I had to come find you."

Ashley went on to explain that she'd been in touch with Brady and even though he hadn't been able to find Jenna, Ashley had a strong belief she could. That she might somehow connect them. Even if their lives had moved on.

"And now . . ." Jenna sat back down on the bench beside Ashley. "Thank you. Can you please . . . would you send me those pictures?"

"Definitely." Ashley took Jenna's cell number and texted her the photos.

Jenna looked at them again. "Do you know what hospital he's at?"

"The article said Oklahoma University Medical Center." Ashley looked like she didn't want to say whatever was next. "The last I read, they were concerned. He might not survive."

The face of Brady Bradshaw filled her heart and soul. Jenna closed her eyes for a short while. When she opened them she had to blink back tears to see Ashley clearly. "Thank you. For coming." She shook her head. All of this was so crazy. "I can't believe you'd drive so far."

"Brady's waited more than a decade." Ashley's smile was as kind as it was sad. "The least I could do is take a day to come find you. Especially if . . ."

If he didn't make it. That's clearly what Ashley didn't want to say. Jenna hung her head and tried not to fall to the ground weeping. Brady had been alone all this time, thinking about her, missing her. Why hadn't she ever gone back to the memorial?

So what if he hadn't called her? If she could change things she never would've been so hasty. If she could go back to her seventeen-year-old self, she would've called him or figured out a way to meet up with him somewhere. Anything to see him again.

Ashley checked her watch. "I need to go." She paused. "Can I . . . pray for you? For Brady?"

"Please." In that moment Jenna knew she would've been friends with Ashley Blake. If she had more time to get to know her, or if they lived in the same city. She reached out her hands and took hold of Ashley's.

With heads bowed, Ashley prayed. That Brady would be healed of his injuries and that somehow Jenna and him might find the friendship they'd started years ago. And she prayed that God would help them both in whatever the coming days held. Then she thanked God for helping her find Jenna. Just when it mattered most.

They both said amen, and stood. Without

hesitating, Jenna hugged Ashley. "You're the nicest person. Thank you for coming." Again, Jenna could barely breathe. But this time it was out of fear. Fear that she might miss the chance to see Brady.

Jenna looked at her phone. "I need to call the hospital." She hesitated. "Is it okay if I text you? To tell you how he's doing?"

"I'd love that." Ashley smiled. "My husband and I will pray." They shared another hug and Ashley walked off to the parking lot.

For a minute Jenna dropped back to the bench. If not for the hard slats beneath her legs, she'd have to wonder. None of this felt real. As if she'd blink and be in bed. Waking up from the most amazing, terrifying dream. She knew where Brady was, and that he hadn't forgotten her.

But only in time to learn he was fighting for his life.

And in that moment she made a decision. She was going back to Oklahoma City this summer anyway. To take her parents' pictures and precious items and make their part of the memorial right. While she was there she would see Brady. That is if he was still . . .

She picked up her phone and searched the number for the OU Medical Center. A minute later she was talking to a nurse. No, she wasn't family. Yes, she knew him well. She closed her eyes and prayed God would understand the stretched truth.

She had known him well eleven years ago.

Finally the nurse came back on the line. She couldn't give specific details, but she could say this: Brady was still in a coma.

Tears filled Jenna's eyes as she hung up. God was working in this. He had to be. Hadn't Jenna just been praying for their paths to cross? Whatever Brady faced, Jenna would find him.

Suddenly an idea hit. This was the first Wednesday in May. Next week was the last of the school year. She scrolled through her contacts and called another number. A long-ago friend of her mother's. Yes the woman was home this summer, and yes she had two spare bedrooms.

"Come for as long as you'd like, Jenna." The woman sounded as friendly as Jenna remembered. And just like that she had a place to stay.

Back in the break room, she mentioned it to her teacher friends. "I found the woman my mom used to work with in Oklahoma," she told them. "I'm thinking of taking an adventure. Driving there for the summer."

A few of her friends looked less than

happy for her. "An adventure? To Oklahoma?"

"Sure." She wasn't ready to talk about Brady yet. What would she say? "I've been planning it for a while. I want to add pictures and special things to my parents' memorial. I've never done that." She paused. "Anything's an adventure if you make it one."

"Sounds like a second-grade lesson." One of them laughed. "Whatever, Jenna. When you come home after a few days give us a call." She looked at the other girls in the room. "We're spending a month at the lake."

No chance of that. In Jenna's mind it was settled. When the school year was behind her, Jenna would pack her things and head for Oklahoma City. And as soon as she possibly could, she would find her way to the OU Medical Center and a boy she had met in 2007.

Brady Bradshaw.

Ashley drove home from Columbus in disbelief. Brady had looked for Jenna since they were seventeen. Now, because of her dad's brilliant idea, Ashley had found her in less than a few weeks. Whatever had happened in Jenna's personal life since that long-ago day at the Oklahoma City memorial, she still cared about Brady.

That much was obvious.

The whole way home Ashley prayed for the two, that Brady would recover and they'd find their way together. Even for just one more day.

So neither of them would have doubts about what might've been.

Ashley parked in the driveway just before the kids were scheduled to get home. She'd had her phone off while she drove but as soon as she turned it on she saw the text from Jenna.

Brady was being moved out of ICU. He was still in a coma, but he had turned a corner.

"Oh, dear God, thank You." Relief washed over Ashley as she made her way inside.

That night after the kids had finished their homework and headed to bed, she found Landon in the kitchen, doing the dishes. She had told him only that the day had been a success and that she'd give him the details later.

This was the moment.

Ashley came up behind Landon at the sink. "You're the most amazing man." She worked her hands around his waist. "Have I told you that lately?"

"Yes." He turned in her arms and faced

her, his hands still wet with sudsy soap. He dried them on his jeans. "Tell me again."

"You" — she kissed him on the lips — "my Prince Charming, are the most amazing man I know."

"Mmmm." He returned her kiss. "You're my favorite princess. In case I haven't told you lately."

She laughed lightly. There was nothing like the love she felt for Landon, the love they shared. "You wanna hear about it?"

"Must be really good." He took the dish towel and gave her a light smack with it. "Otherwise you wouldn't have made me wait."

"Walk with me." She took his hand. "Outside. It's a pretty sky."

This was something they'd done a lot of when they were dating, when they were still figuring out whether they'd find a way to make things work. Tonight was the perfect time to talk under the bright sky. Especially since they were good again, since the fight was behind them.

Once they were outside, they walked to the stream behind their house. Along the way Ashley caught him up on what had happened. "God was ahead of me at every turn. I found Jenna, no problem." Ashley raised her brow. "Of course, at first I think she thought I was some crazy person. But when I said Brady's name, her expression changed. From that point on I had her attention, for sure."

"She's not married anymore? You're sure?" Landon looked concerned. Understandably. He and Ashley had agreed this wasn't something to do if Jenna were still married.

"Her husband left her." Ashley let that sad detail sit for a moment. "We prayed before I left. And by the time I got home she'd texted me. Brady's out of ICU."

For a long time Landon only looked at her in the moonlight. He slid a piece of her dark hair behind her ear. "You realize we're having a conversation about perfect strangers." He smiled at her. "As if we know them."

"Yes." Ashley made a nervous face. "It's true. This sort of thing could only happen to me."

"Absolutely. But I'm glad I stepped out of the way. Because you were right, Ash. God wanted to use you. I believe that." Landon's smile dropped off. "Sounds like the accident was serious. Keep me posted on how things turn out."

"I promised her we'd pray. You and me."

"Okay, then . . . let's do it." Landon pulled her into his arms and prayed out loud. For a couple of people they didn't know named Jenna and Brady, and that Ashley would always be drawn to help people.

Even total strangers.

15

Brady wasn't sure if he was in hell or not. His head throbbed and he couldn't speak. Whatever had happened to him, he couldn't move his arms or legs. Couldn't turn his head from side to side.

Still somewhere deep in his subconscious he had the slightest sense that maybe he wasn't in hell. Heaven, either. Just possibly, he might actually be alive. Not because he felt himself getting better.

But because he kept seeing Jenna in his dreams.

Like a favorite movie on replay, the memory would start at the beginning. The day he and Jenna spent together. Brady couldn't take a deep breath. Everything was numb, and the pain throughout his body consumed him. Even so, images from years ago were taking shape in his heart once more.

Brady felt his head sink deep into the pillow. Then he did what he'd done every time

Jenna filled his mind and heart.

He let the memory come.

He'd always thought of them as part of a club. The wanderers who made it to the memorial every April 19. The ones who walked along the chain-link fence alone and without words of any kind. All of them had lost someone.

Brady never asked who, never talked to anyone at the memorial. Even when he saw the same people year after year. He never spoke to a single person until 2007.

The year he met Jenna.

He was reading the offerings left on the fence when he spotted her. Golden dark red hair, beautiful green eyes. A face that took his breath even with the sorrow written into her expression. He was about to walk by, wouldn't have interrupted her moment.

But just as he was about to miss her, their eyes met.

They exchanged names, and he showed her his arms. Proof he'd been in the building that terrible day. At one point he asked her to feel his scars. She did, and her touch was the softest thing he'd ever felt.

He could still feel her fingers against his skin.

She had no reason to trust him, but a connection happened between them. They spent an hour at the Survivor Tree, and all the while he could feel himself drawn to her. And his attraction gradually turned into something deeper.

She told her story and when she finished, when they realized they had been only a couple of five-year-olds when the bomb went off, Brady had reached for her hand. And for the first time in all his life he felt something he'd never felt before.

He felt complete.

Her hand was made for his, and gently he ran his thumb along her fingers. For a minute or so he didn't say anything. He didn't want to ruin the quiet understanding between them. Like they were both still just two kids missing their parents.

Jenna's expression was different than any Brady had ever seen. And somewhere along the course of the day, Brady knew what it was. Empathy. The empathy he had missed every day since. Jenna's eyes held a kindness and understanding, the sort that could only come from someone who had been through it. She was another grown-up five-year-old who had lost everything that April morning.

As the day played out, the weather changed. It grew colder and they took a walk. All the while Brady wanted just one thing: for the day to never end. One of the best parts of their time together was the conversation they had before they walked to the coffee shop across the street from the memorial. They agreed that people talked about the bombing like it happened to the city.

When really it happened to the two of them.

Personally.

Then they got deeper still. Jenna admitted how she used to imagine that her parents were traveling somewhere far, far away and one day they would walk through the door and they could all be together again. Brady admitted that he had thought something similar. They talked about how they used to pray that God would return their parents, that life might miraculously find its way back to what it once had been.

Before the bombing.

That's when they discovered something else they had in common. One more connection. Both their mothers had come to their rooms every night and said the words "Love you to the moon and back."

After that he was hooked. He might only have been seventeen, but he knew he wanted Jenna in his life as long as he lived.

Then Brady shared something else he hadn't shared with anyone before. He told her about his disconnect with God. Jenna felt the same. She said she was frustrated with God. Why would He take her parents?

Brady would never forget the walk back to the memorial. The wind was in full force and he took her hand again. When he eased his fingers between hers, the feeling sent chills down his arms and legs. She looked just like Emma Stone, only prettier. Jenna was definitely prettier.

Brady couldn't remember everything else they talked about. But he would remember the feel of her hand in his as long as he lived. Finally the clouds had broken open and it started pouring. They ran into the museum to get out of the rain and there they found their way to the picture.

The one before the bomb went off.

They talked about how Brady and his mom could've run errands another day, and maybe her parents might've stayed home from work that April 19.

And then it was time for Jenna to go.

Brady still held her hand, still had his fingers between hers. They swapped numbers and he promised he would call. He had to call. He was sure he would.

No one had ever connected with his soul

the way Jenna had.

They promised at least to talk when the next anniversary came around. But then Jenna smiled at him. "A year is a long time."

"A week's a long time." They were standing so close. He wanted to kiss her, but it wasn't the time. He stared at her number. "I'll call you soon. It'd be nice to get to know you." He felt his smile drop off. "Outside the club, I mean."

"I'll never forget today." Jenna took a step closer to him. "You're the only one who knows just how I feel."

"You, too." He couldn't keep from telling her how he felt. He practically whispered the next words. "I want to kiss you, Jenna."

She looked like she wanted that, too. But she only smiled. "I think we should wait."

"Yeah." He could feel himself flirting with her. "Come here."

They were only inches apart. Jenna did as he asked and it took all of his willpower not to kiss her. Instead, he took her in his arms and held her. The hug wasn't something passionate.

It was deeper than that.

Like two people who'd been lost and now were found.

The dream was fading, at least it felt that

way. Brady could see light through his closed eyelids. He could hear sounds. He still couldn't lift his head or turn it, couldn't move his hands or feet or shift his position. And he certainly couldn't talk.

Someone was saying something about levels or numbers, vital signs. Something Brady couldn't make out. It was a guy and he was still talking. "Brady? Brady, can you hear me?"

He tried to close his eyes more fully. He didn't recognize the voice of the man. Why would he be talking about numbers? Where was he, anyway?

Then another voice spoke closer to him. A woman's.

"Brady . . . can you hear me?"

The sound worked its way through his consciousness and straight to his heart. *Jenna? Jenna, is that you?* Only his words didn't come out very loud. They didn't come out at all.

The voice came again. "Anyway, it's me. Jenna. I've been living in Columbus, Ohio. Teaching."

Brady tried with everything in him to sit up straight and open his eyes. Tried to shout that yes, he could hear her and yes, he knew who she was. He was dreaming still, of course. He had to be. Jenna wasn't in his life except when he dreamed.

But for some reason in his dream he couldn't move.

"You're probably wondering how I found you." It sounded like she was crying. She sniffed. "You know that woman? Ashley Blake. She found me, Brady. She drove all the way to Columbus and found me at my school." Another pause. "I came here as soon as I could."

Jenna was still talking, but Brady couldn't make out the words. Ashley Blake? Ashley had found Jenna? That could only mean one thing.

Maybe he wasn't dreaming after all.

16

Jenna hadn't been to the Oklahoma City memorial in eleven years. Today was as good a time to go back as any. She'd been in town three days, and this morning her mother's friend, Allison Wessel, made her breakfast. They chatted for an hour before Allison headed to the inner city medical clinic where she worked.

Talking to Allison was like getting a glimpse of what it might've been like if Jenna's mother had lived. Allison had worked with Jenna's mother. Same floor. But on April 19 she had taken the day off.

A random doctor's appointment saved her life.

Before she left for college, Jenna used to stop by Allison's house once every few weeks. Jenna always had the feeling she was visiting with her mother. Never mind Allison's brown skin and deep brown eyes. In the woman's presence, Jenna was home.

Back then they would share coffee and catch up on Jenna's schoolwork and friendships and dreams. Usually they'd end up laughing about something, and then before Jenna would leave, the conversation would turn to Jenna's mother.

"It should've been me," Allison would sometimes say as they hugged goodbye. "I wasn't married. I didn't have a little girl waiting at home."

"No." Jenna would shake her head. "You can't say that. No one should've died that day."

Now, Jenna had a clearer understanding. It was her parents' time. They loved God. They believed in Jesus. They had gone home to heaven together. Period. Whenever she was tempted to doubt God or spiral into a whirlpool of whys, Jenna would remember Romans 8:28. The meaning stayed with her every day. *In all things God works for the good of those who love Him.* No matter what dark alley her thoughts sometimes took, that truth remained.

God was working good out of what had happened.

Even if sometimes Jenna didn't see it.

She kept the radio off as she drove. Her friendship with Allison Wessel was one good thing that had come from her parents' death. The woman hadn't believed in God before the bombing.

Now she talked about Jesus like He was her personal friend.

The connection between Jenna and Allison had returned the moment Jenna walked through the woman's door. Allison had hugged her and looked long at her face. "I'm glad you're here."

"Me, too." Jenna embraced her again.

Allison's kindness had made it possible for Jenna to come to Oklahoma at all. She wouldn't have had enough money to stay in a hotel for more than a few days. But now she had all the time in the world.

The whole summer.

Which gave Jenna this day to see the memorial and then return to the hospital. She'd been there every day since getting into town. Brady was still in a coma. Because he had no next of kin, the doctor deemed it necessary to share Brady's progress with her.

His doctor had said Jenna was the only person other than his fellow firefighters and a sweet older couple who had been by. The only ones who had seemed to care.

Brady had two broken legs and a fractured spine. His right calf and thigh were seriously burned and he'd been fighting pneumonia since he was admitted. His lungs seemed to be healing, so that was good. Apparently, his helmet had protected his face, but not necessarily his head.

"Brain damage is possible," the doctor had told her yesterday. "He may never wake up. These things are hard to diagnose until he's conscious."

Jenna had decided to stop asking questions. Instead she spent most of her time at the hospital praying. Because only God knew what the future held for Brady Bradshaw.

She reached the memorial and parked several rows from the front. The anniversary had happened nearly a month ago, but still the place was busy. Jenna had read about the fascination. Oklahomans came because they wanted to pay their respects. Make a statement that something like the bombing would never be ignored.

The victims would never be forgotten.

But it wasn't just Oklahomans who made their way to the memorial. Some were like the woman Jenna had met at school, Ashley Blake. A visit here was part of a road trip or a spring break. Jenna sat in her car and stared at the gates. The towering walls that stood adjacent to each other at one end of the memorial.

She wore her key today. The one with *9:03* engraved in it. Yes, healing had begun then. But healing could take a while, that was the thing.

The past pressed in around her, pulling her from the car. She took a bag from her backseat, the one with her parents' pictures and personal items. These were the reason she'd planned the trip, after all. She stepped out of the car.

A cool breeze drifted over the parking lot. Jenna wore a long-sleeve lightweight sweater and dark jeans. A wide-brimmed hat and sunglasses would keep the moment private.

Which was how she wanted it.

Her first stop was her parents' chairs and then she walked over to the Survivor Tree. Every step of the way she caught herself thinking not so much about her parents, but about the boy who had made her part of the club. At the bench next to the tree, Jenna sat and closed her eyes.

Without her faith, she wouldn't be here. It had been the biggest part of her healing.

Run to Jesus, she had told herself over the years. Stop trying to live life without Him. And along the way, she had become a new person.

Free. Whole. Ready to live again.

Yes, she would always miss her parents.

She would wonder why they had been called to heaven so soon. But she wasn't angry with God. She loved Him.

He was with her, every day of her life — even when she was mad at Him. And one day she would see her parents again.

Jenna drew a quick breath. Had Brady ever returned to God? Was he still determined to keep his distance?

She held a map of the memorial grounds, and she stared at it. There she saw something she'd missed the day she'd met Brady. On the east end of the memorial were several slabs of concrete from the original structure. Etched into them were the names of more than six hundred people who had been in the building and survived.

Brady's name. She had to find it. She walked closer, right near the gate that read 9:01. And there, in alphabetical order, were the names of those who — like the slabs of concrete — had withstood the blast.

It took seconds to find his name.

Lord, would you heal Brady, please? Breathe Your strength through him by the power of Your Holy Spirit. I can't believe this is it for him. He needs You, Lord.

He had lived through the most terrible thing once.

He would live through it again. She had

to believe it.

On her way into the building, Jenna stopped in the victims' room. There she met up with a volunteer who took the items from her bag. Along with photos she gave the woman an engraved key chain from her parents' fifth anniversary and the bookmark her mom had treasured, the one with the quote from *Little Women.* Her dad's Bible and some dried flowers. An old penny dated the year her parents married.

Small things, but still important.

The lady assured Jenna that her parents' memorabilia would be placed in two separate side-by-side glass boxes for visitors to see.

"We'll have it put together by the end of the week," she said.

Jenna looked again at their pictures and she could feel the memories come to life.

She might've only been five years old, but she remembered them both. She could still hear her mother's voice, feel her arms around her daddy's neck. She could see their eyes, the way they looked into hers. Yes, she was glad she'd come today. Glad she'd brought the items for her parents' part of the memorial. However sad, it was important that people know who Bill and Betsy Phillips were. Proof that her parents had lived and mattered. A way for everyone who passed by to see something of who they had been.

Before she left, Jenna found the glass box for Sandra Bradshaw — Brady's mother. Inside was a photo of a woman and a little boy — clearly the two of them. Next to it was what looked like a copy of a child's drawing of the moon and stars. Beneath the image, in childish writing, the words *To the Moon and Back — Brady Bradshaw — Age 5.* Jenna felt her heart breaking.

A final look at the other glass boxes and photos that lined the walls of the room and Jenna took a step back. *God, remove me from this place. I've had all I can take. I want to be with Brady.* She turned and walked back to her car. Something told her she needed to hurry, that her voice was important to him. Not just that, but her faith, too.

Because if Brady ever needed God it was now.

Something was different about Brady. Jenna could tell as soon as she entered his hospital room. She put her things down and stood at the side of his bed.

"Brady, it's me. I'm back." A quick pause and she searched his face, his arms, his bandaged right leg. Looking for any sign of

276

movement. There was none. "Brady, it's Jenna." She studied his still handsome face. "If you can hear me, move your fingers. Open your eyes."

There was a sound at the door and Jenna turned. A man wearing an Oklahoma City Fire Department shirt stood there. Clearly another firefighter. He stepped inside, hesitant. "Hi." His eyes moved to Brady and then back to Jenna. "I'm Eric." He walked in and shook her hand. "Eric Munez. I work with Brady."

Jenna introduced herself. She paused. "You're probably wondering why I'm here." She could sense that much.

"He didn't . . . mention you." Eric looked like he felt bad making the admission.

She wouldn't have expected Brady to talk about her to his work friends. He hadn't seen her since they were seventeen. The fact that he'd written her a letter every April 19 and left it at the memorial was far more than she'd ever imagined.

She took one of the chairs near Brady's bed and motioned for Eric to take the other. "It's a long story."

He seemed willing to listen, so for the next ten minutes she told him about meeting Brady and how the impact of that single day had remained. For both of them. "When

I heard he was here" — she looked at Brady. He still hadn't moved — "I had to come."

"Wow." Eric leaned forward, his elbows on his knees. "Brady never talked about it."

"I'm guessing he didn't marry?" Jenna had visited Brady's Facebook page, but there was no relationship status listed.

"No." Eric took a deep breath and stood. He walked to the side of Brady's bed and stared at his friend. "Never married. Barely dates." Eric looked back at Jenna. "His whole life's his work."

Jenna knew Brady's injuries were caused by the fire. But she didn't know more than that. "Do you know how he got hurt?"

"Yeah." Eric nodded. His eyes grew distant. "I was on the roof with him. At the edge." He clenched his jaw and exhaled. "He took the middle . . . the most dangerous spot . . . so I wouldn't." His eyes met hers again. "I have a family. He doesn't. If something happened he wanted it to happen to him."

Her heart melted. "That's the Brady I met years ago."

"He shouldn't be here. Falling through a roof like that, he never should've made it." Eric turned and leaned against the bed rail, facing Jenna. "God has a plan for Brady. That's what I keep telling him."

"He must." Jenna looked at Brady. "His doctor keeps saying it's a miracle he's still here."

"I begged God for his life." Eric sighed. "Brady's a hero. Heroes shouldn't die fighting fires."

"All firefighters are heroes." Jenna believed that.

Eric nodded. "Brady's different." He told her how Brady served Oklahoma City a dozen ways. At least. The downtown mission, the children's hospital, whenever there's a project benefiting just about anyone. "Brady's there."

Jenna was about to ask if Brady believed in God, whether that was part of his motivation to help others. But before she could find the words, there was a stirring in the bed.

Jenna was on her feet. Eric turned and watched Brady. He was lifting his fingers. Just the slightest wiggle, but still it was something.

"Brady . . . hey, man, can you hear me?" Eric took hold of Brady's hand. "You're crazy, Bradshaw. You never shoulda gone that far out to the middle."

The slightest groan came from Brady. Jenna walked to the other side of the bed and waited. She didn't want to confuse him.

And since Eric's was a voice he was familiar with, she kept quiet.

Another moan came from Brady's lips. This time Jenna watched him squeeze Eric's hand, just enough for them to know. He could actually hear Eric's voice. Over the next hour neither of them left the side of his bed.

Brady's doctor came in, checked his vitals and confirmed the obvious. He was waking up. "Take it slowly." The doctor nodded at both of them. "He'll want to hear your voices, but he'll be very tired. I'll come by every few minutes to check on him."

Again Jenna didn't want to say anything. *He wouldn't know my voice if I was the only one in the room,* she thought. Now that he was stirring she wondered why she was even here. The shock of seeing her might be too much. If she'd been alone with him, maybe. But for now she would wait.

Another hour passed and Brady seemed to grow agitated. He was trying to open his eyes, trying to form words. At least it seemed that way. Finally, just as Eric was getting ready to leave, Brady spoke. "Wh . . . where?" His voice was a raspy whisper. But the word was clear.

"Brady." Eric bent over the bed, their faces close. "You're at the hospital." Tears filled Eric's eyes. He was a tough-looking firefighter, built like a tank. But here he was just a guy pulling for his friend. "Can you hear me?"

This time Brady nodded. The motion was clear and undeniable. "Wha . . . happened?"

Jenna stood a few feet away. Tears filled her own eyes. This was the answer she'd prayed for. However long the journey ahead, at least Brady understood what his buddy was saying.

Eric clearly didn't want to tell Brady too much. He wiped his tears, his voice strong. "You're okay, man. You're going to get through this."

The effort of trying to talk must've been too much because Brady fell asleep again. It was just after two o'clock. Eric had to leave, but he gave Jenna his number. "Call me if he wakes up more than this. I want to be here."

She nodded and thanked Eric. Thanks to him she now knew more about the years she'd missed with Brady. She sat by his bed and pulled up the photo Ashley Blake had sent her. The one with his letter.

God, I don't know what You're doing. But I can feel it. Please . . . give Brady a miracle. Give us both one.

Exhaustion came over her. Sitting here

watching Brady was taking its toll. Wondering what he'd say when he woke up again, or if he would wake up at all. Jenna was about to leave, head back to Allison's house for a nap, when Brady started moaning again. He turned his head a few inches in each direction, clearly agitated.

No one else was in the room, so Jenna took hold of his hand.

A rush of memories came over her, the way his hand had felt eleven years earlier. His skin was rougher now. Firefighter hands. But they were as warm as they'd been that far-off spring day.

Jenna stared at him. Should she speak to him? Now that he was coming to? She held her breath and decided she had to say something. Brady wanted to find her. It mattered to him. Maybe it would give him a reason to fully wake up if he knew she was here. "Brady . . ." She could feel her heartbeat in the hollow of her neck. "Brady, it's me. Jenna."

His restlessness suddenly stopped. He went still and then just as quickly he began to move again. And this time, finally, his eyes blinked open. Not all the way, but enough to squint at her. He turned his face in her direction and blinked a few more times.

"Jenna." Her name on his lips was unmistakable. "H-how?"

Every word took all his energy. Jenna could see that. Tears blurred her eyes. "Brady, I'm here. I found you."

His eyes closed again, but he knew. She was absolutely sure he knew. Not because he was able to look at her or say her name. But because of the way he squeezed her hand and ran his thumb along her finger.

Just like he'd done more than a decade ago.

17

Brady had been awake for two weeks.

He was still in the hospital, but earlier today they had moved him to rehab, four miles away and closer to his fire station. Though he had some swelling in his brain, miraculously he had no permanent damage. So it was time for him to get serious about his recovery, his doctor told him. Brady was all for that.

He had a reason to live now.

Jenna was helping him get set up in his new room. Eric came by every few days, and the Fishers, too. Cards and balloons from his other firefighter friends lined the shelf in the corner of the small space. A window spanned the area adjacent to his bed, and a television hung on the opposite wall. The place was very much like a hospital room, except instead of heart monitors and IV stands there were exercise machines. Pulleys for stretching and pushing and teaching Brady how to move again.

Brady watched Jenna, the way she moved, the efficient way she had of putting his things in their proper place. Everything about her was familiar. Not because they'd spent so much time together, but because he had memorized every detail about the hours they had shared.

He would never forget them.

"You're supposed to be sleeping." She smiled over her shoulder at him. "The doctor said, remember?" For a moment she studied the room. Then she took the chair by his bed. "You'll need your strength."

I need you, he wanted to say. But he kept his thoughts to himself. He didn't want to scare her. He leaned back into the pillow. "I'm not tired."

She took hold of the arms of the chair and watched him. "The doctors forgot they were dealing with Superman."

"Exactly." He laughed and winced at the same time. Any movement of his chest still hurt. He began to cough and with the energy it used to take to finish a two-hour workout, he pushed himself higher up in the bed. When he'd caught his breath he used the button on the side of his bed to move to a sitting position. "Okay." He gasped. "Sorry." He steadied himself, refusing another wave of coughs. "Maybe not Superman."

A smile lifted the corners of her lips. A seriousness came over her. "You are to the people in that retirement home." She stood and came closer, poured him a fresh cup of water and handed it to him. "Eric says the whole place would've burned down if you hadn't held the hose on the middle for so long."

"I don't know." Brady closed his eyes for a long moment. He was more tired than he wanted to admit. Again he looked at her. "Better me than him."

"He said you'd say that." She angled her head, studying him. "You need anything?"

There were a hundred ways he could answer her. But he only smiled and shook his head. "I'm okay."

"You need more water."

"True." He swigged back half of it and then looked at her again. "Thank you, Jenna." Her name on his lips still was more than he could believe. "You don't have to stay."

"I'll leave soon. I'm in town because I pulled together photos of my parents for the memorial. Photos and a few personal items. I'd never done that before."

"Oh." He felt the slightest disappointment. She wasn't here for him, after all. "Glad you did. That's important."

"Right now, what's important is you." She leaned toward him, her eyes dark with worry. "We need to get you walking."

Brady stared at her. He couldn't talk. Couldn't do anything but look at her. Not because of his injuries, but because he felt like he was caught up in some beautiful dream. Her being beside him, the two of them so close like this . . . none of it made sense.

"You're really here?" He held out his hand. She looked the same as when she was seventeen, but more beautiful. She had a confidence that hadn't been there before. "I keep thinking I'm dreaming."

She slid her fingers between his. "I'm here, Brady."

He was still on medication for pain, and his mind wasn't fully clear. Details about the accident were gone, probably forever. The swelling in his brain meant that some days he still struggled to remember his address. But even if he were completely recovered it would be difficult to comprehend that a stranger named Ashley Baxter Blake had actually found Jenna.

And even harder still to believe was the fact that Jenna had come to him. That she had stayed these last few weeks. He'd had surgery on his legs and now both of them had been fitted with metal rods. His spine had been fused to help his back heal and he'd had a skin graft operation for his right calf.

But she was here. That was all that mattered.

His doctor had said there was no telling how well he'd walk or if he'd walk. Fire-fighting was almost certainly out of the question. Brady didn't believe a word of it.

Jenna had found him. Anything was possible.

"You're a miracle." She released his hand and took a step back, toward the door. "You look so much better than you did. Even a week ago."

He couldn't stop watching her, couldn't stop staring into her eyes. "You texted Ashley, right?" Sometimes he felt like he was repeating himself. But he tried not to let that bother him. This part was critical. Ashley needed to know. "You told her I'm okay?"

"I did." She leaned forward. There was no end to the concern in her eyes. "You want something?"

"The last eleven years back." He smiled and forced himself to relax against the bed again. "But no food. Thanks." He checked the clock on the wall. "You leaving?"

"In a bit. I told Allison I'd make dinner." She hesitated. "I'll get a cup of coffee and come right back. At least for an hour or so." She moved closer to the door. "We still have a lot to catch up on."

"I like it." He watched her go. Their conversations had been in fits and starts. When they weren't being interrupted by a doctor or a therapist or a nurse drawing blood, he'd been sleeping. But every day he was a little more awake, more able to carry on a conversation.

Brady closed his eyes. No one had thought he'd live through the trauma. But here he was. Coughing every few minutes, still working to clear his lungs, still fighting to prove the doctors wrong. Now that he'd lived, they were worried about his future.

Not Brady. He was sure he'd beat the pneumonia and walk again. Convinced he'd fight fires once more and live the way he'd done before the accident. The only thing that worried him was losing Jenna.

He'd gotten the basics about her last eleven years. She'd finished college and moved to Columbus to teach. There she'd met and married some jerk named Dan who walked out on her. Brady clenched his jaw.

If only he'd found her years ago. He opened his eyes and stared out the window. Or if he'd run into Ashley Blake sooner. Outside the sky was cloudy. Rain hit the window and ran down toward the world below. How could any guy walk away from Jenna?

She returned with a coffee and sat in the chair near him. This time they talked about Jenna's school, the kids she taught and how much she loved it. "I'm connected. I have my friends and my church." She slid the chair closer to his bed. "My students. Life is good."

Brady listened, taking in every word. This wasn't the first time she'd talked about loving her life in Ohio. Her work and her church. Brady felt a piercing fear. The old Jenna had loved Oklahoma. She didn't believe in God and she hadn't had her heart broken by a guy. Was Jenna too different now? He didn't dare think about the possibility. Back then they'd had everything in common. Now he wasn't sure.

Best not to think about it. He could fall through the roof of a burning building and survive near death on a dozen different levels. But if all this was only leading to another terrible goodbye, Brady wasn't sure he could stand it. He took another sip of water. "Did you ever think about making a life here?" The question had come before, Brady was pretty sure. But he couldn't remember her answer. And he had to know.

"I didn't." Her reply came as quickly as the sadness that filled her eyes. "I couldn't . . . you know, drive by the memorial every day. Hear about the bombing every April." She shook her head. "I needed a life away from this."

He nodded. "I guess for me . . . it was too late for that. It already defined me. What happened that day." He paused. "It still does."

"I get that."

An older nurse came in then. "You need to sleep, Mr. Bradshaw. Your first rehab is in two hours."

"I'm not tired." He grinned at the woman.

She cast a wary look at Jenna and back at Brady. "I see that." Patience didn't seem to be her strong suit. "Either way, I need you to sleep."

Jenna took the hint. As soon as the woman was gone she stood and reached for Brady's hand once more. "Work hard this afternoon." She smiled, her eyes locked on his for a long few seconds. "I'll be here tomorrow."

"Okay." He savored the warmth of her

touch. If only he could freeze time, hold on to this moment forever. "Thanks again. For being here."

She smiled at him. "I'm glad I found you."

He grinned. "You did actually talk to Ashley Blake, right? She's not an angel?"

Jenna laughed, and the sound filled the room like the most beautiful song. "Yes. I texted her. She and her husband are praying for you."

"Well, then." He was procrastinating; doing everything he could to keep Jenna beside him a minute longer. "You better go."

"I better." Her eyes sparkled. He had the feeling she didn't want to leave, either.

He sighed. "Bye, Jenna."

"Bye, Brady." She released his fingers, took her bag and headed for the door.

With everything in him, he wanted to get out of bed, take her in his arms and ask if she felt the same way he did. He certainly hated seeing her go. But the nurse was right. Rest was the only way he'd be able to work hard enough to walk again. And he had to walk again.

So he could do the other thing he'd forever wanted to do.

Take Jenna Phillips on a date.

18

As May became June, Jenna could feel herself falling. Her summer in Oklahoma City was like something from a movie. The sound of Brady's voice, the way she felt when he watched her. Some afternoons she could barely breathe for the effect he had on her.

Her new life had taken on a different kind of routine. When she wasn't with Brady, she and Allison would share breakfast on the weekends and sometimes they'd work in Allison's garden or take a trip to the library. Other times they'd sit at the neighborhood pool and talk. But only when Brady was busy.

During the week Jenna would find a few minutes to talk to Ashley, catch her up on how Brady was doing. The two of them had gotten close. Jenna could tell they were going to be friends, just like she had believed that day when Ashley came to her school.

Just yesterday Ashley had asked about the future, whether Jenna saw any hope for her and Brady.

"That's tough." Jenna felt comfortable sharing this. Ashley seemed to understand the situation better than almost anyone. Even Brady. "We're very . . . different. Especially in our faith."

Deep conversations happened between Ashley and her nearly every morning.

Then, in the afternoon, Jenna would head to the rehab facility.

Brady worked hardest when she was there, Jenna was convinced. Each morning the therapist would teach him the day's routine, and when Jenna arrived she'd cheer on his practice. She'd go home for dinner and then return for another few hours with Brady.

Today Jenna parked in her familiar spot and headed into the facility. If things went right, this would be Brady's first day on his feet. They'd gotten him up several times already, but with a lift and only to keep his circulation going. This would be Brady's big test, the chance to see the full extent of his damage and just how far he had to go to walk again.

Jenna knew something was wrong as soon as she entered his room. He was sitting on the side of the bed, his shirt off, his muscled back to her. Sweat glistened on his arms and shoulders and his head hung in defeat. He sounded out of breath.

Should she leave or find his therapist? Maybe he didn't want her to see him right now. She stopped and was about to turn around when he must've heard her. He looked over his shoulder and the muscles in his jaw flexed. He shook his head. "Go, Jenna." His voice was tight, like he was speaking through clenched teeth. "I can't see you now."

"Okay." Jenna stepped out of the room and walked to the nurses' station. She waited until Brady's therapist, Kyrie, spotted her.

The woman was from Kenya, a strong, no-nonsense type. Today, though, her face was marked with compassion. She motioned for Jenna to follow her down the hall and when they were out of earshot, Kyrie turned to her. "It was a rough morning for your friend."

"I see that." Jenna felt her heart start to pound. "Did . . . did you get him on his feet?"

"I tried." Kyrie narrowed her eyes. "It didn't go well. The combination of pain and muscle atrophy. The rods in his thighs." She shook her head, clearly discouraged. "I have to be honest, Jenna. Some people never regain use of their legs after an injury like his."

Please, God, no. Jenna could feel the blood draining from her face. She turned and took a few steps in the direction of Brady's room and then back toward Kyrie. "Brady has to walk again." Tears welled in her eyes as she looked at the therapist.

"I feel the same way."

Jenna's head was spinning. Walking was all Brady talked about. That and how happy he was that she was here, that they'd found each other again. She managed to speak. "Is there a way . . . some sort of test to know? Whether he'll walk?"

"Not at this point." Kyrie sighed. "He has feeling. It's really a matter of whether he can tolerate the process."

Tolerate the process? Jenna wanted to laugh at the woman. Of course Brady could tolerate the process. He had fallen through a burning roof. He had lived his whole life in foster care with no one to love him. And he had waited for her eleven years without giving up.

Jenna forced herself to sound polite. "Ma'am. Brady can handle anything."

"Well then." Kyrie nodded toward his

room. "Maybe he needs a little encouragement."

"From me?" Jenna thought about how
he'd looked, how he had asked her to leave.
"He sent me away."

"They all do at first." Kyrie stood a little
straighter, more hopeful. "You say he can
deal with anything. So go back in there and
get him on his feet." She patted Jenna's
arm. "I'll be right back to help."

A sick feeling came over her. In the weeks
since she'd been in Oklahoma, she hadn't
once seen Brady down. Never experienced
a single moment of the utter defeat she saw
in him today.

Jenna steadied herself and walked toward
Brady's room. With every step she found a
new level of determination. If he needed
someone to push him, she was up for the
task. She reached his room and walked
inside. He was still sitting on the side of the
bed facing the window, his shirt still off.
But his breathing was more normal and he
wasn't as sweaty.

Again he turned to her, his expression a
mix of despair and frustration. "I said go,
Jenna." He faced the window again. "I
can't . . . I can't have you see me like this."

"Like what?" She set her bag down and
walked to him. So she was right in front of

him. "Kyrie says you need practice."

He lifted his face to her. Tears pooled in his eyes and his lip quivered. "Practice?" He laughed, but it was more of a cry. "Jenna, I can't put weight on my feet." He shrugged his bare shoulders. "My legs won't work."

"They will." Jenna was acting. All she wanted to do was run out of the room and let Kyrie take over. She was scared to death he might be right. But Brady needed her strength, not her fear. "Come on." She held out her hands. "I'll help you."

Jenna heard someone at the door. She looked up to see Kyrie. The woman had her hands on her hips. "You can do this, Brady. Use your thighs."

"My thighs?" He was shaking now. As if just the thought of standing again was more than his body could take. "I don't have thighs, Kyrie. I have metal rods. Remember?"

"Okay, so you're bionic." Her voice didn't hold a drop of compassion now.

Jenna understood. Brady needed tough love. Otherwise he wouldn't push himself to the next level. She still stood in front of him, arms stretched out toward him.

"You got the prettiest girl in physical therapy willing to help you." Kyrie clucked her tongue. "Use your metal rods, then. And push from your heels. But get that specimen of a body up." She raised her voice. "Now, Brady. Do it now."

Anger flickered in his eyes and Jenna watched it catch, watched it burn through his whole being. He gritted his teeth and took hold of both Jenna's hands. Then with an effort that took Jenna's breath, Brady pushed off his heels until his body began to rise from the bed.

"Good." Kyrie came a few steps closer. She nodded, emphatic. "That's it, Brady. You got this."

Once Jenna had watched a documentary on a woman who had gotten lost in the jungle and nearly died of malaria. That was how sick Brady looked now. Every inch of him was shaking and sweat streamed down his face.

"Breathe." Kyrie stayed back far enough to let Jenna do the assisting. "You gotta breathe, Brady."

A rush of air came through his clenched teeth, his face red from the exertion. When he was almost fully upright, he hit a wall and dropped back to the edge of the bed.

"There. See." Kyrie gave a firm nod. "Don't tell me you can't, Brady. You're one of Oklahoma City's finest." She had a fervor in her voice. "You most certainly can and you will." She turned to Jenna. "Next time don't let him fall back to the bed. I want him on his feet for three minutes. Then he can rest." She pointed at Jenna. "And don't you do the work. You're just there for support."

Clearly satisfied, Kyrie smiled at Brady. "Again, Mr. Bradshaw." She headed toward the door. "Come on. Again."

Kyrie left the room and Jenna stared at Brady. His sides were heaving, and he looked ready to pass out.

"Is she kidding?" Brady's eyes found hers. The anger was still there, but something else now.

Hope.

Jenna grabbed a towel from the shelf in the corner of the room. She could hardly wipe the sweat from his body. But he needed help. She handed him the towel. "Where's your shirt?"

"Drenched." He took the towel and ran it over one arm and then the other. His movements were slow and shaky. "I've never been so tired."

Jenna thought about what Kyrie wanted. She found her confidence and stood in front of him once more. "Let's try it again."

Brady ran the towel over his forehead and then tossed it on the bed. He searched

Jenna's face. "You're serious?"

"Kyrie's serious." She forced a determined smile. "You ready?"

He laughed, his breathing still fast from the previous attempt. "Do I have a choice?"

"Apparently not." She held out her hands. He gripped her forearms, and she could feel him trembling. "You sure you want to do this?"

She wanted nothing more. "That's why I'm here."

Brady positioned his feet, his heels and he clenched his jaw. His determination was like a physical force. Gradually, one inch at a time, he lifted off the bed until he was upright. Jenna's breath caught in her throat. "You're doing it . . . You're standing!"

As soon as she said the words, she felt his body give out. This time, though, instead of dropping to the bed he leaned into her. His chest pressed against her, his body hot and shaking. He hung his head, clearly embarrassed. "I'm sorry. You don't have to do this."

"It's okay. I want to help." A million thoughts fought for her attention. He was taller than she remembered and somehow he smelled amazing. Which didn't actually make sense. Maybe it was his shampoo or the lotion they used to keep his skin from chafing while he lay in bed.

Whatever it was, Jenna could barely focus. She could feel him breathing, feel his heartbeat against her body. He struggled with his balance, but he remained close to her. "How long?"

Jenna hadn't been keeping track. She swallowed, trying to find her own stability. "A minute. At least a minute."

Finally he looked down and stared into her eyes. But only for a second. Never mind the hardship he was working through or the fact that this was merely an exercise. The attraction was absolutely there for both of them.

Like all he wanted to do was kiss her. And all she wanted was for him to do it.

He steadied himself, easing back some so he was bearing his own weight. "Longest minute of my life."

And mine. She kept her thoughts to herself. She glanced at the wall clock and the second hand. "One more to go."

He looked at her again. His arms and body still shook, and he was sweaty all over. But he managed to find a smile. "I have a question."

"Go ahead." She braced herself so he could lean against her if he needed more support.

"So . . ." His eyes searched hers as he blinked a sweat drop from his lashes. A single laugh slipped from between his lips. "How am I supposed to think about standing . . . when all I want to do is kiss you."

She felt the heat in her cheeks even before he finished his sentence. "I was sort of thinking the same thing."

For the next ten seconds she was sure he was going to kiss her. But his strength was giving out. "Jenna . . ." He was breathing harder, the strain pushing him to the edge. "I have to believe . . . there will be a better time."

She laughed and lost her balance. He dropped back to the bed and she narrowly avoided falling on top of him. Instead she landed beside him. Despite his exhaustion they were both laughing now. Laughing so hard that they fell back onto the bed, side by side.

Kyrie walked in then. "The goal is to be standing." She gave them a stern look, but her tone told them she was teasing. "Let him rest for ten minutes."

"Yes, ma'am." Jenna scrambled to sit up. She wondered if Brady's heart was beating as hard as hers. Whatever was happening between them, she couldn't stop it.

"You're right about one thing, Kyrie."

Brady was still lying on the bed. He grabbed the towel and wiped his arms and chest and face again. Then he shot a teasing look at the therapist. "She kept me on my feet longer than you did."

"I figured." Kyrie shook her head and left the room. "Ten minutes. That's it."

And so it continued. Every ten minutes for an hour, Jenna would act as support for Brady as he practiced standing. And every time he seemed to do all he could to keep from looking at her. They weren't going to kiss. Brady was right, of course. This wasn't the time.

But Jenna made a note to bring him a few new T-shirts tomorrow. She could only take so much.

As June played out Brady proved everyone wrong, even himself. Two weeks after checking into the rehab facility, with Jenna at his side, Brady took his first steps. After that there was no stopping him.

Kyrie explained it best. The body remembers. Once Brady started working the muscles in his legs, his memory took over. That, and the fact that Brady had been in top physical condition at the time of the accident, meant he would get stronger every day.

The third week of June, Brady was discharged. Jenna was there when it happened.

His doctor told him the good news. Brady's legs were strong, his lungs were fully functioning and the swelling in his brain had completely subsided. "You're healed, Brady. Someone must've been praying for you."

The doctor's mention of prayer was the only moment that day when Brady looked indifferent, irritated almost. Before they left, Kyrie scheduled outpatient therapy a few times a week. "It'll be a year before you feel like you did prior to the accident." She smiled at him. "Keep working, Brady. Every day." Then to Jenna, "You stay on him. He'll get there."

There was nothing but joy between them as Jenna pulled up the car and loaded his things. Brady made it to her passenger door without any problem. Fifteen minutes later, she walked with him into his apartment and suddenly his eyes lit up. "The letters!" He motioned to her. "I'll be back."

He returned with a manila envelope and then he nodded to the living room. "Sit with me." He took her hand and they sat side by side on his sofa. "I want you to read them."

Jenna took the envelope and opened it. Inside were the letters he'd written to her.

One every year since they met. "I wish . . ." She looked at him, deep into his eyes. "I wish we could go back and live those years again."

"Me, too."

She read one of the letters while he watched her. The sound of their heartbeats filled the inches between them. "Thank you. For these." She stood. "I have to go, but I'll read them later."

"Okay." He looked relieved. "I'm just glad you finally have them."

They walked to the door and before she left he took her in his arms. This time he didn't need any help keeping his balance. He ran his thumb along her cheekbone and seemed to get lost in her eyes. "Jenna." His voice fell to a whisper. "Will you . . . go out with me tonight?"

She wanted to tell him yes, of course. Being out with him was something she'd dreamed about ever since that day in rehab, when they had almost kissed. She was about to respond when he moved closer.

"Before you answer . . ." He ran his hands down her arms. Jenna could smell the mint on his breath, feel the heat from his body. He framed her face with both hands. "I need to thank you. For helping me." He searched her eyes. "You're the reason I'm here."

Jenna had never felt more attracted to any guy in all her life. She grinned at him. "I loved it." This was intoxicating, standing here in his embrace. The way his strength had returned. Her voice was barely audible. "The first day on your feet was the best."

"What a mess I was." He chuckled under his breath and his eyes found a place in her heart that was his alone. He eased back some and his laughter faded. For a long time he only looked at her. Straight to her heart. "Even so . . . I'll remember it forever."

She felt her breathing pick up. "You told me we needed . . . a better time to kiss."

"Exactly." His voice fell to a whisper, his fingertips soft against her cheeks, a mix of strength and tenderness. "Like now."

And in slow motion the moment she'd longed for was happening. His lips found hers and the kiss was more wonderful than anything she could've imagined. Despite the time they'd spent together at the hospital and rehab center, Jenna was almost certain she was dreaming.

He drew back a few inches. His eyes told her he felt the same way. "I've dreamed of this as long as I can remember." He kissed her again, and she knew. She would be his forever. The kiss was everything they'd both thought about and hoped for. Not since she'd arrived in town.

But since they were seventeen.

19

The Baxter family's Fourth of July picnics at Lake Monroe were always epic and this year figured to be another memorable one. Everyone had set up their tables and blankets near the grassy shore, and now Ashley and Cole were trying to organize what had become their latest tradition. The one Ashley loved best.

A sand castle contest.

Each family was responsible for building a single sand creation. Their dad and Elaine would create one, too, so in all there would be six entries. Cole had come up with a voting system. It was a complicated but effective idea: each person could choose two sand castles, a first and a second place.

Every first-place vote was worth ten points, and a second-place vote was worth five. Also, you couldn't vote for your own sand castle.

Once Cole was done explaining the rules

Luke yelled out, "There will be a test on this later, in case some of you weren't paying attention." He pointed to a few of the younger kids and then he chuckled. "No, really. You can help us grown-ups."

Everyone laughed and Cole set a timer. One hour to build the best sand castle. Dayne and Katy and their kids were there, too, and this year they'd brought a dozen different-shaped buckets and turret molds and shovels. Kari and Ryan provided each team with a box of decorative seashells.

When Devin saw the supplies he announced that the news should cover the competition live.

"It'll probably come to that at some point." Ashley's dad chuckled.

"Yeah." Brooke put her arm around Peter. "Then the Olympics."

"For now, though" — Cole looked at the families — "it's just us. Best sand castle competition ever."

The setting sun, in part, dictated the time limit. Landon leaned close to Ashley seconds before the starter went off. "This is us, baby. It's our year."

Ashley nodded. "I can feel it."

Cole gave the countdown. "Five . . . four . . . three . . . two . . . one!" He raised his fist. "Start your castles!"

Ashley loved her family, every wonderful crazy person in the mix. The groups dashed to the supply pile and found what they needed to start building. The way Ashley saw it, her family had the edge. They had the most kids and they had Cole. Who had been planning the Blake Family Castle Idea since May.

The idea was a secret, of course. But now that the time had come, there was no more hiding. They were about to build Aslan, the lion from Narnia. Cole huddled the family together. "I didn't know about the sea-shells." He couldn't have been more serious. "I think we just won."

"Why?" Devin's expression went blank.

"Because." The answer was clearly obvious to Cole.

Ashley looked from one boy to the other and Janessa did the same thing.

"Okay." Landon looked at the setting sun. "Tell us about the seashells! Time's a-ticking."

Cole lowered his voice. "We'll use them for the mane."

"That's it." Amy clapped her hands. "You're right. We just won!"

Ashley smiled to herself as they got busy. She was in charge of building a short castle-type wall around the spot where Aslan would sit. Landon and Janessa would dig the moat around the outside of the wall.

And Cole, Amy and Devin would work on the lion.

"Plus" — Cole was now working furiously, building a smooth platform for Aslan — "we have two artists in our family." He grinned. "Mom . . . and Amy."

Ashley caught the way his compliment hit Amy. The look on her face as she basked in her cousin's praise was priceless. Ashley shared a quick glance with Landon. He smiled.

He had seen Amy's reaction, too.

The whole family worked so hard and so fast that the hour flew by. As the minutes ticked down, Cole gave warnings. Finally time was up. They were all out of breath, talking and celebrating and covered in sand.

Ashley put her arms around Landon's waist as they surveyed their work. Landon chuckled. "It's actually pretty amazing."

"It is." Ashley grinned. Aslan looked very much like a lion, and sure enough, the seashells made his mane look beyond majestic.

"Of course" — Landon kissed the side of her head — "Cole's right. It isn't really fair that we have two artists on our team."

"True." She gave him a sheepish look.

Each team took a turn revealing what they had created. In the event it wasn't obvious — which for some was the case.

Luke and Reagan's family had made the White House. Though Tommy admitted that he got confused and tried to do the Lincoln Memorial halfway through.

"Our team was definitely a little unclear." Luke laughed. "But it looks good. Whatever it is."

Kari and Ryan and their kids had created an all-sand football stadium. "It's supposed to be Clear Creek High." Kari took a bow. "We think we nailed it."

The Kensington Palace replica was done by Brooke and Peter and their girls. "Because it's supposed to be a castle." Hayley clapped and high-fived her older sister. "Right, Maddie?"

"Yes, that's right." Maddie linked arms with her and waited.

Dayne and Katy's family had made a theater, complete with rows of seats — each topped with a seashell.

"Very nice." Cole nodded. "When it comes time to judge, don't forget the little touches." He winked at Landon. "The details all matter. Speaking of which . . ." He motioned to Ashley. "Mom . . . tell them about ours."

Ashley took a quick breath. "Ours is Aslan of Narnia."

"Are you serious? The eyes look like they're real." Brooke put her hands on her hips. "Ash, how can we compete with you?"

"The eyes weren't mine." Ashley beamed at her niece. "They were Amy's."

"Way to go, Amy." Tommy clapped for her.

"And don't forget the seashell mane." Cole stepped back so everyone could see it. "Papa, it's your turn."

Ashley turned to her dad and Elaine. They were down the beach a little bit, and Ashley and the others didn't see their creation right away. But now that they all walked closer, Ashley knew what it was before her dad said a word.

"It's the Baxter house." He put his arm around Elaine's shoulders. "The place where it all began. The house that will always be home."

"Talk about details." Ashley stared at the house. She stooped down and looked more closely. "Seashell shutters. That's brilliant."

Somehow her dad and Elaine had even managed to capture the front porch and the basketball hoop in the driveway.

For a long time, the adult kids stood around, staring at the design. Tears filled Ashley's eyes and when she looked up from the sand house she saw she wasn't the only one.

"How can you look at that and not see a million memories?" Kari folded her arms. "Dad, Elaine . . . it's beautiful."

"It was his idea." Elaine smiled. "I thought it was a good one. Especially today."

Elaine was very deep and this was a perfect example. She might never have lived in the house, the one Ashley and Landon called home now. But Ashley's mother had lived there. And since she had started the Fourth of July picnic tradition, it was only right that her memory carry on.

Even in a sand castle.

"And instead of a moat it has a pond and a stream." Devin cheered, both arms in the air. "That's amazing, Papa! Way to go, both of you."

Cole gave Devin a look. "It's a competition." He lifted his hands and let them fall again. "Probably don't sway the votes to another team."

Everyone laughed and Cole handed out scoring sheets along with a quick refresher on the intricate voting system. The whole group walked around choosing a first and second place.

"No comparing notes," Cole directed. "This is serious stuff!" Even he chuckled at his words.

Ashley loved that he could poke fun at himself. He came by his competitive nature honestly. But at least he knew when to back off. Ashley couldn't always say that for herself.

Voting was simple for Ashley. She wrote her name, made her picks and handed her sheet to Cole. She was also careful to take pictures of each of the sand creations. The only way any of them would remember exactly what they'd done here today.

Landon made his selection quickly, too. Same with Kari and Ryan. The four of them walked up the hill to the nearest picnic table while the others were still deciding.

Landon and Ryan sat on top of the table while Ashley and Kari used towels to brush the sand off their arms. Kari was still laughing. "We might just be the most fun family on earth."

"Absolutely." Ashley dropped her towel near a pile from earlier in the day. Then she sat on the bench and leaned back against Landon's legs.

Kari did the same, resting on Ryan's knees. Only then did she turn to Ashley. "So whatever happened with that guy you met at the memorial? Brady, right?"

Ashley had kept Landon up on the latest,

but she and Kari hadn't talked about it since the day she found Jenna and learned Brady had been injured fighting a fire. Ashley looked over her shoulder and grinned up at Landon. "It's all good news, right?"

"It's a miracle." Landon shook his head. "I mean really. I have to admit, I thought maybe Ashley had gone off the deep end on this one." He sighed. "But wait till you hear."

"Yeah, I wondered, too." Ryan leaned forward. Both he and Kari were listening intently.

Near the water the rest of the family was finishing up their selections. Some of them were headed up the hill already. Ashley needed to make the story quick. "So you know how I went to Columbus and talked to Jenna in person?"

"Naturally." Kari nodded. "Like any sane person would do."

"Yes. Right." She laughed at herself. The whole story was pretty crazy. "Well, so, Brady was still in a coma and Jenna could hardly wait to go see him."

"She left work?" Ryan looked confused. "I thought she was a teacher."

"School was getting out the next week." Ashley's tone grew more excited. "So she moves to Oklahoma City for the summer because she knows someone who lives there."

"She moved?" Kari's eyes grew wide. "I can't believe it."

"Right, and then Jenna stays by Brady's bedside in the hospital until he's well enough to be transferred to a rehabilitation center." Ashley looked back at Landon and he pulled her gently up to sit next to him.

"Sounds familiar, right?" Landon looked at the others and back at Ashley. "I wouldn't have survived if you hadn't been sitting there all those days, Ash."

She felt sick at the memory. Landon had been fighting a house fire when he found a little boy, overcome by the smoke. Landon had saved the boy's life, but in the process nearly lost his own.

Ashley let the memory linger for a few seconds before she continued the story. She looked from Ryan to Kari. "So then he gets to rehab and it doesn't seem like he'll be able to walk again. Because his legs are a mess and his spine's fractured."

Ashley felt Landon shudder beside her. He took a deep breath. "Such a tough job, fighting fires."

"Absolutely." Ryan put his hands on Kari's shoulders. "You're all heroes."

"It's true." Ashley kissed Landon's cheek.

"So get this . . . Brady learns to walk. But only because of Jenna. Because she won't let him give up." She finished the story with the news Jenna had shared with her this week. "And now they're dating!"

"They are?" Kari stood up. "I can't believe this."

"Not because of Jenna." Landon reached for Ashley's hand. "Because my wife won't take no for an answer."

Dayne and Katy had come up the hill. Katy looked pensive as she stood next to Dayne. "Sitting at a hospital bedside while someone you love fights for his life. A little close to home." She looked at her husband. "Right?"

"Definitely." Dayne looked at Ashley. His memory was there for all of them. The time Dayne's car had been run off the road by paparazzi. The day he almost died. Dayne drew a deep breath. "Anyway . . . back to you, Ash. Talking about that firefighter you're helping?"

Ashley smiled. "Yes." There were no secrets in a family like theirs.

Cole was running up the grassy embankment, and behind him the rest of the family followed. "The votes are in!" He jumped onto the center of a picnic table. "I'm about to go from sixth to first place."

"You mean last place?" Maddie was clearly teasing. "Come on, Cole. Someone has to be last."

"Besides, there's always next year." Ashley's dad raised his brow. "Losing is a part of life. Even when it's all in fun."

Everyone agreed.

"Okay, here goes!" Cole looked to the bottom of the sheet of paper. "In sixth place we have Uncle Luke and Aunt Reagan's family."

"Yay for the half White House, half Lincoln Memorial!" Tommy started giggling and in a few seconds he was doubled over laughing. "Still . . . sixth place isn't bad. And first place for originality!"

Ashley savored everything about the moment. Her family was hilarious. And yes, this was the best Fourth of July picnic yet.

As the laughter quieted, Cole found his announcer voice again. "And in fifth place, Uncle Ryan and Aunt Kari's family with the Clear Creek Football Stadium!"

A round of applause showed the appreciation. Landon leaned over to Ryan. "Don't tell the team."

Ryan grinned. "Don't worry!"

Jessie, their oldest, shrugged. She looped her arms around her brother and sister. "It was the best sandy football field on the lake.

That's for sure!"

More laughter and then Cole revealed fourth place going to Dayne and Katy and their kids, and third place to his own family's creation. "Aslan of Narnia!"

Ashley was proud of Cole. He had dreamed about this contest for weeks and worked on figuring out a scoring system. She would've guessed they finished first by the enthusiastic way he ran up the hill with the results. But evidently he had taken the message to heart. This was about the family having fun.

Not about winning.

Besides — as her dad had said earlier — losing was part of life.

Second place went to Brooke and Peter's family, and the sand replica of Kensington Palace. Hayley jumped around and hugged Maddie, then her mother. She was one of the happiest people any of them knew. She might as well have won the Olympic medal for sand castle building.

"Which means, first place goes to . . ." Cole did a faux drumroll on his knees. "Papa and Grandma Elaine for the Baxter house."

Ashley smiled, her heart full. Was there ever any question?

A round of high fives and congratulations

came from the others. Ashley watched her dad hug Elaine and kiss her. The two of them had married several years after Ashley's mother died. Elaine was a very special woman, for sure. In fact, not long ago for a school project Cole had met with Ashley's dad so he could tell the love story between him and Ashley's mom. Cole's Grandma Elizabeth. Elaine was not only supportive of the project, she encouraged it.

It was evident today that nothing about that project had harmed her dad and Elaine in the least. Ashley was glad. She loved seeing her dad so happy.

"Let's take a look once more at all the sand castles." Ashley's dad led the way down the grassy bank, Elaine at his side. "Before the sun goes down."

Just then a couple of ski boats sped by not far from the shore. They weren't doing anything dangerous, really. But Ashley watched as the boats kicked up a wake and then zipped off across the lake.

"The wild ones come out on the Fourth." Landon shaded his eyes from the setting sun.

Before anyone could say anything else, a series of waves reached the shore and washed up against the winning creation.

Cole ran toward it. "Wait!" He was a few

feet away when the house, weak from the wave, melted into a pile of mushy sand.

For a few seconds all anyone could do was stare. Then Cole glanced back at his papa. "All that work . . ."

Ashley looked at her dad, but he was smiling, his eyes deep with nostalgia. "Isn't that just how it is, though? You build something here on earth thinking it'll last forever." He drew a slow breath. "When really it's the people who last. The souls of people. Their faith and their God. That's what endures."

"True." Ashley walked up to the collapsed house and took one of the seashells. She studied it for a few seconds. "All of that and something else." She smiled at her dad and held up the shell. "The memories."

Kari joined her and took a seashell from the pile, and then Ashley's other siblings did the same thing. Because whether it was a sand castle or Kensington Palace, their dad was right. Time would take the things they treasured here on earth.

Even, one day, the Baxter house.

Which was why, at the end of a day like this, Ashley was grateful. Not only that her family enjoyed celebrating the Fourth of July this way, but that each of them loved Jesus. Because one far-off day on the shores of heaven, the sand castle contest could

involve the entire family.
Not just the ones here today.

20

This summer was easily the most beautiful of Brady's life, and yet he had the worst feeling. The sense that life with Jenna wasn't just beginning.

It was ending.

Brady tried not to think about it, tried not to read into some of her comments or expressions. She had read every letter he had ever written to her, and they'd talked about them. Each one seemed to draw the two of them closer.

In fact, their good times were better than Brady ever imagined they might be. But so far Jenna hadn't wanted to discuss what they were going to do next, after summer. Sometimes at night he'd lie awake remembering every wonderful thing that had happened since she'd walked back into his life, and then the fear would hit.

Summer was almost over.

School had a start date, first full week of

August for teachers. When that day arrived, Jenna would be there. Not in Oklahoma City with him.

That much was certain.

Columbus was a thousand miles away. A thirteen-hour drive on a good day.

That wasn't all.

Lately she'd been mentioning her faith more often. It was becoming the religious elephant in the room. Eleven years ago they were the same, raised with their parents' faith but certain God had forgotten them. He had taken away the people they cared about most, and He hadn't answered any of their prayers since.

Back then they agreed on every point.

Now, though, Jenna spoke like someone who definitely believed in God. She talked about wanting to know God's will and several times she had referenced her certainty that God had great plans for His people.

Whatever that meant. Because how could God's great plans include what happened at the Murrah Building?

Brady gripped the wheel of his pickup. He was five minutes from the place where Jenna was staying. Today they were doing something new. Riding bikes together. Kyrie thought it would help his recovery to use his upper leg muscles. A bike ride through the park had been Jenna's idea.

When he didn't think about her increasing penchant for faith or the fact that summer was fading, Brady put his concerns out of his mind. Their chemistry was crazy amazing, and even though Jenna seemed careful not to spend time at his apartment, she clearly felt as much for him as he felt for her.

Brady pulled up in front of Allison's house and hurried out of his pickup. Not because he was late. Because it felt so good to be able to move. To order his legs to take a stretch of sidewalk at a fast clip — the way he had done all his life — and for his body to follow through.

He still hurt, still woke up each morning stiff and achy. Kyrie said that was to be expected. But the more he moved throughout the day, the better he felt. And every day he could move a little more.

Jenna opened the front door before he reached the top of the steps. "You're getting around so well." She shut the door behind her and joined him on the porch. "You're the hardest worker I know."

This was something else he'd noticed. She never invited him inside. They'd hung out every day for the past few weeks, and yet they'd been alone only a handful of times.

And almost never lately.

Brady let it go.

"I found the perfect park." Jenna moved to the edge of the porch. "Fifteen miles of paths and they rent bikes right near the parking lot."

"Sounds good." He took Jenna's hand as they walked back to his truck. If this summer was all they ever shared, if he had to live the rest of his life without knowing the sweet look in her eyes or the feel of her lips against his then he would at least have the memories of these weeks.

The feel of her fingers between his.

He opened the truck door for her and before she stepped inside, he pulled her into his arms. "Is Allison home?" His voice was softer than before. Full of a desire he could no longer avoid.

"She's not." The want in Jenna's eyes mirrored his own. But again she stopped short of inviting him in. "Brady . . . I can't . . ."

"Shhh." He put his finger to her lips, and then, like he was dying to do, he kissed her. "I missed you."

This time she kissed him and when she finally stepped back, her cheeks were red. "I missed you, too." But as soon as she said the words the look in her eyes changed.

There it is again, he thought. *What is it?*
He walked to the driver's side and climbed
in. Every move made him aware of his healing injuries. But nothing hurt more than
her hesitancy or doubt. Whatever it was.

Forget it, Brady. He started the truck and
pulled away from the curb. She was here.
She was real and she was his. There was
nothing to fear. He forced himself to relax.

The radio was on. Country music. Something by Thomas Rhett. He turned it down
and glanced at her. "I used to pretend you
were in the car behind me." He grinned.
Anything to hold on to the good between
them. "Did I ever tell you that?"

"No." She turned in her seat so she was
facing him. "Like I was driving behind you?"

"Yeah." He looked straight ahead again.
"I couldn't find you. So I let myself believe
you were there." He raised his brow in her
direction. "Does that freak you out?"

She laughed. "I mean, it's sad, but no." A
quick pause. "Of course, if you actually *saw*
me in the car behind you I'd have to wonder."

"It never got that bad." Not quite true,
but Brady liked the easy banter too much
to be too honest now. There were definitely
times when he looked in his rearview mir-

ror and saw her. His imagination was that strong.

"I have to say, I never pretended you were in the car behind me." Jenna looked relaxed, happy.

"Never?" He mouthed the word in her direction. Then he feigned a knife through his heart. "Ouch." Another glance in her direction. "And the mall." He allowed a quiet laugh. "I pretended we were shopping in different stores. That we'd meet up for lunch, but then . . ." His laughter faded. "Lunch never came."

Jenna watched him, her expression tender again. "I never got to the place of seeing you where you weren't." She didn't look away. "Every time I remembered that day, I was sure there was a reason you never called. Like you had a girlfriend. Or maybe you'd just moved on like the rest of the club."

He nodded a few times. "The club." They were almost at the park. "I stopped looking for familiar faces after you didn't come back the next year. Since then . . ." His voice trailed off. "I guess I haven't thought much about the club."

They reached the park and Brady found a spot at the back of the lot. More walking. Better for his recovery. He'd been worried about getting on a bike. Before the accident, his workouts were hours at a time. He could've biked up the side of a mountain. Thirty miles would be a cooldown.

But now, he wasn't sure he'd find his balance, or if his legs would move the way they were supposed to. Also it was hotter than it had been all month. Hot and humid. Some days Brady still felt his energy drop off, sometimes without warning.

Not that it mattered. He would get through this bike ride no matter what toll it took on him. Clouds gathered in the distance and Brady remembered that thunderstorms were forecast. Maybe they should cut the ride short.

Jenna looked up. "Glad we're starting now." She didn't say what she was probably thinking. That the worst thing would be for them to get caught in a storm. A slippery path could make even the simplest ride hazardous.

They rented bikes from a booth near the parking lot. Jenna climbed on hers first, and Brady stayed behind her. If he couldn't work the pedals he didn't want her to see him fall. He clenched his teeth, his determination fierce. His first attempt was a fail. He slid off the seat, his legs on either side of the frame.

Then in a single motion he tried again and he was on, his feet and legs working just as they should. Jenna looked back. "You've got it!"

There was a humiliation in realizing that anyone was celebrating the fact he could ride a bike. Especially Jenna. But in this situation Brady didn't care. He might as well have won gold in the Olympics. He was riding a bike! Nearly three months ago he had almost died. And now he was pedaling through a city park with Jenna.

Life was good.

They rode four miles of path before taking a break. Jenna's idea. Brady had water bottles in his backpack and he grabbed one for each of them. She took a long sip. "How do you feel?"

He looked at her, searched her face and her eyes. "Perfect."

"Good." She drank more water, put the lid back on and handed him the bottle. She seemed to notice the storm moving closer on the horizon. "Maybe we should turn back."

"Another couple miles." He breathed in deep. "I've never felt so alive in all my life."

He wanted to kiss her again, take her in his arms and get back to the bike ride later. But today couldn't be about that. He wanted to know her heart, her thoughts. What she wanted for tomorrow and next month and ten years from now.

The conversation they both seemed to keep avoiding.

Brady led the way this time. His legs didn't hurt, and by the end of the next few miles he had forgotten about the rods in his thighs or the approaching storm or the fact that the summer was waning.

After a while, they reached a grove of flowering dogwoods and black walnut trees. They stopped their bikes and climbed off. Only then did Brady realize he was breathing too hard. *Exhale. Just exhale.*

"You okay?" Jenna walked her bicycle beside him and leaned on the seat. Her eyes clouded with worry. "We should go back."

"No. I'm . . . fine." *Another few outbreaths.* There. He felt the panic subside. He could fill his lungs with air again. "I'm a little rusty. That's all." He wanted to talk about something else. "I love trees. I always have."

"Me, too." Jenna lifted her eyes to the branches overhead. "Ever since that first time at the memorial."

"Yeah. Who knew so much heart and emotion could come from an elm."

"Mmmm. True." Jenna smiled at him. "I

333

see the branches like arms, lifted to heaven. Praising God. Because the creation can't do anything else." Her eyes were flirty, her tone carefree. This wasn't one of those moments, where she almost seemed like she was testing him, his faith.

But the comment rubbed Brady like sandpaper. Did she really believe that? Trees had no choice but to praise God? He clenched his jaw. The idea was ridiculous. He looked at a grove of oaks up ahead. *Calm, Brady. Don't ruin the moment.* He forced himself to relax. "You know what I see when I look at a tree?"

"Tell me." She tilted her head back.

The wind in her hair was a vision that for a long moment left Brady speechless. He took a deep breath and tried to focus. "I see *The Swiss Family Robinson.* A mom and dad, a couple imaginative brothers. All of them ship-wrecked together, making the most of it." He paused. "I saw that movie a dozen times when I was in middle school. I had the same foster family for three years. It was their favorite film."

"I remember it." Jenna looked up at the highest branches. "I loved how they survived together."

"Yes." He caught a few glimpses of her, face lifted toward the sky, understanding how he felt about something as simple as *The Swiss Family Robinson*. How did she do it? Whatever his heart felt, hers felt, too. Even now. More than a decade later. Still, there was a part she wasn't connecting with. "Don't you get it, Jenna?"

"Get what?" She looked at him.

"God didn't let our families survive together. So how could the trees be praising Him?"

She looked hurt by his remark, but before she could say anything the first clap of thunder hit.

"Come on." He took a few steps and climbed back on his bike. "Now we really do need to get back."

Lightning split the clouds as they turned around and set out. Ten minutes later the sky opened up and rain poured hard and intense around them. Brady had to yell to be heard over the sound of it. "There!" He pointed to a picnic shelter twenty yards ahead.

Wind whipped against them as they pedaled the last few feet to cover. They pulled their bikes under and rested them against the wall. Brady was breathing hard, the effort taking its toll. Jenna was out of breath, too.

Both of them were drenched.

Brady leaned against his bike and faced her. He laughed, but it was more out of desperation. His legs shook and he wondered if he might collapse. "I've . . . got nothing left." The storm raged outside, but they didn't have to yell now.

Worry changed Jenna's expression. She pointed to a picnic table. "You need to sit down."

She was right, but he couldn't move, couldn't take a step. "It's . . . okay."

The handlebars were pressing into his back, and suddenly Jenna seemed to notice. "Here . . . let me help." She moved the bike so he could rest against the wall.

His breaths were shallow and fast, his body struggling to get oxygen. *Relax . . . inhale.* She stepped back, watching him, clearly concerned. He followed his own orders and after a minute or so his breathing steadied.

"The wind's crazy." She looked suddenly afraid. "It's not a tornado, right?"

With his remaining energy, he pulled his phone from his pocket. His hands trembled as he checked his weather app. He clicked on the radar and saw the banner across the bottom. SEVERE THUNDERSTORM WARNING. He stared at the sky and put his phone away. The clouds were blacker than before.

"No tornado. Not yet, anyway."

Lightning crackled on either side of the shelter. Thunder shook the ground and Jenna jumped. "That was close." Her teeth chattered, her hair wet against her face. "You think . . . we're okay here?"

His energy was coming back. Just enough for him to realize what was happening around him. She was scared. If she needed protecting, he was the guy. He found his footing and held out his hands. "Come here." He willed himself to find the strength to hold her. "I've got you, Jenna."

She slipped her arms around his waist. "I'm afraid."

"I know." He ran his hand along her back. "I'm here."

He could feel her heart beat, her breath against his neck. The storm was getting worse, fierce hail and pounding rain battering the roof and sides of the shelter. It felt like dusk, the clouds were so dark now. Before he could check the radar again, the alert on his phone buzzed. "Hold on." He took his phone from his pocket again and read the notification. "Tornado warning."

"Brady!" She was more panicked, more afraid. Her eyes locked onto his. "What do we do?"

"We'll be okay." He would keep her safe,

whatever he had to do.

In the distance sirens began to sound, their haunting rhythmic cry filling the air, mixing with the whistling wind and hail. Brady still felt shaky. The weakness wanted to consume him, but he fought it. Jenna needed him. His eyes darted around the shelter.

At the same time the wind grew stronger, howling and almost drowning out the wailing sirens. Brady needed a plan. There were four picnic tables under the covering. The table in the back corner was probably the safest. "Come on." He took her hand and led her to that one. "Get under it."

They scrambled to the ground and he made sure she was under the table before he took refuge beside her. She was shaking, and Brady realized the temperature had dropped. Twenty, thirty degrees maybe. Classic tornado weather.

A sound like a barreling freight train came next. Brady had to yell to be heard. "Hold on to me!"

Jenna did as he asked. She grabbed his waist and held on like her life depended on it. For all Brady knew, it did. He wrapped his arms around her body and clung to her.

"Jesus, help us!" Jenna cried out the words.

And even there, hanging on to each other beneath a picnic table in the middle of what seemed like a tornado, Brady felt the name grate against his soul. *Jesus?* She was crying out to Him now? The flicker of a thought ran through his mind.

Why would Jesus help them? He hadn't helped their parents.

Stop, he told himself. *Focus.* The most important thing was protecting her. The shelter started to shake and suddenly sections of wood pulled away and disappeared.

Jenna buried her face in Brady's chest. She was still praying, at least it sounded that way. It was too loud to hear her. Brady put one hand over her head and the other tight against her back, holding her as close as he could.

Next it was the roof. The half by the entrance collapsed in a sudden ground-shaking crash. Their bikes were buried in the rubble.

Right where they had been standing.

Jenna had her eyes closed, her face still pressed against him. She didn't know yet what had almost happened. The storm roared overhead and then, gradually, the sound began to lessen. More thunder and lightning, but the tornado sirens stopped.

He breathed against her hair, holding her.

That was close. Way too close. Adrenaline continued pumping through his arms and legs. "It's okay." His heart still raced. "It's over."

They climbed out from under the table and Jenna held on to him again. Only then did she see the collapsed roof and their bikes, somewhere under the debris. "If we hadn't . . ." She turned and eased her arms around his waist. "If you hadn't . . ."

She didn't have to finish her sentence. If they hadn't gotten under the table, they could've been killed. Brady had responded to storm scenes where people had died in lesser situations.

A ton of roofing and brick and wood collapsing over them? He shuddered. "I'm glad we moved when we did."

"It all happened so fast." She stepped back and held on to his forearms. "I mean, ten minutes ago we were riding our bikes and now . . ." Tears shone in her eyes. "Brady, we could be dead."

The storm was passing, leaving only the subsiding wind and rain and an occasional rumble of thunder. Never mind the broken pieces all around them, all Brady could see was her face. Her unforgettable green eyes.

"Jenna . . ." He eased his fingers along her cheeks and into her wet hair. His voice grew quiet. "I wasn't going to let anything happen to you." He allowed himself to get lost in her. "Not ever."

Like the tide against the shore, they came together. The attraction, the chemistry between them was stronger than the storm. Brady's kiss came in a rush of passion and intensity, more than before. Everything about it was like a dream. Before, Jenna had always seemed so careful when they kissed.

But here, now, there was none of that. Nothing could've stopped the moment. The kiss grew until it felt almost desperate. This was Jenna, in his arms. The one he'd looked for and longed for half his life.

Finally he drew back, his breathing fast. He released his hold on her and looked at the scene around them. Beyond the damaged shelter a few trees were down. Nothing like the destruction Brady had seen from other Oklahoma tornadoes. But bad, all the same. He reached for her again.

"We need to go." Fear returned to her eyes. "We need dry clothes. And you're not supposed to be out this long."

Brady nodded. She looked so beautiful. All he wanted to do was live in this minute forever. He would've stayed here all week if it meant not letting go of Jenna. But she was right. His adrenaline had worn off and the tired feeling was back. They were both drenched as he took her hands, and that's when he noticed it. Something in her touch was different. Like her heart had pulled away in a matter of seconds.

Brady knew deep in his gut that the change had nothing to do with the storm or their soaking wet clothing.

He hugged her again, but it didn't last as long. He studied her eyes, her expression. There was no time like now. He tried to draw a deep breath and failed. It didn't matter. He had something to say. "Can we talk? Before we go?"

Jenna relaxed, and nodded. "Okay." The concern was definitely there. Concern or hesitation. Something. "We should."

He wanted to kiss her again. But he wanted answers more. "Something's different. With you . . . with us."

She didn't deny it. She only looked at him, straight to his soul.

"Why?" The thudding in his chest came harder, faster. His legs felt weak. "What's . . . going on?"

Jenna placed her hand against his cheek. "Summer's almost over." She shrugged one shoulder. "I'm going home soon."

Panic wrapped its fingers around his throat. "Jenna . . . I spent years looking for you." He forced a single laugh. "You think my feelings are going to change because summer's over?"

She lowered her hand. This time she eased her fingers between his, but she focused on a spot on the floor. When she looked up, there were tears in her eyes again. "We . . . whatever we have . . ." She shook her head. "It isn't going to work."

He needed to sit down. "I'm . . . sorry, I . . ." His legs buckled and he dropped to the picnic bench.

"Brady!" She was instantly beside him.

He hated this. Hated his weakness. "I'm . . . okay."

"You're not." She put her arm around his shoulders. "We can talk about it later."

He couldn't let his body beat him. Not now. He gripped the edge of the bench. "I'm fine . . . we can talk —" Dizziness swept over him. He was wet and shivering. He closed his eyes and hung his head. "Jenna . . ."

"What can I do?" She sounded anxious again. "Should I call someone?"

"No." He was light-headed, trying to grasp what she was saying, why she was willing to let things fall apart just because school was starting. The thoughts chased each other around his mind, making the dizziness worse. He was so thirsty. More than ever in his life. "Water. Please."

He could feel her get up, hear her take a few steps. But then she stopped. "It's all buried. We have nothing."

Brady drew a few breaths. Deep as he could get them. What was he supposed to do? The last thing he wanted was a crew of paramedics running down the bike path, trying to rescue him. He was fine. He had to be fine.

He was still hanging his head, still trying to stop the rotating. An idea hit him. Something that couldn't hurt, given the situation. He tried to concentrate. Tried to stop the dizziness twisting his insides. *God, if Jenna is so sure about You, fine. If You're real, get me out of here. Give me the energy to get up. Make my head stop spinning. Then I'll know.*

"Brady?" She was still worried. "Can you hear me?" Jenna was sitting beside him again.

Thirst was still an issue, but he wanted to answer her. He blinked and his eyes opened. He blinked again.

The dizziness was gone.

He sat straight up and felt his heart skitter into a strange rhythm for a few seconds. What was this? How could the faintness be gone seconds after he asked God to prove

Himself?

Coincidence.

Brady breathed deep and this time he felt his lungs fill with air. The way they were supposed to. His energy was returning, that was all. Random perfect timing.

He put the thought out of his head and turned to Jenna. "That was weird." He tried to smile. "It hit so hard."

"Like the storm." Her face showed how worried she was. "You okay?" She had her phone out. "I can call for help."

"No." Brady stood. His balance was almost perfect. "I'm not dizzy anymore." He looked at the sky. It was still stormy. "We should go." He reached for her hand and they made their way through one of the gaping holes in the side of the structure.

At the same time a park truck drove up. The driver saw Brady and Jenna and stopped. "Everyone okay?"

"Yes, sir." Brady felt well enough to walk on his own. As he made his way toward the pickup he noticed something. His shaking legs, his shallow breathing. The weakness and spinning. All of it was gone. Brady pointed to the collapsed shelter. "We rented bikes, but . . . they're buried." He looked at the driver. "Could you please give us a ride back?"

The man dropped them off at the parking lot, where the bike stand was also in a heap of rubble. Brady opened the door for Jenna, but he was too tired to help her into the truck. It took him nearly a minute to walk around the front of the rig and climb inside.

On the drive home, several times Jenna urged Brady to see the doctor.

"I'm okay, Jenna." It was the truth, at least physically. If she wanted to worry about anything, she should worry about his heart. About both their hearts.

After that they drove in silence. Not his choice. This wasn't how he wanted the day to finish. But she didn't seem to feel like talking. He wanted to hear more about what she was thinking, and why she thought this beautiful thing they'd found had to end.

As they pulled up to Allison's house, Brady didn't walk her to the door. Jenna seemed in a hurry, and she said something about needing to get out of her wet clothes.

Brady's desperation mixed with panic. This couldn't be the end. "Tomorrow?"

Jenna nodded. "Yes." She watched him for a long moment. "Ten o'clock?"

"Ten."

"Thank you." She hesitated before climbing out. "For saving my life today."

He tried to find a lighthearted smile. But

it wasn't possible. "It's what I do."

She nodded, never breaking eye contact. Then she managed a little wave and mouthed her next words. "See you."

Brady wanted to scream. Why did they have to end the day now? Like this? She could've come to his apartment and they could've watched a movie or played backgammon. He wouldn't push things physically, if that's what she was worried about. They could've sat at the table and talked for all he cared. Anything but spend the evening alone when she was right here.

When it was still summer.

But she was already walking toward the house. He sighed, frustration taking jabs at him. "See you, Jenna."

She was too far away to hear his words. She waved once more before she went inside, and with no choice left, he drove home. He could feel her pulling away. Like some dream, destined to end too quickly, their time together was almost over.

Sure, she could tell him why tomorrow. They could work out the details and come to an understanding. But that wouldn't change the fact.

Jenna was leaving.

She was going back to Ohio and that would be that. When he was home, he stretched out on his bed and stared at the ceiling. That whole talking to God and his symptoms going away was nothing. Brady was strong. His body was fit. He would've gotten better with or without his challenge to God.

If God were real, this wouldn't be happening. He never would've allowed them to find each other, only to take Jenna away again.

Brady blinked back tears. Once Jenna was gone, he would fall back into his same routine. He could already see it: working and volunteering and trying to make his way past April 19, 1995, 9:02 A.M. But this time missing her and longing for her wouldn't last eleven years. Brady was sure.

It would last the rest of his life.

21

Jenna was grateful Allison had her Bible study that night. She couldn't have stayed up chatting, pretending everything was okay. Not when her heart was breaking. Allison would've seen through her façade and asked her about it.

And Jenna wouldn't have known what to say. She was still processing the answers herself.

But by the next morning when Brady picked her up she couldn't run from the truth anymore. She had the answers, and they weren't good. She wore the key necklace today, the one she'd had engraved years ago. The one she would give to Brady, no matter how much her heart was breaking.

If only he shared her faith. If only he had found his way back to Jesus. Every day Jenna had tried to gauge Brady's interest in God. She would talk about something being a blessing or she would refer to how the

Lord was working in her life. Every mention of anything spiritual only irritated him. Confused him.

Jenna could tell. His eyes gave him away. Since yesterday's storm, Jenna had replayed over and over the promise she'd made to God. The promise she'd made to herself. Brady was nothing like Dan, but the fact remained: Brady was determined to spend his life far from the Lord. He had alluded to that just before the tornado.

Which meant one thing.

She had to keep her word. Even if walking away from Brady Bradshaw was the hardest thing she'd ever have to do.

From the moment Brady picked her up, his steps were sure, his face alive with energy. Not the broken guy from yesterday's storm experience, for sure. As she climbed into his truck, she ran her fingers over the engraved numbers on the key. She had no idea how he would take the news. She would have to tell him sometime today. Later. So they'd have at least a few good hours.

He smiled at her. "Hi."

"Hi." Her heart hurt. The subtle smell of his cologne mixed with the leather from the seats. She returned the smile, but the whole time she could feel the sadness coming.

If only he didn't take her breath away every time they were together. She stared at her hands for a moment. *God, change his mind about You. Please, get his attention.*

Before he pulled away from the curb, he glanced at her necklace. "I like that. A key." He seemed so much stronger today. "It's different."

"Thanks." She looked out her passenger window. *Different.* The word lodged in her soul. That was the problem now. As much as they had in common, when it came to what mattered most they were different.

Their plan today had been set since the beginning of the week. They had decided to go to the memorial. Brady wanted to see about getting a sapling from the Survivor Tree for Amy, Ashley's niece. And Jenna needed to see her parents' memorial boxes. The way they looked with the photos and items she'd brought from home.

Still, the whole day seemed like a last-ditch attempt to Jenna, on both their parts. Maybe if they spent a day at the place where they had met they would figure out a way past their differences, a way around the logistics.

And they'd never have to say goodbye.

Before they reached the memorial Brady stopped at the coffee shop, the one they'd visited together all those years earlier. On the way in, he put his hand ever so lightly at the small of her back. The feeling was electric. One thing was sure. No matter what happened after today, Jenna would never forget him.

Never love anyone the way she loved him.

Everything about being back in the café put Jenna's heart on high alert. She had to fight to keep from drowning in Brady's presence. The way his voice soothed her soul, the feel of his arm against hers as they waited for their drinks.

Since Brady had been well enough to get around he had teased Jenna that she was a coffee addict. "It's a teacher thing," she always told him. As for Brady, he had given up coffee his first year as a firefighter.

Now, though, when she ordered a caffe breve, he stepped up beside her, his eyes sparkling. "Make it two, please."

"Yes, sir. Two." The guy behind the counter entered the order.

Jenna looked at Brady, confused. "Two?"

"One for me." He elbowed her gently in the ribs. "I gotta broaden my horizons a little, right? Get out of my box."

Something in his tone made her laugh, and he started to laugh, too. And Jenna realized something. They hadn't done much of this recently. Between his injuries and rehab and the desperate feeling that they were running out of time, they hadn't laughed.

The exhilaration and joy that came with it felt wonderful.

When their coffees were ready Jenna put a cardboard sleeve on her cup and Brady did the same. He winked at her. "You're the expert."

"Definitely." She loved this, the way she felt around him. She couldn't help herself. That was the problem: this feeling, the way she fell into his gravity, could never be enough. She would keep her promise to God, no matter what.

Even if it meant losing him.

As they walked out of the coffee shop, Brady put his arm around her. The touch of his fingers against her shoulder sent chills down her. If she stayed another week, no matter what her convictions, Jenna was certain of one thing.

She'd never go home.

As soon as they were in the truck, Brady took his first sip of coffee and started to make a face. But then his eyebrows raised and his expression relaxed. "What in the . . . Are you kidding me? No wonder I gave it up."

"What?" She laughed. "You mean because it's so good, right?"

Another sip and Brady sank back in his seat. "This is amazing." He pointed at her, his eyes sparkling. "When I'm addicted a month from now, it'll be your fault."

"Guilty." With everything in her she wanted to stay here, hold on to the moment. Forget about the conversation that would come later. But even as she laughed again, she knew. There was no way to save what they had found.

They reached the memorial ten minutes later, and the place was nearly empty. As they walked onto the grounds, Brady stopped. He looked around and breathed deep. "I can't believe you're here. The two of us like it was that day."

The smell of jasmine filled the air, the summer sun warm on their skin. "I remember everything about it." She faced him. This couldn't go on. Jenna had to say something. "Brady . . . we need to talk."

He searched her eyes, and gradually his smile faded. A dozen thoughts seemed to flash in his expression. Was something wrong? How could she ruin a perfectly good day? Didn't she know how he felt about her? Without a single word, Jenna could see it all. But he said only "Sure."

They didn't have to talk about where they would go, which of the benches they would sit on. Without a word they started walking toward the Survivor Tree. They still had their coffees, but with his free hand, Brady took hers.

She didn't resist. There were only so many hours like this left.

They made their way up the stairs and sat on the bench closest to the tree. For a few minutes they stared at it, drinking their coffee. Lost to yesterday.

When they finished their drinks, Brady took both cups to a nearby trash can. With his every step, her every heartbeat, Jenna could feel the sorrow build. If only there were some other way.

Brady returned and sat facing her. He put his arm up along the back of the bench and watched her. He seemed in no hurry. "What's on your heart, Jenna?"

So much. She wanted to grab his hand and run as far away from here as she could, to a place where Brady's eyes could finally be opened to God. Or where she could break down and cry for a hundred days.

The last thing she wanted was to tell him the truth.

She didn't look away. First things first. "Brady . . ." She drew a shallow breath and pushed ahead. "I have to leave tomorrow morning. I found out last night. We have a mandatory teachers' meeting Monday."

His expression was something Jenna had seen before. When she was in high school some kid had walked up and sucker punched a boy. Jenna was right there, headed to lunch. She saw the whole thing. The approach, the swing. And the way the other kid looked after the hit.

Pale and shocked and in pain.

The way Brady seemed now. He fell forward a little and shook his head. His voice was quieter than before. Like he couldn't get enough air to fully speak. "No . . . warning?"

"I'm on call after the first of August." She exhaled, desperate for things to be different. "Today's the fourth, Brady. The only reason I didn't leave sooner . . . was you."

He stood and paced a few feet toward the tree and back again. "I thought school starts in September."

"Not in my district." Jenna felt her stomach tighten. If only that were all she had to tell him.

Brady took his seat again. "So that's what this is all about? The way you . . ." He glanced around, like the words might be swaying from the branches of the old elm.

"I don't know, the way you've been different this week?"

She stared at him, into his eyes, willing him to understand. "That's not why."

This time he didn't say anything. He just waited, his eyes on hers. Didn't move. Didn't blink.

"Brady . . . every time I mention God, you get mad. Things get tense." She wasn't finding the right words. "It's not like you don't let me talk about Him. But you just . . . you don't believe, do you?"

Shock and anger painted broad strokes across his expression. "I can't believe you're asking me." He shook his head. "You already know the answer, Jenna. It's practically all we talked about the day we met."

"Exactly. That was a long time ago, Brady. I've changed since then." Jenna didn't mean to raise her voice. But the memorial was still nearly empty. She needed him to understand how difficult this was for her. "I hoped you had, too." Tears clouded her vision. "I prayed you had."

Brady looked sick to his stomach. He released a sound that seemed part disbelief, part heartache. "You've gotta be kidding me." He stood and walked to the tree again. For a long time he stayed there, facing the trunk, his back to her. A couple times he seemed to grab a deep breath, probably struggling for control.

The ground could've opened up and swallowed her and she wouldn't have noticed. All she could feel was her world falling apart. Tears ran down her face. *God, why? Please, would You help us? How am I supposed to leave?*

With all her heart, Jenna wanted to go to him. But what would that do? She couldn't take him in her arms and kiss him, couldn't comfort him. The truth was there now, out in the open for both of them to see.

Goodbye wasn't far off.

Finally he returned to the bench. His eyes were red and damp. "Come on, Jenna." He held out his hand. "Let's go see your parents' memorial boxes."

She took his hand and all of her senses were fixed on that one feeling. The warmth of his fingers between hers. "Okay." It was time. This was why she'd come to Oklahoma City. She would see the project through, even as her heart was breaking.

They stood and walked into the museum, through the building and into the area with the individual glass memory boxes. The moment they entered the room, Jenna saw the one for her parents.

Brady stayed with her as she went up and

put her hand over their names. Neither of them spoke. Not for a long time.

"Tell me." Brady's voice was soft, kind. "Why these things?"

Jenna fought the tears gathering in her eyes. She steadied herself. "The little Bible in the corner, that was my dad's. He kept it in the kitchen."

Brady listened, his eyes on the objects in the glass boxes.

"He had his own personal Bible." She managed a smile. "It's in the top drawer of my dresser. But that one" — she pointed to the small leather-bound book — "that was the one he'd pull out during dinner."

"While you ate?" Brady's tone was kind, his frustration with God seemingly on hold for now.

"Yes." She turned to him. "The Psalms tell about the Word of God being like honey. My dad used to say a few minutes in the Bible was like dessert."

"Hmm." Brady's expression grew softer. "Must have been a good dad."

"He was." She looked at the box again. "That bookmark was my mom's. She loved to read. Her mother gave it to her when she was a little girl."

"Must've been hard to let it go." Sadness crept into Brady's tone. "For the memorial." He moved closer. The heat from his body warmed her.

She told him about the other items. The key chain and a dried flower her dad had given her mother the day Jenna was born. The pictures didn't need explaining. They showed the reality of Jenna's former life. Happy couple. Happy little girl.

All of life ahead of them.

There was one more piece, one more truth he had to hear. She looked deep into his eyes. "Every day without my parents I want to remember . . . that God alone lets me live in the healing. I'm a survivor because of Him. Because He has my parents safe in heaven and one day . . ." Her voice broke. She blinked back the new tears. *Let him hear this, please.* "One day I'll be with them again. And when that time comes, I want the people I love . . . to be there, too."

Quiet fell over the moment. She didn't want to move on from here. What could she say? There was no way around the goodbye ahead.

Brady broke the silence first. "My mom . . . she believed." He looked from the glass box to Jenna. His voice fell to barely a whisper. "Look where it got her."

Jenna understood. Without a different view of the heartache in the world, it was impossible to understand how a great and loving God could allow tragedy on earth. Scripture offered a chance to make sense of it all. But it was never easy. Even for her. She breathed in, thinking of a way to respond. "She's with Him now. She's having the happiest time, so happy we can't even imagine it."

He considered that for a long moment. Then he did a slight shrug. "I don't know, Jenna. I'm not sure."

"I am." Her answer was quick. "You know what your mother is doing right now?" She didn't wait for his response. "She's praying for you. That you'll see each other again one day."

Brady flexed his jaw. Whatever he was thinking, he didn't speak it.

They walked together to his mother's glass memory box. "To the moon and back." He put his hand over the top of the container and his gaze seemed to fall on the page with the childlike artwork. "I drew that for her just before she died."

Tears filled her eyes again. "I'm sorry, Brady." She paused. "For both of us." This would probably be the last time Jenna visited the memorial. She didn't like thinking of her parents here. She liked thinking of them in heaven.

With Brady's mom.

He released her fingers and turned to her. His eyes were full of love and hurt. "Why, Jenna?" He seemed to search for the place in her soul where the answers lived. "Why is it so important that I believe?" He put his hand on her cheek, his fingers in her hair. "I love you. Isn't that enough?"

She couldn't breathe, couldn't turn and run. Couldn't do anything to stop the way her heart was breaking. Brady Bradshaw actually loved her after all this time. The whole scene felt like something from a dream, except for one thing. This wasn't a beginning.

It was an ending.

And suddenly nothing could've kept them apart. She closed the distance between them and said the only words that mattered in this moment. "I love you, too, Brady." Tears spilled from her eyes. "I always will." She struggled to speak. "I always have."

"Then why?" His voice was broken, as if he was completely unable to make sense of what was happening.

She had no words. Not now. Not here. Brady leaned in and in a blur of the most wonderful, most gut-wrenching seconds, he kissed her. Here, in the exact spot where he had almost kissed her years ago. Like they'd come full circle.

Their tears mixed and the taste was salty on her lips.

Another kiss and then Jenna pulled back a few inches. "Brady . . . I can't." She stared at the ground and then at him. "Please . . . can we leave?"

His hand was still on the side of her face. But gradually his expression showed the beginning of defeat. He nodded, searching her eyes. "Okay."

They were headed toward the door, when Jenna saw the wall. The one with the time stamp engraved on it. Suddenly she didn't want to leave. Not yet. Not until she'd explained herself a little better. "Wait. I want to show you something."

"Jenna . . ." He stopped and crossed his arms. Like he couldn't stand to draw out this terrible goodbye for another minute.

"Please, Brady . . . it's important." She led the way outside to the survivor wall, the one she'd visited last time she was here. Even if he'd seen it a dozen times, she wanted him to see it again.

When they were standing in front of the cracked slab of concrete, she pointed to his name — engraved with the others who had lived through the bombing. "See."

Brady looked confused. "What? My

name?" He shrugged. "So?"

"So . . ." She turned to him and searched his eyes. *Please, God, let him get this.* "You're a survivor, Brady. It says so right there in that piece of the building. God let you survive." She paused, letting the weight of this hit him. "And He did that for a reason."

She felt the key around her neck and in that instant she knew what she had to do. She looked around and spotted a bench nearby. "Can we sit here . . . for a minute?"

"Why?" He took a step back. "I mean, Jenna . . . what's the point?"

She felt terrible. All she wanted was for him to kiss her again. But there was no way back. She would do this one last thing for Brady, then she would say goodbye. Forever. Because of her love for God she'd found the superhuman strength to do something she wasn't sure she could ever do.

Push Brady away.

She found her voice. "After all we've been through . . . I can't leave without giving you something."

He stared at her for a minute, looking like he had just lost his best friend. "Okay."

This was hard for him. Hard for both of them.

His hesitation didn't last long. With a slight sigh of what seemed to be resignation, he reached for her hand once more. It was one thing to stop him from kissing her, but she wouldn't resist him taking her hand. When their fingers were together, their hearts were, too. That had been true from the beginning.

Jenna sat on the bench and Brady did the same. Their knees and shoulders were touching. She took a slow breath. "Do you remember what the time stamp on the wall stands for?"

"The 9:01?" He clearly knew the memorial grounds well. "There are two walls, Jenna."

"Not that one." If only she could fix the brokenness inside him. "We can't go back to 9:01. None of us can." She hesitated. "I'm talking about the other wall."

Brady nodded slowly and looked at the wall at the other end of the pool. "I know it." He sat a little straighter, almost as if he were squaring off with the wall. Like the two of them were enemies somehow. After a long moment he shook his head. "I never got there. 9:03."

Give me the words, God, please. Help him hear me in his heart. She held her key necklace and looked from it to Brady. "You said you liked my necklace. Look at it."

A quick hesitation and then gently he took

the key and stared at it. The realization hit him all at once. She could see it in his eyes. He nodded slowly and lifted his face to hers. "The minute healing began." He looked at the key again. "You live in 9:03. Life after the bombing."

"Yes." She blinked back her own tears. The story needed to be shared. "I had returned to God before I met Dan. I met him at church, so I thought he believed the way I did. The way my parents did." She caught a tear with her fingertips and tried to focus. "But in the months after we married, I found out he didn't. He only pretended to believe in God."

Brady was listening. His expression held a layer of sympathy that hadn't been there before.

The sun was hot overhead, but Jenna barely noticed. "Dan stopped going to church with me, stopped wanting to talk about the Bible." She could picture herself back then, married and alone. "I thought he might be having an affair with one of our neighbors. But before I could figure it out, he was gone." She blinked back another wave of tears. "I never heard from him again."

For a while Brady said nothing. "I'm sorry."

"It's okay." She sniffed and shook her head. "I've been over him for a long time. I'm at peace." This was the part she wanted him to understand. "But after he left, I made God a promise. I said I'd never fall in love with an unbeliever again. Never."

Brady's understanding was instant. He released her hand. "So that's it." He nodded and folded his hands. For a long moment he stared at the ground. Then he looked at her. "I get it." His hint of a smile didn't reach his eyes. "You made a promise to God. So I'm not the guy."

He looked off, but after a few seconds he turned to her again.

"Jenna, I would do anything to keep you here with me." He leaned closer, looking into the deepest places of her soul. "I would say anything." He hesitated. "But I will never lie to you." The hurt in his eyes intensified. "I don't believe. I can't."

His words were like so many bullets. But she ignored them. There was something she had to do.

The key was still between her thumb and forefinger, her eyes on his. "This is called a Giving Key. It's meant to be given away." She paused. "I bought it because I hoped . . . I prayed . . . that one day we'd find each other and . . . and you'd believe in God again." She wiped another tear.

He seemed to feel the news to his core. Any slight smile faded, and he clenched his jaw. "I'm not there, Jenna. I'm sorry."

Her tears came harder now. With her fingertips she dabbed beneath her eyes. "I understand." *Composure, Jenna. You can't break down.* She drew a deep breath. "I see that now."

"And it's why you and I . . ." His eyes were damp. "Why this can't work."

"Yes." That was it. She'd said everything there was to say. "I'm sorry, Brady. I promised God for a reason." She hesitated. "It's a reason that still matters."

There was one more thing she needed to do. Jenna unclasped the key necklace and clutched it in her hand. "This is yours. I've wanted to give it to you for a long time." She held it out to him.

"I can't . . ." He shook his head. "It's yours."

"I'm there, Brady. Like you said, I live in 9:03." This time she took hold of his hand and gently placed the necklace in his palm. "It's yours now. And as long as I live I'll pray you get there someday."

He looked at the key for a long moment, at the time stamp at the center. Then he slipped it into his pocket, his movements slow as if he didn't want to damage the chain. His eyes found hers again. "Thank you." Brady stood. There was nothing more to share, nothing else to discuss. Despite the hurt in his eyes, he held out his hand one last time. "Come on. I'll take you back."

As they walked past the reflecting pool Jenna caught the image of the two of them. And in that instant she saw what Brady saw. Two people desperate. Holding hands so they wouldn't fall to the ground. Heartbroken.

Changed forever by the bombing.

When they reached Allison's house, Brady came around to her side of the truck and helped her out. It seemed his physical strength had remained today, no matter how much the conversation had destroyed him.

Both of them.

This was it, the goodbye Jenna had known would happen. The one she had dreaded more than any in all her life. Brady closed the passenger door and leaned against the truck.

When he took hold of both her hands, she didn't resist. Instead she came closer, inches from him. "I hate this."

For a few seconds, determination flashed in his eyes. Like he might beg her to change her mind or let go of her promise to God. But the look was gone almost as soon as it came. "So that's it? You leave tomorrow . . . and don't look back?"

All she wanted was to be in his arms. *Something hopeful. Think of something hopeful.* "You know how to reach me."

"Why?" His eyes were dry now, marked by futility. "Jenna, you've made up your mind. You need to keep your promise." He released her hands and slid his into the pockets of his jeans. "This is it." He paused. "Right?"

Jenna stepped forward. "I don't want it to be." She felt herself melting, falling into him. The space between them closed and she put her arms around his neck. "I love you, Brady."

That was all it took. He placed his hands on either sides of her face, his fingers up in her hair, and like that his lips were on hers. The kiss was slow and unforgettable. A dizzy mix of longing and desperation and finality.

She could've stayed there forever, but one kiss became another and another. And a minute later, Jenna knew it was time. If she didn't step away from Brady Bradshaw now, she never would.

Her breathing was jagged, her lips still

hungry for his, but she did the thing she could never have done in her strength. She pulled away and took hold of his hands. They were trembling, tears brimming in their eyes. "Goodbye, Brady."

"I love you. I always will." His voice said he was past asking why, past trying to figure out a way to make her stay. "Goodbye."

Jenna let go of his hands and moved back a few feet. "I love you, too." She hesitated. "If you change your mind . . . you know where to find me."

His eyes told her he understood. Not if he changed his mind about her. But if he changed his mind about God. "I can't, Jenna." His voice was barely a whisper. "God took the only people I've ever loved." He blinked back tears. "I can't believe in a God like that."

She looked at Brady for a long moment, memorizing him, certain that for everything they shared, this really was goodbye. Not just for a while.

But forever.

By the time she turned and headed up the steps into Allison's house, she was crying hard. She closed the front door behind her, leaned against it and slid down to the floor, her sobs coming from a place so deep and raw, Jenna wasn't sure they'd ever stop.

She heard Brady start up his truck, heard him drive away. As he left, Jenna realized they hadn't gotten a sapling for Ashley's niece. It was another loss, though it paled in comparison to losing Brady.

Jenna wasn't sure how much time passed. Ten minutes or fifteen. Thirty. But suddenly while she was sitting on the floor, while sadness racked her body and made her wonder how she'd ever move on, she had an idea.

A crazy idea.

Her phone was in her pocket, and she pulled it out. Through bleary, tear-soaked eyes she began to write a text message. She explained the situation and asked for help. Any help at all. Then she sent it to the one person who might be able to do something, the person who would always want Brady and Jenna to find a way.

Ashley Baxter Blake.

22

Ashley got the text during the seventh inning of Devin's summer league baseball game. As she pulled her phone from her purse, she figured the message must be from Amy, who was playing with Janessa at the playground adjacent to the ball diamond. But it wasn't.

It was from Jenna Davis.

Landon was sitting beside her, cheering for Devin's friend, who was up to bat. Landon didn't seem to notice as Ashley shaded the phone screen to read it. The baseball game faded as the words came to life.

I'm sorry to bother you, Ashley. I would've called but I can't stop crying, and I had to talk to you. I said goodbye to Brady a few minutes ago. Forever. Like I told you, we're too different. He doesn't believe. Which means I have to let him go. I knew you'd understand.

Ashley's heart immediately engaged. She hadn't heard from Jenna in a few days and she'd wondered how things were going. Clearly not well.
She kept reading.

This is the situation. What I never told you. A few years ago I promised God I wouldn't fall in love with someone who didn't believe in God. If I couldn't share my faith with the person I fell in love with, then I wouldn't fall in love.

Well, with Brady it's too late. I love him more than I've ever loved anyone. But he won't believe. He can't. He still blames God for what happened on April 19, more than twenty years ago.

I understand that, really. But that means we're too different. I can't consider having a relationship with him. All of which is destroying me. I'm devastated. We both are.

Tears stung the corners of Ashley's eyes. *Oh, no.* Brady didn't understand what he was walking away from, how complete his healing would be if only he'd turn his heart over to God. *Dear Lord, this is terrible.* Ashley found her place and finished reading the text.

I don't know, I just thought I would tell you. Could you please pray for Brady? Pray that something happens to get his attention, to show him about God. Pray that he'll change his mind and choose to believe. The way his mom believed before she died.

Otherwise, this summer has been beautiful. I couldn't help but fall in love with him. But I can't let things continue. Not unless he changes.

I guess I'm asking you to pray for a miracle. I know this isn't your problem, but I appreciate all you did to get us together, and I just thought . . . I knew . . . that you would pray. I'll call you soon. Thanks again. Jenna.

Ashley sighed as she lowered her phone. *Dear Lord, please speak to Brady. Let him hear Your voice. Give him a miracle, Father, please.* Ashley lifted her eyes to the action on the field.

Devin was walking up to bat.

"You got this, Devin . . . nice and easy!" Landon's tone was positive. Devin had struck out twice already this afternoon. But Landon's encouragement was endless. Another reason Ashley loved him so much.

With the count two and one, he connected with a fastball. Devin hit it over the shortstop into left field, right in the gap.

Ashley and Landon were both on their feet as Devin tore off toward first base. He beat the throw by a mile, prompting the entire fan section to clap and cheer. Ashley high-fived Landon and then sat down. "Yes! He needed that." She looked up. "Thank You, God."

As Landon sat, too, Ashley remembered the conversation they'd had this morning over breakfast. God probably doesn't care about hits and strikeouts. But He's absolutely concerned with His children.

When they finally got home, Ashley and Landon poured glasses of iced tea and went out onto the front porch. The sun was setting, and the summer breeze was cooler than before. The humidity less intense.

They had just leaned back in the porch swing when Ashley gasped. How could she forget? "Jenna's text!"

"What?" Landon glanced at her, clearly concerned. "Jenna who?"

"Jenna." Ashley sat up straighter. "The young teacher from Ohio."

Landon seemed to process that for a moment. Then it gradually hit him. "The firefighter's girl. From the Oklahoma City memorial?"

"Yes." Ashley smiled and put her hand on Landon's knee. "I love how you keep track of my craziness."

"I'm good at it." He grinned. "Okay, so what's this text?"

"I'll be right back." She handed her iced tea to Landon and ran into the house. Once she found her phone, she returned and took her spot beside Landon again. "Listen to this. It's from Jenna. About Brady."

"The firefighter." Landon looked slightly unsure. He set their glasses down on the table next to the swing.

"Yes. The firefighter." Ashley couldn't wait to read the text. She started at the beginning. "Okay, here's what she said: *'I'm sorry to bother you, Ashley. I would've called but I can't stop crying, and I had to talk to you . . .'* "

Landon put one knee up on the swing like he wanted to be completely focused as she read. When she finished, Ashley set her phone on the porch railing. Then she turned to Landon. "Isn't that terrible?"

"Yes." Her husband was serious now. "It's

377

very sad. After they had such a great summer." He looked at her for a few seconds, his brow raised a little. "You're not going to Oklahoma tonight, are you?"

The hint of a smile tugged at her mouth. She leaned close and kissed his lips. "No, Landon . . . I'm not going to Oklahoma."

He was quiet for a minute. "I have an idea."

"Uh-oh." She felt the sparkle in her eyes. "Don't tell me *you're* going to Oklahoma."

"No." He smiled. "What if you text him? Tell him you've been praying for him." Landon leaned forward. "Just see where it goes. Maybe God will open a door so you can talk to him about faith."

Ashley felt her heart soar. "Why didn't I think of that?"

"Because" — Landon kissed her again — "we're a team."

"Yes." She ran her fingertips over his brow. "We are that. Your heart to mine, Landon Blake. You are the brush I paint with in life."

"And you" — he searched her eyes, the two of them lost in the moment — "are the colors in my painting." He leaned back and grinned.

"Let's pray for him. For a miracle."

"Yes."

Landon led the prayer, and it was beautiful. That God would change Brady's heart and that he would see that the God he'd been avoiding was the very same God who had brought Brady and Jenna together.

When Landon was done, they stayed there on the porch swing, quiet in the gentle breeze. And Ashley did just what Landon had suggested. She sent Brady a simple text:

This is Ashley Blake. God keeps bringing you to mind. This probably seems a little out of left field. But I thought I'd let you know anyway.

She reviewed it and then read it to Landon.

"Perfect." Landon smiled. "That should start the conversation."

Ashley hit send and waited. It wasn't until later that night when she was curled up in the living room recliner reading Devin's book report that Brady texted back.

Hi Ashley. I know you mean well, and I appreciate that. But please keep God out of this. He took my mother and does nothing to stop the tragedies and heartbreak in this world. You want me to believe in a God like that?

Ashley sat up a little straighter and read

his message again. She could almost hear the anger and hurt in his voice, almost see the pain in his eyes. His questions weren't easy.

Lord, what am I supposed to tell him? How can I get him to understand that You're real and You care? She looked out the window at the dark night.

My daughter . . . remind him that in this world you will have trouble. But I have overcome the world.

The words ran through her soul as if God were sitting beside her in the living room. Ashley felt chills on her arms. *Lord, is that You?* The message was clear, and it was something Brady needed to hear. The world had trouble. It always would. But God had overcome the world.

That's what she needed to tell Brady.

She started to text, and then changed her mind. A real conversation was the only thing that could help at this point. She was sure. But even so she was afraid. What if he got mad or thought she was being too pushy? What if she made things worse? *Okay, Father . . . give me the words. Please.* She took a deep breath and placed the call.

Brady answered on the second ring. "Ashley."

"Hi." The two of them had never actually

talked. "I thought it would be easier if I called. Jenna has kept in touch all summer. I feel like I know you."

He sighed. "I can't . . . Ashley, I'm not interested. I'm sorry."

Ashley held her breath. *Please, God . . .* "I want to answer your question. That's all."

"My question?"

"Yes." She exhaled. At least he was still on the phone. "You asked why you should believe. How you could believe in a God who allows pain and suffering." Her heart was pounding. "May I answer?"

Silence filled the line for a long moment. "I really don't want an answer." He drew a sharp breath. "All right. Go ahead. Maybe I should hear this."

Yes! She walked out onto the back porch and stood at the railing. The stars danced overhead. "Your mom believed in Jesus, right?"

"Yes." His answer was quick, frustrated. Barely patient enough to listen. "Right up until a terrorist took her life."

"Okay." Ashley gripped the wooden rail. "So if she was a Christian, she believed in the Bible. And she believed in Jesus."

"She did." Brady paused. "She loved the Bible." His voice softened a little. "At least from what I remember."

Ashley stared at the sky, but suddenly all she could see were the words to the Scripture. "In the book of John it says in this world you will have trouble. It's a promise." She let that sink in. "But then it says to take heart . . . Because the Lord has overcome the world."

He didn't say anything for a few beats. He paused. "Take heart? So, we're supposed to chock it up to earth. These things happen?" His tone was gentler. But the hurt remained.

"It's *just* earth. I think that's the point." Ashley didn't want to talk longer than he was willing to listen. She tried not to be wordy. "See, all of us deserve."

"Ashley . . ." He sounded tired. "I know this."

"Okay." She leaned against the rail, her eyes still on the sky. "I guess all I'm saying is that this isn't the end. Every one of us will die." She was careful not to rush her words. Not to sound forceful. "Jesus offers us a life rope out of this place. Because as great as it is . . . it's not heaven."

Another pause. "Thank you, Ashley. Really." He was only putting up with her. She could tell. "I gotta go."

One more thing. That's all she wanted to tell him. "You can see your mother again. If you believe Jesus died for your sins, if you accept that gift, you will join her in heaven." She hesitated. "Just think about that. And know this, Brady. I'm praying for you. That God will show you somehow."

Silence.

Ashley looked at the phone, to be sure he was still on the call. "Brady?"

"You think . . ." His voice was more emotional. "You think she's in heaven? You believe that?"

"Absolutely." Ashley felt a ripple of hope. Finally, he was hearing her.

Brady was quiet again. When he spoke, his words were softer. "I need to go, but thanks." He hesitated. "Really."

She offered to talk to him again, if he needed anything. He seemed genuinely grateful, and then the call was over. Ashley stared at the phone. The whole conversation had lasted just under eight minutes.

Was it enough to make a difference?

Ashley wasn't sure. But there was one thing she could do, whether he called her again or not.

She could pray.

Brady didn't work that Sunday. He had planned to go to the river with a few buddies from the station. But ever since the call from Ashley, all he could do was think about what she'd said.

The only way to see his mom again was to believe. Believe in the very God who had taken her from him. His thoughts battled and fought for position in his aching heart until all he could do was deal with them.

And there was only one place he could do that.

He arrived at the memorial an hour after it opened. This time it was more crowded, not that it mattered. Brady didn't see the people around him, didn't hear their voices. Sunglasses on, he walked to the bench where he and Jenna had sat two days earlier. The place where she had told him why she couldn't stay. Why it wouldn't work between them.

Brady sat, and for the longest time, he only stared at the wall and the time stamp six feet high, engraved at the top.

9:03.

Jenna had found her way there, found a way to believe in God and move forward in her healing. She was a true survivor. No doubt. Ashley's words came back to him. If he believed, he would see his mother again. In heaven.

He was contemplating it all when a tall blond guy walked up and sat on the other side of the bench. "Serene, isn't it?"

Brady was confused. Had he looked like he wanted company? He nodded. "Definitely."

The guy held out his hand. "I'm Jag. Good to see you again."

"Brady." The sun was bright on their faces, so Brady kept his sunglasses on. The stranger wore none. Even so, the sun didn't seem to bother him. He wasn't even squinting. "Have . . . we met?"

"A long time ago." Jag smiled. "You were five. And one other time not too long ago."

"Okay." He had no memory of the man. But something about him was familiar. Brady could see that now. Was he part of the club? "Why are you here?"

Jag stared at the wall across from the reflecting pool. "Do you know the motto of the memorial?"

"The motto?" Brady sat up straighter. Who was this guy?

"Yes." Jag turned to him again. "Come to remember. Leave with resolve."

Brady hadn't heard that. "I thought I knew everything about this place."

"It's on their website." Jag hesitated, his eyes locked on Brady's, like the guy could see straight through his sunglasses. "You've spent a lot of time here. Remembering."

How did the guy know? Despite the sum-

385

mer sun, a shiver ran down Brady's spine. "How . . . ?"

"You lost your mother here. I know that." Jag put his hand on Brady's shoulder. "A lot of people lost much on these grounds." His look grew more intense, and at the same time, more peaceful. "Leave with resolve, Brady. Resolve to move on. Resolve to make this world a better place." He paused. "Resolve to believe. You know why?"

"Why?" Nothing about the conversation made sense. How did Jag know him? And how could he know about Brady's beliefs?

"Because . . . God loves you. More than you know." Jag stood.

"How do you . . . ?" Brady's voice trailed off. He had a dozen questions, but before he could ask a single one, Jag shook his hand again. "By the way, there are a few saplings at the main office."

"At the office?" Brady's head was spinning. The man knew about the saplings?

"You were looking for one, right?" Jag smiled.

"Yes. For a little girl. But there weren't any left until . . ."

Jag took a step back and pointed to the museum. "I found two. They're holding them."

"I . . . that's amazing." Nothing about this

made sense. Brady felt tears in his eyes. "Thank you."

"I gotta go." Jag stepped away. "See you around, Brady. Leave with resolve." With that, the man turned and walked off toward the museum.

"See ya . . ." Brady's words became a whisper.

Brady stared at the time stamp on the wall. What in the world had just happened? How had the stranger known him when he was little? The guy couldn't have been more than ten years older. And what about the two saplings?

Brady turned to look at Jag again. The guy should've been twenty, thirty yards ahead on the sidewalk. But he wasn't.

The path was empty.

Another shiver ran through him. Where had the guy gone? Nothing about the last few minutes made sense. Brady blinked a few times. *Could the guy be an angel?* He let that thought sit for a few seconds. No. That wasn't possible.

For the next hour Brady stayed there, sitting on the bench, thinking about Jag and his words. Leave with resolve . . . Resolve to believe. Whoever the guy was, his message came at the exact right time.

Suddenly the words from Jenna and Ashley ran through his mind.

Words from the Bible.

In this world he would have trouble. That was true, right? That was the whole problem, the trouble in the world. The way evil seemed to win far too often and pain seemed ignored by God.

If there was a God.

But what if there was? What if He really was the way Ashley had described Him? Brady felt the warmth of the sun to the center of his being.

Or maybe that was the conviction spreading from his heart to his soul.

Could they be right? Jenna and Ashley? Was it possible that God loved the world so much that he sent Jesus? Not to protect people from the pain of earth, but to save them from it? Not as the reason for the bad things in the world.

But as the rescue.

Brady pictured his mother, the hazy memory he still carried with him. Yes, her body had been destroyed by the bomb. But because of her faith, Jesus had rescued her. Lifted her right out of the rubble and into His kingdom.

Life to life.

Suddenly, Brady understood what Jag had told him. This was his place to remember.

More times than he could count, he had come here to honor his mother, to recall her talking to him. *I love you to the moon and back, Brady. To the moon and back.* Yes, he had come here to remember.

Now it was time to leave with resolve.

Like Jag said.

Brady took a deep breath and felt an urgency rise within him. He had to exit this place, had to get out of the memorial. With a final look at the time stamp he hurried to the office. There they were. Two saplings from the Survivor Tree. Just like Jag had said. He carried them to his truck and set off through the city. He knew exactly where he had to go, what he had to do.

Minutes later he was knocking on the door of Cheryl and Rodney Fisher.

Cheryl opened the door. Her eyes lit up. "Brady! Why . . . what are you doing here? You look all healed up." She stepped back. "Come in. Rodney's in the other room."

Brady was breathing hard, his heart and head pounding. He remembered a detail from the last time he was here. How Rodney had prayed that something would happen. Something that could only be from God. Like Jag, whoever he was, suddenly appearing.

Like Jenna.

He steadied himself.

"Mrs. Fisher . . . I want to talk. About God."

"Hallelujah." She whispered the word. Her smile was as warm as the summer sun. "I knew you'd ask one day."

He stepped inside and like that his tears came. Quietly, without fanfare. They spilled from his eyes down the sides of his cheeks. "I . . . I have so many questions."

Cheryl took him in her arms. "You came to the right place, Brady." Then she looked straight at him. "Rodney and I . . . we have answers."

Brady nodded and found his composure. He felt a peace and acceptance he hadn't felt since Jenna left. And for the first time something told him the feeling wasn't from the Fishers.

But just maybe from God, Himself.

Answers weren't enough.

That week fighting fires and responding to accident calls, Brady thought about the things he'd heard recently. First from Ashley, then from the Fishers. God was the rescue in hard times, not the reason for them. Jesus loved Brady enough to die for him. On and on it went. The people he loved had answered every question Brady asked, except the one that bothered him still.

Why?

Why did God take his mother when he was so little? Why did He do that to Jenna? And so, though Rodney and Cheryl had done their best to help Brady believe, he had walked away from their house that day unconvinced.

He couldn't get past the idea that God could've stopped the tragedy, prevented the bombing altogether. A quick zap from heaven and the terrorist never would've made it to the Murrah Building.

No fertilizer bomb. No explosion. No devastating destruction.

Brady and Jenna would still have the people they loved. Same with countless others changed by that April day. Confusion about his questions consumed Brady's every waking hour.

But they didn't work their way into his bedroom until one stormy night later that week. Brady couldn't fall asleep. His legs and head ached — something that had been happening less and less frequently. Every ten minutes he had to find a different position — his right side, his left. On his back with one arm over his head.

Whatever he tried he couldn't get comfortable.

He couldn't remember actually falling asleep, but in a blurry instant Brady was in the burning warehouse again. The one where he nearly died. Blazing fire exploded all around him and he was pinned beneath the rubble. Suffocating. Dying.

Help me! he cried out, but no one could hear him. What was happening to him? Why was he reliving the ordeal all over again? The heat grew more intense and Brady could see the skin on his hands start to bubble.

Help me, someone!

And then suddenly he could see his mother calling to him. Pretty and kind with the most loving eyes. And she was yelling for him, crying out for him.

"Brady! Come home!" She held out her hand, but it didn't reach him in the fiery debris. "Please, Brady . . . I'm waiting for you! Come home!"

"Mom . . . I can't move!" Brady screamed the words. "Send someone! I'm dying."

He couldn't breathe, couldn't keep his eyes open much longer in the searing heat. And his mother's hand was right there, right in front of him, but he couldn't grab it. Like it was more apparition than reality. Still he could see her, hear her. Even above the roaring fire.

Come home, Brady! Please, come home!

One last time, Brady tried. With everything in him he shouted at her. "Send someone to help me!"

And the moment the words left his mouth a man appeared. Tall and strong, he tossed aside burning pieces of roof and red-hot metal beams like they were made of paper. One after another, the man moved scorching sections of building away from Brady. He could see the man now. Surreal blue eyes. Blond hair. Even in the midst of the terrible fire Brady knew who it was.

Jag.

The stranger at the memorial.

"It's time to come home, Brady." Jag took his hand and helped him to his feet, and at the same time the heat and fire and flaming debris around them disappeared. Brady's skin was normal and he could breathe again.

Jag's eyes pierced his own. "Your mother is waiting for you. Your Father, too."

With a shattering gasp, Brady opened his eyes and sat straight up, tangled in his bedsheets. His shorts and T-shirt were drenched with sweat, his lungs heaving. "What in the . . ."

He jumped out of bed, eyes wide, and

looked around. No fire, no broken building parts pinning him to the ground. His breaths came in rapid succession. He was in his bedroom, whole and alive and exhausted.

But unlike any other dream Brady had ever experienced, this one had been real. He could remember every detail. Smell them. Feel them. And then — in a slow and steady rush — a strange reality dawned on him.

Jag — whoever he was — had rescued him from the warehouse fire.

There was no other way Brady would've escaped from the collapsed building that day. No one in the department knew how he'd made it out alive. And not only that but maybe Jag had rescued him from the Murrah Building. Wasn't that what he'd said the other day at the memorial? That he'd seen him when Brady was five?

A shiver ran down his arms. And now that same Jag had been part of his dream. The man's words echoed again. *It's time to come home, Brady . . . Time to come home.*

He could see his mother crying out to him, begging him to join her.

Brady's heart pounded against the wall of his chest. What did it mean? What was the message? Was Jag a person or was he . . .

could he really be an angel? His mind flashed back to their conversation at the memorial.

Brady had no way of knowing for sure. But Jag's message was unmistakable. There was a reason Jag had freed him, a reason his mother had appeared to him in the dream.

And slowly, like all of his life had led to this moment, Brady dropped to his knees. His legs and arms shook and his heart raced within him. He grabbed the edge of his bed and pressed his forehead into the mattress.

All of it was real. The rescue at the warehouse, the dream, and the cry from Jag and his mother. It was time for Brady to come home. Time for him to stop fighting against the God who was clearly pursuing him.

"I'm sorry, Lord." Brady whispered the words into the fitted sheet. "I'm so sorry."

With everything in him he could feel himself changing.

The dream had changed everything, and with his entire being Brady suddenly believed in the truth that his mother was safe in heaven and that he would see her again. And in the reality that Jag had been sent to rescue him. He believed in the obvious fact that Jenna had come back into his life for a reason, and he believed in something else, something he had never expected to believe in again.

Brady Bradshaw believed in God.

23

Rain was forecast that August morning, so Ashley had moved her painting of the Survivor Tree into the kitchen. She was nearly finished. Amy knew, now, that the painting was for her.

Ashley could hardly wait to hang it in her niece's room.

She stood in front of her easel. It had been nearly a week since her call to Brady. If he'd found God, she knew nothing of it. A few days ago she'd received a random text from Brady asking for Ashley's address. She figured maybe he was going to send her a card or a letter. She had texted back that she was still praying for him, and he had thanked her. That was it.

Jenna hadn't reached out again, either.

The paint on the end of her brush was more brown than green. She dipped the bristles in the palette. Today she was high-lighting the trunk of the great elm. Bringing it to life, she liked to say. This part of painting required her greatest skill, her most careful hand. She was focusing on a specific area when the doorbell rang.

She set down her brush and frowned. If someone had come up the drive, she hadn't heard the car. It was too early for the kids or Landon to be home. And her father and Elaine were out of town for a few days. Maybe it was one of her sisters.

She padded across the wood floor to the front door and opened it. For a few seconds she didn't quite understand what she was looking at. Who she was looking at. But then her mind began to right itself.

The man standing on her porch was Brady Bradshaw. He had to be, right?

He was dressed much the way he'd been that day at the memorial. Dark jeans, sweatshirt. In his hands was something Ashley couldn't believe. She lifted her eyes to his. "Brady?"

"Yes." His expression was humble, his face kind. "It's me."

"Is that . . ." Ashley looked at his hands again. He was holding a sapling, a small baby tree with its roots covered in a paper bag.

"It is." Brady smiled. "It's from the Survivor Tree." He handed the bundle to Ashley.

"You asked about getting one for your niece."

She took the tree and stared at it. This was the only thing Amy had wanted for the better part of a year. Ashley couldn't move, couldn't do anything but gaze at the little sapling. "I . . . I can't believe it." She stepped back and ushered Brady inside. "Please . . . come in."

"I need to go." Again his tone and expression were gentle. The frustration from the other night completely gone. "I have to make it to Ohio before school gets out."

Ashley searched his face. Had he really said that? Did he mean . . . ? "You're going to see Jenna?"

"Absolutely." Brady reached out and shook Ashley's free hand. "Thank you. For calling me." A single laugh and he raised his brow. "That couldn't have been easy."

"It wasn't." Ashley still didn't believe this was happening. "What are you saying, Brady? You believe?"

Brady's smile filled his face. "Let's just say God got my attention. I've been praying about seeing Jenna ever since I left home."

Joy came over Ashley all at once. She set the sapling on the floor and hugged Brady. Then she stepped back and squealed. "Are you serious? Brady . . . this is amazing."

He couldn't stop grinning. "I can't say I have it all figured out. But I believe." For the next few minutes he told her about an older couple, the Fishers, and how he had gone to their house the day after Ashley called. And then he told her about his dream.

Ashley could hardly wait to hear more of the story. "So these people . . . the Fishers . . . they're Christians?"

"Definitely." Brady raised his brow. "They've been waiting for me to ask them about God for years."

The feelings in Ashley's heart were more than she could comprehend. She listened while Brady told her about how the Fishers had opened the Bible and looked at a dozen different verses from John and Romans and James. "And then, my dream . . ."

He seemed overcome by a rush of emotion. He shook his head. "There's more to it. I don't know. After that, I could see. Clearly." The corners of his lips lifted again. "For the first time since I was that five-year-old little boy waking up in the hospital."

Ashley thought about her painting. If anyone would want to see it, Brady would. "Let me show you something. In the next room."

The two of them walked into the kitchen

and Ashley pointed him to the painting. His eyes softened and he nodded slowly. "It's perfect. Beautiful." He looked at her. "You must've been really affected by the memorial."

"Because of my niece. The one I sent you the message about." Ashley stared at the image. It was almost finished. "Amy, my niece, she lives with us."

The situation seemed to make sense to Brady now. "She lives here?"

Ashley told him about Amy, how her family had been killed in a car accident, and how she was determined to live a life that made them proud. And that was the reason she wanted a sapling from the memorial.

Again Brady stared at the painting. "No wonder she loves the old tree."

"Exactly. Amy . . . she draws strength from her faith every day."

Each word seemed to land deeply on Brady. "What a wonderful truth." He pulled his phone from his pocket and looked at the time. "I need to get on the road."

Ashley led him back to the foyer and Brady motioned to the sapling. "Tell Amy to take good care of the tree." His smile faded a little. "And tell her I'm proud of her. For being a survivor."

"I'll tell her." Ashley was touched that he

would go out of his way to come here.

For a few seconds, Brady hesitated. "Can I ask you for something?"

"Of course."

"Follow me." He stepped outside.

The air was warm, but clouds gathered in the distance. All of Bloomington embracing another summer day. She walked beside him to his truck, and saw it before he said anything. There in the bed of the truck.

Another sapling.

"You got one, too." Ashley looked at Brady as he opened his door. Was he taking the little tree to Ohio? A possibility dawned in her heart and worked its way to a hesitant smile. "You're taking it to Jenna?"

His eyes lit up with what looked like hope. "Just pray for us. For a second chance."

Ashley nodded. "I will. Absolutely."

Brady hugged her again and then he slid behind the wheel and closed the door. Ashley watched him go and a thought occurred to her. She wasn't watching a frustrated, hurt young man set off to whatever was next in his life.

She was watching a miracle.

Jenna Davis was in the last half hour of the first Friday in the school year when the principal stepped into the classroom and

402

motioned for her. The woman's face didn't look alarmed. But there was an urgency in her expression all the same.

The new second graders sitting at their desks noticed the interruption. Jenna smiled at the children. "One minute, boys and girls. Please stay in your seats."

She walked to the door and moved into the hall with her principal. Ms. Brown spoke first. "You have a visitor. Waiting in the office." She raised her brow slightly. "Please come straight there ten minutes before the bell rings." The woman smiled. "I'll have the vice principal take your students to the buses."

A visitor? Who could possibly be here for her? "A man or woman?"

Ms. Brown paused. "A man." She smiled. "A very handsome one."

Who would be here? And why come to the school without contacting her first? Jenna had no idea. "Thank you. I'll be there." She returned to her class. And just like Ms. Brown had said, ten minutes before the bell rang, the vice principal arrived to take over.

Jenna thanked him and grabbed her things.

On her way to the office, she tried to imagine who could possibly be waiting for her. The dad of one of her new students, maybe? One of the little girls had told her yesterday that her daddy wasn't married and he wanted to take Jenna on a date. Jenna hadn't given any thought to the matter.

But now . . .

Curiosity fueled her pace, but it wasn't until she turned the corner and could see the glass wall of the main office that she stopped short. The man was there, standing near the counter. Jenna could only see his back, but his shoulders were familiar. His dark hair, too.

What?

Could it be . . . ?

She walked to the office door, her heart racing. As she stepped inside, he turned and saw her. Jenna's breath caught in her throat and she brought her fingers to her lips. It was him.

Brady Bradshaw. Standing three feet away.

"Jenna." He moved toward her. No man had ever looked better. But there was something different about him. Like the hurt was gone for good. He kept a slight distance between them, but his eyes didn't leave hers. "Can we talk? Outside?"

If the office staff was watching the moment play out, Jenna wasn't aware. All she could see was Brady, all she could hear was his voice, soothing the hurt she still carried in her heart.

She nodded. *Breathe, Jenna. You have to breathe.* Was she dreaming? "I . . . I can't believe you're here."

He smiled. "I'll explain everything." He followed her outside. Not until they reached the school's front walk did they both stop. "I can't believe you're really here, Jenna."

"Brady . . ." Tears sprang to her eyes. Again, something was different about him. She could sense it. "Tell me I'm not dreaming."

He took her in his arms and held her the way she was aching to be held. They stayed that way for a long moment and then Brady whispered, "I believe, Jenna."

"What?" She eased back and searched his face. "You believe?"

"In God." His eyes were damp. "It's a long story. God spoke to me in a dream." He smiled and she could see he was absolutely telling her the truth. "I'll tell you everything later, but God changed my heart. My mind. I've given my life to Him."

His life? Brady was a believer now? Jenna couldn't stop her tears. "You're serious?" She reached for his hands. Her knees were shaking, her hands trembling. The feeling of

405

his fingers between hers was too real for this to be a dream. "Is that . . . why you're here? To tell me?"

The smile started in his eyes. "It's part of it." He released one of her hands and motioned toward the grassy yard in front of the school. "I have something to ask you."

Only then, as Jenna turned, did she see what he was looking at. She gasped and stared at the scene.

Half the school was gathered on the lawn, watching them. The only bare spot was a small circle of grass. And at the center . . . a small potted sapling. "Brady?" Her voice was part cry, part whisper. *How could this be happening? When had he made a plan with her school?* Jenna could barely breathe. *Was he going to . . .*

She couldn't finish the thought.

It was all too good to be true.

"Jenna . . . come on." This time he led her toward the crowd. With a hundred teachers and students watching, Brady stopped at the center of the open patch of grass and picked up the little tree. He held it out to her. "It's a sapling."

She took the gift as tears fell down her cheeks. "From the Survivor Tree."

"Yes." He nodded. "I thought it would look good in our backyard."

She was laughing and crying at the same time. *Their* backyard? This was really happening. *Dear God, I can't believe it . . .* Her heart was bursting inside her.

Brady was still looking at her, taking his time. "I talked to the fire department in Columbus. They're ready to hire me . . . and I'm ready to move here. Depending . . ." He took the sapling from her and set it on the ground. Then he took a ring from his jeans pocket and dropped to one knee.

A buzz ran through the crowd standing nearby, but Jenna couldn't hear a single word, couldn't focus on anything but Brady.

He held the ring up to her. "Jenna, I'll never love anyone but you. To the moon and back." Tears fell onto his face, but they didn't dim his smile. "Will you marry me?"

Her hands flew to her mouth and she nodded. Then she took the ring as he stood. "Yes, Brady." She had kept her promise to God, and now she would pledge Brady her life, her heart. "A million times yes."

The teachers and students burst into applause; several of them had their cell phones out, capturing the moment. Brady slipped the ring on her finger. Then he took tender hold of her face and kissed her. "I have a long way to go. A lot to learn and understand." He kissed her again. "Together, Jenna," he whispered. "We'll grow closer to God. Every day of our lives."

"We will." Her tears and laughter mixed. "I love you."

"I love you, too." Their lips met again, and around them the crowd cheered.

Jenna would remember this moment forever. She was certain. Everything she had prayed about was happening in a single instant. Brady was here and he was hers. But so much more than that, he believed now. She couldn't wait to hear what had happened, how the old couple had helped him.

She looked at the ring and then back at Brady.

They were both survivors now. And the sapling would grow up in their backyard, somewhere here in Columbus. They didn't need the memorial any longer. They were whole and alive and the future was theirs.

Brady kissed her once more. "I can't wait to be your husband. God has great things ahead for us, Jenna. I know it."

Chills ran through her as she nodded. "He does." And suddenly she felt like a princess again. Princess Jenna. Not just because she was going to marry Brady Bradshaw after all these years.

But because she was going to spend eternity with him.

Amy's heart was full. The family had gathered that Saturday to celebrate her birthday. And for another reason. Amy walked into the backyard where her cousins and aunts and uncles, and Papa and Grandma Elaine were already gathered. Papa and Uncle Landon had the shovel ready.

Today they were going to plant her little survivor tree.

Amy had chosen the spot, not far from her grandma Elizabeth's rose garden. Aunt Ashley had agreed it was the best place. The tree would give shade to anyone who wanted to smell the roses.

That sounded like a nice idea to Amy. Plus it was close to the house. So Amy could always do her homework out there or sit against the trunk when the tree got bigger. Just to think about God and life.

And the family she had waiting for her in heaven.

"Okay . . ." Uncle Landon walked up and handed her the sapling. "Are you ready?"

Amy nodded and grinned at her uncle. "I can't wait."

Cole came up and put his arm around her as she carried the little tree to the hole her

Uncle Landon had dug. "You're amazing, Amy. If I haven't said that enough."

"Thanks, Cole." She smiled at him. He was always kind, always looking out for her. Today was no different.

As they reached the spot, Cole dropped back. "This is all you, Amy."

She nodded. Then with all her family gathered around, she stepped up to the hole and set the baby elm inside. Uncle Landon had already uncovered the roots, so it was ready to be planted.

Amy knelt down in the dirt and positioned the tree so it was straight. She looked over her shoulder at her papa and Uncle Landon. "Is that good?"

"Perfect!" they both answered at the same time. Aunt Ashley and the others gave her a thumbs-up and nodded. "Perfect," they all agreed.

And so it was. Amy took handfuls of the dirt piled near the hole and pressed them around the roots so the tree wouldn't fall over. When it was steady, she stood and took the shovel from her Uncle Landon.

This part was a surprise. She scooped one shovelful of dirt and sprinkled it on the roots. Then she looked at her Aunt Ashley. "Your turn."

"Me?" Her aunt looked surprised.

"Honey, this is your tree. You can do it."

Amy had been waiting for this day for months. She looked around at her family. "What happened to my mommy and daddy, what happened to my sisters when they went home to heaven that day . . . it happened to all of us." She didn't want to cry, but tears came anyway. She blinked a few times. "We're all survivors."

Everyone had tears now, even Cole.

Her throat was tight. For a few seconds she couldn't talk, but then she did a little cough and her words came. "Please . . . I'd like everyone to pass the shovel and put some dirt in the hole. So we all plant this tree together." Her tears made it hard to see, but she smiled anyway. "Okay?"

Everyone nodded and moved in closer. Aunt Ashley went first and then Uncle Landon, her papa and Grandma Elaine, Amy's aunts and uncles and all her cousins. Cole was last, and when he was done he handed the shovel back to her. "You finish, Amy."

She smiled and put the last few shovelfuls around the tree. Then she and Cole got on the ground and patted the dirt in, nice and tight. When they stepped back, Amy could see the elm clearly. Not just how it looked today, a baby tree in brand-new dirt. But how it would look a year from now. Twenty years from now.

Their very own survivor tree.

Her papa looked around. "Let's pray."

Amy wiped her eyes. "Yes." Praying was just what they needed to do. She held out her hands. Cole took hold of one, and Aunt Ashley the other. Then everyone else added in and they made a circle around the sapling.

"Father, it's like Amy said." Papa's voice was tender. "We are all survivors because of You. We have lost much, but through Your strength we have also loved much. Please, Lord, let this baby elm tree be a reminder to us that You are for us, not against us. You are the Healer of our broken hearts. And one day You will bring us home with those who've gone before us. Thank You for Amy. In Jesus' name, amen."

Amy's family started talking all at once, about how pretty the tree was and how well they'd planted it. Everyone came up and hugged Amy, and they hugged each other. Their voices and smiles and faces filled Amy's soul and her tears stopped.

What they'd done today would stay in Amy's heart forever. Her idea had worked. That all of them would take turns planting the tree. The Baxters were always stronger this way. Together. They were Amy's family, her favorite people on earth. Survivors, all of them.

And now they had the little tree to prove it.

ACKNOWLEDGMENTS

No book comes together without a great deal of teamwork, passion and determination. That was definitely true for *To the Moon and Back*!

First, a special thanks to my amazing publisher, Judith Curr, and the team at Howard Books. Judith, at the Simon & Schuster offices, you're known as the Rainmaker. How blessed I am to be working with you and your passionate team. You clearly desire to raise the bar at every turn. Thank you for that and for everything!

A similar thanks to Carolyn Reidy and my family at Simon & Schuster. I think often of our times together in New York and the way your collective creative brilliance always becomes a game changer. Thank you for lending your influence in so many ways. It's an honor to work with you!

This story is so very special because of the incredible talents of my editor, Becky

Nesbitt. Becky, you have known me since my kids were little. Since the Baxters began. How many authors actually look forward to the editing process? With you, it is a dream. And always you find ways to make my book better. Over and over and over again. Thank you for that! I am the most blessed author for the privilege of working with you.

Also thanks to my design team — Kyle and Kelsey Kupecky — whose unmatched talent in the industry is recognized from Los Angeles to New York. Very simply, you are the best in the business! My website, social media, video trailers and newsletter along with so many other aspects of my touring and writing are what they are because of you. Thank you for working your own dreams around mine. I love you and I thank God for you every single day.

A huge thanks to my sisters, Tricia and Susan, along with my mom, who give their whole hearts to helping me love my readers. Tricia as my executive assistant for the past decade, and Susan, for many years, as the head of my Facebook Online Book Club and Team KK. And Mom, thank you for being Queen of the Readers. Anyone who has ever sent me an email and received a response from you is blessed indeed. All three of you are so special to me. I love you and I thank God for each of you!

Thanks also to Tyler for joining with me to write screenplays and books that — for now — readers don't even know about. You are a gifted writer, Ty. I can't wait to see your work on the shelves and on the big screen. Maybe one day soon! Love you so much!

Also, thank you to my office assistant, Aurora Galvin. You create space for me to write! This storytelling wouldn't be possible without you.

I'm grateful also to my Team KK members, who use social media to tell the world about my upcoming releases and who hang out on my Facebook page, answering reader questions. I appreciate each of you so much. May God bless you for your service to the work of Life-Changing Fiction™.

There is a final stage in writing a book. The galley pages come to me, and I send them to a team of five of my closest, most special reader friends. My niece Shannon Fairley, Hope Painter, Donna Keene, Renette Steele and Zac Weikal. You are wonderful! It always amazes me the things you catch at the final hour. Thank you for loving my work, and thanks for your availability to read my stories first and fast.

Also, my books only happen with the help

of my family, especially my amazing husband, Donald. Honey, thank you for your spiritual wisdom and leadership in our home, and thanks for talking through books like this one from the outline to the editing. The countless ways you help when I'm on deadline make all the difference. I love you!

And over all this is a man who has believed in my career for two decades: my amazing agent, Rick Christian of Alive Literary Agency. From the beginning, Rick, you've told me to dream big, set my sights high. Movies, TV series, worldwide reach. You imagined it all, you prayed for it to be. You believed. While I write, you work behind the scenes on film projects and my work with Liberty University, the Baxter family TV series and details regarding every book I've ever written. You are brilliant and driven, compassionate and dedicated. I used to dream of having you as my agent. Now I'm the only author who does. God is amazing. Thank you, Rick, and thank you for praying for me and my family. That most of all.

Finally, my greatest thanks to God Almighty, who is First and Last and all things in between. I write for You, through You and because of You. Thank you with my whole being.

Dear Reader Friend,

On a cloudy day several years ago, I stepped foot on the Oklahoma City National Memorial. I walked the grounds and touched the Survivor Tree and stood for fifteen silent minutes near the chairs representing those killed. Long before I left that day I was sure of two things.

First, the memorial is one of the most beautiful, reflective places I've visited. And second, I knew I'd write about it one day.

You may be too young to remember much about April 19, 1995. But either way the terrible tragedy of that day happened. Lives were lost, families were ripped apart, and Oklahoma City was forever changed. The United States was impacted for all time.

I hope as you read Brady and Jenna's love story that you found yourself connecting to the tragedies and hard times in your own life. The truth is this: God wants to make good out of your darkest days. And as time passes, He wants you to find love and hope, redemption and healing.

Beauty from Ashes.

As with my other books in this new Baxter family collection, this story and the ones to come will allow us the chance to live with the Baxters. We will see what matters to them, and how their work and family affect the people and culture around them.

The next Baxter book, *When We Were Young,* is another of those! I know you'll love it! These are among the most favorite books I've ever written. I'm grateful you're sharing in the journey!

Being back with the Baxter family has been the greatest gift. Always when people ask, "How are the Baxters?" I have an answer. I honestly do. I see them at work and play, holding close conversations, and looking for new horizons. Participating in adventures.

You've probably heard by now that the Baxter family is coming to TV. The series is expected to become one of the most beloved of all time. I know you'll be watching. You can find out more details about that and how to connect with me on social media or through email at my website — Karen Kingsbury.com.

But in the meantime, I'll see you in the fall with my next book.

Because the Baxters aren't just my family. They're yours.

And with them at the middle of our lives, we are all connected.

Until next time . . . thanks for being part of the family.

Love you all!
Karen Kingsbury

THE BAXTER FAMILY:
YESTERDAY AND TODAY

For some of you, this is your first time with the Baxter family. Yes, you could go back and read twenty-some books on these most-loved characters. The list of Baxter titles — in order — can be found at www .karenkingsbury.com/baxters. But you don't have to read those to read this one. In fact, there will be other Baxter books coming in the next few years. These books are a collection, and can be read in any order.

If you wish, you can begin right here.

Whether you've known the Baxters for years or are just meeting them now, here's a quick summary of the family, their kids, and their ages. Also, because these characters are fictional, I've taken some liberty with their ages. Let's just assume this is how old everyone is today.

Now, let me introduce you to — or remind you of — the Baxter family.

The Baxters began in Bloomington, Indiana, and most of the family still lives there today.

The Baxter house is on ten acres outside of town, with a winding creek that runs through the backyard. It has a wraparound porch and pretty view and the memories of a lifetime. The house was built by John and Elizabeth Baxter. They raised their children here. Today it is owned by one of their daughters — Ashley — and her husband, Landon Blake. It is still the place where the extended Baxter family gathers for special celebrations.

John Baxter: John is the patriarch of the Baxter family. Formerly an emergency room doctor and professor of medicine at Indiana University, he's now retired. John's first wife, Elizabeth, died long ago from a recurrence of cancer. Years later, John remarried Elaine, and the two live in Bloomington.

Dayne Matthews, 43: Dayne is the oldest son of John and Elizabeth. Dayne was born out of wedlock and given up for adoption at birth. His adoptive parents died in a small plane crash when he was 18. Years later, Dayne became a very visible and popular movie star. At age 30, he hired an attorney to find his birth parents — John and Elizabeth Baxter. He had a moment with Elizabeth in the hospital before she died, and years later he connected with the rest of his biological family. Dayne is married to Katy, 41. The couple has three children: Sophie, 8; Egan, 6; and Blaise, 4. They are very much part of the Baxter family, and they split time between Los Angeles and Bloomington.

Brooke Baxter West, 41: Brooke is a pediatrician in Bloomington, married to Peter West, 41, also a doctor. The couple has two daughters: Maddie, 20, and Hayley, 17. The family experienced a tragedy when Hayley suffered a drowning accident at age 4. She recovered miraculously, but still has disabilities caused by the incident.

Kari Baxter Taylor, 39: Kari is a designer, married to Ryan Taylor, 41, football coach at Clear Creek High School. The couple has three children: Jessie, 17; RJ, 11; and Annie, 8. Kari had a crush on Ryan when the two were in middle school. They dated through college, and then broke up over a misunderstanding. Kari married a man she met in college, Tim Jacobs, but some years into their marriage he had an affair. The infidelity resulted in his murder at the hands of a stalker. The tragedy devastated Kari, who was pregnant at the time with their first child, Jessie. Ryan came back into her life around the same time, and years later he and Kari married. They live in Bloomington.

Ashley Baxter Blake, 37: Ashley is the former black sheep of the Baxter family, married to Landon Blake, 37, who works for the Bloomington Fire Department. The couple has four children: Cole, 17; Amy, 12; Devin, 10; and Janessa, 6. As a young single mom, Ashley was jaded against God and her family, when she reconnected with her firefighter friend Landon, who had secretly always loved her. Eventually Ashley and Landon married and Landon adopted Cole. Together, the couple had two children — Devin and Janessa. Between those children, they lost a baby girl, Sarah Marie, at birth to anencephaly. Amy, Ashley's niece, came to live with them a few years ago after Amy's parents, Erin Baxter Hogan and Sam Hogan, and Amy's three sisters, were killed in a horrific car accident. Amy was the only survivor. Ashley and Landon and their family live in Bloomington, in the old Baxter house, where Ashley and her siblings were raised. Ashley still paints and is successful in selling her work in local boutiques.

Luke Baxter, 35: Luke is a lawyer, married to Reagan Baxter, 35, a blogger. The couple has three children: Tommy, 15; Malin, 10; and Johnny, 6. Luke met Reagan in college. They experienced a major separation early on, after having Tommy out of wedlock. Eventually the two married, though they could not have more children. Malin and Johnny are both adopted.

In addition to the Baxters, this book has revisited the Flanigan family. The Flanigans have been friends with the Baxters for many years. So much so that I previously wrote five books about their oldest daughter — Bailey Flanigan. For the purpose of this book and those that might follow, here are the names and ages of the Flanigans:

Jim and Jenny Flanigan, both 46. Jim is a football coach for the Indianapolis Colts, and Jenny is a freelance writer who works from home. Bailey, 24, is married to Brandon Paul, 27, and they have one child, a daughter, Hannah Jennifer, almost 1. Bailey and Brandon were once actors in Hollywood — Brandon, very well known. Today they run the Christian Kids Theater in downtown Bloomington. Bailey's brothers are Connor, 21 — a student at Liberty University; Shawn and Justin — both age 18 and seniors at Clear Creek High; BJ (James), 17, a junior in high school; and Ricky, 15, a freshman.

In addition, Flanigan family friend Cody Coleman has resurfaced in recent books. Cody lived with the Flanigans when he was in high school and had a long-standing crush on the family daughter, Bailey. But all that changed when Brandon Paul entered the picture. Even before the relationship between Brandon and Bailey got serious, Cody began to have feelings for Bailey's former college roommate, Andi Ellison. Over the following years, Andi and Cody shared two failed engagements. Now, though, the two are married and may appear in future story lines.

ONE CHANCE FOUNDATION

The Kingsbury family is passionate about seeing orphans all over the world brought home to their forever families. As a result, Karen created a charitable group called the One Chance Foundation.

This foundation was inspired by the memory of her father, Ted C. Kingsbury. Ted always said, "Life is not a dress rehearsal. We have one chance to love, one chance to truly live!"

Karen often tells her reader friends, "You have one chance to write the story of your life!"™ Now, with Karen's One Chance Foundation, readers can join her in the belief that all of us have one chance to make a difference in the lives of orphans.

In the Bible, James 1:27 says people with pure and faultless religion look after orphans. The One Chance Foundation was created with that truth in mind.

If you are interested in giving to Karen's

One Chance Foundation and having your dedication printed in one of Karen's upcoming novels, visit www.KarenKingsbury.com. Below are dedications from some of Karen's reader friends who have contributed to the One Chance Foundation:

- To my mom, Vivian! I Love you To The Moon and Back! I thank God for YOU! Shelly
- In memory of my brother, John Fosmer. Love you "To the Moon and Back," Eleanor
- Endre, you and me under the full moon. What a gift! Love, Catherine
- In loving memory of my mom, Annabell! Love your daughter, Adelia Rippetoe
- To Shannon — love of my life — my best friend & my "lil' monkey face." Love, AC
- Tammy, you are my best friend and I would be lost without you! Love, Lisa
- Caryn and Jared, God bless your marriage! We love you to the moon and back! Love, Mom & Dad
- Love to my granddaughter Emma Nelson of Bloomington, IN. Your Grammy Dena Patrick
- I love you, Moma! Thanks for being

the Jenny to my Bailey. Love, Little
Lulu

- Hudson & Nolan, we love you to the
  moon and back! You are our greatest
  joy. Love forever, Mama & Daddy
- To Gloria, the most godly woman I
  know and the best mom! I love you!
  Jessie
- To my daughter & friend, Melissa
  Milkie. I wanted to see your name in
  an inspirational book, as you so gra-
  ciously dedicated your books to me.
  You, Michael & Mark are the best hap-
  penings of my life. — Love, Mom
- To my big sister & first best friend,
  Elizabeth! I love you so much & I am
  so proud of you! Love, Lydia
- To my family — Rick & Cori (grand-
  children, RT & Ali, AJ & Josh), Ron &
  Kori. 8 Blessings from God! Luv you,
  G'ma Margery
- In loving memory of our mom, Hazel
  Owens, who read all of your books,
  Love & miss you always — Barb and
  Jean
- Dottie, 12.24.60–7.3.11 Always in my
  thoughts; Forever in my heart! Love,
  Mimi
- God is doing great things through you,
  Evan Miller! Proverbs 3:5–6 #Pray4Ev

- To Dennis — the love of my life. You are missed. Love, Mary Mikel
- Aunt Faye — my 2nd Mom — you taught me the love of books. Love, Sharon
- To my family: B, R, P, J, T, A, A, A, C, N, R, M, L & M, all in God's loving care! B+R 50yrs!
- In Loving Memory of the Most Amazing Mom, Patti Berg! Blood did not define family . . .
- In loving memory of sister Martha Elizabeth Offer, 1986–2012. Miss you! Love, Sarah
- To Kurt — Celebrating 35+ yrs of loving you to the moon and back! Forever, Sheila
- Mom — Words can't express how truly thankful we are for you. Love, Kristen & Kade
- In Loving Memory of My Husband, Jay — Janice Helmkamp
- To my babylove, thank you for helping me chase sunbeams to the sun. Love, Staci
- In Memory of "My Chuck" . . . "Remember When" — Sharon Crist
- Jonnye Dickson, thanks, Mom, for encouraging my reading. Love, Annette
- Tara and Mary — Dedicated to our

friend Eva Mayer. Love you to the moon and back!

- Karen Taylor — Miss you, Mum & Dad, always here for you, Sandie. Love you all forever
- MaryBeth Cannon, I carried you in my womb for 9 months, in my arms for 2 months, and I will carry you in my heart forever. LOVE, Mom
- Aunt Pam, your encouragement and support mean more to me than you will ever know!! Love, Jonica
- Precious Kennedy Grace, Be Humble & Kind. Live Boldly. Papa & Lala Love You BIG!
- Mom/Tammy: Just like you always say, "Love you to the moon & back!" Daidra & Family
- To my sisters Becky & Missy for loving our family To the Moon and Back! Rose McCauley
- Diane K. Weimer: With love and thanksgiving for my son Theron Edward Weimer, Jr.
- Grandma MaryAnn Marley, We love u 2 the moon & back! Nicole, Renee, Sophia, Annette
- In memory of Robert Perez, my husband and best friend — always and forever!

- Jocelyn Tow . . . no one will ever know how much we love you, not even you! Love, Mom and Daddy
- I Love You, Katy Goll! You're Amazing! Love, Your Husband, Raymond
- Jodi Jordan, my daughter: I love you to the moon & back!! — Your mother, Joyce
- To our Law Enforcement Officers. Thank you for your service! May God bless you! — Mary Johnson
- Vernon, I would do it all over again. It's hard to believe we have celebrated 52 years already. Love & prayers, Sharon
- Natalie Garber — "And Beyond." Happy Graduation. Reach for the stars. Love, Memaw
- In memory of Donna. You're always in our hearts. Love, Your Family and Friends
- To my Grams in Heaven, I will always love you to the Moon & Back! Love, Shelly
- Helen A. Smith, Forever my Best Friend. I LOVE YOU MORE! Love, Littlefoot
- Dr. Wilcox, loving and sharing Jesus for 42 years! Best 1st grade teacher ever!

- To Barb Rysavy, an example of love & grace! Thanks for the gift of life! Love, Sue & Karen
- In honor of my best friend and beautiful mom, Cindy. I love you more! — Becca Turner
- To Maw: Thank you for always being our angel here on earth. You've loved us through it all & we love you always. You show Jesus Eyes to everyone. Love, Hope & Kingston
- Mom, we miss you but know you are watching over us from Heaven. Love always, Lydia Seabron
- Fred, we miss you and love you so much!! Love, Jerri Ann, Dawn, Kevin, Katie, William
- Mom, my true Strength, Grace, and Faith. Love, Dad (Matthew Landavazo)
- Allie & Hannah, you're a gift from God. I love you to the moon & back! Love, Mom (Lauren Morris)
- To Justin, Kellie, Faith, and Carl! I love you "to the moon and back"!!! 731 Aunti Joni
- To Arleen, my mom and best friend! I love you forever!!! Joni xoxoxo . . .
- To Jennifer Powell & Janet Tilford: My Power 100 Heroes!! Thank you for the

hours of love & support you give each week as you "walk the talk" in helping all of us become healthier. God bless you! — Janice Kukkola-Miller

- To our precious daughter Angela Dilling from Romania, an angel messenger sent from God. With love, Mom and Dad, Ellen & Pete Miller
- To Tina Dunson & Joyce Bush, Your lives are an inspiration to all! With love, SB
- Tori Brianne, You are precious beyond words; we love you, TTMAB! — Dad, Mom, Landon & Cade

ABOUT THE AUTHOR

Karen Kingsbury, #1 *New York Times* bestselling novelist, is America's favorite inspirational storyteller, with more than twenty-five million copies of her award-winning books in print. Her last dozen titles have topped bestseller lists, and many of her novels are under development as TV movies and major motion pictures. Her Baxter Family books are being developed into a TV series slated for major network viewing sometime in the next year. Karen is also an adjunct professor of writing at Liberty University. In 2001 she and her husband, Don, adopted three boys from Haiti, doubling their family in a matter of months. Today the couple has joined the ranks of empty nesters, living in Tennessee near five of their adult children.

The employees of Thorndike Press hope you have enjoyed this Large Print book. All our Thorndike, Wheeler, and Kennebec Large Print titles are designed for easy reading, and all our books are made to last. Other Thorndike Press Large Print books are available at your library, through selected bookstores, or directly from us.

For information about titles, please call:
  (800) 223-1244

or visit our website at:
  gale.com/thorndike

To share your comments, please write:
  Publisher
  Thorndike Press
  10 Water St., Suite 310
  Waterville, ME 04901

WALKING ON MY GRAVE

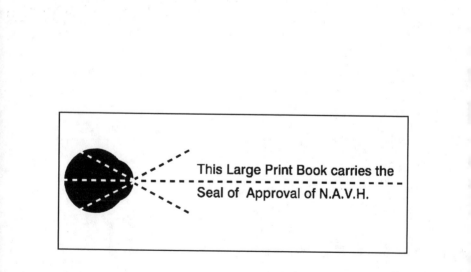
This Large Print Book carries the Seal of Approval of N.A.V.H.

WALKING ON MY GRAVE

CAROLYN HART

THORNDIKE PRESS
A part of Gale, Cengage Learning

Farmington Hills, Mich • San Francisco • New York • Waterville, Maine
Meriden, Conn • Mason, Ohio • Chicago

GALE
CENGAGE Learning®

Copyright © 2017 by Carolyn G. Hart.
A Death on Demand Mystery.
Thorndike Press, a part of Gale, Cengage Learning.

ALL RIGHTS RESERVED

This is a work of fiction. Names, characters, places, and incidents either are the products of the author's imagination or used fictitiously and any resemblance to actual persons, living or dead, business establishments, events, or locales is entirely coincidental.
Thorndike Press® Large Print Mystery.
The text of this Large Print edition is unabridged.
Other aspects of the book may vary from the original edition.
Set in 16 pt. Plantin.

LIBRARY OF CONGRESS CATALOGING-IN-PUBLICATION DATA

Names: Hart, Carolyn G., author.
Title: Walking on my grave / by Carolyn Hart.
Description: Large print edition. | Waterville, Maine : Thorndike Press, a part of Gale, Cengage Learning, 2017. | Series: A death on demand mystery | Series: Thorndike Press large print mystery
Identifiers: LCCN 2017011421 | ISBN 9781410496829 (hardcover) | ISBN 1410496821 (hardcover)
Subjects: LCSH: Large type books. | GSAFD: Mystery fiction.
Classification: LCC PS3558.A676 W35 2017b | DDC 813/.54—dc23
LC record available at https://lccn.loc.gov/2017011421

Published in 2017 by arrangement with The Berkley Publishing Group, an imprint of Penguin Publishing Group, a division of Penguin Random House, LLC

Printed in the United States of America
1 2 3 4 5 6 7 21 20 19 18 17

To Michelle Vega,
in thanks for your kindness and patience.

CAST OF CHARACTERS

Annie Darling — The tap of a cane sets off a scramble to save a woman's life.

Max Darling — Catches a look of fear on a bank teller's face but doesn't know who frightened him.

The Incredible Trio: Mystery Author Emma Clyde, Civic Volunteer Henny Brawley, and Annie's Ditzy Mother-in-law Laurel Roethke — Use their unusual insights in the search for a would-be murderer.

Police Chief Billy Cameron — He doesn't believe everything he's told.

Mavis Cameron — Police dispatcher, crime tech, and Billy's wife.

Sargeant Lou Pirelli — A tough cop with a soft heart.

Officer Hyla Harrison — Pays attention to faces.

Gazette **Reporter Marian Kenyon** — The first to know.

Bar and Grill Owner Ben Parotti — Listens

7

to his customers.

Ves Roundtree — Knows someone walked on her grave.

Katherine Farley — Will do anything to save her husband.

Bob Farley — Drives to the remote north end of the island on a foggy afternoon.

Adam Nash — Selling his yacht won't bring in enough money.

Fred Butler — Tells Ben Parotti about his future plans.

Gretchen Roundtree — Cool, collected, backed into a corner.

Curt Roundtree — Always puts himself first.

Jane Wilson — Dreaming of a June wedding.

Tim Holt — Wants to buy some property cheap for a can't-miss development.

Estelle Parker — Furious at the idea of suicide.

Joe Mackey — A neighbor who calls 911.

Roger Clark — A business appointment takes a dark turn.

Bill Hogan — Plays dominoes at Parotti's Bar and Grill on Saturdays.

TIMETABLE

Friday, February 5 — Ves hosts a dinner party.

Thursday, February 11 — Ves hurries up the stairs.

Wednesday, February 17 — "I do not intend to die."

Friday, February 19 — A discovery on Fish Haul Pier.

Monday, February 22 — Pirate gold beckons.

Tuesday, February 23 — Blood on a doorjamb.

Wednesday, February 24 — Silence in an office.

Thursday, February 25 — Shots in the night.

Friday, February 26 — Billy Cameron hears a confession.

Saturday, February 27 — The grandfather clock strikes at quarter after seven.

1

Katherine Farley looked down at the bright and inviting brochure. Instead of the bamboo forest and charging black rhinoceros, she pictured Ves Roundtree, springy reddish curls framing a tight narrow face. Ves radiated energy, competence, intensity. Sharp lines at the corners of Ves's eyes and mouth revealed the gnawing mind-set of a worrier, a woman who had scrabbled for what she had and could always imagine disaster looming.

Katherine turned a page of the brochure.

"Doesn't it look great?" Bob's tenor voice was eager.

Katherine smiled at him. She could see herself and Bob in the mirror behind an old saloon bar they'd installed at the end of their long living room, which overlooked the marsh. It had cost a pretty penny to buy the bar and arrange for its shipping, but that was back when they had plenty of money. The bar was a restored relic from a shuttered saloon in an abandoned cattle drive town. Now the golden oak bar and brass footrail gleamed with polish, as bright as when long-ago adventurers, con men, prospectors, and cowboys drank mule kick bourbon and eyed saloon girls. She appraised her reflection clinically, medium height, nice figure, sleek black hair drawn back in a chignon, aristocratic features that were a dime a dozen in period films, dark eyes that had once been merry. Her smile was easy, though that took every ounce of her steel will. She wanted to rush across the room, take his dear face in her hands, love him riotously, ferociously, as if champagne-drenched nights could still be theirs. Nothing would wound him more than to know her thoughts. She was careful to keep her tone light. "You, me, and a herd of gazelles. Add gin and tonic and I'm sold. The safari looks grand." Grand and expensive. Very expensive.

His gaunt face, still handsome despite deep furrows grooved by pain, lighted with an eager smile. For an instant the past overlay the present, and it was like seeing Bob when he was strong and able to walk easily, didn't have to hobble with legs encased in braces, a cane in his left hand.

Unchanged was his sandy tousled hair, intelligent dark brown eyes, bony nose, squarish chin. He one-handedly propelled the wheelchair, which he used at home, and rolled up to her. "We get a big discount if I book next week. We'll save a bunch of money."

She listened as if enthralled, hearing the wanderlust, the hunger to go and do and be, the need for variety and new experience despite the maimed right arm that lay useless in his lap and the weakened legs. She listened and knew the cost of such a trip mounted into the thousands, thousands they didn't have, thousands he no longer earned because the hand with fingers locked into a claw had been his painting hand, the thousands she had never earned with her drawings that achieved acclaim but sold for modest sums in the galleries. She was the one good with figures. She took care of bills and investments. Now she scraped to get them from month to month. She'd missed the last mortgage payment. But to see him eager meant everything to her. There were so many dark quiet days when he withdrew, and the dullness in his eyes broke her heart. Ves Roundtree could make the safari possible. She would . . . and if she wouldn't . . .

■ ■ ■ ■

Jane Wilson cupped her chin in her hand, listened as Tim excitedly described his plan for a shopping center on the mainland ". . . right there on the highway. I've researched the property. A great place to stop between Charleston and Savannah. It can't miss. You and I together can make it happen."

Jane felt the usual bubbling of desire deep inside when she looked at Tim. His strong-boned face enthralled her, thick brown hair above a high forehead, strong nose, chin with a hint of a cleft. His dark eyes held the promise of passion, his full sensuous lips worked magic when he held her. She knew she was nice-looking but no more than that. She was so ordinary compared to Tim. Her mind drifted back in memory to that moment on the beach when they'd met. She'd thought herself alone. She'd stood staring up at the Mediterranean mansion, golden in the sun, tears streaming down her face. He'd loped to her side, face drawn in concern, bronze and muscular in a life-guard's red swim trunks, binoculars dangling from one large hand. "Hey, what's wrong?" It seemed right to tell him, swiping the tears from her face, about the days when her mother was Mr. Roundtree's secretary and how in the summers Mr. Roundtree insisted Jane was welcome to play in the pool or on the beach and join her mom for lunch. "He was such a good man. When my mom was so sick — she had cancer and the insurance wouldn't cover some of the medicine — Mr. Roundtree helped us out. And he came to her funeral. I didn't even know until after he died that he'd left me some money."

Tim had been so interested. "So you're an heiress. First time I've ever met an heiress. That's neat."

She'd been quick to explain that she didn't get any money when Mr. Roundtree died. "He set up a trust. His sister Ves gets everything for now. When she dies, the money is split up. Originally he included my mom, but after she died, he put my name in instead. I have to be alive when Ves dies or my share goes to the others."

Tim grinned. "Better take care of yourself. How does it feel to be in line for some big-time swag?" She'd laughed and shaken her head. "I'll be an old lady before Ves dies. She's only in her forties and she's a dynamo." To Jane the prospect of lots of money seemed unreal. But she would always appreciate the note sent to her after Mr.

Roundtree's death and his tribute to her mom: *Nellie was as fine a person as anyone I've ever known. I wish she could have lived and taken that trip to Ireland she always wanted to. Naming you in the trust is my way of saying thank you to her for years of hard work.* Jane kept the letter in her jewel box. As for the money, it was a gift that might come someday . . .

"Hey, Jane, didn't you hear what I said?" Tim was smiling, but his gaze was intent.

She reached for her glass of wine. Tim had ordered expensive wine. She looked desperately around the crowded dining room for inspiration. He'd brought her all the way to Savannah for a fine dinner, and she'd stopped listening. She felt a moment of confusion, Tim talking about his plans, his big grandiose pie-in-the-sky plans, because how could he ever get enough money to buy that kind of land and build a shopping center? "Oh," she said in a rush, "the center would be wonderful, wouldn't it?"

His face lightened. He reached across the table, took her hand. "All I need is backing. You can tell Ves Roundtree about the center and we'll promise her a cut of the profits." He was pleased, excited.

She felt a sweep of panic. She didn't want to ask Ves Roundtree for money. "I don't

16

know if she'd be interested." She saw darkness in his eyes. If she made him mad, that warm, intimate smile would disappear. "Oh, I don't know, Tim. I can try" — she didn't want to ask, she had no right — "but I know she'll say no."

Curt Roundtree glared at his mother. "I missed out on a chance to sail to the Bahamas on Buster Gordon's yacht."

Gretchen Roundtree spoke in her usual breathy, catchy voice, but her tone was firm. "We will go to dinner, and I advise you to be charming." She looked at her son and remembered how appealing he'd been as a little boy, reddish hair in shining ringlets, a cherubic face, gurgling laughter. As an adult, in years if not in behavior, he still had reddish curls and a broad, freckled face and he was always ready to laugh or make others laugh. His wanderlust lifestyle was made possible by rich dilettante friends who welcomed him for a stay of a week or a month at no expense to him. A generous monthly check from Gretchen took care of other expenses, but he counted on snagging rides in friends' private planes or on yachts for carefree — accent on *free* — holidays in Snowmass or Bermuda, depending upon the season. Friends assumed he was wealthy, because he had no job.

Gretchen was blunt. "The money spigot is turned off. No more checks from me. I'm working at a cosmetics shop to pay the food bill. Either you sweet-talk Ves out of some money or find a job." She knew the last would get his attention.

Curt's blue eyes were cold. "If the old man hadn't been such a bastard, I'd never have to worry about money."

"But he was, so you better do as I say."

"Where'd your money go?"

Gretchen shrugged. She felt a twinge of the old bitterness. Rufus had been glad to see her go. She'd agreed for $2 million. Curt didn't know how much his father had paid, but he saw her travel in style from Nice to Venice to Bar Harbor to Scottsdale. She, too, was adept at snagging invitations to stay with wealthy friends.

She looked at her son, knew they were two of a kind. Curt took his thrills from diving from a cliff in Acapulco or skiing off trail in avalanche country or daring a night at a seedy bar in Amsterdam.

She enjoyed another kind of daring, but that avenue was closed to her now. Not only closed, but she was pushed to the brink by a blackmailer. All she could do was pay up.

"I had some expenses." Gretchen's voice

was tight. A cold-eyed youngish trophy wife had a damning photo in her cell phone, and her price for silence was high. Gretchen had returned to the island and the condo Rufus had provided, taken the job at Perfumerie. She could no longer mail checks to Curt.

She felt the old flash of anger at her former husband. Why couldn't he have left his millions to Curt? It was stupid to expect Curt to become some kind of financial wizard just because Rufus was a success. She still had the letter from Rufus that the lawyer sent after his death: *. . . better for Curt to make his own way, better for him as a man. He should be in his sixties before Ves dies, and by then he will have learned the value of work.*

"The money's gone. I don't have it anymore. I'm going to ask Ves to advance me enough to open a dress shop in Buckhead." Fifty thousand dollars would get her started, fifty thousand and some new credit cards that weren't maxed out. She imagined an elegant shop in Buckhead. If she drew the right kind of women and offered to bring the finest in couture to their homes, she would see the houses, learn enough to engage in her favorite trade. "That's my plan. I suggest you figure out one for yourself."

■ ■ ■ ■

Adam Nash exuded an aura of success, an aura he'd carefully cultivated over the years. Tall, well built, with a leonine head of silver hair, his chiseled features were quite perfect for a captain of industry, a spellbinding orator, a financial seer. He instilled confidence. His expression was benign, a steady gaze, a slightly raised eyebrow, a pleasant smile, as he listened to the luncheon speaker.

There was no hint of the panic flaring deep inside, like a rat twisting to be free of a trap. He had a couple of weeks at most. He could juggle figures until then, but he must have an infusion of cash no later than the end of February. Eighty-six thousand dollars. It might as well be eighty-six million. He had borrowed on the house. His Lexus was leased. He'd had no luck selling the yacht. Even if it sold, that wouldn't be enough. He'd clear only forty thousand. He needed eighty-six thousand. His credit was no good. He couldn't borrow. He had many high-flying friends but none of them would write him a check for that kind of money. There was no family to call on. His last remaining relative, a down-at-the-heels cousin, died last year. He wished he could demand the return of jewelry he'd lavished on a succession of women, but they cared no more for him than he for them. When there was pleasure, fine. When bad times came, he was alone.

He was at the head table as befitted a leading resident who was currently president of the community drive. He maintained his pleasant expression as he gazed at the audience. He saw Ves Roundtree, wiry reddish hair, nervous gestures, thin bony shoulders hunched as if poised to spring at any moment. She turned toward Ben Parotti, her conversation animated.

Ves Roundtree. She was his only hope.

Fred Butler, his round face expressionless, methodically counted out twenties. His hands moved a shade slower than usual, a calculated response to the customer's rudeness. "Nine hundred and sixty. Nine hundred and eighty. One thousand." He took his time as he slipped the bills into a white envelope, pushed the envelope across the wooden counter to a tall, slender woman with upswept dark hair and a supercilious stare, her attitude one of impatience. "Can I do anything else for you, Mrs. Crain?" His tone was bland.

She scooped up the envelope, the emerald

21

on one slim finger gleaming in the beam from the overhead light. She flipped through the bills, turned away without speaking, her Jimmy Choo high heels clicking on the marble floor of the bank.

Fred hated the way he felt diminished. Most of the rich women on the island were nice. Not Viola Crain. She often looked through those she considered her social inferiors or gazed in disdain as if observing some lower life-form. Fred wished he could tell her that someday he'd be rich, too, and, when he was, he'd . . . What would he do? He didn't live in her world. But when he was rich maybe he could join the country club. Or maybe he'd go to Mexico. Americans — rich Americans — lived like princes there.

He looked at Estelle, the other teller, nodded toward an inconspicuous door. She gave him her usual sweet smile. In the right kind of world, people like Estelle would be rich, not Viola Crain. He put the See Next Window sign out and moved quickly. He turned the knob, slipped through the opening, closed the door behind him. He hurried to the break room and poured a mug of coffee. The bank had good coffee. He picked up a glazed doughnut from a half-empty box open on the counter. At the

Formica-topped table, he took an end seat. He dunked the doughnut in the coffee, took a bite. The sugar lift was immediate.

He swallowed coffee, felt better. When he was rich, he wouldn't be ignored by people like Viola Crain. People treated you differently if they knew you had money. Or were going to get money. They'd all been nice to him at the dinner in Rufus's memory. When he was rich, he'd enjoy the best of everything, go to a fabulous Caribbean resort. Images of coconut palms swaying in a breeze and azure water soothed him. They would all live high after Ves Roundtree died and the estate was divided.

He didn't understand why Ves kept on working after her brother left her all that money. Or why she hadn't moved to Rufus's mansion on the beach. Instead, she rented out the luxurious home during the season to rich Yankees. He felt his usual spasm of irritation. If she had moved out of the family home, he could pursue his plans without worry. But she hadn't moved. She continued to live in her antebellum home, so he had to slip around her property while she was at her shop. He for sure didn't want Ves to find him in her backyard. She had a sharp tongue. Worst of all, he would have to explain. He'd rather die. As for her brother's money, it would be a long time coming, and by then he was positive he could soon be rich all on his own.

He finished the doughnut. As for Ves, wallowing in all that money, why did she think people wanted to know about money they wouldn't see for years? He wasn't the only one who felt that way. Maybe Ves meant it nicely when she had them all to dinner at her house, the ones who would be rich when she died, but it was a reminder that she wasn't old, that she had years to enjoy all that money. The evening was stiff with uneven bursts of disjointed conversation. Those anointed by Rufus to someday share in his largesse were there. Katherine and Bob Farley, the artists; Jane Wilson, Rufus's secretary's daughter, and her boyfriend, Tim Holt; local financial adviser Adam Nash; Curt Roundtree, Rufus's playboy son; and Gretchen, Rufus's ex-wife. Ves included Gretchen Roundtree and Jane's boyfriend at the dinner even though they weren't in the trust.

Yeah, it was a weird night. He particularly remembered Katherine Farley. She was dramatic in a vivid red-and-yellow dress, flamboyant against the gray walls of the small dining room and the shabby elegance of the old and worn Chippendale dining table. Candles wavered when Ves moved in and out of the kitchen to bring the food. In answer to a question from Bob Farley, she said a seafaring Roundtree had brought back a portion of a Buddhist altar screen that hung over the sideboard. Bob had paused and leaned against his cane to admire the screen before he moved stiffly to his chair at the table. Bob recalled a trip he and Katherine had made to the South Putuo Temple in Xiamen and how he'd love to go back, but he and Katherine were planning a great adventure in Kenya for the fall. Jane Wilson, the daughter of Rufus Roundtree's deceased secretary, listened enthralled as Bob talked about travels, his eyes alight with excitement. Jane was a nice-looking girl, an eager face, curly brown hair, big blue friendly eyes. Her boyfriend spent much of the evening describing some kind of real estate project to Ves, who only occasionally turned to Katherine on her left. Curt Roundtree often looked admiringly at Ves and adroitly drew her out about her shop and her recent trip to Egypt. Adam Nash tried to act like a bon vivant. Fred thought his mellifluous voice was smarmy as he meandered on and on about a Broadway show he'd seen last month and the Degas exhibit in Atlanta. Gretchen Roundtree had been nice to him, but he'd never felt comfortable, not all the long evening. He didn't care that the estate was growing, even more money than when Rufus died. He wanted money now. He gulped the rest of the coffee. He intended to have money now. No one was going to stand in his way, though he'd be careful. Very careful.

Fog curled around a fountain midway to an antebellum house. A marble statue of Diana the huntress faced the back porch. One marble hand held a bow, the other a portion of an arrow pointed skyward. No lights shone in the two-story white frame house. A mourning dove made a low throaty call.

A figure in dark clothing lifted an arm, checked the time. A few minutes before five. Ves Roundtree usually arrived home at a quarter after five. There was plenty of time. The visitor eased through the fog, head swiveling from left to right, backpack shifting from the movement. Confident no one was near, the visitor climbed the back steps, crossed to the door. A gloved hand tugged a ring of keys from a pocket, tried several until one fit. The door opened. The intruder stepped inside, slid the backpack free, closed the door.

In the hallway, gloved hands opened the

backpack, lifted out the necessary materials. There was no sound but the ticking of the grandfather clock as the intruder worked swiftly. Perhaps only three minutes passed and the materials were put away, a zipper pulled, and the backpack once again in place. The back door was opened cautiously. The fog was lighter now. A rapid descent of the steps. The figure crossed the yard to a stand of bamboo, stopped in its shadow.

Ves Roundtree drove fast, but traffic was sparse on Sunshine Lane. She turned into her long drive, a graveled lane that ran a hundred yards with dense foliage on either side before rounding a curve. The trees thinned here and she could see the house. She relished privacy. Her nearest neighbor was a twelve-foot alligator in a pond a quarter-mile deep into the woods. The van rattled as she stopped a few feet from the stand-alone garage. She needed to take the van, twelve years old now, to Petty's Garage to see if he could do something about the rattle.

She turned off the motor, opened the door, used the hand grip above the door as she slung to the ground. She'd make some spoon bread, reheat chili from earlier in the week. The evening stretched ahead, quiet, comfortable, uneventful. The week had been tiring, prompting her to choose a bright outfit today, a turquoise knit top and gray trousers and matching turquoise heels. She always wore teetering heels to work. They made her feel young and buoyant.

She moved fast, as she always moved, a tight, tense blur of energy, rushing up the back steps. Her heels clattered on the wooden porch. The door opened, closed.

The chill drizzle didn't take the shine from the morning for Annie Darling. Although she was careful in placing her steps, she felt her usual Monday-morning happiness, a new day, a new week, and at the end of the slick boardwalk the best mystery bookstore north of Delray Beach, Florida, her own wonderful Death on Demand. She never tired, not in summer, fall, winter, or spring, of stopping in front of the plate glass window.

She admired the rocking chair with a pink-and-blue afghan casually draped over the armrest, perfect to suggest contentment with a mystery on a drizzly February day. The new titles were tantalizing: *Cometh the Hour* by Jeffrey Archer, *Jane and the Waterloo Map* by Stephanie Barron, *A Turn for the Bad* by Sheila Connolly, *Here Comes the*

Bribe by Mary Daheim, *No Shred of Evidence* by Charles Todd, *Time of Fog and Fire* by Rhys Bowen, *The Killing in the Cafe* by Simon Brett, and *Fool Me Once* by Harlan Coben.

Shoppers were few and far between in February. Perhaps she'd call Max at his office next door. Confidential Commissions would be quiet as well. Max's secretary, Barb, was in the Caribbean. Max usually kept office hours, though this morning he'd murmured something about dropping by the men's grill at the club since not much was shaking at the office. Max was quite willing to consider any interesting task, puzzle, or question brought to him, but he was equally willing to enjoy peaceful hours without a task. He was probably sharing, in a deprecating manner, of course, his recent hole in one on the third green. Her husband considered downtime God's gift to golfers. It was up to her to set a good example. Nose to the grindstone. Hew to the course. As if reading were ever a task and not a pleasure. She'd make a pot of Colombian, heat up a blueberry scone, build a fire in the café area, and settle down with one of the new books. Would she see what Molly Murphy was up to or plunge into Harlan Coben's new novel?

29

Footsteps sounded behind her. A plethora of footsteps. This was unusual enough at ten A.M. on a drizzly February morning that she turned to look at the hurrying figures. *Oh my.* A quiet, luxurious morning of reading was no longer in her immediate future.

2

Annie Darling maintained a bright smile. The voices rose, the dulcet tone of her ditzy mother-in-law, Laurel Darling Roethke, the gruff bark of renowned mystery author Emma Clyde, the dry, wry contralto of mystery aficionado and indefatigable island volunteer Henny Brawley.

Laurel's husky voice had an otherworldly timbre, as if she conversed with a wise faun in a sun-spangled glen. ". . . swirls of red, white, and blue with stars cascading in the center of the cover, and on the first page of my little publication, it's such a difficult choice, but I believe I will go with *A good friend lifts your heart.*" Laurel's gaze was distant as if she saw beyond the room, the island, perhaps the universe.

Emma spoke with blunt force. "I don't intend to reveal all my secrets in my little booklet, but here's a particular favorite of Marigold's: *A bad dream is your subcon-*

31

scious knocking on the closed door of your mind. What could be more perfect for a collection of wise observations by my dear Marigold and unflappable Inspector Houlihan?" The mystery writer's strong square face was pugnacious, daring the others to disagree.

Annie's gaze was admiring though she secretly loathed Marigold Rembrandt. Emma's sleuth was an officious busybody with all the charm of a wasp.

Henny was upbeat. "I've never flaunted my mystery knowledge —"

Annie suppressed a smile. Henny Brawley and Emma Clyde delighted in sprinkling their conversation with mystery references that demonstrated mastery of the genre. Recently the tone had been sharp edged when they disagreed about the most memorable quote from Agatha Christie's works. Henny's favorite came from *Towards Zero:* A young nurse tells a would-be suicide bitter at being saved, *It may be just by being somewhere — not doing anything — just by being at a certain place at a certain time — oh, I can't say what I mean, but you might just — just walk along a street someday and just by doing that accomplish something terribly important — perhaps without even knowing what it was.* Emma was condescending.

"Pretty, but peripheral. In *Ordeal by Innocence,* Hester Argyle says, *It's not the guilty who matter. It's the innocent.* That" — emphatically — "is the essence of Christie."

"— but I can't wait" — Henny's voice was exuberant — "to share my list of favorite mysteries in my pamphlet."

Annie felt caught in a gossamer web, insubstantial but clinging, immobilizing. Of course, sounds didn't make a web. No matter, she felt enmeshed. She recalled a summer day on horseback as she trotted around a curve and almost barged into a twenty-foot web hanging between two live oaks, home to an industrious golden silk spider. She'd gazed in awe before turning to ride back the way she'd come. Unfortunately, she didn't have a horse at hand. There was no escaping her current entrapment and the apparent rock-solid conviction of Laurel, Emma, and Henny that Annie not only ran a mystery bookstore, she was simply a perfect choice to publish pamphlets.

Laurel waved a graceful hand, nails gleaming with the daintiest of pink polish. "My dears, quiet for a moment."

Emma paused in midbark, raised a demanding eyebrow.

Intelligent, perceptive Henny looked up

from her notebook, her expression quizzical.

Annie was resigned to the reality that Laurel's ethereal beauty misled viewers into thinking she was nothing more than a gorgeous blonde. Annie knew better. Her mother-in-law's Nordic blue eyes held a mixture of sublime confidence and wicked mischief that never failed to send chills up Annie's spine. *What was her Laurel thinking? What was she planning? What had she quite possibly already done?*

Silence fell. She and Emma and Henny awaited a Royal Pronouncement.

Laurel's benign gaze settled on Annie. "Dear child, I sense stress."

Emma gave a huff. "Stress? I can tell you about stress. Right now Marigold is trapped in a cave with a marauding bear at the entrance and a nest of cottonmouths —"

Annie loved the idea of a bear looming over Marigold. She was also tempted to point out that cottonmouths, aka water moccasins, were North America's only poisonous water snake and therefore highly unlikely to be found in the depths of a cave, but confronting a bear or even a nest of water moccasins would be preferable to an Emma publicly challenged.

"— and I have to figure out a way for her

to escape."

Henny tapped her purse. "If she carries a small atomizer of mace, she's out of the cave in a flash."

Emma's craggy face pursed in thought. She gave an abrupt nod. "Not bad." Her tone was grudging.

"Of course" — Henny was quick to apply balm to an even slightly challenged authorial ego — "I know you'd already thought of mace and likely decided for Marigold to use the emergency food kit she always carries in her purse and toss a honeycomb past the bear to distract him long enough to dart to her car."

Emma's cornflower blue eyes were easily read. *Honeycomb . . . that's a genius ploy . . . I certainly had almost thought of it . . . was thinking of her purse . . . Henny has obviously read my books carefully . . . she's a good sort . . .* Pleased, Emma beamed at Henny. "I was just trying to decide which action offered the reader more excitement. I think, yes, the honeycomb." Clearly Emma was now sure she'd created the clever escape route.

Laurel gave her tinkling laugh that reminded Annie of a pixie playing a marimba.

"We've had such a good visit with Annie and given her much to think about. We hope she will be excited to publish our chap-books."

Henny clapped. "How perfect to call our little publications *chapbooks. Chapbook* used to be the common term for any small pamphlet whatever the subject, not just po-etry."

Laurel pushed back her chair, came blithely to her feet. "We've given her a great deal to consider. She has the look of one —"

Annie felt self-conscious as three pairs of eyes settled on her. Was her velour boat neck top too bright a red?

"— needful of a quiet moment to ponder what we've offered. I know we are eager to afford her the solitude necessary for creative genius. I have no doubt" — Laurel's mes-merizing gaze fastened on Annie — "that Annie is already envisioning our chap-books." A nod at Emma. *"Detecting Wisdom."* A nod at Henny. *"Classic Crime."* A modest smile. "And my *Merry Musings, Modest Maxims for Happiness.* I know" — and somehow she was shepherding Emma and Henny down the central corridor toward the door — "we can expect much from our dear Annie."

Annie remained at the table nearest the coffee bar. It seemed hours since the arrival of the Incredible Trio, as she and Max had long ago dubbed his mom, the island author, and mystery guru Henny. Annie glanced at the wall clock. Actually, their visit had lasted less than a half hour. "Why are you such a wimp?" she demanded aloud. Her psyche was defensive, replied hotly, "It would have been rude to refuse to listen." "Did you tell them no?" "How could I tell them no?" But her reply was weak. Just as weak as she was. She might possibly hold up against one of them. When they combined forces, she might as well be an effigy on a tomb. She grinned, picturing herself in marble splendor with three chapbooks clasped to her bosom.

Warm fur brushed against her ankle. She reached down, slipped a hand over Agatha's silky fur. "Do you think I'm talking to you? Of course, I am. Cat's in charge, right?"

In an instant, her sleek black cat landed beside her, turned twice before she settled into a comfortable ball in the center of the table. A throaty purr reverberated.

Annie bent to nuzzle warm fur. "I'm flattered that you waited until they left before you came out. Of course, you were probably eating, and first things first. Agatha, am I a wimp?" Annie lifted her head. The purr increased. "Kind of you to say so. I agree. When the Trio speaks, it's wiser to listen."

She pushed back her chair. Agatha watched with sleepy green eyes as Annie crossed to the coffee bar. She needed a boost. She paused in front of the fireplace to admire the watercolors hanging above the mantel. Each pictured a scene from a mystery novel. The first customer to identify each author and title received a free (non-collectible) book and coffee for a month. As proprietor, it was her pleasure to choose the books. She loved humor, and these books were guaranteed to make readers laugh.

In the first watercolor, a striking young woman in a gypsy dress and an elegant thir-tyish blonde in a kimono stared at a heap of dull glassy pebbles lying on a bunk in a luxurious ship cabin. The younger woman looked puzzled and disappointed, but her older companion, who had an air of sophis-tication, was excited and fascinated.

In the second, a white picket fence gleamed in the moonlight. Four surrepti-tious figures, each clutching a suitcase, peered over the fence at the unlighted wing of a huge old house. There was an aura of stealth in their posture.

In the third, a sour-faced woman in a business suit teetered on the ledge of a fifth-floor window above a busy street. She clutched a rusty drainpipe with one hand, the other gripped her handbag. A crowd clustered on the sidewalk, faces upturned. Two constables dealt with a traffic jam as gawkers stopped to watch.

In the fourth, a beautiful dark-haired woman lying in a hospital bed stared at an attractive blond nurse, a tall, distinguished man with horn-rimmed glasses and a pipe, a short, pudgy, balding man with a paunch, and a sandy-haired man with a worried face.

In the fifth, a slender middle-aged Asian man stared out the fourth-floor window of a frowsy building at a rusty green crane and the wrecking ball swinging toward the adjacent office windows. Below, a potbellied man with a dirty yellow hard hat and a clipboard appeared to be directing the demolition.

Annie filled a mug. When she settled again in her chair, delectable brew in hand, she was smiling and not only because of the watercolors. She gazed around the table. Although she sold books and didn't publish them, creating pamphlets might be fun. She wondered if the creative trio had illustrators in mind. Laurel excelled at sketches and might already have drawings for her chapbook. Annie reached over Agatha to pick up a pink manuscript box tied with red ribbon and topped with an emerald bow. She untied the ribbon, lifted the lid, pulled out a sheet, and read the author's introduction:

MERRY MUSINGS
MODEST MAXIMS FOR HAPPINESS
by
Laurel Darling Roethke

Merry Musings offers maxims guaranteed to make any life happier. Each is a Signpost on a road that twists and turns, climbs, descends to depths, winds upward once again to touch trailing clouds. Live with élan.

Annie turned the page, nodded approval at Laurel's illustration, a burst of fireworks in a splendid shower of red, gold, and green. *Merry Musing One: Catch a falling star before it knocks you flat.*

Annie pondered. At first glance, the maxim seemed simple. But was it? She had the old familiar sweep of uncertainty she often felt when dealing with her mother-in-law. Was Laurel saying each person must be aware of possibilities, make the right move at the right time? Was she saying — ? Annie shook her head. That way lay bewilderment.

40

Annie replaced the sheets in the pink box, reached around Agatha for a gray folder with a gold-embossed title: *Detecting Wisdom.* Emma, of course, was pleased to share Marigold's dictum: *If you can imagine it, it can happen.* Much as she loathed Marigold, the point was well taken. Quickly, she reached for the sheets prepared by Henny. The introduction to *Classic Crime* was pure Henny, unassuming but potent: *A tribute to memorable mysteries.*

Annie scanned the list. She felt, as always, a tiny chill at *The Franchise Affair* by Josephine Tey. Henny's comment: The Franchise Affair *strips away the comfortable assumption that ordinary, decent people aren't vulnerable to accusations of evil.*

As Annie turned over the next sheet, Agatha rolled over on her back, clamped her paws on either side of Annie's right wrist. The cat's green eyes glittered.

"You've already eaten —"

The first tiny tip of claws pricked Annie's skin.

"My mistake." Quickly Annie began to sing, "Chow time for Agatha, chow time for Agatha."

In a smooth undulating move, Agatha loosed her grip, was on her paws, and

41

launched the five feet from the table to the top of the coffee bar.

Annie hurried. Not that her cat bullied her. Of course not. As she poured dry food into the bowl, the front bell rang.

Slow, uneven steps sounded in the central aisle. Ves Roundtree, right arm immobilized in a sling, limped toward her. Ves normally moved swiftly, reddish curls quivering with energy, bright green eyes jerking from face to face, narrow beringed fingers gesturing emphatically.

Annie hurried to pull out a chair. "What happened?"

Ves nodded her thanks as she eased carefully onto the chair, obviously uncomfortable. "A bad fall." She glanced at the table, saw the gray folder, pink manuscript-sized box, and slim sheaf of sheets. "You look busy."

Annie gave a careless wave of her hand. "Nothing that won't keep." Annie knew Ves Roundtree moderately well. Ves's store was at the far end of the boardwalk. She and Ves were active in the Island Council of Retail Merchants. Ves was the current treasurer, Annie the secretary. In good weather, they played tennis on Wednesday afternoons. Ves had a wicked forearm, the arm now cradled to her side. This wasn't the Ves she knew, a woman always in a hurry, bright, so bright she could seem metallic, impatient, never one to curb her tongue, yet a cool thinker on the court, playing each shot to her opponent's weakness.

"I'll get some coffee."

"No." Ves was abrupt in her usual fashion, focused on a goal, not one to waste time. Her reddish hair was drawn back in a bun that emphasized the jut of her cheekbones and the bony point of her chin. "You're sure you have time?"

Annie didn't glance at the clock. It was probably a quarter to eleven, and she'd hoped to call Max and meet for lunch at Parotti's Bar and Grill, but Ves looked upset and worried. Annie gave her a reassuring smile. "Nothing is urgent on a sea island in February. I'm awfully sorry you fell, but if you have to have an accident, now is the time. I don't imagine you have many customers this time of year either."

Ves's stare was hollow. "I didn't have an accident."

Annie sank into the chair opposite Ves. The blunt words hung between them.

Ves talked fast. "I get home about a quarter after five in the winter. There isn't much to do at closing time. I parked in the drive last Thursday. I didn't bother to put the car in the garage. I was in a hurry." A pause, a tight smile. "I guess I'm always in a hurry. Somebody was counting on that. When I get home" — she took a quick breath as if pushing back from a precipice — "I go upstairs to change. The house was just as it always was, a little cool, quiet enough that I could hear the tick of the grandfather clock in the entry hall. I go in the back door and walk to the front of the hall. The house is old and the stairs run right up straight without a turn. There's no carpet on the treads. The steps are wooden. Some of the treads have a kind of hollow in the center. I was almost to the top, maybe four steps, maybe five, and it was as if I stepped on ice. It happened fast. I stepped and my foot slipped. I fell backward." She took another breath. "I ski every January. I close the shop and go to Breckenridge. That's where we always went when I was a kid. I'm a good skier. That saved me. I know how to fall. I turned myself to the right and grabbed at the banister. My hand whacked against the rail, but I hung my fingers around a baluster, caught, held on. I landed on my hip. It hurt like hell. My wrist was bent, but I didn't let go. I huddled there for a few minutes. Finally I got up on one knee and then I was able to stand. I managed to get down the stairs. I grabbed my purse with my left hand, went out the door. I got to the car, drove to the emergency room. Broken collarbone. Dislocated shoulder. Sprained wrist." The clipped words stopped. Her voice was harsh. "I should have been dead."

A slip on slick stairs. A fall. A fortunate twist and grab. "You say it wasn't an accident." Annie's voice rose a little.

"I've had the same housekeeper for fifteen years. Gladys cleans every Monday. She runs a dust mop on the stairs. Those steps are never slick." Ves's lips twisted. "There was no slick step when I went downstairs Thursday morning. There was no one with a legitimate reason to be in my house that day. I didn't spill anything. How did the step turn into a skating rink? Someone made it happen. But there's something worse." Her eyes bored into Annie's. "Someone was waiting outside, watched me come out, get to the car. My appearance must have been a damn big disappointment." The last jerky words were grim.

"You saw someone?" Annie scarcely breathed the question.

Ves shivered. "I saw no one, but I'm sure someone was there, watched me struggle to the van, and, as soon as I left, hurried inside and cleaned up the step. I don't know what was used. Furniture polish maybe. Beeswax maybe. All I know is when I came home from the hospital, I climbed those stairs with a flashlight. I checked every step. The fourth one from the top was clean and dry, not a trace of dust. I ran my hand back and forth, didn't pick up anything. None of the steps" — her voice was heavy — "were slick." She stared at Annie. "I know what happened. I can't prove anything." Her tone was flat. "Something made the step slick. That's why I fell. I've gone up and down those steps for years. Sure, I wear high heels, I move fast. But I didn't trip. My foot came out from underneath me." She gazed at Annie in despair. "You think I'm nuts."

"Of course not." Annie tried to be reassuring. "Obviously something made you fall. Your shoes?"

A tight humorless smile. "I looked at them. I thought if there was something slick on the steps, there should be some residue on the sole of my shoe, but I had walked outside and across the yard. I went to the hospital. By the time I looked, the sole was normal. Then I thought maybe some of the polish, if that's what it was, came off the shoe onto lower steps. Funny thing is, they were really clean, too, but they were last dust mopped Monday. There wasn't a trace of dust on any step."

"Did you call Billy?"

Both she and Ves knew Billy Cameron, the chief of police. Billy was big, stolid, steady, careful, a good man, a good policeman. Ves was an island native. Billy knew her, knew Annie.

Ves turned both hands palms up. "What could he do? There's no evidence of a crime. I know something was put on the step that made me fall, but the step was clean when I came home from the hospital. Billy's a policeman. He needs facts. How do you suppose he'd feel if I gave him a list of names and said one of these people wants to kill me?"

Annie pictured pragmatic Billy Cameron. Billy believed in facts. Accusing people of attempted murder required facts. Ves had no facts. She had claims. A step was slick. Later the step wasn't slick. Annie didn't look at Ves's feet, but she knew the style of high heels — very high — that Ves preferred. Any man might be forgiven for thinking high heels could cause a fall. Ves spoke of a list. A list? Ves scarcely seemed like the kind of woman to be surrounded by mortal enemies. "A list?" Annie knew she sounded incredulous. A list of would-be assassins

47

plotting death for Ves seemed absurd.

Ves gave a weary head shake. "I shouldn't have come. I guess I wanted to tell someone and you're always reasonable and we've worked together a lot lately on plans for the boardwalk shops this summer. That doesn't mean you want to hear about my troubles." She pushed back her chair, lurched unevenly to her feet. "I shouldn't have bothered you. There isn't anything you can do." She turned away.

Annie started after her. "Ves, wait, you can tell me."

At the front door, Ves looked over her shoulder. "It's all right. I need to think it through. It isn't fair to involve you." She opened the door, gave Annie a twisted smile. "Never mind."

The door shut behind her with finality.

As he came through the front door, Max Darling gave a thumbs-up to Ben Parotti, gnome-sized owner of Parotti's Bar and Grill. Ben looked natty in a blue blazer, striped shirt, and khaki trousers. He'd worn overalls until he met Miss Jolene, owner of a mainland tea shop. Transported to Broward's Rock after their marriage, Miss Jolene added style and class to the rustic restaurant: vases with flowers on the tables and the addition of quiches and gelatin salads to the menu. Unchanged was the attached bait shop, coolers with squid and chicken necks, and sawdust floors.

"The missus coming?" Ben's gravelly voice was genial.

"On her way." Max felt inner happiness spreading across his face. Annie was on her way. He walked to their usual booth, sat where he could see the door. She'd swing through in just a moment, dusty blond hair, steady gray eyes, slim and lovely, kindness in her gaze. His Annie. That was still a miracle to him. They'd met in New York, seen each other across a crowded room. He'd known in that instant that she was his. He'd followed her from New York to Broward's Rock when she inherited a mystery bookstore. In her serious way, she'd decided they weren't well suited. He was rich. She was solidly middle class. He was relaxed. She was intense. He defined himself by what mattered to him, people in all their quirky variety, sun and sand and sea, laughter, moments of ease to remember good days and envision better days. Annie epitomized the work ethic, so many tasks to do, so little time in which to do them. He didn't have to work, felt no need to achieve, but to please her he opened Confidential Com-

49

missions and, truth to tell, he enjoyed helping people solve odd and unusual problems, the more odd and unusual the better. At the moment, he had no clients. Maybe Annie would agree to close Death on Demand during the February doldrums and they could take the train from Raleigh to New York, see some plays —

The door opened. Annie saw him, and her face came alight for a moment, followed by a worried frown. She rushed toward the booth.

He stood, reached out. "Hey, what's up?"

Words tumbled, not in her usual happy fashion, but in tight, tense spurts. "Ves Roundtree's in big trouble . . . a list . . . the more I think about it, the scarier it is . . . she told me not to worry. How can I not worry?"

He looked down. "A deep breath." His voice was soothing. "One. Two. Three." He touched her elbow, guided her into the booth, slid onto the opposite bench. "Start at the first."

"The morning started off so quietly. And then . . ."

He listened with an inward smile. Annie was incapable of shortening a report into a crisp summary. She didn't leave anything out, including the literary aspirations of the

Incredible Trio.

Ben stopped for their order. He didn't bother with a pad.

Annie paused in midsentence. "My usual."

Ben glanced at Max. "Grilled flounder, coleslaw?"

Max nodded.

As Ben turned away, Annie called out, "A double shot of Thousand Island on my fried oyster sandwich." She swung back to Max. "Anyway, I'd just taken a peek at the copies they left when Ves Roundtree limped in."

When their food arrived, Annie ate as she described Ves's appearance and her accident. She concluded, "Worst of all, Ves said she had a list of people who wanted her dead." Annie's gray eyes were stricken. "Ves is nice." Warm emphasis. "How could anyone want to kill her? The idea that she has a list of people who want her dead is awful. Imagine how you'd feel" — her gray eyes were huge — "if you thought people wanted to kill you." She put down her sandwich.

This was also Pure Annie. Whatever happened, she could put herself in another's spot and understand their sadness or anger or, in this case, terror. He tried to picture lurking assassins, had no success. His world was always sunny-side up.

Max reached across the table, placed his hand over hers, realized she was shaking. "You believe her."

Annie gazed at him straight, spoke slowly. "She doesn't make things up. She doesn't exaggerate. She doesn't read fiction." A slight tone of astonishment. "She reads about the Tang dynasty and monetary policy and how crows make tools."

Max looked into gray eyes filled with uncertainty and anxiety and understood. In the past she'd often tried to help friends and sometimes she'd been foolhardy, and once she disappeared. The last had shaken him, rocked his world. He'd demanded that she promise never again to become involved in other people's problems. It was a promise she'd tried to keep, hadn't kept. He'd realized she wouldn't be Annie if she turned away from someone in need.

His Annie. Kind, brave, generous. Those steady gray eyes implored him. "I guess," he said gently, "you better go see Ves, find out what's going on."

Annie drove straight to the boardwalk, hurried to Trinkets 'n Treasures, Ves's shop. The front window was dark. A Closed sign hung a little askew on the knobby arm of a wooden chair that might once have been in a monk's spare cell. Ves likely hadn't opened today because she was uncomfortable from her injuries.

Back in her Thunderbird, Annie drove a little too fast, hoping no wandering deer chose this lousy afternoon to cross a road in front of her. It took only five minutes to reach Sunshine Lane and turn into a narrow drive shadowy beneath tree limbs that interlocked. As she came around the last curve, she was relieved to see lights shining on the lower floor of Ves's house. Huge live oaks rose in the front yard. On a misty overcast February day, the gray Spanish moss wavering in the breeze added a melancholy, slightly sinister aura.

The two-story white frame house had upper and lower piazzas with three Ionic columns on either side of the short flight of front steps. Annie pulled up in the single drive and parked behind Ves's van. Out of the car, she walked swiftly on an oyster shell path to the front of the house and climbed the steps. She knocked on the front door.

A clank from inside. A chain being unloosed?

The door eased open, then was pulled wide. "Annie." Ves's tone was surprised, uncertain.

Annie was blunt. "You left because you

thought I didn't believe you. I believe you."

Ves's lips quirked in a lopsided grin. "I live on Sunshine Lane, but you're the first ray of sunshine I've seen today. Come in."

Annie stepped into a hallway with a gleaming heart pine floor. Stairs rose old and straight ahead of her. The hallway held a marble-topped side table. Mail lay in a bronze tray. A mahogany grandfather clock sat against the back wall. To the right was a drawing room with a shabby Queen Anne sofa, two Chippendale side chairs, a fireplace with an Adam mantel. To the left was a small dining room with a long table and a glass-door cabinet filled with china.

The door closed. Ves's green eyes might have held a trace of tears. "Thank you for coming. My brother would have said you're a good Joe. Funny expression, isn't it? But it meant a lot to him. And to me. A good Joe." She stood by the door, gave a quick shake of her head, like a terrier coming out of a pond. "What changed your mind?"

Annie kept her gaze steady. "I've been looking over a friend's collection of mystery quotes: *Unlikely melodrama is the likeliest to happen of anything in the world.* That's why I'm here."

Ves's look was peculiar, probably as peculiar as Jerry North's when his ditzy wife,

Pam, made the observation in *Death Has a Small Voice* by Frances and Richard Lockridge.

Annie flashed a grin. "I can do lots of quotes. Not just mysteries. *A trouble shared is a trouble halved.*"

Ves's face was transformed, a mixture of delight and amazement. *"Quod in communi, est dimidium malum."* She reached out a thin hand, gripped Annie's elbow. "This calls for a celebration." Talking fast though still moving with a jerky pained gait, she guided Annie down the hallway. "Our dad taught Latin at the high school. Did you know Ves is short for Vesta? She was the goddess in the temple who was keeper of the flame. I shortened it to Ves before I was five, and trust me I've avoided flames ever since. My brother arrived with a mop of red hair and that's why he was named Rufus, 'red haired' in Latin. Dad was irrepressible. Rufus and I could spout Latin quotes like some kids do baseball statistics. *Alis volat propriis.* One of my favorites. *She flies with her own wings.*" She pushed through a swinging door into a bright kitchen, waved Annie to a seat at a maple table in a bay window overlooking the garden. "I have coffee, but how about some egg nog, my own recipe, left over from the Death's Head Feast." At Annie's startled look, she gave a bark of laughter. "More about that anon, as a good Latin scholar would say. I'll bring egg nog with coffee for a chaser."

Ves brought cut glass glasses filled with egg nog and two blue coffee mugs. Annie picked up a crystal glass with golden contents, took a taste. Egg nog could be too sweet, too heavy. This was perfection, and Annie was sure the nutmeg was fresh.

Ves eased into the opposite chair. She, too, took a deep swallow of egg nog. "When in doubt, drink egg nog, and you'll know life is good. That's a quote, too, but nobody famous. My mom was convinced homemade food and drink made any burden lighter." She sipped the egg nog, gazed at Annie. "I'd like to halve my trouble. And" — her face clouded — "I'll feel better if someone else knows what I'm thinking. Just in case." The final sentence was somber. She took a deep breath. "I mentioned Rufus, my brother. A good man. A very good and kind man. After college he went to New York. He was a trader." Her voice was vague. "I don't know what he did exactly, but he made a lot of money. He married fairly late, almost forty. He was quite a bit older than I. It's odd how nice men have a tendency to marry bitches. Gretchen was and is a class A bitch.

Gorgeous if you like packaged blondes, always coiffed, sleek as a rat's fur, in my view, never wearing just a dress, always a designer whatever that might as well flaunt a price tag. A tinkling laugh that might have been cute when she was five. She produced an heir, but Curt is lazy on his ass." She gave Annie a quick smile. "I'm telling you my family history because everything's tied up with Rufus. He moved back to the island after he retired."

Annie nodded. She remembered Rufus Roundtree, a big man with a round face, a thatch of red hair salted with white, a booming voice, and a personality that overwhelmed a room. He'd plunged into everything on the island and been generous with donations to the library, the island rec center, the historical society, the art league, and the community charity drive.

"Rufus had a wonderful time. I'm glad about that. He invited me to live with him in his beach mansion, but I've lived in the family house forever. It's home. I don't have a lust for luxury. Anyway, it was grand having him on the island. He died last year."

Annie remembered the headline in the *Gazette:* ISLAND PHILANTHROPIST FELLED BY HEART ATTACK.

"I wasn't surprised that he made me the

life income beneficiary of his estate. I thought it was fair enough that I would enjoy the income and that at my death the estate would be divided equally among six people he chose. It was his money. He earned it. I've enjoyed not having to worry about money for the first time in my life. I know he would be pleased to know — and" — her lips quirked — "maybe he does know — how much pleasure he's given me. I went to Cairo last month and brought back tons of wonderful curios from the Khan el-Khalili bazaar." Her eyes gleamed. "Chess boards with mother-of-pearl inlays, bedouin jewelry, brass hanging lamps . . ." She trailed off. "But" — her voice was ragged — "if he knows how much I've enjoyed the money, he knows what's happening now. I'd hate for him to know that his generosity put me in danger." A somber look. "Last week was the anniversary of Rufus's death. I thought it would be nice to invite the beneficiaries-to-be for a dinner remembering him. I intended to give them an accounting of the estate. Martin Ford at the bank is the trustee — he sends me quarterly updates. He and I have taken good care of the assets. I've had a few extravagances, but the estate is larger than when Rufus died. I took the trip to Cairo, bought a new car and a new furnace for the house, but the estate's grown by almost two hundred thousand. If the remaindermen, as they are called in cold legalese, inherited today, each would receive about three million dollars. There are six of them: Katherine Farley, Bob Farley, Jane Wilson, Curt Roundtree, Adam Nash, and Fred Butler." Ves's face looked thinner, narrower. Her fingers fastened on the coffee mug, but she didn't lift it. "They all came to dinner, plus Gretchen, Rufus's ex, and Jane Wilson's boyfriend. I think Gretchen was especially frosted that Curt didn't inherit immediately and would have to wait for Ves to die. Six million for a couple of artists, no cut for his son. But Gretchen came to the dinner. It's a dinner I'll always remember as the Death's Head Feast. Before that gala evening, most of the beneficiaries had contacted me, asked for money. The exceptions were Bob Farley and Fred Butler. Probably Bob knew Katherine had her hand out. Anyway, I've liked Fred better than the others ever since. I turned them all down. I was bland, said I was honoring Rufus's wish that I enjoy the estate now, and they would receive their portion on my death." Ves's chin jutted. "The night of the dinner, we had those stiff exchanges, you know the kind. *Are you watching* Down-ton Abbey? *What do you think about the plan for a new high school? Which girl-on-a-train book did you read? Have you priced lobster lately?* I looked around at each one of them." Abruptly, she pushed back her chair, came to her feet. "Let's go to the dining room. I want to show you."

3

Ves flicked the switch. The crystal drops of the chandelier glittered. Gray walls emphasized the ruddy richness of the mahogany table and the mauve drapes. Three Chinese plates in brass holders adorned a Hepplewhite sideboard. Above the fireplace hung an oil portrait of Rufus Roundtree, his large face genial.

Ves stood by the end chair. A silver tea urn stood on the dining room table. "There were so many of us, I put in the center leaf. I sat here with three on one side, four on the other." She touched the back of the end chair nearest the kitchen door. "Fred Butler was at the other end. You know Fred —"

Annie did. He was a cashier at the bank and a steady customer at Death on Demand. Annie found customer reading choices fascinating. Fred was an inveterate reader of thrillers with swashbuckling heroes, the more derring-do the better.

"— a dumpy little guy, wispy gray hair that stands up in tufts around his face. He wears bifocals and peers at you over the rims. Rufus met him at Parotti's. A bunch of mostly older men play dominoes at a round table in the bait section." Her nose wrinkled. "Trust men not to mind a stink. I said that to Rufus once and he laughed and insisted a fisherman likes the smell of live shrimp or mullet better than any whiff of cologne. Rufus got a kick out of Fred, said he could surprise you when you got him talking, that his ideas might be crackpot but they put a zing in his life. Fred said almost nothing at the dinner. No repartee from Fred. Adam took up the slack, a torrent of words. He was trying to exude charm. It was wasted effort on me, I can assure you. Put Adam in a brown suit on a platform with a bottle of snake oil and he'd be right at home — senatorial good looks, a plastic face usually wreathed in a smile, a voice so deep and warm you feel like you've pulled on a cashmere coat. Adam spent most of the dinner one-upping Bob Farley with travel tales.

"Bob was next." Her face was suddenly rueful. "Poor devil. They never mention his accident, but you have to wonder why anybody wants to hang glide. Anyway, he did. Ka-boom. Now he can barely manage to walk and his painting arm is useless. He was a superb artist. I have several of his Low Country paintings at the shop. One I especially love, a sunny summer day and an alligator on the bank, but the alligator's eyes are open and he's looking at a man standing by the lagoon." She gave a slight shiver. "Heat. Menace. Power. Danger. I look at the painting and know in an instant the alligator will attack, take the man over the edge and into the water. I hope" — her voice was thoughtful — "that having been a great painter will see him through.

"Katherine Farley was to my left. She's one of those classic beauties, sleek black hair, patrician features, midnight eyes, though she looked haggard, not her usual gorgeous self. She wore a red-and-gold lamé dress. She kept up a pleasant stream of conversation, travel, the new book by Joyce Carol Oates, her recipe for clam chowder, the sketch she'd just finished of a loggerhead turtle in the moonlight just past the high tide line sweeping the sand with a flipper to prepare a nest for her eggs. But" — Ves sounded hollow — "all the while it was as if she and I were pantomimes in a shadowy background. Her attention was focused on her husband. Yet when she

63

turned to him, she spoke casually. I wondered if I was the only person at the table aware of that tension."

For Annie, the dining room was slowly filling with guests, tuft-haired Fred Butler, smooth-talking Adam Nash, crippled Bob Farley, beautiful and passionate Katherine Farley.

Ves looked at the empty place to the right. "If I were doing that honored-guest kind of thing, I should have put my nephew to my right, but Curt drives me nuts because all he does is play. I like people who work whether they have to or not. Rufus tried to fix it where he had to shape up, but Curt sponges off his rich buddies. Gretchen, my ex-sister-in-law, isn't an heir. I called her to ask how to get in touch with Curt, and it would have been rude not to include her. Anyway, I put Tim Holt to my right. I like his get-up-and-go." A smile. "He's one handsome guy. Big, curly brown hair, a lifeguard in the summer. I'm not sure what he's doing now, general handyman work. Ben Parotti uses him for some repairs."

Ben Parotti owned not only Parotti's Bar and Grill and the *Miss Jolene,* the ferry that plied between the island and the mainland, he was involved in several businesses and owned a great deal of property.

"Tim's ambitious. I heard all about the shopping center he wants to build near the ferry landing on the mainland, how the property was available, how he was looking for backers, how much the construction would cost, the possibility of anchoring with a Winn-Dixie, and on and on and on. I already knew about it. Jane came to see me at the shop and finally — she was very diffident, I'm sure he would have been disappointed — she said she wondered if perhaps I might consider investing in a wonderful construction site. I heard her out and gave her my standard reply to all the prospective heirs: no." Ves's chin looked very pointed. "Rufus gave the money to me to enjoy. I intend to do so. But Jane's a nice girl. Her mother was Rufus's secretary and she died of cancer. I remember Jane being at Rufus's big house with her mom during the summers, a little girl with pigtails. Now she's grown up and grown up very nicely, pretty brown hair, a sweet face, beautifully dressed. An Escada blue print sheath dress with cap sleeves. Gorgeous. Nothing she could afford. She works at a secondhand store up the street from Parotti's, and that was someone's discard. Luckily for Jane most rich women are a perfect size eight, so she can enjoy finery as long as she doesn't mind secondhand. She didn't have much to say at dinner. Tim was talking as fast as he could to me. Curt was on her left. He ignored her and put himself out to be nice to me. Gretchen was on her best behavior, favoring me with warm smiles and approving nods when I talked to Curt.

"Gretchen" — Ves's tone was considering — "was her usual vision of perfection. Blond hair gleaming and a face that really didn't look much past thirty. She must spend a fortune on cosmetics. She wore a stunning short-sleeved black lace minidress. She even tried to be charming to Fred. He was on her left at the end of table, but he perched on his chair and stared at her like an urchin meeting high society. She valiantly kept trying." There was grudging appreciation in her tone. "Very unlike her usual disdain for peasants. Believe me, I saw that in operation when she was married to Rufus. I was one of the peasants then."

Annie pictured Ves at one end, fish-out-of-water Fred at the other, Jane's hunk boyfriend Tim, quiet accommodating Jane, playboy Curt, and sleek Gretchen on one side, vivid Katherine, talkative Bob, and pompous Adam on the other.

"That's the lot. I don't hire a server when I have people for dinner. I cleared the plates.

Jane offered to help. As I said, she's a nice girl. I thanked her but said no. I took the dishes out to the kitchen, stacked them in the sink, got the dessert. When I pushed through the swinging door, everyone stopped talking. Their heads turned and they looked at me. I felt like stone. I couldn't move. Time stopped. I started shivering." Ves's green eyes were enormous with a curious emptiness. "My mother always said when out of nowhere you suddenly feel scared, can't breathe, sense darkness and danger, when you feel like that, someone is walking on your grave. That's what happened to me when I came in the dining room with the tray that night. Someone was looking at me and seeing me dead, wanting me dead. Walking on my grave."

". . . and Ves stood in her dining room and saw them looking at her." Fire crackled in the grate. Annie stood in front of the fireplace, but the warmth didn't dispel her inner chill, the same chill she felt that afternoon when she'd seen doom in Ves's eyes. She took a breath, knew her voice was uneven, choked. "Ves said, 'Someone was looking at me and seeing me dead, wanting me dead. Walking on my grave.' "

Max looked at her with concern in his

dark blue eyes. Her gaze moved to their guests. Each face reflected an intensity and, more, resolution. Henny Brawley, Laurel Roethke, and Emma Clyde excelled in discovering truth among lies. All three were immersed in island society with knowledge of an astonishing range of personalities from the aristocratic to the disreputable.

Max, relaxed in a plaid flannel shirt and brown corduroy trousers, lounged comfortably in his red leather chair, plump white Dorothy L contentedly asleep in his lap. He stroked her smooth fur. Handsome Max, strong, powerful, gorgeously male. His dark blue eyes said, *Don't be scared, don't worry, I'm here, I'll always be here.*

Henny projected competence, intelligence, wisdom. Silver-streaked dark hair framed a narrow, intent face. She was elegant in a gray turtleneck, cream suede jacket, gray slacks, and ankle-high boots.

Laurel Darling Roethke, golden hair in shining ringlets, lake blue eyes slightly dreamy, had a faraway look of introspection, as if she summoned an inner muse for consultation.

Emma Clyde's primrose blue eyes glowed. She sat with broad stubby hands planted on her knees. "I like it. I like it!" So might the Sphinx appear if garbed in a red velvet caftan: huge, imposing, solid.

Four faces turned toward Emma. Annie frowned. Max's blond brows rose in surprise. Henny's gaze was questioning. Laurel exuded placid understanding.

Emma was not without perception. There might have been a tiny flush in her heavy cheeks. "Not to say I am wishing Ves ill. Certainly not. But don't you see? How often can murder be prevented?" Her spiky hair, a subdued russet tonight, seemed to quiver with eagerness.

Laurel cooed, "Quintessential Emma. Right to the point. A rapier to the heart." A gentle smile for Annie. "Whether you realize it or not" — was there just a hint of a patronizing tone? — "you've come to us to winnow out a Prospective Murderer. That is the only result that will assure Ves's safety." Laurel's smile was confident. "I have no doubt we shall prevail. Now, we have six heirs —"

Max interrupted. "They are actually contingent remaindermen beneficiaries."

Emma was brusque. "They get the money. If they are alive when Ves dies. If one of them pops off before Ves, the share is divided among the survivors. We can call them heirs no matter what the proper term is."

Laurel gave her son a consoling glance. "So well meant, my dear, so exquisitely legal, but let's keep this simple. Six people will benefit if Ves dies. Gretchen Roundtree and Jane's young man could also profit because of their association with the heirs. Now" — a pause to be sure everyone was attentive — "we know these facts. Each heir except Fred Butler and Bob Farley has asked for money. Ves sees no reason to disburse any sums in advance. One of those who will inherit decided to kill Ves. Last Thursday shortly before five P.M. Prospective Murderer, hereinafter known as PM, entered Ves's house in some fashion" — a careless wave of pink-tipped fingers — "a skeleton key, an unlocked window. Old houses pose no obstacle. PM greased a step on the staircase, exited, waited, observed her arrival, likely heard her cry out, but, and this is a most interesting and curious fact, PM didn't rush to the house immediately to clean the step. PM waited. In a few minutes an injured Ves comes outside, limps to her car. When she was gone, PM entered the house, removed the slick substance from the stairs, departed. What does this behavior tell us?"

Henny's dark eyes gleamed. "PM is agile.

We can delete Bob Farley from our suspect list."

Emma was brusque. "Not so fast. Bob gets around on a cane. He has a handicapped-equipped car. Movement takes him longer, but he could have managed." She nodded emphatically, shaggy short cut hair quivering.

Max's admiring nod at his mother was, in Annie's estimation, a trifle overdone.

Laurel's dreamy gaze settled on Annie. "What else can we surmise?"

Annie said uncertainly, "Uh, PM's pretty smart." Annie knew she sounded lame, and Max didn't have to look at her so kindly.

Henny jumped right in. "Annie's right. PM doesn't jump to conclusions."

"Thinks before acting," Emma added.

Laurel was encouraging. "And?" She turned her hands over in a graceful gesture encouraging class participation.

Max punched his right fist into his left palm. "Ves's death has to be an accident." He spoke rapidly. "If Ves is found dead and it's murder, the police immediately want to know cui bono."

Laurel clapped in pretty appreciation of her son's acumen.

With an effort of will born of long prac-tice, Annie maintained an agreeable expression. But honestly, sometimes Max's and Laurel's elevated opinions of each other were a little hard to tolerate.

Emma, never enamored of anyone else's cleverness — after all, she was the clever one — kept to the point. "PM came equipped to get into the house with a substance, possibly furniture polish or floor wax, to smear on an upper step, and cleaning equipment to remove all traces. Likely had a backpack, wore gloves."

Annie tried not to sound grudging. "It does appear that the intruder —"

"PM," Laurel said pleasantly, but firmly.

Annie would have engaged in a verbal joust with Laurel but it would save time to acquiesce. "PM intends for Ves's death to appear accidental."

Laurel nodded approvingly. "And that" — her husky voice was full of cheer — "means we do not have to worry about Ves being knifed or shot. Accidents take time and effort to create. Fortunately, we have no cliffs."

Annie almost mentioned the reddish unstable headland bluffs buffeted by swirling currents, but she understood Laurel's point. The island had no handy canyons or gorges or narrow mountain trails, and Ves would surely not stroll near water's edge alone with any of her recent dinner guests.

Emma's square face folded in a frown. "True enough. Ves may be quite safe, since she survived the fall."

Annie hoped she didn't detect a shade of disappointment in Emma's voice.

Henny's glance at Emma was slightly chiding. "I wish we could be confident no more attempts will be made." Her intelligent face was grave. "We can't make that assumption. But, as Laurel pointed out, accidents require thought, planning, the right particular moment. Failed brakes in a car. Perhaps a shove over the railing of the *Miss Jolene.* I believe Ves is one of the islanders who always gets out of her car and climbs to the upper deck for the crossing. Annie can suggest she not do that until we discover the identity of her attacker."

Annie was cautiously hopeful. "You say that as if you think there is a way to figure out who waxed the step." Annie backed closer to the fireplace, seeking its heat to ward away the cold image of a watcher in the shadows near Ves's backyard.

Henny nodded in agreement. "We know the Prospective Murderer was physically present at Ves's house at approximately five P.M. last Thursday. Where were Katherine and Bob Farley, Jane Wilson and Tim Holt,

Curt Roundtree, Gretchen Roundtree, Adam Nash, and Fred Butler at that time? We will find out."

Emma was gruff since she hadn't made the proposal. "Better to have Max nose around their finances, see who needs money now, ASAP. Then we can focus on the likeliest suspect."

Laurel's smile was kindly. "Ranking the depth of monetary desperation can be a challenge. I address that in my collection of *Merry Musings: Sufficiency for one is deprivation for another.*" A benign smile. "Or, even more apropos: *Happiness comes from giving, not taking.* However, Emma's point is well taken. I'm sure Max will see what he can discover about their bank accounts and current financial statuses."

Max's expression was wry. "Easier said than done."

Emma's shoulders squared. "Sounds like shilly-shallying to me. I suggest we lay our cards on the table." A vigorous nod.

Laurel's eyelashes fluttered.

Annie watched in fascination as Laurel murmured, not quite loud enough for Emma to hear, what was clearly another quote from *Merry Musings: Indulge a friend's weakness for trite pronouncements.*

"And," Emma continued forcefully, "shoot

a warning shot across the bow."

Laurel winced.

Emma bowled ahead. "Just like Inspector Houlihan says to Marigold in the new book: *Don't hesitate to be tough.* It's one of my favorites from *Detecting Wisdom.*"

Henny smiled serenely at Emma, but her voice was firm. "A careful perusal of Earl Derr Biggers's *The House Without a Key* yields this observation from Charlie Chan: 'I have many times been witness when the impossible roused itself and occurred.' Our aim is to discover the whereabouts of Ves's guests at the time the step was doctored without their realizing that five P.M. Thursday is important. Let's move with the silence and stealth of a panther so we don't alert our prey that we are in pursuit. There is always time to be tough" — an admiring nod at Emma — "but circumspection will better serve us when we talk to Ves's dinner guests."

4

Laurel sat with a partially open window in her green convertible and observed Tim Holt loading boxes in the back of a black pickup truck. The truck wasn't new but it was clean and well kept. Quite an attractive young man with curly brown hair and strong features. He moved with easy grace. She enjoyed young men, so virile, so . . . She must focus on her task. She smoothed back a curl, opened her oversized calico catchall bag, lifted out a legal pad. She opened it to the first sheet and admired the schedule she had produced quickly and efficiently last night. Dear Max had perhaps been too generous in his praise. She made no claim to brilliance, except perhaps in the sheen of her golden curls. She had never succumbed to an overinflated view of herself. That would never do. After all, when one was fortunate enough to be beautiful, graceful, and perceptive, tributes naturally flowed.

She glanced at her darling serpentine watch, a gold-and-silver band coiled around her forearm from a tail embedded with tiny emeralds to an almond-shaped timepiece, a gift from a young man in Dallas. Texans topped her list of manly men. It was one minute to nine. The plan was as choreographed as a Broadway musical. She, Henny, Emma, Max, and Annie would approach Ves's dinner guests on a precise schedule to be sure their quarries had no opportunity to collaborate on a version of last Thursday afternoon.

Laurel stepped out of her Porsche, welcomed the breeze that fluttered her hair and she knew becomingly molded her pale blue dress against her. She didn't bother to lock the car. She turned to a fresh sheet in her pad, perched the pad against her left arm, and strolled unhurriedly to the recently waxed truck. She noted the painted sign on the driver's door: HOLT ODD JOBS.

A thud as he slid a crate into the bed of the pickup. Despite the chilly temperature, Tim Holt wore a short-sleeved tee. His jeans hung low on his hips and his sneakers were well worn.

Laurel admired the ripple of muscle in his near arm. Very nice. "Tim Holt?"

He turned and looked at her as men usually did. Men were so predictable. He stood a little straighter, brushed a smudge of dust from one arm. "I'm Tim Holt." His voice was low, the kind of voice a man might use in a bar when he turns to a woman sitting alone next to him, an attractive woman who might be willing to play.

Laurel beamed at him and, regretfully, made her tone a trifle arch and definitely not beguiling. "I've been asking around." She gestured vaguely behind her, perhaps implying she'd dropped into some of the downtown shops. "I'm looking for young people for a survey. I'm L. D. Roethke from Consumer Characteristics Commission. I have a few questions and, of course, CCC offers remuneration for your time. Fifty dollars. I do hope you can help us out today."

As she'd expected, his brown eyes glinted at the fifty-dollar offer. "I've got a few minutes. What do you want to know?"

Laurel delved into her bag, pulled out a pen and a crisp fifty-dollar bill. She pinned the bill against the pad with a thumb, held the pen with her other hand. She spoke in a rush, a canvasser with a canned presentation. "A little bit about CCC first. We are seeking to determine buying habits of consumers ages eighteen to thirty with an emphasis on late-afternoon activities. Our specific time frame is from four to six P.M. To avoid the distractions of the incipient weekend, which can easily distort buying patterns, we focus on Thursdays. Now" — she gave him an encouraging look — "please tell me where you were at four P.M. this past Thursday."

He leaned against the back fender. "Thursday." His face crinkled as he concentrated. "Let's see. I needed a battery for my cell phone . . . No, wait, that was Wednesday. Thursday . . . I picked up a riding mower at the inn, took it over to Haney's Repair. Shot the breeze with Big Al in the back shop. That was my last job. I dropped by the fish market at Parotti's around five, got a pound of shrimp, took it over to my girlfriend's house."

"I guess she was glad to see you with something for dinner."

"Yeah. We fixed gumbo."

Laurel leaned nearer as he talked, her eyes widening. "I think I know why you look so familiar. Was it Friday? No. Before that. Oh, Thursday, it must have been Thursday. Where was I?" She pulled out a small notebook, riffled through several pages, looked up in satisfaction. "Sunshine Lane, of course. Did I see you around five o'clock?"

He grinned. "I wasn't anywhere near Sunshine Lane. Jane lives on Bluefish Road close to the church."

At nine A.M. Annie glanced in the display window of You Want It, We Have It. Floor spots angled up to illuminate a tan-and-gold sweater dress draped over a shabby rattan chair, a bright pink suit spread on a worn blue sofa, a man's tweed coat with leather elbow patches dangling from a slightly listing coat tree, and a cocktail dress with spangles pinned to a makeshift clothesline. The effect was cheerful and inviting, the displayed items freshly cleaned and pressed, the window clear and sparkling, the flooring obviously old but gleaming with a high polish. Annie felt a pang. How long had it been since she mopped the flooring of the Death on Demand display window?

She noted the store hours as she opened the door: 9 to 5 winter hours. A bell jangled as she stepped inside. Her nose wrinkled at a combination of potpourri, furniture polish, and dust, not casual house dust but dust embedded in old books, rugs, and cushions.

The store was long and narrow, racks of clothing interspersed with wooden chairs, side tables, sofas, and filled bookcases. A rattle of steps, and a young woman hurried forward. Honey brown hair framed a gentle face with a high forehead, slender nose, generous mouth, and soft chin. A Donna Karan striped pullover sweater was flattering to her willowy figure. Gray wool trousers bunched stylishly over low silver leather boots. The outfit new might have cost around $1,000. Annie wondered what the markdown was in the store.

Big blue eyes were quick, understanding Annie's appreciative glance. "I'm a walking ad for the store. These clothes came in a couple of weeks ago and were priced at twelve dollars each for the top, slacks, and boots. And" — a happy gurgle as she came nearer — "I get an employee discount. If you're interested in clothes, we have some real prizes." She carried a can of furniture polish in one hand, a cloth in the other. "Feel free to browse. Clothing is sorted by size, casual wear in the front, dressier as you go to the back." She skidded to a stop in front of Annie, looked at her with sudden recognition and perhaps a dash of surprise. If she recognized Annie, she knew well enough that Annie had no need to shop for fine clothes at a used store. "Oh, hi. Are you here to check out the books? We have all kinds. Not like your store, of course." A shy smile. "I'm Jane Wilson. My mom loved mysteries, especially old ones. I used to look for her favorites in your used books. They made her happy."

Annie nodded quickly. "I remember you." Jane's face had been thinner, graver when she used to shop, buying books for a woman who had not long to read. Annie glanced at a nearby bookcase, squinted. Was that an early edition of *The Album* by Mary Roberts Rinehart? She resolutely returned her gaze to the shop assistant. "I wish I were book hunting today. Instead, I'm here for the Island Council of Retail Merchants. We're asking around about store hours, thinking we might come to an agreement for all the shops to close at the same time in the winter. I know you close at five, but I'd like to get your input. We decided to focus on Thursdays. We're asking everyone to give us an estimate of their traffic between four and six." Annie pulled a note card and pen from her purse. "How many customers did you have last Thursday from four o'clock until you closed?"

Jane gestured toward the back of the store. "Come sit down."

As they walked down the center aisle, Annie felt a little ashamed at the subterfuge. Jane Wilson had no reason to suspect this visit was anything other than what it seemed to be, and she was responding quite openly. Would she be this relaxed if she had anything to hide about last Thursday afternoon?

Annie knew the answer. If Jane had crept across Ves's backyard with furniture polish in her hand and murder in her heart, she would have no difficulty presenting an innocent face to the world.

At the end of the corridor, Jane gestured to a blue easy chair for Annie. She put the can of polish and the dustcloth on a table, settled in an upright wooden chair. She crossed one leg over the other, hooked her hands around her knee. "Four to six? Usually it's quiet as a graveyard here from four to five when I close."

"You closed at five Thursday?"

"I stayed a little later. I didn't get away until about ten to six."

There must have been a late customer. This nice girl would have an alibi. Annie was glad. She smiled. "I know how it is. Someone comes in at closing time and they are looking for something and you don't say a word about turning off the lights."

Jane smiled in return. "That happens. But this past Thursday I ducked out in the afternoon. I put up the Back Soon sign. I'm the only one here, but my boss told me at

83

the start if I need to do something, go ahead and just stay open a little later to make up the time. She doesn't live on the island anymore. She moved to Montana. She's trying to sell the store now." Jane looked around. "I like it here. I like seeing the clothes come in. She buys them all over the place. I got a box from Pasadena last week. It's been fun and there's lots of downtime." She gestured at a laptop lying on the table. "I'm taking some classes online until I save enough to go back to school. But Thursday I went to the hospital to visit a friend — well, I think of her as a friend even though she's lots older, but she was so sweet to my mom when she was sick. She came and stayed through some bad days. She doesn't have any family, and I could tell she was kind of blue. She's very nice but very serious."

Annie knew at once. "Pamela Potts?" Annie had been by to see Pamela at the hospital as well. Knee replacement. Pamela, blond, placid, immensely serious, was always the first to bring a casserole or offer to help when trouble struck.

Jane nodded eagerly. "Isn't she swell? I guess most everyone on the island knows Pamela. Anyway I was there longer than I intended so that's why I stayed open late

Thursday."

"Did you have any shoppers?"

Jane shook her head. "Nobody came in. I sorted through that box of clothes from Pasadena. I found a gorgeous tulle skirt that needed mending. I wish I had somewhere to wear it. Someone will love it now."

"So you were late getting home."

Jane shrugged. "I got home a little after six."

Henny Brawley followed Emma Clyde's new Rolls-Royce as it turned onto Bayberry Lane, a narrow rutted sandy road. She was perhaps twenty yards behind the crimson Rolls-Royce. Emma's previous Rolls had been bronze. Henny grinned at the contrast between Emma's majestic conveyance and her own shabby old black Dodge. Henny wasn't envious. She enjoyed outings in Emma's chariot, but she knew everything was fleeting. Each moment had a brief life and was gone, never to return. Prized moments were never about riches, not jewels nor silks, not fine cars nor mansions, not stacks of cash nor stock certificates. Prized moments were a look of love, a gentle touch, the sight of a cat's grace, sunlight slanting through a stained glass window. Emma enjoyed her car, but it was a plaything.

Emma's prized moments were the pleasure of crafting a sentence, the joy of creating an illusion that seemed real to her readers. Henny immediately thought of Maureen Summerhayes speaking in *Mrs. McGinty's Dead:* "I never think it matters much *what* one eats . . . or what one wears . . . or what one does. I don't think *things* matter — not really." Maureen Summerhayes would have understood Emma Clyde.

The Rolls glided to a stop in front of a two-story wooden building and parked next to Katherine Farley's gray Lexus. A sign hung above the steps to the piazza: FARLEY STUDIO AND GALLERY.

Henny drove another hundred yards around a grove of pines to a cottage on pilings very similar to her home on a neighboring marsh. She parked on a sandy drive behind a Honda van with a lift on the back for a wheelchair. She noted a similar lift at the top of the steps.

As she shut the door of her Dodge, Henny looked out at the winter-pale stubble of spartina grass, took a deep breath of the familiar pungent marsh odor. She never tired of the marsh, enjoying the greening grasses in spring, steaming mud flats in summer, migrating birds overhead in autumn, raccoons fishing for clams in winter.

She climbed the stairs to the landing and knocked on a weathered front door.

"Come in." Bob's voice was muffled.

Henny reached for the knob, turned. The door swung in and she stepped inside.

Bob Farley was seated in his wheelchair by the windows overlooking the marsh. He looked at her and there was politeness, but no warmth in his face. He finally managed a cursory smile and seemed to rouse himself. "I haven't seen you in a while. Come in."

Henny had often visited the studio when Bob and Katherine held receptions to display their latest work, his oil paintings of marshes, ocean, beaches, and Low Country wildlife from foraging raccoons to attacking owls, and Katherine's clever pen-and-ink sketches of islanders at work or play. Henny especially treasured two sketches of the *Miss Jolene.* In one, holidayers arrived on the ferry, pale faces eager. In the second, vacationers departed, faces sunburned, noses splotched with zinc oxide, looking back across the water as if trying to hold on to lazy days and wet feet in warm sudsy water and frosty bottles of beer and no thought for tomorrow.

Henny settled on a rattan chair and smiled at Bob, keeping her expression bright and open with no hint of how painful it was to see the gauntness of his face and the immobile arm that had once created such beauty. She hurried to speak. "It's been much too long. Ves Roundtree told me about the safari you're planning to Kenya." She opened her purse, drew out a manila envelope, handed it to Bob. "I wanted to bring you the guidebook from the trip I made last year to Samburu. I hope you can include that reserve in your itinerary. Absolutely rugged country, but I saw some amazing animals, a herd of Grévy's zebra and more than a dozen Somali ostrich." She chattered on. "Our guide was a Cornell graduate, and he told us the status of endangered animals and especially the need to protect elephants."

Bob pulled out a guidebook, glanced down, made no effort to open it. "A safari. Yes. We've talked about that." His voice was dull. "You're very kind to think of us. I'll show Katherine." The guidebook rested in his lap.

Henny felt as if she pushed against a gate that wouldn't open. "I've been carrying it around ever since last Thursday. I dropped by about five, but you weren't here and Katherine's car was gone, too, so" — a cheerful smile — "I called to be sure you'd be here this morning. I waited a little while Thursday but you didn't come home. What took you out on such a foggy afternoon?"

Bob Farley stared out at the marsh, but Henny knew he wasn't seeing a vee of pelicans or the ripple of the incoming tide. "Thursday." He turned toward her. "I was here Thursday." His expression was remote. "You must have come by Wednesday." He again stared out the windows at the marsh. Sudden deep lines indented his face on either side of his lips. "It was foggy then, too. When the fog hides the marsh, I feel trapped. I got out for a while. I took a drive. Wednesday." He pressed one thin hand against his cheek.

When fog settles on the island, wreathes in the trees like an old woman's straggly gray hair, pools into cottony mounds where roads dip, islanders drive cautiously, if at all.

Henny was casual. "I thought I dropped by Thursday, but perhaps I'm mistaken."

"I was here Thursday." There was the slightest emphasis on *here*.

Henny had a sense that his words meant much more than she understood. Was his insistence that he was home Thursday an effort to distance himself from Ves's house?

"I don't suppose Katherine was out in the

fog either day."

His gaze moved to a photograph of a laughing Katherine on a sunny day, barefoot on the beach, breeze-stirred sea oats behind her. "She hates driving in fog. She hates fog. But she had a delivery Thursday afternoon." A long pause, then he said in a weary tone, "I promised her I'd stay home. So I did."

"The blossoms are always six petaled and a rich cream color." Katherine Farley gestured at a watercolor in the center of one wall. "The flowers bloom from May to July at the top of the stalk. The dagger-shaped leaves at the base have a sharp tip and they really hurt." There was remembered discomfort in her voice. "I was sketching them, my camp stool toppled, and I brushed some spines as I went down. But I love that painting. It was worth the pain."

Emma disliked cold weather. In a puffy quilted beige caftan with occasional chartreuse spots, she resembled a mobile stuffed leopard. That her appearance might amuse some was of no matter to her. She relished comfort and dismissed fashion as irrelevant. She sat with her usual imposing posture in a solid oak Stickley cube chair with a comfortable red leather back and cushion. A number of sketches were spread on a cocktail table in front of her.

Katherine perched on a wooden bench near the table. This morning she was austere in a heather matte knit jersey sweater, blouse, and slacks. With her smooth black hair drawn back in a bun, her chiseled features, and intent expression, she reminded Emma suddenly of a monk in a brown wool robe.

Emma listened to Katherine while she plumbed the vagrant thought. There was nothing remotely monklike about Katherine. Except, yes, there was an intensity, an almost frightening sense of leashed power focused elsewhere. Although she was making an effort to be charming to a prospective customer, she was jerky in her speech, obviously under some kind of stress.

Emma was brisk. "I'm glad I caught you in the studio today. I dropped by last Thursday around five. I supposed you'd already closed up for the day."

"Thursday? I was making a delivery. I'm sorry I missed you. And glad you came back." Again there was an effort at charm.

"I am, too. Very impressed with your drawings," Emma pointed at a pen-and-ink sketch of a large herring gull, blue-gray wings tipped with white, a white body, a bright yellow beak with a small red dot.

Emma knew her seabirds, recognized the herring gull in summer or fall finery, the feather color and red dot beak indicating the season. "I rather fancy a wall of herring gulls. I'd like to commission you to do perhaps a dozen sketches for me. I'd like some of the gulls swimming or cracking clams or nesting. The sooner the better." She spoke with the imperious assurance of a wealthy woman quite willing to pay whatever it might take to achieve her current whim.

Katherine tried to keep her voice even. "A dozen sketches? I'd consider that, though it would require my putting aside some current projects."

Emma placed her square strong hands on the armrests, preparatory to rising. "I don't want to put you behind."

Katherine leaned forward and spoke in a rush. "Oh no, nothing due anytime soon. I'd be delighted to undertake the commission. A dozen sketches?"

Emma nodded. "That's settled, then. Appreciate your cooperation." As she came to her feet, she watched Katherine's taut features relax, saw a tic at the corner of one eye, and knew she was seeing a woman desperate for money, pressed for money, willing to make any accommodation for money. Emma had known hard times. She was rich now. She had not always been rich. She remembered the hollowness when there were bills due and not enough money to pay them. "I understand this may interfere with other projects. Perhaps a thousand dollars a sketch."

Katherine's eyes widened. "A thousand . . ." Twelve thousand dollars.

Emma was gruff. "This means quite a bit to me." If everything worked out and she wasn't talking to a future felon, she would enjoy the herring gull sketches in her terrace room, and she would be glad she'd been able to stave off the dogs of poverty nipping at Katherine for a while.

Emma scooped up her oversized puffy cloth purse, a matching blue with tan spots, fumbled past a notebook, several pens, a cellophane bag of salt water taffy in assorted flavors, an iPad, an iPhone, three copies of her latest Marigold paperback, a change purse and billfold, an island map, an Amtrak schedule, a menu from Paula Deen's restaurant in Savannah, this morning's *Wall Street Journal,* pulled out her checkbook. "Be glad to pay half in advance." She patted a zippered compartment that held a fifty-dollar gold piece now worth $1,500, her nose-thumb to the days when she'd had coffee for breakfast, a candy bar for lunch, and a Big Mac for dinner, when her change stretched that far.

Max skirted his silver Lamborghini, walked to their new runabout, a beige VW that he considered hardy enough for any island road. Its compact size avoided low-hanging branches and spiky underbrush. The car was a recent purchase, an unspoken statement to Annie that Confidential Commissions, his somewhat ambiguous business, would continue.

Not long ago, he'd announced NO MORE: No More trying to solve mysteries, No More danger for Annie. Annie promised to stay out of other people's troubles, but when a close friend was embroiled in a murder, Annie put her promise on hold. That's when he understood that Annie had to be Annie, and he loved her because she cared about him, cared about others, cared about justice and honor and decency. So Confidential Commissions began a new chapter, and he bought the VW knowing there might be times when he wanted to drive about the island without attracting notice. He liked people, was good at finding out information. He understood the logic of checking out everyone who would profit when Ves died, but independent testimony would be definitive. If he found a nosy neighbor who saw one of the dinner guests on Sunshine Lane last Thursday around five P.M., they would have their answer. As he drove, he enjoyed a triumphant moment imagining how he would reveal the perp's identity to Annie and the Incredible Trio and, at their exclamations of amazement, smugly say finding out was just a matter of legwork, good old-fashioned sleuthing.

He drove past the entrance to Sea Side Inn. He reached the main road that looped around the entire island, and turned left, heading for the older residential area where antebellum homes were interspersed with cottages, an occasional doublewide on blocks, and a few modern ranch-style houses.

Since he and Annie had moved to their antebellum house on Bay Road, he'd become familiar with this end of the island. Sunshine Lane intersected Federal near Morgan Manor, one of the island's loveliest old homes, a three-story gray-green tabby home that sat far back on a lot behind several majestic live oaks and huge weeping willows. The house was almost always in shadow. One massive live oak was known as the Hanging Tree. A daughter of the house, learning of her lover's death at the Battle of Honey Hill, took the veil especially made for their planned wedding and hung herself from a high limb.

Max was glad to swing past the house onto Sunshine Lane, leaving behind the looming mansion and long-ago grief. Sunshine Lane was a gravel road. Loblolly pines crowded close on either side. The shadows from the trees belied the name. Every thirty or forty yards white signposts carried house numbers. Ves's address was 207. No houses were visible from the road. Instead, narrow drives plunged into deep woods.

There would be no nosy neighbors to ask if they'd seen anyone near Ves's drive. An Oscar Mayer Wienermobile in all its orange-and-yellow glory could have wallowed up and down Sunshine Lane and never been noticed. No structures were visible from the lane because of the towering pines.

Max reached the end of Sunshine Lane, made a U-turn. Ves's drive mirrored the lane, a narrow road with pines pushing close on either side. He drove slowly, followed a curve into a clearing. He knew from his gardening mother that Ves had used native grasses for the lawn. A single-lane cement drive ended at a separate frame garage. Any car in the drive would be instantly visible to

Ves when she arrived home. Max parked and walked around the garage. A neat vegetable garden ran from behind the garage to the woods. No one could have parked there.

Max frowned and returned to the drive, studied the back of the house. The backyard was huge but offered no hiding places for a car. But someone entered the house, applied a slick substance to a step. The intruder had either arrived on foot — very unlikely — in a car, or on a bike. Max walked past the garage. He stopped next to a stand of bamboo and surveyed the yard. He had a good sense of geography. In good weather, he and Annie often took their old-fashioned bikes out for a ride, sometimes following a path down to the sea, sometimes to the marsh, sometimes winding behind homes. He walked swiftly across the backyard, plunged into the woods, found an asphalt trail about twenty yards from Ves's property line. He remembered this trail. It connected with several paths, making Ves's house easily accessible to anyone with a bike.

He returned to the backyard. A bike would work, but if he planned to arrange a fatal accident for anyone, he thought he'd want to have a car handy for a quick departure. He passed a fountain, noted Diana with a bow and broken arrow, climbed Ves's back steps. He knocked.

No answer.

Ves wasn't home yet. He checked his watch, pulled a ring of keys from one pocket. The fourth key unlocked the back door. He stepped inside, felt an odd sensation knowing he was repeating the actions of Ves's attacker. He walked to the front of the hall, turned to look up the steep stairs. The ticktock of the grandfather clock seemed loud. Max pulled a small laser flashlight from a pocket. He aimed the beam at the worn wooden treads, climbed swiftly. He slowed near the top. The fourth step looked unnaturally clean. He knelt, pantomimed pouring something onto the step, pretended to cap a can or canister, rose, and went down the stairs and outside, locking the door. He strode across the yard to a stand of bamboo that offered a good vantage point to watch for Ves's arrival and be unobserved. He stopped by the bamboo, looked at his watch. Not quite four minutes.

Max folded his arms. The unknown visitor waited for Ves to come home, waited to see what happened. If she hadn't broken her fall, if all had been quiet, the waiting figure would have cautiously eased into the house. If Ves had been lying dead at the foot of the stairs, the mission was a success. If she were injured, unable to move, there would likely have been another blow to her head, one that would appear consistent with a fall.

Instead, Ves limped outside, made it to her car.

The would-be murderer wanted her death to appear accidental, so Ves was allowed to drive away. Then a hurried return to the house to clean the step. Likely the cleanup, while thorough, was done in haste just in case Ves called the police on her cell.

Max frowned as he walked back to the VW. Instead of a triumphant revelation of the attacker's identity, he had paltry bits of information. The house was accessible on a bike. If the attacker drove a car, it must have been hidden somewhere. There were no shoulders on Sunshine Lane, pines thick on either side right up to the graveled road. He was almost to the entrance to Sunshine Lane when he jammed on the brakes, rolled down the window, and backed up a few feet. He stared at a broken frond of a resurrection fern. His gaze dropped. In an instant, the engine was off and he slammed the driver's door shut. Ruts. The indentations were faint but there were definite ruts. There had once been a road here. Traces of it angled past ferns and a bayberry bush. He pushed past the ferns and plunged into gloom. He walked ten feet, twenty, and felt a sense of success. Crushed vegetation indicated a car had come this way, likely stopped where he was standing.

Max was thoughtful as he walked back to the VW. He should have remembered there were many homes on the island where people could come and go and never be noticed. Finding out who wanted Ves dead was not going to be easy. Max checked his time. A quarter to ten. He slid a rarely used prepaid cell from his pocket. He didn't use his regular cell, to avoid being identified on caller ID. The prepaid cell revealed only the caller's number, and that was fine. He dialed.

"Perfumerie. Gretchen speaking. How may I help you?"

Max enjoyed occasional roles in the island's summer theater. He affected a breezy, good ol' boy ebullience. "Goofy Sullivan, pal of Curt's. Here for a spot of golf and somebody gave me a heads-up, said Curt might be here. Like to look him up." He listened. "Thanks a bunch."

5

The sweet scent of gardenia mixed with a hint of ginger pleased Laurel as she stepped inside the elegant small shop on Main Street. Three mirrored kiosks with cushioned stools were arranged in a semiprivate curve to the right. To the left and ahead were counters filled with every variety of cosmetic, probably including the bright green malachite paste used as eye shadow by Cleopatra. A verse from Ecclesiastes was a favorite of Laurel's: "What has been will be again, what has been done will be done again; there is nothing new under the sun." Some might find the message chilling. Laurel in her own mystical way felt part of a continuum of time. Besides, beautiful women owed a duty to themselves to always appear at their best.

Gretchen Roundtree in a becoming pastel blue smock came eagerly around the back counter. "Laurel, I've been thinking about you. We just received the newest Crème de la Mer moisturizing cream." Her smile looked almost genuine.

Laurel chided herself. That beaming smile was likely genuine. A commission on several jars of Crème de la Mer would be a tidy sum for a February sales day.

With murmurs that reminded Laurel of starlings in a cluster, they exchanged pleasantries of the feminine sort — *How lovely you look today. Such a pleasure to see you.* — as Laurel settled on a cushioned stool. While Laurel studied her reflection in the three-way mirror, Gretchen brought a tray with several small jars and tubes, and perched on the next stool. Gretchen gently removed Laurel's makeup. "I have a new ointment you will simply adore, perfect for your flawless complexion."

Laurel selected three lotions, two ointments, and a delicate mauve shade of eye shadow. At the checkout counter, Gretchen swiped the items, rang up the sale. She was so perfectly the well-bred society woman fallen on hard times in a job requiring finesse and charm. The lines near her eyes and lips were a little deeper than when they'd last met. She'd smoothly but determinedly plied Laurel with every possible high-end product. Was Gretchen desperate enough for money to slip through the fog to her ex-sister-in-law's home with murder in mind?

Gretchen looked up and their gazes met.

Before the automatic smile transformed Gretchen's expression, Laurel sensed a crackle of anger and desperation.

Laurel picked up the shopping bag with her purchases. "I'm glad you were here today, Gretchen." A slightly reproachful laugh. "I was soooo disappointed when I came by last Thursday around five and you weren't here. The hours say ten to noon, two to six."

"Thursday." Gretchen's face was utterly still, her blue eyes watchful. "That must have been the afternoon I delivered some purchases to the inn." Her tone was careless, as if it didn't matter.

Laurel remembered, from the last presidential campaign, clips of a politician speaking followed by clips of a dog barking, presumably in response to lies. She smiled at Gretchen. "Do you hear a dog barking?"

Gretchen's eyes were blank. "I don't believe so."

Laurel smiled. "It must just be me. I was sure I heard a dog barking." As she drifted to the door, she mused about the possibilities. Dogs can detect cancer, find the lost, protect the weak, rescue the drowning. Perhaps there was yet a new frontier. Which breed was most likely to detect insincerity, a cardinal sin to dogs? A basset hound? A cocker spaniel? A Labrador retriever?

Laurel smiled as she started her car. Henny had a new dog with a pointed nose, a low-slung body, and a ferocious guttural bark. Cinnamon was an odd mixture of a basset hound and a German shepherd. If only she could be trained to bark at lies.

The island bank was small with a tiny lobby and two tellers. It boasted a marble floor, however, and the bank president's office, behind an oak door to Annie's left, was large and sumptuous. She stood in the center of the lobby on one side of a circular glass counter that held an assortment of slips to make deposits or withdrawals. She wondered what had compelled a half dozen islanders to arrive at the bank promptly at ten A.M. She continued her charade of adding and re-adding figures until there was no line.

Fred looked a bit dazed. She'd overheard several conversations, including a brusque customer who demanded to know why he couldn't get all the cash right now, this was a check from a reputable company, what

104

did he mean it would have to clear, that was a crock, and if there was another bank on the island he'd be the first to sign up, and that's what happened when people had a monopoly.

Annie's tone was commiserating. "Hi, Fred. Always fun to deal with the GP, right?"

He looked frazzled, his tufting hair exaggerated by several frenzied swipes. He poked his bifocals higher on his plump nose and made an effort to smile. "Nice to see you, Annie." He glanced at the checks on the counter. His taut shoulders eased and he took a deep breath. "Got some deposits today."

Annie usually used the bank drive-through. She banked the old-fashioned way. As far as she was concerned, taking a picture of checks and clicking to deposit was an open invitation to a hacker, even though Max insisted mysteries had made her paranoid and she needed to join the electronic world. She insisted she wasn't paranoid, simply careful, and she'd bank electronically when hacking no longer occurred. "All deposits."

Fred turned to his computer. His plump fingers tapped without hesitation.

"I missed seeing you when I was here

Thursday afternoon."

She was watching closely and didn't miss the fraction of a second when he stiffened.

"Uh, no."

"Where were you?" Bright, friendly.

A door opened behind him. Quick footsteps sounded. She nodded hello to big, red-faced Martin Ford, the trust officer, lifted her voice just a little. "Yes, I missed you Thursday afternoon. Were you on a holiday?"

Martin stopped behind Fred, gave him a poke in one shoulder. "I'd guess Fred would prefer a holiday. Unless he thinks the dentist is a barrel of fun." Martin gave a deep-throated laugh that sounded like an elephant's trumpet before he swung away to push through a gate into the lobby. He was still laughing as the front door closed behind him.

"Bless your heart." Annie leaned on the ledge. "Who's your dentist, Fred?"

Fred hooked a finger over his collar, tugged. "Nobody on the island. A dental surgeon in Chastain."

Annie was eager. "Someone asked me just the other day if I knew of a dental surgeon. What's his name?"

Fred's voice was thin. "Charles Garcia." He handed her the deposit slip.

On the sidewalk outside the bank, Annie turned to her left, walked briskly past several shops and an old modest hotel with clientele that returned year after year. The wind picked up as she stepped onto the boardwalk. Whitecaps rippled across the harbor. The berth for the ferry was empty, the *Miss Jolene* likely just now reaching the mainland.

Annie reached her goal, a worn phone booth, one of the last public pay phones on the island. Annie pulled, and the door grudgingly opened far enough for her to slide inside. Her nose wrinkled at a sour smell and her right shoe stepped on something sticky. She used her cell to get the number of the office of Charles Garcia, DDS, in Chastain, scrambled for change, dialed, fed the coin slot.

"Dr. Garcia's office. This is Chrissy. How may I help you?" The voice was young and pleasant.

"Hello. Chrissy. This is Agnes Morrison for Cadillac Dental Pan. I'm simply calling to confirm the appointment last Thursday afternoon for Dr. Garcia's patient Fred Butler."

"Hold on."

Annie pictured pinafores as she listened

to a sprightly violin rendition of "Hi-Lili, Hi-Lo."

The young voice returned. "Excuse me. What was the patient's name?"

"Fred Butler."

The violin music resumed. Annie hummed along. She didn't mind admitting she loved a great many unsophisticated things, including fried chicken, Edgar Guest, Thorne Smith's Topper books, six-foot-tall sunflowers, week-old kittens, and old June Allyson movies. She sang a verse, broke off when the music was interrupted.

"There appears to be some mistake. Dr. Garcia doesn't have a patient named Fred Butl—"

Annie interrupted with a quick laugh. "I'm in error. I meant to dial the number on the line above. Sorry to have bothered you." She depressed the cradle.

She took a deep breath of the sea-scented air when she stood on the boardwalk, scraped her right shoe bottom on a board. Still sticky. She moved to the sandy border of the walk, swiped her shoe back and forth. Better. She turned to stride back to the bank, ready to confront Fred Butler, ask what he was doing Thursday afternoon since he wasn't at the dentist's office as he claimed. She jolted to a stop. She and Max and the Incredible Trio were trying to garner information without alerting a Prospective Murderer. Fred was safe for the moment.

Henny Brawley looked at Ben Parotti and gestured at the front door. "Here comes Marian. What's her favorite breakfast?" Marian Kenyon, the *Gazette*'s star reporter, was moving fast, her leather shoulder bag banging against one hip.

Ben didn't hesitate. "French toast with whipped cream and caramel syrup, sausage patties, and a side bowl of sliced bananas. Black coffee."

Henny laughed. "And she's skinny enough to fit into a straw. Bring it on. The sliced bananas sound good with some whipped cream." She'd enjoyed her usual bacon and eggs at shortly after six and watched dawn send fingers of light across the dark marsh. "Coffee black."

Ben didn't bother to write down the order. He waited until Marian plopped into the seat opposite Henny. His smile was fond. "You newlyweds behaving yourselves?"

Marian's narrow face came alight. "We wouldn't dare do otherwise. Those joined in matrimony by Captain Ben Parotti know it would be the brig if we transgressed." She reached up a thin hand, squeezed Ben's wrist. "Oh, Ben —"

He spoke hastily to head off an emotional moment. "I hear Craig's the new City editor."

Diverted, Marian's grin was supercharged. "He started this week. Walt said he'd sweated through his last July here. He's retired to Colorado Springs to write a bodice ripper but I told him those went out with panty hose. Craig's loving the city desk."

"Hope he knows the island's pretty sleepy. Not a lot of news."

Marian shook her head like a terrier with a rag doll. "Not so. There's always news."

As Ben started to turn away, Marian looked surprised.

Henny laughed. "He already has the order. I asked him what you like. I know you're always hungry even though it's midmorning. Consider it a bribe."

"Bribe?" Marian leaned her elbows on the table, dark eyes bright. "What's up?"

Henny picked her words carefully. Marian was smart, quick, always alert for a scoop. "You know more about everybody on the island than anybody but Father Morris, and what he knows never leaves the confessional."

Marian's bony face was intent. "I'm listening."

"I'm looking for gossip, fact, surmise, or questions about several islanders."

"What's in it for me?" Marian had her quid pro quo look.

Henny was grave. "I won't have anything to —"

Ben arrived with a tray, placed a plate before Marian, a bowl and small pitcher of cream before Henny. Steaming mugs for both of them.

"— share with you if your information helps solve a problem. Least said, the better at that point. If things go horribly wrong, I'll tell you everything I know."

Marian dabbed a chunk of French toast in caramel syrup. "Sounds like I get the story if there is a story. Okay. Run the names by me." She spoke with her mouth full. She cut another portion of French toast with the edge of her fork, used her left hand to tug a laptop out of her purse. She set the laptop up to the left of her plate.

"Katherine and Bob Farley."

Marian ignored her laptop. "You consider yourself a friend of theirs?"

Henny was startled. Ves Roundtree's safety was her objective, the objective of Laurel and Emma and Annie and Max. The Farleys? She liked them. If neither had attempted murder, she wished them well. She said the words aloud. "I wish them well." With an unspoken caveat.

"So maybe" — Marian added another splash of caramel syrup — "you're worried about them. I hear a lot of things I never repeat. If someone has a problem according to island know-it-alls, I file it away under Rumors." She pointed her fork at the laptop. "There's nothing but good stuff in the *Gazette* files about Katherine and Bob. But an unnamed source told me Katherine and Bob are broke on their ass and the bank is about to call some loans due." Marian's face scrunched in thought. "I understand people have problems. I've been there. Maybe it's money. Maybe it's his bunged-up body, but something's wrong big-time with Bob. Somebody I know, a bird-watching nut, was out near Gurney Point Wednesday afternoon."

Henny knew the remote area on the northern tip of the island. Swirling, tricky currents raced against a reddish clay bluff, eroding a foot a year, making the water murky, making a maelstrom at high tide.

Marian looked wry. "The bird-watcher spotted a peregrine falcon and was ecstatic, and here came Hyla Harrison on her yellow scooter."

Police Officer Hyla Harrison was a familiar sight to islanders on her bright yellow scooter.

"My guy was scarcely breathing. And, of course, the put-put of the scooter spooked the falcon. My guy was ready to storm out of his spot behind a pine to ream out Hyla, then he got interested. She rolled the scooter behind a bayberry bush and went up the trail, disappeared in the fog. Then he thought maybe he better stay where he was, maybe she was after someone and something criminal was going on. About this time an SUV pulls around a bend, parks at the foot of the trail. Bob Farley, my guy knows him, got out and somehow, hard to imagine doing it with bum legs and a cane, Bob labors up the trail. My friend said he looked like a crooked scarecrow in the fog, was hardly visible. My friend had binoculars, but the fog got thicker and he couldn't see either Bob or Hyla. A few minutes passed and Bob came hobbling down the trail. Hyla was behind him. He climbed in the SUV, drove away. Hyla got her scooter and left." Marian lifted bony shoulders, let them fall. "Maybe he was out there to look at the water. Not that he could probably see much in the fog. On a clear day you can see the water foam when it hits the rocks, hear it gurgle and suck." Marian speared a piece of banana, dipped it in whipped cream. "Hyla waited until he'd driven away before she left."

Henny felt as if she stood on the bluff and fog swirled around her. Now she knew where Bob Farley was on Wednesday afternoon. She remembered his bleak expression when he told her he'd promised Katherine he'd stay home Thursday. She'd sensed darkness and now she understood. He claimed he'd stayed home on Thursday. Perhaps that was true.

Marian took a big swallow of coffee. "Who else is on your prom list?"

"Jane Wilson."

Marian looked blank. "Don't know the name." She turned to the laptop, tapped, clicked several times. "Only *Gazette* mention is in the obituary of her mother. I knew her mother. She quilted, won some prizes at the fair."

"Tim Holt."

Marian muttered to herself as she checked. "Rings a bell. Yeah, here it is, arrested in a big melee during a summer beer bust two years ago, no charges filed. Last summer swam out despite shark sighting to rescue a teenager caught in an undertow."

Another click. "Good-looking dude. A shot of the lifeguards at the start of the season."

"Adam Nash."

Marian's expression was sardonic. "Best friend to rich old ladies. I'd sooner trust a barracuda. Something about his eyes. Kind of a dull green. They remind me of pond scum. Before Craig and I got back together, I used to go out to the Country Place."

Henny knew about the old plantation house with a roulette wheel, slots, and poker.

"Adam was a regular. He gambled big-time. That's the only thing I know about him that doesn't fit his civic leader profile. So far as I know, he's never landed in any trouble, and I'd know."

"Fred Butler."

Marian rolled her eyes. "Fred reminds me of wilted lettuce. But" — she brightened — "he gets interesting if you ask about Black Jack MacDougal. Fred has a man crush on pirates. Ginger —"

Henny often played bridge with the *Gazette* Lifestyle editor, whose Southern charm masked the instinct of a piranha when she was on a story.

"— did a feature on him about hidden gold on the island. She said he's a little unhinged on the topic. She was kind enough not to point out that pirate maps are an industry and so far as she knows nobody's ever found any buried gold. Otherwise, Fred's a fussy old maid, no wine, no women, no song."

"Curt Roundtree."

"Rufus Roundtree's son?"

Henny nodded.

Marian shrugged. "Never made any waves on the island."

"Gretchen Roundtree."

Marian considered another bite of French toast, regretfully shook her head, put her fork and knife on the plate. "Funny you should ask. This is pure speculation, but I learned about an interesting coincidence. I e-mail with an old friend who works on a Phoenix paper. She said there was a rash of jewel robberies last spring. Rich ladies went beddy-bye, and when they woke up the next morning, jewelry was gone from the boudoir. There were house guests. Turns out Gretchen was in the houses when several robberies occurred. Or had recently been a guest. No one's been arrested. The last robbery was in late April. My friend wanted to know what I could find about Gretchen. I did some checking. Gretchen came back to the island May fourteenth. Also interesting to note, no more jewel thefts have occurred there. But" — a Gallic shrug — "Gretchen has been working in a makeup bar so she's either the world's most cautious thief, frugal with the proceeds, or she's innocent." Marian picked up her coffee mug. "I have to hand it to you. I thought for sure I'd see a connection when I heard all the names. Not so. Are we playing a new version of that brain teaser where you're supposed to spot a common denominator?"

Emma Clyde's sharp blue eyes noted scuff marks on the floor of the poorly lit corridor. Adam Nash's office door needed screws tightened in the upper hasp to right a tilt. She touched the knob, pulled her hand back. She burrowed in her purse for a package of wet wipes, cleaned the knob. She found a Kleenex, wrapped the wipe in a ball.

Opening the door, she stepped inside. No one sat at a receptionist's desk. Emma strode forward, spotted a wastebasket, tossed her trash. Two unoccupied easy chairs sat on either side of a coffee table. She looked past the chairs at a door with a frosted glass panel.

She knocked twice on the door, turned the knob.

Adam Nash looked up with a frown. He was in his shirtsleeves. Interesting. She'd not imagined he wore suspenders. As always, he appeared immaculate. It was surprising he tolerated the slovenliness of a building that needed a better effort from the cleaning crew. Perhaps he was in arrears on his rent and in no position to make demands.

Adam's frown was replaced with an ingratiating smile. He came to his feet. "Emma, it's wonderful to see you. You're looking splendid."

"Glad I found you in." She charged to an apple red chair in front of his desk and plopped down. "The financial news out of China continues to be worrying."

He immediately was judicious, ponderous. "Have to keep a sharp eye on commodities. In times like these, it's good to seek a safe harbor . . ."

Emma listened as he extolled several financial havens he highly recommended, all of which would pay handsome commissions to him. Emma was not a woolly minded writer when it came to investments. She could talk currencies, dividends, and mutual funds with ease, but she kept her gaze wide and admiring. "Oh my, it's all so complicated."

He was instantly reassuring. "You have come to the right place, Emma. I'll be glad to take charge of your portfolio —"

She watched his eyes, saw the eager, hopeful, desperate glint. Pond scum accented by avarice.

"Well" — she tried to sound anxious, not a usual tone for her — "I just haven't made up my mind what to do. I'm talking to several people." She rose. "I'll need a financial statement. Just to be sure your firm is in good order. I know you won't mind sending it. After all" — an arch smile — "if you are to know all about my finances, it seems fair enough for me to know about yours."

Adam pushed back his chair, came to his feet. His face was no longer alight. "That's not customary."

She gave a bark of laughter. "I think you know I don't give a rip about customary. But it's up to you. Send me your financial statement. Or don't." She paused at the door, appraised him with cold blue eyes. "I believe in people keeping office hours. I do when I'm working on a book. You weren't here the day I came by. I decided to give you another chance. But I don't understand why your office was closed a little before five on Thursday."

"Thursday? If you knocked —"

Emma was brusque. "Turned the knob.

119

Door was locked."

"I was here." His voice was flat. "I was working on some figures, didn't want to be disturbed."

Max knew a dozen ways in and out of the Sea Side Inn. He parked in the west lot, strolled to the terrace. On a chilly February morning the umbrellas were furled at the tables around the pool. One hardy swimmer stroked methodically. Max used the back entrance. He didn't need to check the note in his pocket. Gretchen hadn't hesitated to give good old Goofy her son's room number. Interesting that he wasn't staying with his mother.

Max walked up to the second floor, stopped at room 227. He held a clipboard in his left hand, knocked with his right. He assumed a pleasant, slightly vacuous expression. He'd taken pains with his choice of clothing, a navy polo that was slightly worn, chinos, loafers.

The door opened. "Put it —" Curt Roundtree's freckled face looked annoyed. "You're not room service."

"Sir, I'm canvassing —"

"Good for you." The door slammed shut.

Henny pulled into the oyster-shell lot north

120

of the police station. She spotted Hyla's yellow scooter parked neatly next to a rack that held several bikes. The island was small enough that it was easy to commute to work in fair weather on a bike. Henny sat with her hands resting lightly on the steering wheel, the driver's window rolled down. She knew and respected Officer Hyla Harrison, who had joined the force a few years ago, seeking a new place, a new life. She'd been an officer in Miami and seen her partner shot and killed. Hyla was reserved, retiring, intelligent. She would never divulge information about an investigation.

But, as Henny had learned long ago in teaching, there are many different paths to the same goal.

Hyla came swinging around a palm tree on the oyster-shell path to the parking lot, slender, trim, moving with a purpose.

Henny opened her door, slammed it shut, turned to the path, her face transforming into recognition. "Hyla." Henny hurried toward her. "I'm glad to see you. I was going to drop by this morning and say hello after I talked to Mavis." Mavis Cameron was Police Chief Billy Cameron's wife as well as a dispatcher and a crime scene tech. Henny patted her purse. "I'm hoping to recruit Mavis to help serve chili at the

Friends of the Library supper. Can I can count on you as well?"

Hyla stopped, her freckled face pleasant. As always she was immaculate in a crisp uniform. "Chili supper?"

Henny gave her a brilliant smile. "Two weeks from Tuesday at the library. Two bucks a bowl, corn bread and iced tea free. Can you help? We need servers there at five thirty, doors open at six. Runs to eight o'clock."

Hyla pulled a small notebook from a back pocket, flipped it open. "Will do."

"Wonderful. Free chili for the volunteers. And" — Henny reached out, touched Hyla's sleeve — "on another matter entirely, I like Katherine and Bob Farley. You went above and beyond the call of duty to let Katherine know. I want to thank you."

Hyla's fair cheeks turned pink. "Nothing special for me. Part of the job. Knew it was a near thing. Have to alert a family member."

"Katherine's been worried about him. Their good fortune you took action."

Hyla's narrow face was grave. "I was on my way home and I came up beside his van. I looked up. I saw his face. I saw trouble. Funny thing, when I was in Miami I had a friend in the K9 unit. Her dog always knew when somebody was going to die. That's how I felt. I lagged back, followed him. He wasn't looking in his rearview mirror. I guess he was thinking a lot of things but not about the road behind him. Pretty soon I figured out where he was heading. I went off trail. I got to the point and hid my scooter. I hiked up the trail, waited there in the fog. If he didn't come, well, I was just going to be late getting home, no big deal. But he came. When he got close to the edge, I started talking to him, slow and easy."

Ves Roundtree stood near the mantel, her left hand tight on the ivory head of her cane. Her reddish hair was subdued into a chignon, which emphasized the dark splotches beneath her eyes, the pallor of her fair skin. She had the aura of a woman who'd suffered either a debilitating illness or a psychic shock. She pressed her lips together.

Annie felt sure that in its long history the old house had no doubt witnessed joy and sorrow, but this might be the first time murder was the focus of those gathered.

Emma Clyde, imposing in a maroon velvet caftan, occupied most of the Chippendale sofa. Emma's blunt chin jutted. She was in her combative mode. Laurel Darling Roethke, ethereal in a pale blue dress, perched lightly at one end of the sofa. Her dark blue eyes were concerned. Henny Brawley sat with her usual erect posture in a straight chair near the fireplace. Always intuitive, Henny looked uneasy.

Annie sat stiffly next to Max on the brocaded love seat. She had a sense of something momentous about to happen, like a jagged bolt of lightning when the sky hangs purplish and heavy before a summer storm.

Ves had listened without comment as each of them spoke, her thin face taut and intent. Abruptly, her lips curved in a wry smile. "Clever devils, all of you. If I'd tried to ask each of them where they were at five on Thursday, I'd have asked straight out. Instead, none of them have any idea I'm aware. I suppose my murderer thinks I was so shaken by the fall, I didn't question why I fell. It would have been nice if I could drop a name from the list. I'm inclined to drop Bob Farley. Climbing the stairs to fix a trap and climbing them again to remove any evidence would require a huge effort. But the rest of them" — she ticked them off one by one — "are fair game. Katherine needed money before Bob went to Gurney Point. Now she must be desperate. Fred Butler didn't go to the dentist. Something was important enough to him that he lied to his supervisor. He has a nine-to-five job. If he wanted to get to my house before I got home, he had to get off work. Jane Wilson says she stayed late at work. Was it simply a coincidence her late day was Thursday? Her boyfriend claims he was at her house."

Laurel was pleasant but definite. "It sounded at the time as if she was there, too."

Ves nodded. "To be fair, maybe he didn't intend to imply Jane was there, maybe he has a key. He told you where he was and didn't think her late arrival mattered. He's obsessed with his plan for a shopping center. If he's counting on Jane's inheritance, he must feel very certain she'll marry him. He's a possibility." Ves massaged one cheekbone. "I wish I had a fortune wheel and I could give it a spin and it would stop at the most likely. The arrow might point to Gretchen. She has a substantial monthly income from her divorce settlement. She's always been a big spender, loved going to high-society places, Martha's Vineyard, Scottsdale, Rancho Mirage. When she came back to the island, ended up working at the cosmetics shop, I thought maybe she was trying to set a good example for Curt. But now it looks like she's in big trouble. No wonder she wants money. It looks like she pilfered one time too many, got caught in the act, and came up against somebody as ruthless and greedy as she is. She must be paying big-time blackmail. If she's cut Curt off, that makes two of them that would enjoy my obituary." She glanced at Emma. "I'll be interested if you get a financial statement from Adam. If you do, you can bet it's fake."

"I was quite effective as a possible client." Emma was amused. "In any event, he didn't learn the purpose of my visit. The criminal has no inkling an investigation is underway. I employed a technique I've utilized in many books. As Marigold is quick to say: *Casual conversation has been the undoing of many.*"

Annie was incensed. Emma's authorial ego apparently knew no bounds, but this wasn't the time or place to indulge her. Annie leaned forward. "I think —"

Henny gave Annie a warning glance. "I agree with Annie. We can't do better than to call on Emma for guidance. We are fortunate Emma is sharing with us one of the entries in *Detecting Wisdom.*"

Annie was unimpressed. What did Emma mean? Did she have any idea what she meant? Undoing of whom?

Emma basked in Henny's admiration. "Precisely." Emma nodded approvingly at

Henny. "As I reported, either Katherine Farley or Adam Nash could have been here Thursday afternoon. I can't prove it either way. But I can tell you that Katherine Farley is a shaken woman. She looked eons older than when I saw her at the market last week. Eons. Moreover, her conversation was disjointed. She scarcely seemed to pay attention to what I said, though she obviously is desperate to make some sales. Katherine Farley deserves serious consideration." A decisive nod as she scooped up cashews from a pottery bowl.

Ves had insisted on iced tea or sherry for the ladies, a beer for Max, and had placed bowls on side tables with cashews, walnuts, and spiced pecans.

Ves picked up a glass of sherry with her left hand, lifted it in a toast. *"Quod ad summam illam."*

Annie looked at Max. She depended upon him for Latin translations.

He murmured, "That's the sum of it."

Ves sounded reflective. "One of my father's favorite lamentations when everything's gone to hell. He always said it mournfully when the Dodgers lost. We're talking the Brooklyn Dodgers, and they seemed to love to lose. Dad would murmur, *'Quod ad summam illam.'* That's how I feel, like an old Dodgers fan. You've all gone to bat for me, but we haven't scored a run." Her voice was brittle. "Nobody has an alibi for five o'clock Thursday afternoon. Everybody needs money, even Jane Wilson. She hated asking me, was backing toward the door the whole time, but that young man has her under his thumb." A cold smile. "He doesn't mind asking. He was still pleasant after I said no, I'll give him that. Which means my future — if I have one — is up to me. Someone who ate at my table wants me dead, tried to kill me, slipped away in the fog. So, what am I going to do about it?"

Max was firm. "Go to the police. You should have made a report Thursday."

Ves arched a sardonic brow. "Billy Cameron's a good guy. He'd listen. He'd come out, look at the step, maybe bring a crime tech, check for traces of wax or polish. What if they find it? What's he going to do? Arrest everybody on the island who has some floor wax or furniture polish?" She laughed without humor. "I don't believe in wasting time. His or mine. I've got some ideas. I'm not done. But I want to thank all of you." Her tone softened. "You are my friends. You've tried, done your best. Now it's up to me to spin the wheel. Is it Katherine or Bob Farley, Jane Wilson, her boyfriend, Adam

Nash, Fred Butler, Gretchen Roundtree, Rufus's son? I will find out which one came. I will survive."

Again she lifted her glass, her gaze intense, her hand steady. She had the air of a soldier before battle, hearing the far off rattle of guns. *"Audentes fortuna juvat."*

As the Lamborghini leapt forward, Annie turned toward Max.

He spoke before she asked. "Fortune favors the bold."

The car plunged deeper into the shadows beneath interlocking tree limbs. Annie stared into the night. "What is Ves going to do?"

6

Annie sketched three chapbook covers, shooting stars for Laurel's *Merry Musings,* a mélange of famous titles like spokes around a wheel for Henny's *Classic Crimes,* and a huge magnifying glass for Emma's *Detecting Wisdom.* This was going to be fun. Each chapbook would be distinctive: pale blue background for Laurel, simulated parchment for Henny, a police blotter format for Emma.

There was silence in Death on Demand except for the rustle of paper and Agatha's purr when Annie paused to stroke her sleek back. Annie enjoyed quiet mornings at the store, though she knew she should be unpacking new books, *Midnight Sun* by Jo Nesbø and *Breakdown* by Jonathan Kellerman. Instead of being relaxed and content, she felt uneasy. Every so often her gaze returned to the first entry in *Detecting Wisdom: A scared rat has sharp fangs.*

Maybe she should go see Ves, warn her . . . That was the problem, wasn't it? Ves knew she was in danger. Annie didn't have any bright ideas on what Ves should do.

The front doorbell rang. "Hey, Annie."

She heard Max's voice with delight, came to her feet. Maybe he had thought of something. Somehow she felt sure his morning, too, had been preoccupied with concern for Ves. She met him halfway up the center aisle, gave him a hug. "You know what to do."

He looked startled. "Did Ves call you?"

She had the feeling they weren't communicating. "Call?"

Max hunched his shoulders. "She called the future heirs, plus Gretchen and Jane's boyfriend, said she had an announcement about Rufus's will and to be there at eight o'clock, hung up. I'm supposed to get there a few minutes early."

Annie was eager. "I guess she'll call all of us. That way we can speak up if anyone tries to change their story about Thursday afternoon."

Max looked uncomfortable, stared at a poster for the new Alpine mystery by Mary Daheim, muttered, "I don't think so." He cleared his throat, talked fast. "She wants me to stand next to her, look menacing. She

131

said there's nothing menacing about you or Laurel or Henny or Emma. If she included all of you, the gathering would seem like a party. She said a good time wasn't on her agenda."

Annie pointed at the yellow walkie-talkie, which looked out of place on the coffee table in their den. "It's set on receive."

Max promised to put the other one in a good spot in Ves's living room. "I wanted to use my cell phone on speaker, but I found the walkie-talkies we take when we camp. The sound should be a lot clearer."

Laurel's smile was approving. "Max thinks of everything."

In the interests of maintaining a cordial relationship with her mother-in-law, Annie did not inform Laurel that her pink cashmere top made her look like a birthday cake and that it was Annie who dug the walkie-talkies out of the attic and insisted Max take one with him.

Emma glowered. In her black — was she making a statement? — caftan, she reminded Annie of an irascible cat when the doorbell rings too many times on Halloween. "Since when is Max menacing?"

"Max is perfectly capable of looking menacing," Annie said hotly.

Laurel no longer looked like a pink confection. Her tone was dulcet with underlying steel. "Max is a blue belt."

There was a moment of silence.

Laurel offered, "Orange belt?"

Henny rushed to the rescue. "Black belt." She laughed, a good-humored laugh. "Face it, ladies. Testosterone counts. Of course Ves wants a tall, strong man at her side when" — a quick breath and the smile was gone — "she confronts a murderer."

Max answered the doorbell. Fred Butler was the last to arrive. When he saw Max, his eyes widened, looked huge behind the thick lenses of his glasses. The breeze lifted the gray tufts on either side of his head, giving him the appearance of a befuddled owl unsure if he'd reached the right roost. "Uh." He started, stopped.

Max held the door wide. "Everyone's in the living room. Come right in."

Fred gave Max one more puzzled glance, moved hesitatingly to the left. The only sound was the slap of his shoes on the heart pine floor. There was silence in the living room.

Ves sat on the brocaded love seat. Her springy reddish curls looked youthful but her face was tight and thin. The dark green of her silk blouse emphasized the brilliance of her eyes. She nodded at Fred, used her cane to gesture at a wooden chair. Fred scuttled to the chair, took his place.

Max stopped just inside the archway, stepped to one side of a wrought iron stand that held a bust of Minerva. Ves had chosen the spot before the company arrived, said, "Whoever waxed the step is a gambler. I don't expect anyone to clutch a hanky and faint when I talk. But it won't hurt for you to be on the lookout for . . ." She'd trailed off. "I don't know, maybe a hint of panic? Anything that doesn't look normal. And you're a big strong man, ready to pounce." He maintained a bland expression and carefully did not look at the walkie-talkie in the bookcase by the fireplace. He'd shoved the unit between two large dark tomes. It would be noticeable only to someone studying the shelves.

Ves used the cane for leverage to rise to her feet. "I have an announcement to make." She moved slowly, the cane thumping with each step. She reached the archway, turned to face the room, standing about two feet from Max.

Every eye followed her. There was a general air of uncertainty and a hint of irritation.

Fred Butler sat with his shoulders rounded and tight, chin low enough to hide his neck. Adam Nash smoothed back a lock of silvered hair, maintained his usual dignified posture, but a reddish flush stained his cheeks. He was accustomed to deference, likely found the assembly odd, the ambience unpleasant. Curt Roundtree, casual in a short-sleeved polo and khakis, slouched comfortably in a wicker chair, but the intensity of his gaze indicated close attention. Gretchen Roundtree nervously fingered a gold filigree necklace, dark brows in a tight frown. Jane Wilson's young, rounded face puckered in concern as if she found herself in the middle of an argument and wished she weren't there. Tim Holt was in his work clothes, a flannel shirt, jeans, and boots. He looked at Jane, gave a shrug as if to ask what the hell was going on. Despite the haggard paleness of Katherine Farley's face and the almost fervid glances she darted at her husband, she was her usual elegant self, dark hair shining, a beige textured top and black slacks and heels. Bob Farley's gaze slid past Ves with every indication of disinterest, a man enduring a social evening until he could go home.

"Each of you will be wealthy when I die." Ves spoke in a thin, clipped voice. "One of you" — she took her time, gazed directly at each in turn — "tried to kill me last Thursday."

This was the moment, if there was to be a moment, the instant when shock might reveal a look of guilt. Max tried to catch a glimpse of each guest. Fred's plump face sagged and he began to shake. Adam leaned forward, looking predatory and wary. Curt gave a low whistle, raised a skeptical eyebrow. Gretchen sat as still as stone, her fingers clamped hard on the necklace. Jane's eyes widened and her lips rounded in an O. Tim looked blank, then his big mouth twisted in a sardonic smile, clearly dismissing Ves as some kind of nut. Katherine's lovely face was rigid. She clutched Bob's arm, held tight. Bob appeared unaffected, a man only minimally aware of his surroundings.

The moment was past.

Adam Nash lifted his leonine head. "You are obviously hysterical. Of course, you're a woman of a certain age." His tone was disparaging.

Ves gave him a cool stare. "A rather curious response, Adam. Instead of asking what happened, you respond with sexism. But perhaps you didn't ask because you know what happened Thursday."

"You are either hysterical or deranged. To accuse one of us" — his big hand gestured at the others — "of murder is absurd."

"The accusation stands. I do not yet know which one of you committed the crime. I have a friend here tonight" — she gestured toward Max — "as a witness. If I am murdered, he will inform the police about each of you and your motives. Further, I have written an account of Thursday for the police."

Jane Wilson burst out, "Murder? Oh, you must be wrong."

Tim Holt folded his arms, leaned back as if in a theater, a man ready to be entertained. "Are you playing a game with us? I like murder nights, but this is starting to sound kind of crazy."

Gretchen's face was hard. "That is a serious accusation."

"Serious. True. Here's what happened Thursday afternoon . . ." When Ves finished, her mouth twisted in a humorless smile. "What do you do when you know someone tried to arrange a fatal accident? You think, *My God, who wants me dead?* That's where it got easy. Not nice, but easy. I don't have enemies. I never saw any point in quarreling with people. Nobody wants me dead because I cheated them or stole a lover. But when I die, each person in this room will be much, much richer. And" — a slight hesitation, then a shrug — "when I brought the dessert in to the dining room the night we had our dinner, I knew one of you wanted me dead."

Adam sneered. "I suppose one of us stuck pins in a voodoo doll."

Ves lifted a thin hand, rubbed against one cheek. "I grew up here. I can tell you things about voodoo that will make you never want to leave the safety of a lighted room. The room was lighted that night. I had candles in the centerpieces and the chandelier was bright. But one of you had already made the decision that I had to die. I knew it then. I know it now. One of you was here Thursday, came inside, made a high step slicker than a greased pig." She paused, swallowed. "What's worse" — her voice was low — "the murderer waited long enough to watch me limp to my car, then came inside and cleaned the step. I suggest each of you look around because —"

Again Max tried to capture a mélange of faces. As he looked, perhaps too quickly, he had a sense he'd missed something important, an expression, a movement, a glance . . .

"— this may be your only opportunity to

say you spent an evening with a murderer. Now I will speak directly to the murderer. I" — she paced her words — "do not intend to die." Her cane thumping, Ves crossed to a marble-topped table. She leaned the cane against the table, used her left hand to lift the lid of a gilt and black japanned box. Her right arm was still in a sling. She reached into the box with her left hand.

Jane Wilson gasped as a gleaming black revolver came into view.

Ves handled the firearm with ease, pointing the barrel away from the guests. "Colt .45, 1911 model. Semiautomatic. The safety is on. At the moment." She was crisp. "I'm ambidextrous so I'm an equally good shot with my left hand. You will notice I am pointing it to one side and at the floor. That's commonsense handling of a gun. But be aware, whoever comes after me will be shot."

Max eased an omelet onto each plate, carried the plates to the kitchen table. "Mushrooms, ham, onions, Monterey Jack jalapeño cheese."

Annie blew him a kiss and pushed the basket with homemade biscuits to the center of the table. "Honestly, sometimes I wonder how I could be so lucky. A handsome hunk who cooks." She admired her plate, a serving of salsa on one side, three strips of bacon, fresh-cut papaya. She speared a piece of fruit.

Max smiled, bent to kiss the top of her head, took the chair opposite her.

Annie waggled the fruit at him. "You had a ringside seat last night. We heard everything, but I wish we could have seen their faces when Ves said one of them was a murderer."

Max cut a piece of omelet, frowned.

Annie felt some of the morning's pleasure, the toasty kitchen, sunlight shining through white curtains, Dorothy L determinedly jumping to the counter and Max as determinedly removing her, seep away when she saw his worried expression.

Max looked across the table, his blue eyes dark with concern. "Ves wanted me there to watch them. I'm afraid I missed something. When Ves told them all to look around because she thought it was the only time they'd ever see a murderer, I think one of them looked — and saw a murderer."

Annie gripped the plastic handle, pulled the razor tip of the box cutter through plastic tape, flipped up the box flaps. Her nose wrinkled in delight. She never tired of the smell of new books. She approved of the large type chosen for the title of *Missing Pieces* by Heather Gudenkauf, sure to catch the eye of browsers. She lifted out five books at a time, transferred them to a dolly, some destined for the shelves, some for an end cap, a good half dozen had been preordered and would await pickup behind the front cash desk.

She worked steadily until midmorning, felt she'd earned a cappuccino. With whipped cream. And a cherry. She settled at the table near the coffee bar, sipped her reward, and faced the fact that she was restless and uneasy.

Agatha landed lightly next to the cup, gave it a dismissive glance, lifted limpid green eyes to stare at Annie.

Annie often shared thoughts with Agatha. "I'm scared for Ves. So she's handy with a gun. How can she be alert twenty-four/seven? She thinks she's warned off an attack. But it looks to me like telling them she knows one of them is after her changes everything. The killer wanted her death to be an accident. No questions. No problems. Now that Ves is making sure the police will know about the trust, the murderer might as well kill her any way possible. He — or she — can lurk in the woods with a rifle and pick Ves off. Or wait until summer and she goes out for a swim and run her down with a motorboat. Or monkey with her brakes. I don't think threats will stop this murderer."

Agatha abruptly crouched, peered down the corridor. In a swift move, she flew through the air, raced in a blur, scooped up a toy mouse, tossed it in the air, caught it.

Annie took a last sip from her mug. Everything was out in the open now. There was no need for subterfuge or subtlety. Annie nodded decisively, pushed back her chair. So far as she knew, only one person had lied about their whereabouts Thursday afternoon. Maybe there was a good reason. Or a very bad one.

Annie stepped into the bank, still uncertain how to approach Fred. He'd had the hunted air of a high schoolboy busted with marijuana when Martin Ford came up behind him and laughed when Annie asked if Fred had been on a holiday Thursday afternoon. If Fred hadn't looked so uncomfortable, she might not have called and discovered that Fred had not been at the office of a dental surgeon as he'd claimed. Should she ask him straight out, say she'd called the dental office and mentioned him and how he'd been there Thursday and thought so highly of Dr. Garcia and been surprised —

Her interior monologue broke off. The only teller on duty was Estelle Parker. Annie hesitated. Maybe Fred was on break. Estelle had a tired but pleasant face. She was nearing retirement and often talked about her plans, she was going to go home to Idaho, live with a younger sister. Annie came up to the counter, was glad there were no other customers. "Hi, Estelle. Looks like you are handling everything alone this morning."

Estelle's placid face was untroubled. "I guess Fred has the day off. Mr. Ford forgot to tell me, and he took the early ferry this morning. He's picking up his wife at the airport. Anyway, it's been pretty quiet. They should have told me." It was as near as Annie had ever heard Estelle sound aggrieved. "Fred didn't say a thing yesterday about not being here. He said he'd see me tomorrow. Meaning today. But" — a shrug — "he's not here. What can I do for you?"

Annie shook her head. "I wanted to tell Fred about a book I thought he'd enjoy. I'll check back another time."

Max drove the VW with the windows down.

He braked by the sidewalk in front of the bank

Annie, her curls windblown, her soft tee molded to her by the breeze, pulled open the passenger door. "Do you have the address?" She slid onto the seat, turned toward him.

Max wanted to drive home, fast, and open the windows in their bedroom to welcome in the breeze and turn to Annie —

"You did get the address?" A pause. A swift smile, a head shake. "Max, be serious."

He was serious. Maybe later today . . . Right now Annie was focused on the tuft-haired teller. Okay, they'd go see Fred, then he'd bring her back to her car, suggest they meet at home for lunch. When they were home . . . "I have the address. I'm in the VW, the better to pretend no one sees us. Always glad to drop everything" — his tone implied he'd been hard at work though he suspected Annie knew he was enjoying a cheerful practice session on the indoor golfing green at Confidential Commissions — "and join you in" — a suggestive pause — "the frolic of the moment. But why do you want me to ferry you to Fred's house?"

"You were there."

Max blinked. "At Fred's house?" Sometimes Annie lost him.

She laughed. "At Ves's last night, so Fred knows you're helping Ves."

The VW turned onto a sun-dappled street with modest one-story homes. "Is my presence supposed to instill panic in his heart? Am I the strong silent sidekick and you're the inquisitor? That I can do. What are you going to say? *Fred, I know you were at Ves's house and she told everyone about her fall and you lied to me the other day about going to the dentist on Thursday so what's the deal?*"

"Absolutely." Annie was combative. "It's very strange that he didn't come to work the day after Ves had them to her house."

Max's tone was light. "As in, one action is caused by another? Let me see. It thunders. Dorothy L comes into the room. Dorothy L made it thunder. Ves warns the murderer. Fred doesn't come to work so he's the murderer."

"Maybe." She didn't laugh.

Max slowed, checking addresses. "Here we are." He pulled up in front of a one-story frame house painted a cheerful yellow. A white picket fence enclosed the small yard.

Annie popped out of the car and headed for the gate.

Max caught up with her. He was firm.

"You do the talking. Ask the man why he took the day off. I can't wait to hear his answer."

"I'll ask him why he lied about going to the dentist."

"Now that" — the gate clicked shut behind them — "might elicit a sexy answer."

Again, Annie's glance was chiding. "Do you ever think about anything else?"

"Occasionally." He grinned. "Then I get back to what matters."

The porch was shady beneath an overhang. Two wicker chairs looked inviting. Annie stepped forward, punched the bell.

Silence.

Max gestured at the driveway. "No car. But he may always put it in the garage." Annie rang again.

The only answer was the caw of a crow who'd landed on a porch railing to watch them.

Annie knocked, kept on knocking. Finally her hand dropped.

Max leaned against a porch pillar. "Either he's not home or, as they quaintly said in the olden days, he isn't receiving callers."

Annie glanced at the well-kept bed of peonies. "Maybe he's in the backyard. And he's mulching or trimming or whatever it is gardeners do in February. Let's go look."

She plunged off the porch in her customary rush.

Max followed at a leisurely pace. He came up beside Annie to gaze at the backyard, which offered proof of Fred's gardening bona fides, clumps of azaleas and a bed with winter-blooming pansies. A wheelbarrow rested beside a small flagstone patio. Cotton gardening gloves rested in the barrow next to clippers. "No Fred." Max knew it was a statement of the obvious. They were the only inhabitants of the backyard except for small gray squirrels that darted about their duties and a trilling cardinal in a magnolia.

Annie spread her hand. "Look at the azaleas. They'll be gorgeous next month. He and Laurel could commune about snails and such. But he isn't here. I'll try the bank again tomorrow."

As they neared the street, he put his arm around her shoulders, gave her a hug. "How about we go home and . . . ?"

7

Henny Brawley enjoyed eating breakfast on her porch that overlooked the marsh. She watched the gold and red of the sun spill across dark water. She chose the porch in all seasons, remaining indoors only when it rained. She was comfortable, despite the fiftyish temperature, in a wool cardigan over a turtleneck, corduroy slacks, thick cotton socks, and ankle-high leather boots. A long twitching grayish nose rose above the glass top of the table. Dark eyes gazed at her hopefully. She sliced a chunk of waffle, offered it. "Good morning to you as well, Cinnamon." The dog slurped the waffle from her hand, leaving moist warmth behind.

Henny smiled, poured a little more syrup on the waffle. She liked Fridays, her usual day to grocery shop, exchange books at the library, tend to errands. She was content. Perhaps this afternoon she and Cinnamon would take the north trail at the nature preserve and Cinnamon could sniff the tracks of raccoons and deer.

A muted trill sounded from the pocket of her cardigan. She felt a flicker of surprise. It was early for a call. She pulled out her cell, recognized the caller, swiped to answer. Her voice was perhaps a shade higher than usual. "What's happened?" She never doubted something had happened. Good news rarely came at odd hours.

"Figured you'd be up." Marian Kenyon talked fast. "An early-morning fisherman at Fish Haul Pier snagged more than he expected. He was looking for dogfish and skates, that's about what you find in February, but he caught a floater. Even worse, a guy he knew, Fred Butler, dead, puffed up from immersion. He — the fisherman, not Fred — called the cops. I got it on the scanner. The body's lying on the pier. Poor guy — the fisherman — was a buddy of Fred's. Tough. Doc Burford —"

Henny pictured the big, rumpled island doctor, chief of staff at the hospital as well as the island medical examiner.

"— is here. He said it looks like a drowning, but he'll do an autopsy. You took me to breakfast and you asked about a bunch of people. One of them was Fred Butler. You also said you and unnamed others were trying to prevent something bad from happening. What would that be? A drowning?"

"No." Henny's reply was swift. "It was something else — someone else — altogether."

There was a doubtful pause. "Are you telling me this is one big coincidence? You want to know about Fred in regard to some unexplained bad scenario and he turns up dead and there's no connection?"

Henny frowned. "I don't know of a connection. There was no threat to Fred Butler."

"That leaves coincidence." Marian's voice was heavy with doubt. "I suppose it's possible. And maybe I'll get a free ticket to the basketball finals because I ate cornflakes this morning. You don't mind if I mention to Billy Cameron that you and unnamed others had an interest in Fred."

Henny was blunt. "Why would he care?"

"Cops like to tidy things up. Did Fred fall, did he jump, was he pushed?"

Henny was firm. "You've read too many headlines. There's no reason to believe Fred's death wasn't an accident. Is there?"

Marian was equally firm. "The guy doesn't have on boat clothes. Or a life vest. Dressy casual. That's a tip-off he wasn't out boating and toppled into the water. Besides, he didn't fish or have a boat. I know because I talk to people everywhere from Parotti's to the bank. It's an occupational disease. If Fred boated I'd know about it. Fred hunted for gold. As in buried treasure, but he was otherwise rational. Anyway, he didn't boat or fish. So what's the occasion in February that he *falls*" — her tone put the verb in italics — "from Fish Haul Pier into the harbor? Did he climb up on the rail and sit there with his feet dangling, enjoying a February breeze? That's an accident that smells like old fish to me. Or maybe he went down the ladder on the south side and jumped in."

Henny remembered the ladder and small landing on the south side of the pier.

"I can see Fred doing a lot of things, grubbing around for gold, working in his yard, volunteering at the rec center. I don't see him going out in a boat on a February night. Nix the idea of a boat. So he comes to the pier. How does he 'accidentally' fall in? If it wasn't an accident, we have to assume he jumped. If so, why? If he didn't willingly jump, somebody pushed him. Why would anyone kill Fred Butler?"

Henny held her cell, stared out at the marsh, a vee of pelicans diving down to murky water seeking their breakfast. She didn't believe in coincidence either. But Marian was right. No explanation made sense. If Fred went to the pier, and that seemed odd in itself, how could he have fallen? But the alternatives, suicide or murder, seemed utterly unlikely.

Marian pounced. "Had you seen Fred lately?"

"Not recently." Henny hadn't seen Fred in several weeks. It wasn't her place to reveal Ves Roundtree's near escape or to describe Annie's talk with Fred or Max at Ves's house with a walkie-talkie in place. There might be a good explanation for Fred's drowning, and she had no reason to connect his death with Ves Roundtree's danger, but just in case, the police should be informed. "Annie and Max Darling might know more."

Annie pulled her peacoat tighter across her front. "Do you think Fred didn't come to work because he was dead?" She and Max had been lighthearted yesterday. She had wanted to know why Fred lied about that Thursday but she never thought that Fred, mild-mannered, polite Fred, had entered Ves's house and waxed a step high on her staircase. What should she think now?

The breeze tugged at Max's sweater. "It seems likely, doesn't it? Especially if it turns out he didn't ask for a day off." He lifted binoculars. "I can see him —"

Annie jammed her hands deep into the coat pockets and stared at water rippling under a stiff breeze, not at the clutch of uniforms standing in a semicircle.

"— lying on the pier. They haven't covered him yet. Doc Burford's talking to Billy. I see Fred clearly. A tan pullover sweater, white shirt collar showing, dark slacks. That's what he wore at Ves's house."

Annie still didn't look toward the pier. She didn't want to see Fred's body. If he was dressed as he had been at Ves's house, did that mean he drowned Wednesday night? "If he died Wednesday night . . ." She trailed off.

Max shot her an understanding glance. "Did he leave Ves's and come to the pier? It could be. Doc will figure out whether he died Wednesday night or yesterday."

Annie was glad he didn't go into details about stomach contents and digestion and rigor mortis and the effect of submersion in seawater.

Brakes squealed.

Annie turned. "Ves is here."

Marian Kenyon was at the end of the pier.

She turned to look at the van at the curb. Marian's red sweatshirt was ragged at the hem and her gray sweatpants baggy, her ankles bare above leather loafers. Obviously she'd rushed from her house sockless in whatever was handy in response to the alert about a drowning victim. The breeze roiled Marian's short-cut dark hair. She held a pen in one hand, a notebook in the other. A Leica hung from a strap around her neck.

The van door slammed. Ves came limping around the back, cane thumping.

She, too, looked as if she'd thrown on the first clothes at hand, a gray pullover, black slacks. Since her fall, she'd worn dirt-stained sneakers, likely part of her gardening ensemble. Her tight red curls needed a comb. She was breathing jerkily when she came up to them. "Do they know when he drowned?"

Annie understood Ves's unspoken fear. Had Fred Butler come to her house and left it to deliberately die? She reached out, touched a tense arm. "No one knows yet. If it happened after he left your home, it could mean he was the guilty one." Was Fred a failed murderer afraid he was going to be accused? She remembered an entry in Emma's *Detecting Wisdom* from Inspector

Houlihan, *When a perp panics, anything can happen.*

"He looked scared Wednesday night. But I can't believe Fred tried to kill me." Her tone was incredulous. "He looked absolutely sick when I told about how I fell. Then I warned them with the gun. I thought the gun upset him."

The sound of footsteps, men's deep voices.

Max looked at the pier. "Here they come."

Billy Cameron was in a brisk conversation with Sergeant Lou Pirelli when they reached the steps. The police chief's short-cut fair hair with a sprinkling of silver was bright in the morning sunlight. A big man, he carried his heft with ease. A pullover sweater emphasized broad shoulders. His navy slacks were freshly pressed. Stocky Lou Pirelli, a good five inches shorter, hurried a little to keep pace. Lou was darkly handsome, a superb swimmer, and a regular at Death on Demand. He loved to reread Ed McBain's 87th Precinct books. Hyla Harrison, ginger hair pulled back in a bun, carried a notebook, made notes as Billy spoke.

Billy's tenor voice carried. ". . . billfold contained a fair amount of cash. Put a call out for his car."

Lou responded. "I already looked it up. A

155

2006 Camry." He rattled off the license plate.

"Find out who talked to him last, state of mind, could he swim —" Billy saw Annie, Max, and Ves. He paused, studied them intently, then thudded down the pier steps, Lou and Hyla close behind. Billy stopped in front of them. "Are you here because of Fred Butler?" He saw their faces, jerked a big thumb. "I'll see you at the station."

Billy Cameron stood at the end of the stained Formica-topped table in the break room, which was much larger than his office. Lou Pirelli was to his right. Lou held a pen poised over a notebook. Hyla Harrison was to his left. She'd already clicked on the tape recorder. Annie was next to Hyla, then Max. Across the table, Ves Roundtree sat next to Lou.

Billy kept his expression pleasant, nonthreatening, but he was highly attuned to the faces turned toward him, Annie Darling with sadness and uncertainty in her eyes, Max Darling frowning thoughtfully, always-on-the-move Ves Roundtree oddly subdued. He knew Annie and Max well, had risked his own career to help Annie prove Max's innocence when a young woman was found dead with Max's bloodied tire tool next to her. He liked them. Admired them. Trusted them. Normally Ves Roundtree exuded the fizz of a just-uncapped soda. Not today. That the three of them arrived at Fish Haul Pier in response to news of Fred Butler's death aroused his intense interest. Drownings were usually accidental, a slip on slick wood perhaps compounded by an inability to swim well, or the result of carelessness, venturing into a riptide or not wearing a life preserver out on a boat or too much alcohol. That was his expectation when he arrived at Fish Haul Pier. Now he wondered.

He looked at Annie. "Why did you come to the pier?"

"Marian Kenyon called Henny Brawley. Henny called me."

Another familiar name. Henny Brawley was one of the island's most respected residents.

"Your connection to Fred Butler? Henny's connection?"

Ves clawed through her frizzy hair. "The connection is actually mine. Wednesday night he was at my house. I'll tell you everything." She explained about the brother's estate. Lou interrupted, got the names, repeated them, "Bob and Katherine Farley, Jane Wilson, Adam Nash, Fred Butler, Curt Roundtree."

Ves described the dinner she held to share an account of the estate. "I also invited Gretchen Roundtree and Jane's boyfriend, Tim Holt." She told how she went to the kitchen for the dessert. "When I came in the dining room, it was like teetering on the edge of a cliff. I was terrified. I knew one of them wanted me dead."

Lou held up a hand. "Let me get the dates. The dinner where you brought the heirs up to date on the estate was Friday, February fifth. You fell the following Thursday, February eleventh. You invited those you suspected to your house Wednesday, February seventeenth."

Billy sorted times and dates in his mind, the dinner, the slick step the following Thursday, her return from the hospital and a clean step, her visit Monday to Death on Demand, Annie going to Ves's house and seeing the dining room where Ves claimed someone walked on her grave, Annie enlisting Max, his mother, Emma Clyde, and Henny Brawley to find out where the dinner guests were at five P.M. Thursday, February 11, their lack of success, Ves's decision to summon the dinner guests to her house on Wednesday, Fred's body found Friday.

Billy wanted clarity. "They came to your

house Wednesday, February seventeenth."

"Yes." Ves spoke rapidly. "I also asked Max to come. I told the guests one of them was a murderer and I didn't intend to die. I have a Colt .45. I showed my gun to them."

Billy felt his face tighten. "Attempted murder, but not one of you" — he looked at each in turn — "informed the police."

Ves said wearily, "What could you have done?"

"Quite a bit. We would have investigated. Looked for forensic evidence. Talked to those you suspected." He was brusque. "Fred Butler was one of the suspects. Now he's dead. We don't know how or why he drowned. He may accidentally have fallen from the dock. He may have chosen to die. He may have been killed. If we had been called in to seek the facts about the slick step, it's possible the outcome may have been different." He realized his tone was harsh, regretted his momentary anger, said quickly in a milder voice, "Or possibly not." He looked at Ves. "You have a license for that .45?"

"Yes."

"Very well. Is there any other information that might relate to Fred Butler?"

Annie leaned forward. "Fred claimed he'd gone to the dentist the afternoon Ves fell.

But he looked so scared and uneasy that I checked with the dentist's office. Fred lied. He isn't a patient of the dentist he said he was seeing. I went to the bank yesterday morning." Annie's voice was thin. "He wasn't there. I wanted to ask him why he'd lied."

Billy was grim. "We'll find out."

Marian Kenyon still wore the red sweatshirt and baggy sweatpants. "I came straight from the newsroom. I am starving. Do you have anything but those croissants dabbed with chicken salad that you give to old ladies wearing purple hats?" She stood by the coffee bar, looked hopeful, aggravated, pitiful.

Annie was defensive. "They're great croissants. I get them from a French bakery in Savannah."

Marian flung herself into a chair at the nearest table. "Okay, if that's all you can offer, I'll take it."

"I can do better." Annie hurried behind the coffee bar, bent to the small refrigerator, rose with two foil-wrapped oblongs. "Miss Jolene has a special today on pulled pork sandwiches, crusty buns, and mustard BBQ sauce. I bought two of them." She didn't add that she'd intended to ring Max and invite him to join her in sybaritic indulgence, but Marian was in need of sustenance. Annie unwrapped the sandwiches, placed them on a paper plate. "I'll pop them in the microwave."

Annie fixed Marian an espresso, always her jolt of choice, and herself a glass of unsweetened iced tea, added, true to her Texas roots, a basket of corn chips and green chili salsa. The microwave pinged. She served the sandwiches on cheerful yellow plates.

Marian sighed happily. As she ate, she complained. "Henny Brawley is like somebody in witness protection who won't give out a peep unless the DOJ signs on." Another big bite. "Apparently you are the DOJ. When I tracked down Henny, she said to ask you, it wasn't her place to say anything. Something funny, as in *peculiar* not *humorous,* is going on and I want to know the link between now-deceased Fred Butler and the other people Henny asked about. I smell a story like Agatha" — a nod at the black cat regarding them steadily from the counter of the coffee bar — "smells pulled pork." She attacked the remainder of the sandwich. Marian was a dog with a bone and she didn't intend to let go.

Annie cut her sandwich in half, scooped salsa with a chip.

Marian devoured the last of her sandwich, still looked pitiful. "I don't suppose you have another sandwich."

Wiry, bony, fast-moving Marian never gained an ounce, and she was always munching on something. Annie used her knife to slide her untouched half onto Marian's plate.

"Thanks." Another mumble. "Why is Henny mum and what's up? Obviously Henny alerted you to the gathering on Fish Haul Pier unless you have a scanner at your bedside. You must have more than a passing interest in Fred's demise since you and Max showed up this morning."

Annie knew Marian well. Marian could be trusted. "It all started . . ."

Marian's dark eyes widened as she listened. At Annie's conclusion, she immediately fastened on the salient facts. "Fred lied about the afternoon somebody greased a step, and Wednesday night Ves waggled a gun at her chosen suspects." The reporter's gamine face drooped with regret. "I could write a hell of a story about Rufus's estate and the dinner party and the slick step and Ves confronting the heirs, but I can't use any of it, not even as deep background. Not unless I want to see the *Gazette* sued for libel. I can't name people as possible mur-

162

derers without one of them scurrying to a lawyer, even though it looks like Fred was the perp. You've squelched my hopes for a scoop, but Fred's flop in the harbor may make sense." She wiped a smear of mustard sauce from her chin, leaned back in the chair. "Re: Fred, accident doesn't seem likely. There's no reason to suspect murder. Looks to me like he jumped. The autopsy report won't be out for a couple of days but Doc Burford told Billy unofficially that he estimated the body had been in the water between thirty to thirty-six hours. That puts him in the drink Wednesday night. Do you know what time the confab at Ves's broke up?"

"Max got home about nine twenty."

Marian finished her espresso. "That works for Fred to be at the pier by half past nine. Maybe he hung out there for a while, nerving himself up to take the plunge." Her expressive face was somber. "Jeez. Can you imagine . . . I don't want to imagine. We cling to life like barnacles to a boat bottom. Doesn't matter how rough the water gets, how dirty." A pause. "Most of us."

Annie felt a wash of sadness. What a way for a life to end. "He must have felt pretty desperate."

Marian's eyes narrowed. "I guess he was.

Ves confronts the heirs. Fred jumps. Cause and effect. Who goes to the end of Fish Haul Pier on a cold February night? Maybe a hot couple not worried about the weather. Not a middle-aged bank teller fully dressed in casual clothes, no fishing rod, not that people fish there after dark anyway. He had no reason to be on the pier. He either climbed over the railing or he went down that ladder on the south side of the pier. Why? To stick a toe in the water? Not likely. Billy figures he climbed up on the railing at the end of the pier. He had on leather loafers with pretty worn soles and Billy thinks he got up on the railing, teetered there, slipped, and fell to his right."

Annie stared at Marian. "What crystal ball was our police chief consulting?"

Marian gurgled. "I'll share that with him. Actually, it's good old-fashioned cop think. There's a contusion on the right side of Fred's head and that fits with standing on the railing and falling to the right."

Annie was startled. "Maybe somebody hit him and dumped him over the railing."

Marian was dismissive. "Who wanted to kill Fred? A jealous husband? An aggrieved bank customer? Did Fred have a secret life unknown to others? Was Fred a sleeper agent for Red China and he'd decided to turn in his chopsticks? Murder requires a motive."

Annie knew Marian was right. Domino-playing Fred Butler was not a likely candidate for a lurid love affair or nefarious activities. But it was possible there was more to Fred's life than Saturdays at Parotti's and working in a bank.

Marian lifted bony shoulders, let them fall. "I asked, pretty pro forma at this point, but I get paid to ask questions, was it maybe a mugging gone wrong? But who gets mugged at the end of a fishing pier? Billfold was in his back pocket. Forty-two dollars in cash, one credit card. Car keys in left front trouser pocket. Car parked in the Fish Haul Pier, nicely locked, no evidence of any damage." Marian arranged her knife and fork at the side of the empty plate. "Thanks for a lunch befitting a foraging reporter. And now I know a lot more about certain people's financial prospects than they'll ever dream. But hey, I don't gossip. Just for my own enjoyment. As for Fred, people will wonder why he jumped, and only a few of us will ever know."

Annie tried to concentrate on the chapbooks. Maybe an inner chant would get her in the groove. *Chapbooks, chapbooks, chap-*

books. She knew she was guilty of undisciplined thoughts. She could start off wondering about goldfish and pop to the name of Wiley Post's monoplane the *Winnie Mae* to wondering if panda fur smelled as sweet as a cat's to a passionate diatribe against rosemary as a seasoning ever for anything. At the moment, despite her best effort to focus on Henny's copy: *Juanita Sheridan was as adventurous as any of her fictional heroines . . .* Now her mind tugged at Fred's lie about Thursday. He could have been at Ves's house and when Ves warned them, did he think she would find out and did he decide to jump at that moment?

The front door opened. The ping sounded like a text message. Her thoughts careened again. Death on Demand needed something more dramatic to announce customers. A bugle call? The *Inner Sanctum* creaking door? No, something about the island. Hey, maybe the sound of an alligator. That would be cool, a low, throaty growl, almost like the rumble of distant thunder.

The thump of a cane brought her to her feet. Ves Roundtree came down the center aisle. She looked uncertain of her welcome. "I hate to bother you, but I have to talk to someone." She pulled out a chair, sank into it, leaned the cane against the table. "Billy

166

called and told me Fred's death looks like suicide, that he apparently went from my house to the pier, and jumped. Billy says that makes it likely that Fred was the person who waxed the step, so I can feel safe now. I thanked him, but ever since we talked I've been thinking about it. So here I am, hoping you can help me make sense of everything."

Annie replied quickly, "I'll help if I can."

"I guess I'm looking for someone else's perspective. You may decide I'm nuts. Maybe I am."

Annie shook her head slightly.

"Thanks." A wry smile. "Billy obviously thinks Fred committed suicide because he tried to kill me and he was afraid I was figuring out what happened. That could be true. But I don't believe it. Can't believe it. Maybe I have that thing — what is it? — second sight. Or maybe I'm a melodramatic fool. But I remember the dinner and that awful sensation, someone looking at me and wanting me dead. Fred was his usual self that night, mild, unassuming. I can't believe the death wish came from Fred. If it wasn't Fred, if it was one of the others, and that means Fred committed suicide for some other reason."

"He died Wednesday night." Annie was

making the point that Fred drowned after Ves threatened to shoot if attacked.

Ves's face tightened. "I get it. I scared Fred; Fred killed himself." She brushed back a reddish curl. "They think he went from my house to the pier because he was wearing the clothes he wore Wednesday night. Plus something about how many hours he'd been in the water." She talked fast. "You heard everything that happened over the walkie-talkie. I warned them. I was telling the murderer that I was prepared. Obviously I had no idea which one was guilty. Why would Fred kill himself?"

Annie remembered the voices over the walkie-talkie and Ves announcing, *"But be aware, whoever comes after me will be shot."* If Fred was guilty, he saw doom closing in on him.

Ves ran her fingers through her hair. "I was tough. Like a bounty hunter. But I didn't wave the gun at anybody. I handle guns right. I handled the gun like I could shoot someone. That's scary for someone who doesn't do guns. I put on a big show. But you want to know about me and hunting? I've never killed anything. Ever. Dad and Rufus shot deer, squirrels, whatever moved. I wouldn't go out with them. I shot at pop bottles on a fence railing." She gave

168

Annie an embarrassed look. "I can't even kill spiders. You know what I do when a spider gets in the house? I get a cup and a napkin and I catch the spider in the cup and cover the opening with the napkin and go to the garage and put the spider out in a corner to build a web there. That night when I warned them, I was trying to stay alive. I wanted to scare the murderer. If somebody came in my house and crept into my room and I knew it was Death, maybe I could shoot."

Annie, too, found it hard to imagine shooting a living creature. She'd never understood hunting. To lift a rifle and see a live creature drop to the ground and die appalled her. To shoot a human being would either be incredibly hard or horribly easy.

Ves placed her hands on the table. They looked small, defenseless. "I wanted to scare them. Fred looked scared. Now I should feel home free, right? The big bad murderer is dead. But I don't feel home free. I don't believe Fred tried to kill me. I don't know why he jumped off the pier. I don't think he was a murderer running scared. I want you to know that if my body turns up, you can bet it's not suicide." She pushed up from the chair. "Now I'm going to try and act like everything's okay. Maybe the powers

169

that be have it right. Maybe I don't have to be afraid. If I'm alive next month, I'll start to believe Fred was guilty. Until then, I'm looking over my shoulder."

Max lounged in his very comfortable red leather desk chair with his cell phone and listened as his mother recounted a visit to Ves Roundtree's store.

Laurel concluded, "I am concerned about Ves."

"I'll tell Annie."

"Dear Annie." Laurel's tone was affectionate. "How is she?"

"She's fine." He sketched a rainbow. Nice of his mother to always inquire about Annie. "We're going to Parotti's for dinner."

"I'm sure she's very busy with the chapbooks." A rather lengthy pause.

Max refrained from a reply.

"And you are quite busy, too?"

"Busy?" He looked at his desk, bare except for his favorite framed photograph of Annie, dusty blond hair, steady gray eyes, a face that always tugged at his heart. "Working away." He glanced at the yellow pad in his lap, a rather good sketch of Dorothy L on a windowsill, tail vibrating as she stared at a blue jay. Artistic endeavor surely qualified as work.

"Don't overdo. Love you."

"Love you, too." He tapped off, smiled, and picked up his 3B regular pencil. He could always count on his mother for encouragement. He looked at Annie's photo, said conversationally, "Laurel cautioned me not to overdo." Annie would think that suggestion riotously funny. He tilted farther back. Annie loved to quote Laurel's comment the day his mother looked at him admiringly as he relaxed in his big red leather chair and proclaimed, "Truly a chair for a titan of industry. Perfect for you." Annie later asked demurely, "What does the titan desire at the moment?" He'd replied, "Desire? Only you." Her response had been eminently satisfactory.

Annie waved hello at Ben Parotti, hurried across the old wooden floor to the booth where Max stood waiting. She loved the gleam in Max's eyes and looked back signaling *Yes, I love you, later.* She slid into the booth and he settled opposite her.

"Ma sends her regards."

Annie was immediately on full alert. It wasn't that she didn't welcome good wishes from her mother-in-law, but Laurel's contacts with Max often included plans for Annie that she was determined to avoid. "Laurel?"

There was a flurry when Ben arrived with tea for her and beer for Max and took their orders, the usual, grilled flounder for Max, fried oysters for Annie, coleslaw for both, jalapeño corn bread. ·

Max poured his beer into a frosted mug. He thought it more tactful not to mention Laurel's delicate reference to the chapbooks. "She said she was certainly surprised about Fred Butler. She always thought he was the nicest man. Ma said she believed that an accident occurred. And that's what she'd told Ves. She wanted to know if you'd talked to Ves."

"Ves came by the store." Annie wouldn't forget Ves's tight face as she announced if anyone found her dead, it wasn't suicide.

"Ma went to Ves's shop." His face crinkled in a frown. "She said Ves was a nervous wreck and her hand went down below the counter when the door opened. Ma had a feeling there was a gun down there."

Not even the high gleam of his varnished desk looked bright on a cloudy Monday morning. Billy Cameron arranged several folders. He opened Doc Burford's autopsy report.

White male. Age 46. Height 5'7". Weight 182 pounds. General health excellent. Cause of death: drowning. Body recovered 8:06 A.M. Friday, February 19. Immersion in water estimated at 30 to 35 hours. Puts approximate time of death between 9 P.M. February 17 and 8 A.M. February 18. Slight trauma to right frontal lobe.

At the top of the page, Doc Burford had scrawled in a thick black ink: *Trauma could have been sustained if he balanced on railing, slipped, struck his head on the way down.*

Billy knew Fred Butler as he knew most of the island residents. He had always found

Fred genial and courteous at the bank, friendly at Parotti's on Saturdays. Billy thought of him as steady, dependable, precise, careful. He was not a man who would miscount your money. Billy balanced that picture against Ves Roundtree's claim that Fred was frightened Wednesday night. Why? Was he the kind of person who always thought a barb was directed at him? Did Fred immediately assume the worst — *she doesn't like me, she's angry with me* — when he encountered any kind of snub? Did Fred think Ves was accusing him of waxing the step? That was possible. If Fred took Ves's accusation personally and if he was guilty, had he fled to Fish Haul Pier and, in a distressed state, lost his balance and fallen? Or had he hurried to the pier, frantic that he would be accused of plotting a death, and jumped into dark cold water?

Billy turned his chair toward the window. The sun was bright this morning. A stiff breeze laced the harbor with whitecaps. He considered what he knew. He'd sent officers out across the island seeking information. Fred Butler had no boat. He did not fish. He could not swim. He was not seen, so far as they could discover, after he drove away from Ves Roundtree's house around nine o'clock. Officers had no luck finding anyone who had been in the vicinity of the pier that night. The temperature was in the forties and there was a slight mist, so it wasn't surprising no one was strolling on the boardwalk. Why would anyone go out on the pier on such a night? That question definitely held true for Fred Butler. Why did he go to Fish Haul Pier? He wasn't the outdoor type. But he definitely went to the pier, went into the water from the pier.

Three choices: accident, suicide, murder. Billy shook his head. Accident and homicide seemed unlikely. That left suicide, which strongly suggested he feared exposure as a would-be murderer.

Death on Demand bustled with vacationers in June, often painfully sunburned and seeking books to read in the shade of beach umbrellas. Annie wondered if they realized sunlight reflected off sand and an umbrella alone wouldn't suffice. A wide-brimmed hat, filmy long-sleeved white top, and towel-draped legs were also advisable, plus plenty of sunscreen. But it wasn't June. It was a foggy Monday in February and only she and Agatha were in the store. She frowned, pulled her cell from her pocket, swiped, knew caller ID identified her to Marian, dispensed with a greeting. "Anything new about Fred Butler?"

"I just got off the phone with Billy." Marian's raspy voice was matter-of-fact. "Presser at ten A.M. to announce official cause of death: drowning. No judgment as to whether he died accidentally or on purpose. If there's a recent life insurance policy, it might be voided if his death is ruled a suicide. Anyway, the case is closed as far as the police are concerned. Billy will announce that Butler was wearing a dressy casual shirt and slacks and loafers, that his billfold and car keys were recovered, that his body showed no evidence of trauma other than a bruise on one temple that could have resulted from striking the pier railing. The presser wraps it up. I'll write the story and readers can draw their own conclusions. Now I've got to run — an alligator on the back porch of the library. Says he won't leave unless he gets the latest Joyce Carol Oates. I want to get there before the critter guy does. It will make a great photo. Wonder if they'll let me shove a stack of books up by his snout. The alligator's snout, not the critter guy's. I can see it now — Shakespeare's comedies, Edith Wharton, maybe Plato, and, of course, Oates's latest. An erudite alligator. I like it." The connection ended.

Another day, another focus. A man drowned one day, a perambulating alligator the next. This afternoon's *Gazette* would have a fun story by Marian and, if she knew Marian, a photograph of an alligator facing a stack of books. Annie picked up the copy for Henny's *Classic Crimes*. She needed to finish editing the Incredible Trio's manuscripts. Max had found a program that would make printing the chapbooks a snap. Emma's birthday was next week. If she hustled, Max was sure he could get the chapbooks done in time for a party. She looked at Henny's comment about *Rebecca* by Daphne du Maurier. *One of the great opening lines in fiction: "Last night I dreamt I went to Manderley again." The tone captures the foreboding and unease that permeate the story of a second wife who lives in the dead Rebecca's shadow. Brilliant.*

Annie agreed. First sentences could be the topic of a great essay, starting with Mary Roberts Rinehart's "One day last fall I ordered the swimming pool destroyed" in *The Swimming Pool* to Rhys Bowen's "Weather outside: utterly bloody!" in *Malice at the Palace*. Maybe she should put together her own chapbook, *Fabulous Firsts*. The weather had been cool and misty Wednesday night —

She gripped the soft lead pencil. Where had that come from? But she knew. She couldn't push away the fact of Fred Butler's death and Ves's insistence that Fred wasn't the would-be murderer. She glanced up at the wall clock. In a few minutes, Billy Cameron would announce death by drowning. And implicit in the bare facts was the likelihood of suicide. Apparently there was no family to mourn him, to face the misery of what-ifs. Everyone on the island would read this afternoon's *Gazette,* including Ves Roundtree. Ves grappled with a different kind of what-if.

Annie had a sudden clear memory of Fred's round face when she spoke to him at the bank, the widened eyes behind the bifocals, the quick panicked glance at the bank manager. He'd been scared that he would be caught out in a lie about his dental appointment. She wished she had been at Ves's house Wednesday night. Had Fred looked scared in the same way? Maybe he was simply scared of unpleasantness, and what could be more unpleasant than realizing you are a murder suspect? Maybe he was afraid word would get back to the bank. People who worked at banks could never afford a whiff of scandal. She wished she had a better sense of who Fred was. If he committed suicide — She frowned. There was no *if* about it. He committed suicide. The question was why. Unless there was something else going on in his life that led him to the end of the pier, the inescapable conclusion was that he was guilty of the attack on Ves and afraid he'd be caught out.

But Ves was sure she was still in danger.

Annie slapped her hand on the table. Papers slithered. Agatha stared at her reproachfully. "I'm sorry, sweetie. But it's awful to be afraid. If we were positive that Fred jumped because he set the trap, Ves could feel safe again."

Agatha's green eyes were unblinking.

"If we knew what Fred was thinking . . ." Her words trailed off.

Fred's state of mind. Unless something had been troubling him, unless he had been in a depressed mood, then clearly he left Ves's house and jumped because he had tried to kill her. It shouldn't be hard to find out about his demeanor in recent days. Was he happy or grim? If there was no hint of depression, Ves could put her gun back in the closet, not be fearful at every footstep.

Annie picked up her cell to call Billy, slowly put it down. The case was closed. But she wasn't bound by any rules.

■ ■ ■ ■

Annie felt sadness when she stepped into the bank lobby. Estelle Parker's kind face had a look of shock. She wore a navy silk dress, and Annie was sure the choice was a tribute to Fred, a way of saying, *I'm sorry, I won't wear something cheerful today, the first day here without you.*

Estelle saw Annie, tried to smile, blinked.

Annie hurried across the lobby to the counter. "I wanted to tell you how much we'll miss Fred."

Tears brimmed in Estelle's blue eyes. She snatched a tissue from a box. "I'm just sick. Fred and I have been here for such a long time, almost thirty years. He came two years after I started. My Jim was still alive and Fred was just out of high school and he and Evie were newlyweds. We used to go bowling together." Tears slid down her fair cheeks.

Annie reached out, touched a plump hand. "I suppose he was depressed. Maybe he was sick."

Estelle wadded the tissue into a ball. Pink flooded her cheeks. "There's some awful mistake. Fred was fine. I know he was fine. We told each other things. He'd just got a good report in his checkup. He told me he had low cholesterol and his blood pressure was excellent. He was kind of proud. He was fine except for his teeth, and I don't know how much longer he had to go with that. He'd gone to the dentist every Thursday afternoon for a few weeks. But that's all that was wrong with him." Her face puckered. "He was happy as could be on Wednesday. He said his research — he loved to check through old histories and things like that — finally put him on the right track and he'd have some exciting news for me one of these days and when he did we'd go into Savannah and have a fancy dinner some Saturday. The police have it all wrong. He never jumped into the water. Never. It makes me so mad they are acting like he jumped just because it was odd to go out on the pier. Maybe he felt like a walk. Maybe he got dizzy. But he never jumped in the water. He wouldn't. He never missed Wednesday-night prayer meeting. He kept on going after Evie died — she died having a little girl who didn't live either — so why would he jump into water over anything else? He told me he didn't want to live without her, but he had to do what God said and she and their little girl were in Heaven and someday he'd see them. Oh, it makes me so mad, everybody acting like he committed suicide."

Annie said slowly, "He'd gone to the dentist every Thursday afternoon for a while?"

"Maybe three or four weeks, every Thursday afternoon. He never said exactly what it was. Maybe one of those awful new implant things. I don't know. But other than the dentist, he was fine." Her eyes flashed. "He was happy as could be on Wednesday."

Annie walked slowly across Main Street. The day had turned pleasant and sunny, the temperature nudging into the sixties. Did she need to call the dental office, see if Fred had been there on other Thursdays? The receptionist had been firm. Dr. Garcia had no patient named Fred Butler. Why did Fred leave work early on several Thursday afternoons? Where did he go? What did he do? He wasn't waxing a step on Ves's stairs the other Thursdays. Perhaps this was just an anomaly, a piece of information that led nowhere. The important takeaway from Estelle was Fred's state of mind. He wasn't a man struggling with depression. He was looking forward to the future when something good happened because of his research.

This fact, and she trusted Estelle's judgment, went a long way toward confirming Fred's decision to jump from the pier resulted from the confrontation at Ves's house Wednesday night. She tucked away the knowledge that didn't fit, Fred's false claim to be excused from work on previous Thursdays.

She lifted her hand, pulled open the heavy front door of Parotti's Bar and Grill. She was just inside when Ben came bustling toward her. Of course, he was on his way to the ferry for the afternoon run to the mainland. She'd arrived just in time. "Ben, I have a quick question."

"Fire away." He teetered on his feet, like a boxer ready for the bell.

She grinned at him. "You love running the *Miss Jolene* better than anything, don't you?"

His leprechaun face crinkled. "Reminds me of the days when I was a young man on freighters. What can I do for you?"

Ben kept his ferry punctual. Annie talked fast. She had a little speech prepared. "I'm putting together a memory book about Fred Butler for Estelle Parker, and I want to talk to some people who knew him well. He played dominoes here, and I wondered if you can give me the names of some of his friends."

"Nice thing to do." Ben patted her shoulder. "Talk to Bill Hogan at Gas 'n Go. He works the afternoon shift." Ben rocked back and forth faster, a man with a job to do. "You can include a tribute from me. Fred ate chili and corn bread here Tuesday nights and we had a right good talk last week. He said he had about decided to run for mayor. He was going to talk to folks, see if he could get support. I told him I'd back him. You know the trouble we have with Cosgrove."

Everyone dislikes somebody, and the penguin-shaped mayor topped Annie's list.

"Fred wanted the town to get behind new basketball courts at the Island Rec Center. Cosgrove opposes it. Fred was a good man and he loved this island and he had lots of hopes and plans for it."

Annie pulled up to the service pump. Gas 'n Go, which belonged to Ben, had two pumps, one self-serve, the other attended. She rolled down her window.

A tall lanky man in overalls approached. "Fill 'er up?"

"With regular. And please check the oil and tires. Are you Bill Hogan?"

"At your service, ma'am."

"Ben Parotti tells me Fred Butler was a

friend of yours." She saw acceptance on the long lean face. Ben's name was about the best recommendation she could have. "I'm gathering remembrances about Fred for a friend and I'm hoping you will share some memories."

"Well." He drawled out the word, bushy eyebrows bunched in concentration. "You could count on Fred. When my boy Rick was hurt in a cycle crash, Fred was at the hospital soon as he heard to give blood, and he went out and fed the chickens and took care of my horses while me and my wife was at the hospital."

"Had you seen Fred recently?"

"Saw him every Saturday, rain or shine. We play dominoes at Parotti's."

"Was he cheerful?"

Bill didn't seem to think her question odd. "Yeah." He sounded sad. "We had a beer after we finished. He was in a great mood. He was always nuts about pirate stuff. I don't know how a grown man could believe in old pirate maps. But he did. I never saw it but he used to talk about this yellowed crumbly parchment map and how he'd found it in the bottom of a trunk he picked up at a flea market. I could've told him they churn those out in prints shops and peddle them to suckers. But I never did. Hell, it

185

made him happy, gave him something to think about. I figure everybody has to have something to hope for. Saturday he said he'd figured out what he needed to do, he'd been counting all wrong. Something about so many paces this way, so many that way. He said it was like having a big lightbulb go off in his brain but it was brighter than any old lightbulb, more like a spotlight. He was sure he'd figured everything out, and it depended on where the arrow would land. I don't know what that had to do with pirates, but he was real excited, said he was going to be rich and maybe he'd take a trip to Paris, he'd always wanted to go to Paris." Bill pressed his lips together for an instant. "Anyway" — his voice was gruff — "I'm glad he was happy."

Annie stepped inside Trinkets 'n Treasures. She liked the way Ves had divided the shop. One side was pricey: the gleam of fine porcelain birds, figurines, and plates, a Sheffield silver tea urn, an antique derringer pistol, Chinese plates, an Egyptian chess set in ivory, two Sevres figurines of Napoleonic soldiers. A comfortable sofa faced the display. The other side was for budget shoppers: cookie cutters shaped like starfish, conch shells, salt water taffy, plastic beach buckets and trowels, kites, flip-flops, sun-block lotion, T-shirts with a T 'n T logo in bright pink, synthetic shell necklaces, a manually propelled scooter, an electric-powered scooter, skateboards, foam boogie boards, plastic beach umbrellas.

Ves came around the desk at the back. She moved slowly, but she was no longer using the cane. "Hi, Annie." She smiled but there were dark patches beneath her eyes.

"I have good news." Annie knew she sounded ebullient. She felt ebullient. She was about to give Ves her life back.

Ves gestured at the sofa. "I'm all in for good news. Are politicians being quarantined in Antarctica? Has the state decided to give a sales tax holiday for the summer? Is Jordan Spieth buying a house on the island?"

"I wish." Annie laughed as she settled on the sofa and turned to face Ves. "It's better than all three combined. You don't have to be frightened anymore. Fred Butler was a happy man. There was nothing wrong in his life. He wasn't sick. He wasn't depressed. He had no worries. He was happy and positive Wednesday. Everything in his life was good until he came to your house Wednesday night."

Ves stared, disbelief mixed with the beginnings of hope. "How can you be certain?"

Annie told her about Ben Parotti and Fred's plans to maybe run for mayor and campaign for basketball courts at the Island Rec Center, his announcement to Bill Hogan on Saturday that he'd soon be rich, his promise to Estelle Parker that he'd see her the next day and they would soon go for a celebratory dinner in Savannah.

Ves pounced. "He said he was going to be rich."

"Pirate gold. Nothing to do with you."

"Pirate gold?" Ves spoke as if the words made no sense.

"He believed in pirates." That didn't sound quite right. "He was into hunting for buried treasure." Ves would be well aware the Low Country had seen plenty of pirates in the early 1800s, and there were many tales of hidden loot, including a stash by Blackbeard. "Apparently Fred had a parchment map and he hadn't been following the directions properly and he'd figured out where an arrow would land and all he had to do was dig. He was really upbeat Saturday."

Ves gestured toward the tacky side of her store. "I have an assortment of parchment maps, all printed this year. I could have given him a half dozen different ones. You say he was happy Saturday. Maybe something happened between Saturday and Wednesday."

"He was happy Wednesday." Annie was emphatic. "He was fine." She frowned. "The only thing I can't pin down was why he lied about going to the dentist on Thursday. That was the first thing that made me think he might have been at your house, then Estelle said he'd been going to the dentist for several Thursdays in a row. He lied about the dentist. I don't know where he was the other times unless he was at your house for several Thursdays but didn't nerve himself up to set the trap until that last Thursday."

Ves pressed her fingertips against her cheeks. "Nerve himself up? That wasn't how I felt at the dinner. Whoever wanted me dead wanted it quick, without hesitation. But maybe he was like me. I have a gun. I talk tough. But the idea of shooting anyone scares me. Maybe he came a few times before he waxed the step. I guess I wanted me out of the way so he could really make a search for that treasure."

Annie felt certain that was what happened. All the ends might not be tidily tied, but Ves saw now that there could be only one reason for Fred's death Wednesday night. He went to the pier and jumped in the water because of what he learned at her house.

Annie sniffed appreciatively. "Mmmm."

Max turned from the pot on the stove. "Coming up soon. Will you check the corn bread?"

She moved to the oven, pulled down the door. The corn bread had a golden crust on top. She used a mitt, set the pan on the granite counter. "Perfection."

Max stirred with a wooden spoon. "I put in lump crabmeat as well as the crab claws." He put down the spoon, picked up a ladle, transferred steaming gumbo to pottery bowls.

The phone rang.

Annie had the corn bread loose and turned it onto a rack.

"Bad time to call. Let it go." Max held a bowl in each hand.

Annie pulled the cell from the pocket of her cardigan and checked caller ID. "It's Ves Roundtree. I better answer."

"Sure." He turned and poured the brown gumbo with crab claws, shrimp, lump crab, sausage, and okra back into the pot.

Annie perched on a stool by the center island, swiped to answer, punched Speakerphone. "Hi, Ves."

Ves's voice was low and hoarse. "It wasn't Fred."

Annie felt as if she'd been struck unexpectedly between her shoulder blades. "Not Fred?" Of course it was Fred who'd jumped from the pier. There was no question about that. Annie said firmly, "Of course it was Fred."

"Fred didn't try to kill me." The words came fast. "I started thinking about what Bill Hogan said. And then it hit me, Fred was going to dig where the arrow landed. I went out in the backyard, and there's Diana in the fountain. A long time ago the arrow broke off but that's the arrow Fred meant. I'm sure that's right because I tracked down Bill Hogan. I asked if he knew the name of the pirate Fred talked about and he said yes." A ragged breath. "Fred was looking for treasure buried by Black Jack MacDougal. I know a lot about Black Jack. Our house was owned by Jeremiah Jemson, and he had this beautiful daughter, Isabel. Black Jack was the second son of some English lord. He had no money but was highborn. Anyway, he had good manners and was a regular at grand dinners and dances in Charleston. Isabel visited some cousins there and she met John, as she called him, at a dance. They fell in love. Supposedly he visited the island several times. He roamed up and down the coast near here in the 1820s. I don't know if the romance really happened. Isabel died of the fever when she was nineteen. Black Jack came to see her before she got sick, and legend says he buried a trunk full of gold in the backyard, but when she died he went off to Barbados and was killed in a duel there. So Fred was looking for treasure in my backyard. The past few weeks I found some odd places in the yard where the dirt was soft and had odd lumps. I couldn't figure out what could have caused it."

Max was standing next to Annie at the island. He silently mouthed, "Gophers."

Annie put a finger to her lips.

Ves barreled ahead. "That explains his lying at work. Fred was coming here on Thursday afternoons before I got home from the shop and digging around in my backyard. I think he was here the Thursday someone came here to set a trap for me. Fred had no right to be here. As soon as he saw someone arrive, he slipped away. He might not have known the person who came inside the house. Don't you see, Fred had no idea what had happened to me, that the step was waxed and I fell, until he came here with the others Wednesday night. That's why he was scared. I told them someone had tried to kill me. Fred looked at someone and he was terrified. He knew who the murderer was. Maybe Fred thought about speaking up but he would have to admit he'd been there. Whomever he accused could say *Oh, I dropped by that afternoon to talk to Ves and I saw Fred and he was on the porch.* There must have been an instant when he almost spoke up, but he was too frightened." Her voice was low. "God, yes, he was right to be frightened."

Annie saw the connections, an arrow, Black Jack MacDougal, lying about Thursdays, lumps in the backyard. Fred could have meant Ves's house when he exulted about buried gold. She wasn't convinced. "Maybe that's true but maybe he decided to try and get rid of you and then he'd inherit from Rufus and he'd have the money to buy your house and it would be hard to sell a house where someone had just died, especially if anyone figured out your fall wasn't an accident."

"I told you how I felt at the dinner, the threat was cold, dangerous, hard. Not Fred."

Annie was skeptical. "Why would he meekly agree to meet this scary person at the end of Fish Haul Pier? In the dark. By himself. If he was scared in your living room, how do you think he'd have felt about meeting a murderer?"

Her answer was slow in coming and her tone sad. "Fred would be afraid no one would believe he was innocent if he admitted he'd been in my yard. Maybe the murderer told him since he hadn't spoken up, he was part of a conspiracy, told him to come to the pier around ten o'clock. Maybe Fred refused and the murderer said *Unless you come, I'll go to the police tomorrow and tell them I thought it over and decided I had to report I'd seen you in Ves's backyard, but if you cooperate no one will ever know.* Maybe the murderer told him all he had to do was sign a paper admitting he was in the yard at that time, and the murderer would keep it as insurance that Fred would keep quiet."

Annie remembered Fred's tension when the bank manager kidded him about the dentist. What would happen to his job if the bank learned he'd lied about dental appointments to dig for gold? "He'd be scared he'd lose his job."

"Fred didn't jump." Ves's voice was shaky. "He was stunned, thrown over the railing."

Annie felt breathless. "We need to tell Billy."

"He'll come back at me with all the objections you had. He won't say so publicly but he thinks Fred committed suicide. Billy will say that now there's a reason why Fred was in my yard. Billy will say Fred had no luck digging and thought it would be easier if I died and the house would be vacant. He could search without worrying about me, plus he'd inherit from Rufus. And I brought out a gun and told them I was ready for a killer, and Fred was afraid I'd hear about Black Jack MacDougal and know he was guilty."

"Billy will listen." Annie knew this was true. "I'll talk to him. I'll call him right now."

"It's after hours. I'll go see him in the morning. I want to think about Wednesday night. I want to remember where Fred sat and where he looked. I haven't had time to really concentrate. Something may come to me. I'll meet you in the morning. Nine o'clock."

Annie spoke quickly before the call could end. "Maybe you should go to the inn to spend the night."

"Don't worry. I have my gun. And believe me, I'll use it now. I liked Fred."

9

Annie parked in the lot north of the police station, rolled down the windows. She breathed deeply, enjoying the faint tang from the sea. The Sound was placid this morning. Puffy white clouds floated in a bright blue sky. She glanced at her watch. Almost nine. Ves didn't think Billy would be impressed that Fred was happy until he came to her house Wednesday evening. Billy could point out that suicides often mask their feelings. Annie intended to insist that Fred's death wasn't suicide. Fred was frightened after he learned of Ves's injury. Why? It was logical to assume he was in Ves's backyard on the Thursday she fell. He was looking for treasure in her yard, had likely been doing so for several Thursdays. He was there and saw someone approach the house. Annie hoped Billy would reopen the inquiry into Fred's death. Billy was painstaking, careful. Even if he wasn't persuaded by Ves's argument, he would surely try to find out where Ves's guests were Wednesday night. Doc Burford estimated Fred had been in the water thirty to thirty-five hours when he was found early Friday morning. Fred was last seen leaving Ves's house shortly after nine. Between then and eight the next morning he went into the water.

A deep throaty whistle announced the nine A.M. departure of the *Miss Jolene* for the mainland. Annie enjoyed the ferry, loved to stand on the upper deck, lean on the railing, and watch passing sailboats and shrimp trawlers and the occasional passenger ship.

Annie twisted to look at the street. Several cars, no familiar van. She hesitated, then fished out her cell, texted Ves: *Waiting for you at the station.* She opened the passenger door, climbed out, walked slowly toward the front steps of the one-story brick building that housed the Broward's Rock Police Station. She reached the steps, yanked out her cell. There had been no ping, no reply to her text. Annie found the number for Trinkets 'n Treasures. After several peals, Ves's voice: *We are sorry to have missed your call. If you'll —* Annie clicked off, tried the home number. The phone rang until it switched to voice mail. Annie clicked off.

She hurried up the short flight of steps.

Billy didn't turn on the siren. "Ves Round-tree is all right. Or she's not."

Annie sat tensely in the passenger seat of Billy's Ford sedan. He didn't drive a police car. Maybe most police chiefs used their own cars. She knew she was fastening on an irrelevancy to try and push away fear. Billy had listened to her scrappy recital of what she'd said and what Ves said and responded calmly that more than likely Ves had changed her mind and decided not to show up. Annie knew Ves wasn't eager to talk to the police. She didn't see any point in doing so. "Wouldn't she have called and told me she wasn't coming?"

Billy drove with both hands on the steering wheel. He didn't answer directly. "I'll talk to her."

He swung the wheel, and the Ford turned into Ves's driveway. Annie leaned forward as they came around the curve. She felt a whoosh of relief when she saw Ves's red Dodge van.

Billy pulled up behind the van. Annie scrambled out, came around the car. Billy stood by the Ford, looked carefully at the yard. But Annie was already hurrying toward the back porch. Billy caught up with her. They climbed the steps.

Annie stopped and stared. "The back door's open."

"Right." Billy was calm. "Ves?" He lifted his voice, could likely have been heard from one end of a football field to the other.

Silence.

"Ves?" Annie's voice was sharp.

In two strides, Billy was at the back door. He knocked, a heavy thump that rattled the door, kept on knocking for a minute, possibly more, then let his hand fall.

Silence.

His hand came down, hovered near his holster. "Police. Hands up. Don't move." His voice was deep, commanding. "Police. Hands up. Don't move." He reached out, pulled open the screen door, gazed inside.

Annie saw a brownish smear on the side of the door. "Billy" — she pointed — "that looks like blood."

"Stay there." The order was spoken softly. He stepped inside. "Police." If anyone was inside the house, that shout could not have been missed.

Annie waited uncertainly on the porch. She wanted to follow him. She didn't want to see what might be inside. She heard his progress, repeated shouts of "Police"; "Hands up"; "Don't move."

She waited, hands clenched, listening to Billy's shouts, heard his heavy steps on the stairs. He stepped out on the porch, face creased in a tight frown. "No one's here." He moved past her, thudded down the steps. He strode toward the van.

Annie glanced back at the screen door. Was that blood on the frame? She reached out, then let her hand drop. This might be a crime scene though Billy said the house was empty. She must not touch anything. She hurried down the steps toward the drive.

Billy pulled at the handle of the van door. The driver's door opened and he leaned inside, twisted to look, was out again in a minute. Next came the garage. He slid the door up. It creaked, rose slowly to reveal a dim interior. On the left wall was a workbench, a freezer chest, bike, and a lawn mower.

Billy crossed the concrete floor to the freezer.

Annie tensed as he lifted the lid.

A cursory glance. He lowered the lid.

Annie breathed again. The freezer, of course, was big enough to hold a body. It was horrible to think in terms of a body, Ves's body. But she had to be somewhere. Billy said there was no one in the house. He would have checked every room, the closets, pantry, bathrooms, under the beds. Everywhere. No trace of Ves, and a bloodstain on the frame of the back door.

Billy yanked his cell phone from his pocket, tapped, talked fast. "Possible crime scene. Send Pirelli and Harrison. Bring the forensic van."

Annie knew he was speaking to his wife, Mavis, who worked as both the dispatcher and as a crime scene tech.

He slid the phone into his pocket, looked at Annie. "Will you come to the house with me? You may be able to help." He moved as he spoke.

Annie hurried to keep up with his long strides. As they passed the fountain, she glanced at the statue and Diana's arm drawn back and the small portion of arrow that remained.

Billy held the door. "Don't touch anything."

Annie kept her hands close to her sides.

He stopped in the center of the hall, nodded at the small table with its bronze tray for mail. "Can you identify that purse?"

A green leather tote bag sat on the table. The handles were attached with brass fittings. "That's the purse Ves was carrying yesterday." Annie pointed. "Those are her car keys." The key ring medallion was shaped like a starfish. "If she isn't here, something's very wrong." It wasn't only the smear of blood. "Women don't go out without a purse. If her billfold's in the purse and her cell phone, something's happened to her."

Billy pulled a pair of plastic gloves from a pocket, slipped them on. He stepped to the table, carefully eased the top of the purse apart. "Not zipped. I see a billfold and a cell phone."

"You're sure she isn't here?"

"There is no one in the house." His tone was grim.

"Where can she be?"

A siren sounded in the distance, coming nearer.

Billy Cameron swerved around a bent pine, testament to the force of the wind off the sea. He heard the pound of waves before he reached the edge of the bluff. Twenty feet below, the sea roiled around rocks, hissing and gurgling as the tide went out. Of course Gurney Point has been checked earlier. Searchers covered the island from the northern tip to the marina and shops at the broad southern end. Now the sun was sinking below the western horizon, turning low-lying clouds pink and rose and coral. Volunteers came from all over the island. Boy

Scouts rallied. Shops closed. All day searchers drove island roads, hiked paths, rode bicycle trails, checked lagoons. The chatter on cell phones tallied sites visited. The island was searched as well and thoroughly as possible. There was no trace of Ves Roundtree. Ben Parotti swore she had not taken the ferry. The motorboat used primarily by renters of Rufus's mansion was secure in its boathouse. Rufus Roundtree's house showed no sign of occupancy, doors securely locked, drapes drawn, no lights, no cars in the garage. Billy was sure every accessible site had been scoured. But water was all around them and deep lagoons and forests where no one might venture for years. As hope dwindled, as the sun slid lower and dusk turned the world dim, he came back to Gurney Point. The rocks below would be exposed. Earlier the tide had been high, waves crashing against the bluff, only the tips of black rocks visible in the foam. Now he looked down, used his Maglite, played the beam along the rocks. Once, he stopped and tensed. But that was a log lodged below, not a body. Finally, he turned away. He walked slowly, felt heavy and weighted. He'd not protected Ves Roundtree. Now he could find no trace of her body.

■ ■ ■ ■

Emma Clyde, hair windblown, blue denim caftan wilted, sagged on a red leather sofa. Henny Brawley, equally fatigued, was propped against a wooden arm of a stately Victorian armchair. Henny was in her stocking feet, her mud-stained hiking boots on Emma's front porch. Laurel was pensive, her classic features not so much weary as thoughtful. In a cane chair, she looked safari-ready in an olive top and slacks and hiking boots. Her bush hat lay on the floor beside her.

Annie tried not to be uncharitable, then succumbed. Trust Laurel to be a spot of high fashion during a search of the island. Annie felt Max's gaze, immediately rearranged her face. Bland was always good when glancing at your mother-in-law.

Max's blue eyes were amused. Annie knew she and Max were bedraggled after the long day of looking, he in a flannel shirt and jeans and boots, she in a pink sweatshirt and navy slacks and boots. Their vine-and-bramble-snagged clothing was an odd contrast to the cheerful yellow-and-blue plaid upholstery of Emma's sofa.

"I called ahead." Emma's seaside mansion

was well staffed. "We'll have food promptly."

As if on cue, wheels squeaked and the plump, red-faced cook, her blond curls tightly constrained beneath a chef's cap, rolled in a stainless steel serving cart, the three shelves laden. They didn't have to move. An assistant, a muscular teen probably working part-time to save for college, was close behind. He set up teakwood tray tables for each of them, described the offerings, served them.

Annie was voraciously hungry. She bit into a huge French roll jammed with sliced ham, Havarti cheese, and mayonnaise. Chips served as scoops for a generous serving of guacamole. Iced tea was hugely refreshing. There was silence as they ate.

Emma took charge, as might be expected in the spacious terrace room of her home. "I dropped by the station on my way home. Billy has a command center set up in the break room. The island's been combed, as well as you can comb a splotch of land with some impenetrable forests. I know each of us" — she looked around her terrace room — "went with different parties." Her face softened. "Good turnout. Several church groups, Kiwanis, Boy Scouts, Rotary, Friends of the Library." She turned her strong square hands palms up. "Nothing.

So we're left with these facts: Ves spoke with Annie at six forty-eight P.M. last night. No other calls are recorded on her cell phone. The landline doesn't show any calls yesterday. Ves said she'd be at the police station at nine A.M. this morning. She didn't come. Billy arrived at her house at approximately nine fifteen." She glanced at Annie.

"That's right." It seemed long ago that she'd jounced in the passenger seat of Billy's car to Ves's house.

"Billy found no one. There was a smear of blood on the frame of the screen door to the back porch. Another smear of blood —"

Annie felt cold. More blood.

"— was found on an overturned straight chair in the living room. Billy declined to say if there appeared to have been a struggle. The search of the island yielded no results."

Henny said quietly, "Remember last August?"

Annie remembered. A birder got off trail in the nature preserve trying for a better view of a reddish egret and wasn't looking down and stumbled over the bones of an Alzheimer patient who had disappeared two years earlier. Search parties set out to look for her as soon as she was reported missing but never found a trace.

Emma's square face was somber. "We

have miles of thick woods. A body could lie there forever."

Henny massaged one temple. "Ves left behind her purse, cell phone, car keys. Her van was in the driveway. Bloodstains in the house. I'm afraid we have to conclude she's dead. Her body could have been dumped in the remote woods or in the ocean."

Laurel asked quickly, "Do you know whether the police have the material Ves put together about Rufus's estate and the dinner at her house?"

Emma nodded. "Billy found the sheets upstairs in her bedroom, lying on the dresser." A pause. "The bed was turned down and a cotton nightgown rested on the pillow. The bedroom light was on."

Henny's gaze sharpened. "If one of those present at her house Wednesday night murdered or kidnapped Ves, why was that damning material left behind?"

Annie tried to keep her voice steady. "Murder can't be easy. Those smears of blood, how did they happen? Did Ves struggle? How about the overturned chair? Maybe she was hurt and ran outside. Maybe the killer came after her and caught her and put her in a car and drove away and never thought about the papers."

"Or maybe" — Max concentrated — "the

papers were left to suggest her disappearance had nothing to do with her claims about someone trying to kill her. Maybe the killer wants everyone to think she was hysterical and anything she wrote down was unimportant."

Laurel's tone wasn't chiding; after all, she was speaking to Max, but she said firmly, "I doubt in the heat of committing murder that a criminal was quite so clever. It seems more likely the murderer, not wanting to stay there long, made a cursory search downstairs, didn't go upstairs to the bedroom."

Annie thought Laurel was probably right, but loyalty kept her from agreeing. "Whatever happened, we don't know where Ves is."

Emma cleared her throat. "Billy shared one other fact. A thorough search of the house, van, and garage did not reveal a gun."

Annie firmly believed in the magic-carpet ability of many mysteries to plunge readers into a world they would otherwise never know, Nury Vittachi's Singapore, Ellis Peters's twelfth-century Shrewsbury Abbey, John P. Marquand's China in the years leading up to World War II. She went straight to the romantic suspense section, grabbed

Crocodile on the Sandbank by Elizabeth Peters. She needed comfort after a restless night spent with disturbing dreams, hurrying to Ves's house, finding the open back door, seeing blood stark against white wood. She had woken up exhausted. She knew the right kind of book would make her feel much better. She decided to indulge herself for an hour, then she'd work on the chapbooks. She was luxuriating in the company of insouciant Amelia Peabody in Rome in 1884 when a familiar ring sounded.

She grabbed her cell, expecting bad news. "Have they found Ves?"

Marian's raspy voice was matter-of-fact. "No news. Usually that's good news. But not when you're looking for a body. If they don't find her in the first twenty-four hours, the odds go way down. They brought in some dogs today. Nothing picked up on Fish Haul Pier. Now they're going around to some of the other docks. They think she left the house, by force or on her own, Monday night. Her dinner dishes are in the sink, rinsed but not washed."

Annie remembered the nightgown resting on the pillow. "How about the blood?"

"It's hers. Not much. Traces of her fingerprints in blood smeared on the doorjamb. Billy said so far as they know, no one reports speaking to her or seeing her after you talked to her Monday night. The only new fact is that she was at her shop around nine o'clock Monday night. At least her van was parked in the alley behind the shop and there were lights on in her storeroom. There's a patrol that checks the area —"

As a shopkeeper on the boardwalk, Annie knew all about the patrols, appreciated them though attempted break-ins were rare in winter, happened occasionally in summer.

"— every few hours and the officer knows her van. The alley was empty when he came back around ten. She returned home, because the van is in the drive. Her visit there may have nothing to do with anything. Billy checked and no calls were made or received on the shop phone. Here's what I'm wondering. Ves told you she wanted to wait until morning so she could think about Wednesday night, remember where Fred sat, where he looked. How did she sound?"

Annie could hear Ves's staccato words. "Tense. Sharp. And" — she felt a shiver — "determined."

"Here's my take." Marian sounded sad. "She kept on thinking and she figured out who Fred saw in her yard. And then, hell, I don't know, did she go by and see that person and get fobbed off, you're wrong, wasn't me, hey, we're friends, and she decided she was wrong and came home? I think the killer gave her time to get home, then started after her. I don't see it any other way." A pause. "Somebody got her. I think it was one of the people at her house Wednesday night. Like I told you earlier, I don't gossip. But with Ves missing and Fred likely murdered, Billy needs to know everything about those at Ves's house the night Fred drowned. I told him about the jewel thefts and Gretchen. If she's the thief, she has steel nerves. She looks rich and attractive and she's someone Ves has known for years. How easy would it be for Gretchen to convince Ves that of course Fred hadn't looked at her. Then maybe Gretchen showed up at the house, told Ves she'd been thinking and she was sure she knew who Fred looked at. Once she got inside . . ."

Max tried to appear stalwart. Wasn't that a quality highly prized in the pages of romantic thrillers? "I concentrate better when I'm putting."

Annie's gaze was affectionate and utterly disbelieving.

He plunked his putter into his golf bag and walked to his desk chair with a grin.

She perched on the edge of his desk,

which hiked her skirt to her thighs. "I just talked to Marian. She thinks Ves remembered who Fred looked at Wednesday night."

He forced himself to focus on her face. "And?"

"You were there."

He understood. If Fred was a fortune hunter, if Fred crept into Ves's yard that late afternoon seeking treasure, he was innocent. If someone arrived, he likely slipped into the deep shadow of the pines, withdrew silently, probably irritated at losing precious time to search, time made possible by a lie at work. But he definitely didn't want to be discovered trespassing. When Ves described the slick step and her fall, he realized instantly he knew who wanted Ves to die.

Max squeezed his eyes together, tried to remember. Fred was the last to arrive. He hunched in a straight chair, shoulders rounded. Fred's chair was at the end of the semicircle so Fred was half turned toward the others: florid-faced and pompous Adam, playboy Curt, suddenly expressionless Gretchen, wide-eyed Jane Wilson, mocking boyfriend Tim Holt, elegant and haggard Katherine Farley, impervious and distant Bob Farley.

Max felt frustrated. "The answer's there.

Fred looked at one of them. His head turned, but I was watching the others. When I looked at Fred, all I saw was fear. Ves was right. He stared at a murderer. They looked at each other, and the murderer knew."

Annie gently tried to move Agatha, who was inelegantly sprawled on her back on top of the copy for Henny's chapbook. A low growl was sufficient. Annie reached for the box tied with a red ribbon and topped with an emerald bow. She wasn't cowardly, but only a fool trifles with a growling cat. It might be cheerful to dwell for a moment in her mother-in-law's madcap mind. There wasn't, so far as she knew, anything she could be doing to help find Ves. It was up to the dogs to find her scent. Or her body might be in the ocean, far from discovery. There were places where currents would pull a body out to sea.

Annie was smiling by the time she'd read several entries in *Merry Musings: A dog loves you because you are you. It never hurts to ask. Each person has a story.* And then she read: *Always wonder why.*

Why didn't the killer leave Ves's body where it would be found?

Ves had been adamant that no one had a motive to wish her dead except those who would profit when she died. Yet the lack of a body meant she would not be declared legally dead for seven years. Why remove the body?

Annie frowned, picked up her cell, tapped a Favorite.

Max's voice was warm. "I was thinking about you." A pause, quickly: "You're at the store?"

"Of course. Where else would I be?"

"Anywhere," he answered simply. "Out in a forest hunting for Ves. Nosing somewhere you shouldn't be. Talking to one of her possible murderers."

"That's why I called."

"You're talking to a possible murderer?" His voice rose.

"I'm thinking."

A whoosh of relief. "Think away. That's never a problem."

Annie wasn't sure exactly what he meant, just as she sometimes wasn't sure how a remark from Laurel should be understood. Mother and son often had an uncanny similarity in the innocence shining in dark blue eyes after speaking to her. She rather felt this was one of those times, but this wasn't the moment to delve deeper. "I mean I'm really thinking." She plunged right in. "Is it true that the trust can't be divided unless there's proof of Ves's death?"

"It depends upon how the instrument is written —"

"You sound like a lawyer. I want the bottom line."

He laughed. "If you ask a lawyer, even a nonpracticing one like me, a legal question, you are likely to get a legal answer. In short, no divvying until Ves is declared legally dead. If no body is found, a court can adjudge her legally dead in seven years."

"That's what I thought. So why would the murderer, if it is one of the surviving — what do you call them?"

"Contingent remaindermen beneficiaries."

"Okay. CRBs. A CRB wants a body, right?"

"Presumably."

"Why kill Ves and hide the body?" She pictured a pot of gold at the end of a dark rainbow.

"I see your point. For a con—"

"CRB."

"CRB to inherit, there has to be proof she's dead."

"I thought the whole idea was somebody needed money right now. Seven years is a long time."

Max's tone was thoughtful. "Whether money would be shared before her death was proved is probably up to the trustee. If Ves isn't found and if it seems obvious she's dead, he could choose to make advances to the CRBs and not wait seven years."

"If one of them is counting on that happening, they would have to be pretty savvy. But maybe not. Ves gave money early to Jane to help with her mom. I would guess that portion was subtracted from what Jane will get eventually. The others have asked for money so they knew Ves could make money available and probably think the trustee could do the same if she's still missing in a month or so. But still, why get rid of the body?"

"If there was a struggle" — Max spoke slowly — "the murderer might worry about traces of DNA. Honey, we can't know what happened at her house Monday night. You've done all you can do for Ves. Work on the chapbooks."

Annie nodded approvingly. Laurel's effervescence was on full display in her chapbook. Annie tried to decide which maxim *Of course there are unicorns.* Or *A seashell is like a memory. The life is gone. The beauty remains.* She had a gold link necklace with an unblemished smooth shiny tan-gray olive shell as the pendant. Max

216

gave her the necklace to celebrate their first wedding anniversary. They found the shell while walking on the beach. The necklace afforded her both a shell and a memory.

Her cell rang. Marian. She answered with a lilt in her voice, still thinking about Max and the shell. "Hey, Marian."

"No word about Ves, but we got a body." The words came fast. "A client arrived for an appointment, found Adam Nash dead in his office, called 911 at four minutes after eleven this morning. On my way there."

10

"Can't you go faster?"

Max was temperate. "Whether we show up in five minutes or ten won't make a difference to Adam Nash and certainly not to Billy. We don't have any information to add. Crime scenes go on for a long time. I don't see any point in our going there." He did push a little harder on the accelerator, but was ready to brake if a deer bounded across the road.

Annie stared straight ahead. Max was right. But to receive such a call and do nothing seemed an affront to Adam and Ves and Fred. Maybe it was foolish to go to Adam's office, but there had to be a connection between his death and Ves's disappearance. She turned to look at Max. "Maybe Adam killed Ves and then killed himself."

"Maybe."

"Maybe there will be something in his office that will help find Ves."

Max turned onto Main Street. Three police cars, red lights flashing, were stopped in front of a small frame building in the middle of the block. The lane was closed. He took a look behind, began to back up. "I'll park by the pier."

"Hold on a minute. I'll get out here." When the car stopped, she opened the door, popped out, headed for the sidewalk.

Adam's office building, unlike some of its more prosperous neighbors, was unprepossessing. The wood was weathered, the roof lacked some shingles that had blown away in a recent storm, a ground-floor window had a jagged crack.

As she hurried up the sidewalk, she wondered how prosperous Adam Nash had been. If she were looking for a financial adviser, the building wouldn't inspire confidence. An art gallery occupied the cottage next door. Everything was bandbox perfect, from a small brick fountain in front to red shutters to a pale yellow door that looked freshly painted. Laurel had told her, dark blue eyes dreamy, that light yellow was an earth color and one of the best feng shui colors for a west-facing door. On the other side of the building now bracketed by yellow police tape was the cosmetics shop where Gretchen worked. Across the street were several one-story storefront shops, including the secondhand store managed by Jane Wilson, a quilting store closed for winter, and, behind a white picket fence, perhaps half of the pickets newly painted, stood an old house inhabited by two reclusive sisters. A crowd clustered on the sidewalk, watching the activity. A muscular figure holding a paintbrush stood with his back to the fence, also staring. Annie recognized Tim Holt. The front door of the old house opened and a reedy voice called, "You get back to work or I'll dock you for wasting time." Tim slowly turned to the fence, dipped his brush in a bucket of paint.

Marian Kenyon, the harbor breeze stirring her dark curls, stood as near the entrance to Adam's building as possible, a scant inch away from the taut police tape. She was crisp this morning in a plum blouse and black skirt.

Annie hurried to join her. "What's happening?"

Marian jerked a thumb toward Officer Harrison, trim and alert. "Hyla said the ME's there and the chief and the tech crew. Nobody's allowed in or out until — Oh, hey." She leaned forward as a burly gray-haired man with a big face, now creased in a frown, came through the front door. He carried a small black leather satchel. "Hey, Doc, what can you give me?"

Doc Burford stopped a few feet away. "Victim is Adam Nash. Bullet wound to the chest. Likely fatal on impact. Estimated time of death yesterday between three and ten P.M." He started for the sidewalk.

Marian moved along the tape, keeping pace. "Homicide, accident, or suicide?"

"Homicide. No powder residue on his hands. No gun at the scene."

Billy Cameron liked to hold sheets of paper in his hand, easy to make notations, easy to flip back and forth from one fact to another. This afternoon Doc Burford e-mailed a prelim autopsy report, confirmed death by gunshot. Billy knew what a slug could do to a heart. This slug — he glanced at another sheet, a .45 caliber bullet, so plenty of force — had torn through muscle, shattered bone, exploded the right ventricle. Adam Nash as a living creature no longer existed. He checked other facts.

White male. Age 46. 6'2" tall. Weight 210 pounds. Good physical condition. No trauma other than the gunshot wound. Time of death estimated to be between 3 and 10 P.M. Tuesday, February 23. Body discovered at 11:04 A.M. Wednesday, February 24.

He picked up another sheet.

Officer Hyla Harrison: Body discovered shortly after 11 A.M. Wednesday, February 24, by Roger Clark. Clark told officers hall door ajar when he arrived. The light was on in the anteroom. The door to Nash's office was open. That light was also on. Clark called out. He stepped into lobby, called out again, walked to open office door. Clark saw Nash slumped forward on the desk, blood pooled in front of his head. Clark hurried across the room. He touched Nash's arm, found it rigid, immediately left the office. He did not touch anything. He went into the hall and used his cell phone to call 911.

Billy leaned back in his chair. Ves Roundtree told Annie Darling she wanted to figure out who Fred Butler looked at the night he died. Ves agreed to meet at the police station Tuesday morning. She didn't come. Could she have disappeared on purpose? That was possible, but no one on the island admitted seeing her after Monday night. Ben Parotti insisted she'd not taken the ferry Tuesday. She had no money, no car.

Billy thumbed through the papers. Yeah. Here it was. Officer Abbott called every rental unit on the island. No check-ins Monday night. Was she abducted and killed? That seemed likely now. Adam Nash was shot Tuesday afternoon. Was he shot because he knew something about the deaths of either Fred Butler or Ves Roundtree or was he shot to increase the portion of those who would ultimately profit from Rufus Roundtree's estate? There was as yet no known link between any of Ves's guests last week to Fish Haul Pier, her house with the smears of blood, or Adam's office with the overhead light bright on a pool of congealed blood. He remembered one hot summer day and a trail through a nature preserve. No-see-ums, mosquitoes, and midges swirled around him obscuring the path. Now conjectures and uncertainties deviled him.

His gaze moved back to the autopsy report. There was one solid fact in the welter of information. Adam Nash was killed by a bullet from a .45. Billy straightened, turned to his computer. He tapped the keyboard. In a few minutes he had the information he sought about Ves Roundtree, Bob and Katherine Farley, Jane Wilson, Tim Holt, Fred Butler, Adam Nash, Gretchen Roundtree, Curt Roundtree. Ves

Roundtree and Bob Farley were registered gun owners. Each owned a .45 pistol. No gun was found at Ves's home after her disappearance. He wouldn't know what happened to Ves's gun until her disappearance was solved. Where was the gun owned by Bob Farley? Those not legally registered as gun owners could well possess a gun. Guns were easily come by, legally or not. He picked up another folder. Hyla Harrison had been commended for alerting Katherine Farley about her husband's visit to Gurney Point. The attempt on Ves's life was made the next day. He pushed back his chair.

Emma brandished a rolled-up copy of the *Gazette* as she barreled into Death on Demand. Today's caftan was an eye-popping orange that matched spiky orange hair.

Annie was enjoying the novel pleasure of ringing up a sale to a lean, elderly man who had been excited to find a moderately priced copy of Jack Higgins's first Harry Patterson novel, *Sad Wind from the Sea.* The customer bustled past Emma, cradling his treasure, calling back disjointedly, "Here to visit my sister. I'll be back. You have some fine books."

As the door closed, Emma unrolled the

Wednesday issue, slapped it on the counter. "Hot from the print run. Have you seen Marian's story?" She jabbed at the headline.

Before Annie could reply, Emma began to read in her deep voice:

ADAM NASH SHOT TO DEATH

Island financial adviser Adam Nash, 46, was found dead of a gunshot wound this morning at his office, an apparent homicide victim according to police.

Police said Roger Clark, a client, arrived at Nash's office at approximately 11 A.M. today and found Nash's body. The medical examiner estimated that Nash was killed sometime Tuesday between 3 and 10 P.M.

Police interviewed building occupants but no one reported hearing a gunshot. A ground-floor occupant worked late and did not leave the building until shortly after 9 P.M. Anyone in the vicinity of the building at 203 W. Main who heard a gunshot Tuesday between those hours is asked to contact police.

Emma paused in her recital. "Either the gun had a silencer or he was shot at five-oh-five. Surely that's occurred to somebody in

225

the little brick building." *The little brick building* was Emma's designation for the police department.

"Five-oh-five?" Annie repeated blankly.

Emma shot Annie a pitying glance. "The ferry." The tone of her voice made it sound like *The ferry, stupid.*

Annie understood. The *Miss Jolene* departed on her last run to the mainland at 5:05, horn blaring. A half dozen shots could safely be shot before the ferry cleared the harbor.

"I'll text Billy." Emma was brisk. Her gaze returned to the front page. "Here's the rest of Marian's story."

Police said there was no sign of a break-in at Nash's office nor any disturbance that might indicate a search or robbery. Police said it appears that Nash likely knew his assailant, as Nash was seated in his office chair. Police will interview friends and clients in hopes of discovering a possible motive. Anyone with information about any matter that might have led to his death is asked to contact authorities.

Police declined to speculate whether there is a link between Nash's murder and the disappearance of island shopkeeper Vesta Roundtree. Roundtree did not show up for a scheduled meeting Tuesday morning. Police said a tipped-over chair and two smears of blood in her house suggested a struggle. Roundtree has not been seen or heard from since Monday evening. Her purse, car keys, and van were found at the house. An island-wide search Tuesday yielded no information about her fate. Bloodhounds brought from the mainland had no success in tracing her today.

Police also declined to discuss the drowning death last week of Fred Butler. Butler's body was found near Fish Haul Pier.

Police have not released information about the activities this past week of Butler, Roundtree, or Nash but the *Gazette* has learned from an unofficial source that Butler and Nash attended a gathering at Roundtree's home last Wednesday. Butler's body was found Friday morning. Time of death is estimated to have occurred between 9 P.M. Wednesday and 8 A.M. Thursday. Also in attendance Wednesday evening at the Roundtree house were Katherine and Bob Farley, Jane Wilson, Tim Holt, Gretchen Roundtree, and Curt Roundtree.

Police have asked anyone with information concerning the death of Nash or the whereabouts of Roundtree to contact authorities.

Emma made an exasperated whuff. "Nothing" — now her voice was a bark — "not a single word about why those people were at Ves's house or Rufus Roundtree's estate or the heirs."

Annie said quickly, "Not heirs. Contingent remaindermen beneficiaries."

"They are suspects. Why doesn't Billy say so?" Her face was red with outrage.

Annie imagined Emma as a scaly orange dragon, fire shooting from her square face. "Billy has to be careful. There are libel laws."

Emma brushed away libel laws with a stubby hand. "There are many ways to say things. Anyway, this" — she tapped the front page with a stubby forefinger — "is police malpractice. There's not a word about Ves figuring out that Fred was digging in her yard on Thursday afternoons and saw the person who waxed the stair tread. Not a word about the fact that Fred was happy as a clam until he got to her house and realized he'd seen a murderer at work. Not a word about Ves trying to remember who Fred looked at that night and next thing you know she's nowhere to be found. As for

Adam, I think the killer decided it would be nice to make the pie slice bigger by eliminating another heir. Those people need to be alerted. When you can pinpoint murder to a select circle, don't keep it a secret." She flipped up one stubby finger after another. "Bob Farley. Katherine Farley. Jane Wilson. Tim Holt. Gretchen Roundtree. Curt Roundtree. They need to know. It's up to you and Max."

"Up to us?" Annie was bewildered.

Emma had the grace to look slightly, but only slightly, uncomfortable. "Ves chose Max to be at her house the night she confronted them, so he represents her. These people need to know how all this ties together. I called and told them to come to your house at eight."

"Our house at eight?" Annie knew her voice was high.

Emma tossed her head, and the orange sprigs danced. "Max can report on the status of the investigation. But you know the real reason."

Annie felt like a dazed parrot as she repeated, "The real reason?"

"To warn the damn fools that someone is picking them off, one by one."

Bob Farley looked surprised when he

opened the door. "Hi, Billy." Then his face tightened. He looked toward the two-story studio. "Katherine?"

Billy understood. Though he and Bob were friendly, had sailed together before Bob's accident, he knew Billy's job and sometimes that job was delivering bad news, awful news. He spoke quickly, "Katherine's fine. I saw lights in the studio when I drove past."

Bob looked embarrassed. "Sorry. But things have been weird. Fred drowned and Ves missing and Adam shot. I guess that's why you're here." He held the door wide, swung his wheelchair to give Billy space. He continued talking as he gestured for Billy to take a big wing chair, perfect for his solid frame, and turned his chair to face him. "I'm afraid Katherine and I don't know anything that will help. I thought Ves was being hysterical, claiming someone was trying to kill her. The shoes that woman wears would trip anybody. Maybe she was right, but I can't believe someone pushed Fred off the pier and somehow did away with Ves and shot Adam."

Billy kept his voice pleasant, but his eyes never left Bob's face. "You are the registered owner of a JFX5F25 PX4 Storm Type F Beretta handgun. May I see it?"

Bob's eyes widened and then he laughed, a robust laugh that reminded Billy of the old Bob with the spray on his face as he moved a tiller. He couldn't help but smile in return.

"That's a boost for my ego." Abruptly his face was somber. "Not that I think it's funny that somebody shot Adam. But the idea I'm out roaming around with a gun makes me sound damn vigorous." He turned his chair, wheeled across the room. "I keep my gun in the bedside table."

Billy was right behind Bob as they entered a small, Spartan bedroom with a single twin bed next to windows that overlooked the woods. Billy glanced at the closed door to the right, likely a larger master bedroom with a view of the marsh. In the small bedroom, a bedside table, a plain maple dresser, and a leather easy chair were the only other furnishings. A man's room.

Bob saw Billy's glance. "I don't sleep very well these days." Bob's tone was determinedly upbeat. "I have my own burrow so I don't keep Katherine up." He rolled to the bedside table, reached down, pulled open the lower drawer. He pulled out a wooden case, lifted the lid. His shoulders stiffened.

Billy was just behind him. He gazed down.

The case was empty.

Bob slowly lowered the lid, returned the case to the drawer. He glanced up at Billy. "I thought that's where we kept it. Katherine must have moved it."

"Let's ask her." Billy was still pleasant. He stepped closer, picked up the receiver from the phone on the bedside table. "I imagine you have an extension for the studio."

"Sure. I can call her." He held out his hand.

"I can do it."

There was an instant of silence. Finally, Bob said roughly. "Five five."

Billy tapped the numbers.

Katherine answered immediately. "Bob?" Was there a breathless quality to her voice? She might well have seen Billy's car parked behind Bob's.

"Hi, Katherine. Billy Cameron here. Bob and I were visiting and I wondered if you could spare a minute and join us."

"Has anyone ever told Emma she's an overbearing old bat?" Max measured coffee into the coffeemaker. His jaw jutted.

"Not to her face." She understood his irritation. As he'd pointed out, Billy Cameron might not be pleased to know the people he intended to interview would have a heads-up on the likelihood the deaths of Fred and Adam and Ves's disappearance were connected. At least, Annie assumed Emma's hope was that Max would not only warn them of danger but urge each to immediately contact the police if they had any sense of who might have killed Fred Butler and Adam Nash.

"Maybe it's time someone told Emma." He poured in water, closed the lid, pushed Start. "All right, fresh coffee coming up. I gather we don't intend to offer liquor or wine?"

"It won't" — she felt a slight shiver — "be a bright gathering."

The doorbell rang.

Annie sat in a wicker chair to the right of the fireplace. Max stood to her left. She knew he wasn't comfortable with his role but that wasn't apparent. He looked relaxed, serious, welcoming. To her, he was always Joe Hardy all grown up, blond, handsome, the man you'd like to have at the tiller in a storm.

"I'm sure some of you were surprised when Emma Clyde asked you to be here tonight. Emma is concerned that some of you might not be aware of the background to Ves Roundtree's disappearance. Although the police did not officially declare Fred Butler's drowning the result of suicide, that was the implication. However, now there is good reason to believe he did not commit suicide."

As he spoke, Annie surveyed his listeners.

Gretchen Roundtree's bony face was blank and unsmiling. The gold medallion pattern of her paisley blouse emphasized the blond sheen of her hair. One hand clutched at the black scarf at her throat.

Curt's relaxed demeanor was in sharp contrast to his mother's. Freckled face skeptical, he lounged on a leather sofa in a preppy plaid cotton shirt, chinos, and tasseled leather loafers.

Jane Wilson's apricot cabled V-neck sweater was perfection above cream wool trousers and cream leather heels with apricot banding, but Jane's sweet face looked troubled.

Tim Holt sat with big strong hands planted squarely on the knees of his jeans. He looked fit and muscular in a wool shirt with the sleeves rolled up almost to his elbows. His strong-boned face creased in a frown.

Bob and Katherine Farley sat side by side on a wooden bench. Her sleek black hair fell forward on one side, shading her face.

Bob's hands were clamped on the head of an oak cane. Katherine would have been her usual stylish self in a plaid jacket with three-quarter-length sleeves except for the rigidity of her posture. Every so often she slid a sideways glance at her husband. He stared straight ahead, lips pressed together.

"Annie discovered Fred was happy and excited. His excitement was based on his expectation of soon finding buried treasure —"

Curt broke in, his tone sneering. "Don't tell us there's a hidden cache of gold and somebody bumped him off to get a map with a huge *X* that marks the spot."

Max was unruffled. "I'll lay out what we know. Each of you can make your own conclusion. In regard to treasure, it doesn't matter whether it exists or not. What matters is that Fred was searching for a treasure reputedly buried in Ves's backyard by Black Jack MacDougal, and further" — Max's voice was measured — "Fred was searching late on Thursday afternoons. On Monday night Ves concluded that Fred was in her yard when someone arrived there the Thursday she fell. Fred likely hurried away because he had no business being there. He didn't know about her fall until last week's gathering at her house. Ves realized Fred knew who greased the step."

Each person stared at Max. There wasn't a breath of sound.

"That knowledge led to his murder later Wednesday night on Fish Haul Pier."

Jane Wilson held up both hands as if to ward off the words, the knowledge. "It sounded like he committed suicide in the paper."

"He had no reason to jump into the water." Annie was forceful. "I talked to people who knew him. Everything was fine in his life. Ves called me Monday night, said she was sure Fred had been murdered. She said Fred knew who set the trap on her stairs. He could have spoken up that night at her house, but that would mean he had to admit he'd been there. Maybe he was afraid he'd be accused. Maybe he was afraid he would lose his job because he lied to his manager and said he had dental appointments on Thursday afternoons. Ves said she wanted to concentrate, remember everything that happened in her living room, picture where Fred sat and where he looked. She told me she'd meet me at the police station Tuesday morning. She never came. Instead her back door was open, the lights on, some blood smeared on the doorframe, a chair overturned."

Katherine's voice was strained. "You're saying someone killed her Monday night to keep her from going to the police."

Gretchen came to her feet, glared at Annie. "You're saying one of us killed Fred and Ves."

Max's tone was equable. "We aren't accusing anyone. We're telling you that when Fred Butler left Ves's house last Wednesday he had no reason to jump into the ocean. I saw him that night. He looked afraid. It's obvious he had good reason to be afraid. Then Ves figured out what happened to him. Did she talk to the person Fred saw?" He looked from face to face.

Tim Holt stood also, looked belligerent with the same stance as a bull ready to charge. His face was hard. "Wait a minute. This gets ugly. Now that rich guy's dead." Annie realized he was talking about Adam Nash.

"They say somebody shot him sometime Tuesday. Look, people, he stood to get big bucks when the Roundtree woman dies. What happens to his share of that estate? Same with Fred Butler. And maybe Roundtree's dead." His stare at Max was demanding. "You were in Ves Roundtree's pocket, standing there that night like she needed a bodyguard. You seem to know all about

237

everything. We're told to come to your house tonight. So let's get down to business. When one of them dies, do the ones who are left" — he gestured at Jane, Curt, Bob, and Katherine — "get their share?"

Max spoke carefully. "As I understand the provisions of the trust, upon Ves Roundtree's death, the estate will be divided among the living contingent remaindermen beneficiaries."

Tim's voice was harsh. "You mean them?" A big hand waved toward Jane, Bob, Curt, Katherine.

Max nodded.

Tim looked like a man grappling with a realization that death could strike at any time. "That's a hell of a bad deal. Who's going to keep them safe?"

Max put a bowl of fresh-cut papaya in front of Annie, another at his place. "Your favorite."

She smiled her thanks. She'd loved papaya ever since a visit to Mexico City and breakfast at Sanborns near the Zócalo.

Max sat across from her, his sexy morning self with thick blond hair slightly tangled, bristly cheeks, muscular in a T-shirt and plaid boxer shorts. This morning he was exuberant. "Today is going to be fine. No more Sturm und Drang." He was grave for a moment. "It's tough to wonder what happened to Ves but we can't do anything more for her. Or for Fred or Adam. It's time for us to get back to normal, have an ordinary Thursday. How about we take the boat out for some red snapper?"

"I'd love to" — her smile was bright — "but I have to work on the chapbooks." She wondered why Max, usually so perceptive, never detected the insincerity in her voice in regard to all things connected to fishing. It wasn't, she thought defensively, that she was hyper, but spending hours with a rod and a line waiting for a no doubt sneering fish to be dumb enough to glob onto a tidbit slapped on a hook was not her idea of fun. That didn't even take into account going out of sight of land in a boat wallowing like a drunken sailor. A native of landlocked Amarillo, Annie took great comfort from seeing land, however distantly.

Max's eyes had the dreamy look of a fisherman imagining triumphs. "Wish you could come. But you'll have fun, too."

Annie petted Agatha and took an occasional sip of coffee as she learned more about Scottish-born John Buchan, his pleasure in arduous hikes, his recurring stomach ailments, his service as governor general of Canada from 1935 until his death in 1940. Buchan was revered in the mystery world as the creator of Richard Hannay, hero of *The Thirty-Nine Steps.* Buchan's rousing tales featured admirable protagonists and gave a sense of a long-vanished world. It would be great to use the original cover —

The front bell sang.

Annie looked up the central aisle.

Jane Wilson moved with the grace of a model, strikingly attractive in a cranberry velveteen jacket with a starburst on the lapel, a floral silk blouse bright with dashes of silver and cranberry, and slender-legged black trousers above cranberry leather heels. All was perfect except for the haunting paleness of an open and rounded face not suited for drama. She reached the coffee bar area, looked at Annie. "I want your advice. I hope you don't mind. I closed the shop to come. I'm going to owe so many hours."

"Of course I don't mind. I'll get some coffee." Annie gestured at a table nearer the coffee bar that wasn't encumbered by the chapbook manuscripts. Jane sat at the table, looked stiff and uncomfortable.

Annie hurried behind the coffee bar, reached up to the display of mugs emblazoned with mystery titles. She chose *Some-*

thing Wrong by Elizabeth Linington for Jane and *The Perilous Country* by John Creasy for herself, filled them, joined Jane at the table.

Jane gripped the mug. "Last night" — her voice was uneven — "Max seemed to be saying that one of us killed Fred and Ves and Mr. Nash. Do you think that's true?"

Annie heard a demand for reassurance. She had to answer honestly. "I'm afraid so. I asked around about Fred. He was a happy man until he went to Ves's house that Wednesday night. When she described how someone tried to kill her, Fred was shocked and frightened. Max saw his reaction. So did Ves. Later she figured out what happened, what must have happened. Fred was in her yard looking for treasure when someone came and waxed the step on her stairs. But Fred didn't know about her fall until the night he died. He came there and he looked at someone. He must have agreed to meet that person on the pier. Ves told me on the phone Monday night she was going to see if she could remember who Fred looked at. No one's seen her since. The next night Adam Nash died. Maybe he knew something or maybe he was killed to increase the others' share, but one way or another, all the deaths have to be connected."

Jane brushed back a soft tangle of brown curls. "Tim says anybody who might get money could be killed. He's furious at me."

Annie was puzzled. If Tim was scared for Jane, she'd understand. Why would he be angry? "Furious at you?"

She lifted her chin. "He wants to get married. Right. Now. Today. Then he can take care of me. Either that or I should let him move into my house. He says I can't live there by myself, that anybody could get in and . . . kill me."

"You live alone?"

Jane's glance skittered away. Her pale cheeks were touched by pink. "Tim and I — well, I'm not in any hurry. I'm nineteen. I want to be able to be myself for a while. Tim is a lot of fun and he's ambitious and maybe he's the right one, but I don't want to decide now. Especially not now. Everything is horrible. That nice Fred is dead and Ves gone and Mr. Nash shot." She pressed her fingertips against her temples for an instant. "It's horrible. I don't want to get married when things are bad."

Weddings should be the happiest of occasions on the happiest of days. Annie remembered Laurel's vision for her and Max's wedding. A red wedding gown. Annie didn't care if that was the custom in China, however nicely Laurel intended her suggestion. Annie wore a soft cream dress of her own choosing. Perhaps the dress had the faintest rose tint. Happiness suffused their day, glorious weather, good friends, a traditional ceremony. *"Do you take this man . . . ?"* Of course Jane wanted to marry in joy, not fear.

Jane hurried ahead. "I want a June wedding. That's what Mom and I talked about. Toward the end" — tears glistened in her eyes — "Mom seemed to like to look ahead and she said, *'You'll marry the nicest boy, I know you will.'* Mom and I figured out what kind of dress, ivory with some lace at the throat, and the flowers. She loved chrysanthemums. I told her — I promised her — when I married it would be just the way we planned." Her gaze met Annie's directly. "A lot of people live together now before they get married but I promised Mom I wouldn't do that. Tim doesn't live with me. He has an apartment on the other side of the woods by the harbor pavilion."

Annie knew the harbor park well and the apartment house separated from the pavilion by thick woods. A path led through the trees to the apartment parking lot.

"He's going crazy. He says we have to get

married today or he should come and stay at my house. I told him no. He says he's scared someone will get me. But I told him I promised my mom." She pushed away the mug, her coffee untasted, scooted back the chair, stood. "Thanks for listening. I better get back to the shop. I guess you're right. Fred Butler knew something and Ves figured out who killed him and Mr. Nash was involved somehow. I don't know anything about anyone so I should be safe. I'll be extra careful. I'll lock up real well. And somebody would have to be crazy to keep killing people in Mr. Roundtree's trust."

A sharp nip on one ankle got an immediate response. Annie sped behind the coffee bar and shook dry pellets into a clean bowl. She refreshed Agatha's water bowl, placed it on the newspaper spread out on the floor. She was smiling as she returned to the round table with three separate stacks of manuscript sheets. She was close to completing her copyedit. Next week Max could work his online wonders and soon the chapbooks would be done.

The next author in Henny's list of classics was one of Annie's favorites. John P. Marquand was better known as a literary author but he also wrote thrillers starring Mr.

Moto, an elegant Japanese spy who often challenged American adventurers. In the first Mr. Moto, *Ming Yellow,* a sardonic newspaper reporter and a wealthy American heiress faced a ruthless marauding mercenary who killed as thoughtlessly as a housewife swats a fly.

Annie felt a chill. That's what someone was doing. Killing without compunction. There were six guests at their house last night. One of them had killed three times. Who? Which one was a threat?

Annie picked up a pen. What did they know about the murderer? The murderer was calm and cool, remaining at Ves's house after she drove off, entering the house to remove evidence the step had been waxed. That indicated steadiness under pressure. The murderer made quick decisions. When Fred looked across Ves's living room, the murderer decided Fred had to die. Fred died within hours. Ves wanted time to remember the moment when Fred looked at . . . someone. If she remembered and spoke to the murderer, she was somehow convinced she was mistaken. The murderer must have been glib, projected an image of innocence, then followed her in the dark to make sure she never told anyone of her suspicions. The murderer, like the Chinese brigand in *Ming Yellow,* was focused on more money, always more money, and so Adam Nash died.

Which of the six had these qualities?

Jane Wilson. Her visit to Death on Demand might have been a clever pretense, emphasizing that she could be a victim so of course she couldn't be guilty of the crimes. Jane was young. She loved pretty things. Did she want to be able to buy designer clothes, not pick them up second-hand? She seemed sweet. Did she resist Tim moving in to her house because she wanted to be free to go and come as she wished?

Tim Holt. He was smart, ambitious, had big ideas about what he could accomplish but he needed backing. Big money. He pushed Jane to ask Ves for money. Ves said no. Was Tim willing to do whatever was necessary to achieve his goals? He was strong, could move fast. Did he have a gun? So many islanders owned guns, whether legal or not. They were easy to come by.

Gretchen Roundtree. There had to be a reason she'd returned to the island, taken a job at a cosmetics store. If the story Marian picked up from a newspaper friend was right, Gretchen certainly was pressed for money. She liked to live high. If she was also a clandestine thief, she had a penchant for danger, was quick, almost nerveless, and might right now be under enormous pressure to come up with money to hide a secret that could put her in jail.

Curt Roundtree. He chose not to stay at his mother's house when he was on the island. Was that because he wanted to be able to go and come without anyone's notice? He had a reputation for sponging off rich friends. If he'd worn out his welcome at too many places, if his mother no longer sent him regular checks, his cushy lifestyle might be threatened. He had the appealing look of so many reddish-haired men, a freckled face, a genial expression. Had he used his charm to convince Ves he was innocent? He enjoyed hang gliding, which was thrilling and dangerous. The same could be said of murder.

Bob Farley. His struggle to get around made him an unlikely attacker. But he might exaggerate some of his difficulties. He was not the man he'd once been, a successful, admired artist with a six-figure income. If he and Katherine were short on money, and that seemed to be the word around the island, maybe he was willing to kill to make it possible to travel to exotic places on trips that would require huge sums. His physical disability could have served him well, made him seem unlikely to be a danger. Perhaps Fred wouldn't worry about meeting Bob Farley at the end of Fish Haul Pier.

Katherine Farley. Katherine learned the night before Ves's accident that Bob had tried to commit suicide. She would do anything, everything to keep him safe. Did she think he needed travel, something to live for, a reason to keep going? Did Katherine's fear for Bob drive her to set a trap for Ves? Once the trap was set, the rest followed. Fred's knowledge meant he had to be silenced. Adam? Did he know something or was he killed purely for money? Katherine was smart, controlled, implacably devoted to her husband.

If she had to rank them . . .

But any one of them could be guilty. It was up to Billy to discover the truth.

11

Billy Cameron liked the smell of fresh paint. He noted that Tim Holt was doing a careful job for the Misses Quinton on their picket fence, smooth strokes, no paint spattered on the grass. Tim wasn't in painter's white coveralls. As an odd jobber, he chose to work in a red polo and jeans with one worn knee. He listened as Billy pointed out how he had an excellent view of the frame office building where Adam Nash died if Tim looked toward the harbor. Billy intended to visit the secondhand shop next, then cross the street to the cosmetics store. Of those who had gathered in Ves Roundtree's living room, only Tim Holt, Jane Wilson, and Gretchen Roundtree were in close proximity to Adam's office. "Did you see anyone enter the building?"

Tim looked puzzled. "What time? I mean, I'm only here after lunch. I paint in the afternoons except when it's rainy."

Billy studied Tim's face. He was a personable guy. Nice-looking with a clear bright gaze. If he was the perp, this was a smart answer. The innocent would have no idea what time a murderer arrived. "Anytime that afternoon."

Tim nodded sagely. "So he was killed in the afternoon. I didn't hear anything that sounded like a shot but maybe I wouldn't. I'm working on this side of the fence now so my back is to the street. I took a break around three" — he gestured to his left — "dropped into the shop to see Jane, had a Coke with her. I came back and painted until a little before five. I was getting my stuff together and not paying much attention to anything. I picked everything up and walked over there." He pointed at a black pickup parked in a dusty lot at the end of the street. I kind of noticed somebody going inside the building" — he pointed at Adam's office building — "but not enough to know who it was."

"Man? Woman?"

Tim's face creased in tight lines. "Oh hell, I'm sorry. I just got a glimpse. I thought I saw a swish of gray, like maybe a raincoat or something. That's all I remember. A swish of gray." He hesitated. "I kind of thought maybe it was a woman."

Billy watched him closely. "Why?"

Tim's grin was lopsided, engaging. "A guy doesn't walk like a dame. You know what I mean. But that was just a feeling. I sure can't swear to it."

"If anything comes to you, get in touch with me."

"Sure."

Billy knew Tim watched him as he walked toward the door of Jane's shop. He wondered if Tim would follow, and then he heard a high voice calling out, "Young man, we don't pay you to stand and stare."

He didn't envy Tim dealing with the Misses Quinton. Or to be precise, Miss Priscilla Quinton. The other sister — Imogene — never spoke to strangers. Miss Priscilla frequently called the station. There was a cat in her yard. The light at the corner of the street had burned out. The sound of the jukebox at Parotti's Bar and Grill was too loud.

A bell chimed as Billy stepped into You Want It, We Have It.

Hurried steps from the back slowed when Jane Wilson saw him. He admired her sweater. It was — what did Mavis call it? — yeah, a cardigan, white with colored figures of skaters. A turtleneck blouse was in the same shade of apricot as the skaters, and

251

her slacks were white. A mighty pretty outfit.

Jane's eyes widened. "Is it true that someone killed Fred and Ves and Mr. Nash? That's what Max Darling told us last night. He said we all needed to be careful."

Billy gave her an encouraging look as she described the gathering at the Darling house. No harm done. Possibly, it was helpful to encourage them to be wary. As he tried to calm her, he appraised her wide eyes and rounded face. A picture of innocence. Perhaps. Perhaps not. "Investigations are continuing into Fred Butler's and Adam Nash's deaths and we continue to search for Ms. Roundtree. Were you here in your shop Tuesday afternoon?"

"Yes." A slender hand touched her throat.

"Did you leave the shop between one and five?"

She shook her head.

"Did you hear a shot?"

"No." The word was scarcely a breath.

"Do you have any idea who might have shot Adam Nash?"

She took her time in answering. "I don't know. Max thinks it was one of us."

"Us?"

"One of the people at Ves's house the night Fred died."

"What do you think?"

She shook her head again, didn't speak.

"What color dress did you wear on Tuesday?"

Her eyes were huge, frightened. "A jersey floral dress, big red flowers on a black background."

He nodded. "We'll be in touch." He left her standing in the center aisle. As he crossed the street, he frowned. He had trouble believing Jane Wilson slipped into Adam's office, steadied a .45 with two hands, shot Adam Nash dead. But there were killers with sweet young faces.

Billy's nose wrinkled slightly as he stepped into the cosmetics store. Funny how women liked all these smells. He was glad Mavis didn't scatter perfumes and powders across the dresser, and nobody looked nicer than she did. Her complexion was soft and smooth. He liked the pale pink lipstick she wore and her powder had a nice homey gardenia scent.

A curtain parted at the back. Gretchen Roundtree's welcoming smile froze for an instant before she moved forward with a pleasant expression. "Chief Cameron." Even in a blue smock over white slacks, she exuded an aura of wealth and privilege. He bet she'd cost Rufus a pretty penny. Her blond hair seemed to glisten, her black brows were perfectly arched, her face smooth and unwrinkled. She stopped in front of him. It would be easy to dismiss her as just another rich woman, dabbling in a little shop. But he had a different picture of Gretchen Roundtree after he talked to Detective Morales in the burglary unit in Scottsdale. She hadn't, as Marian had been told, actually been present as a guest in all the homes that were robbed. But she had visited the houses recently, was known to the victims. He looked into alert blue eyes and judged she was capable of planning a daring theft, capable of executing a carefully timed crime, capable of selling stones to a well-connected fence, capable of hiding monies that she wouldn't be reporting to the IRS. Detective Morales was curious about Gretchen's return to the island. "Working at a cosmetics shop?" He'd given a low whistle. "Sounds like somebody has the goods on her." A pause. "She was at a weekend blowout at a mansion just before she left town. No robbery. The wife is about thirty years younger than her rich hubby. She loves jewels. She has a ruby necklace supposedly worth four hundred grand. She still has the necklace. Maybe Roundtree tried a grab, got caught. This new wife has a mean mouth. Maybe blackmail is a thrill.

Something for her bucket list."

Behind Gretchen's slightly condescending expression was a wary, calculating intelligence. Billy had no doubt she would do whatever she needed to do to save herself. He gave her his most stolid cop look. "Were you here Tuesday afternoon?"

Now there was a slight tilt of amusement to her lips. "I work here. Every day. Yes. If it matters."

"It might matter. Did you hear a shot?"

The tilt of amusement fled. For an instant she looked older. Frightened. "No. When was Adam killed?"

He ignored the question. "Did you leave the shop anytime in the afternoon?"

"I closed over lunch. Went home. Came back at one. I closed up and left around five." She looked at him steadily.

If she was in the shop at five, she was in the clear. When pressed, Doc Burford said, with qualifications, that death likely occurred between four and six. Downtown, while not big-city busy, had plenty of occupants between four and six. Billy was sure Adam was shot as the ferry departed the harbor at five. "Around five? A few minutes before? Or after?"

She appeared to concentrate. "I believe it was a few minutes before five." Then she nodded. "Yes. It must have been. I heard the ferry whistle as I walked to my car."

Was she innocent or enjoying inner pleasure as she used the sound of the ferry horn as an alibi?

Chef Max proudly presented the catch of the day, red snapper baked in white wine with onion, green pepper, and succulent mushroom pieces. Cheese grits and steamed asparagus completed the menu. Max was sympathetic when Annie told him about Jane's visit and her determination not to be pressured into a wedding. As Annie washed the dishes, he opined from a comfortable perch on a stool at the central island. "Tim sounds like he's serious."

"About Jane? Or somebody trying to kill her?"

"About Jane." Max popped a small square of toffee in his mouth.

Annie wasn't one to act as a food gendarme, but toffee seemed a bit of overkill after a spectacular dessert, pineapple cookies crunchy with shredded coconut and homemade vanilla ice cream.

"The man wants her. He's crying wolf to hustle her into marriage. A man will do what a man has to do." There was tacit approval in his tone. "I suppose he may really be scared for her, but I don't see someone stalking the surviving contingent —"

"Heirs," Annie said firmly.

"Oh, ye of little legal knowledge. Anyway, you get my point. Fred had to go because he knew about the step. Then the killer decided to dispatch Ves, and somehow Adam got in the mix. Jane's safe. You want a prediction?"

Annie put the last dish in the dishwasher, poured in detergent, closed the door, and pushed Start. She unloosed the tie to her apron, hung it from a peg at the end of the counter. "Love predictions."

"And this one's about love. I'm surprised you haven't picked up on it." Max grinned. "I admit a mere man cannot be expected to plumb — scratch that — divine the workings of female minds. Greater men than I have tried and failed. But this one's billboard plain. Jane isn't in love with Tim. She won't marry him."

Annie looked at him in surprise. "She cared enough to try and inveigle money out of Ves."

Max shrugged. "They probably have a good time together and she wants to have a boyfriend. She won't marry him."

Annie wasn't so sure. "She's young. She doesn't want to be pressured."

Max looked complacent. "You knew we'd get married."

As they walked into the hall, headed for the den, she looked up at him, thick blond hair, blue eyes, Joe Hardy all grown up and sexy as hell. She remembered the first time she'd seen him. She'd known, perhaps not that she would marry him, but she'd known nothing would ever be the same, he was going to matter to her, her life was going to be different.

He watched her face. His smile was smug. "That's what I thought. Jane doesn't feel that way."

They settled on the couch. Max reached for his iPad, Annie for Charles Todd's new book, then stopped. "I'm in a *Topper* mood." She was happy and she wanted a little frosting on that cake.

Max bypassed the iPad, picked up the remote. "Your favorite ghosts, sophisticated and fun. Coming right up."

Annie loved the beginning, the ebullient married couple racing along in George's car, a crash into a tree. Was there ever a cooler couple than Cary Grant as George Kerby and Constance Bennett as Marion Kerby? She knew the dialogue after the crash by heart:

Marion: "Oh, George, you're getting transparent. You're fading."

George: "Say, that's funny. I can see through you, too. Say, who's that?"

Their bodies are lying by the wrecked car.

Marion: "It's us. You know something, George? I think we're dead."

George: "I think you're right. Funny, I don't feel —"

The ringtone "Happy Days Are Here Again" announced a call from Marian. Annie had changed the ringtone after Marian and Craig remarried. But Marian wasn't likely to be calling with happy news, not with everything that had happened the past few days.

Annie tapped Speaker. "Marian?"

"Just got it on the scanner. Shots fired. 225 Bluefish Road. On my way there. Jane Wilson's house. Right around the corner from you."

Sirens squealed behind them. Annie twisted to look. "Police cars. Maybe three."

The Lamborghini squealed around the corner onto Bluefish. Lights blazed from a house midway up the block. Lighted windows marked several houses on the even-numbered side of the street. On the odd-numbered side, two houses were dark. Only the house in the middle had a small light shining from a front window. In the glare of Maglites, Annie saw the gilt numbers, 225, Jane's house.

"We're here first." Annie's voice rose. "Marian got the report at the same time as the call to the police and she was on her way when she called me." The police station was a good six blocks north and east of their house and even farther from 225 Bluefish.

Sirens blared. Flashing red lights whirled. Max pulled to the curb. Police cars raced past, screeched to a stop in front of the house with a dim light shining through a living room window. Police spilled out, took cover behind their vehicles. Shouts. "Police. Hands up. Throw down your weapons. Police."

Max rolled down the driver's window.

Annie felt sick inside. Jane was upset when she came to the store this morning, but she was alive, alive and thinking about the wedding that someday she hoped to have, a June wedding and an ivory dress with lace at the throat. Annie strained to see, yet she looked with dread. Her gaze traveled across the front lawn. Nothing. Which meant she didn't see a body lying on the grass. The steps . . . Nothing there, but to the left of the steps, a huge fern looked askew, its fronds bent and tangled.

Maglites illuminated the yard. The house was well kept, a one-story yellow cottage with a magnolia tree to one side of the gravel drive. A green Honda was in the drive.

Annie scarcely breathed as she stared at a huge royal fern to the left of the front steps. Portions of the fern looked crushed. It was a still night and the flower bed was sheltered from wind. Some of the lower fronds of the fern moved.

A uniformed figure darted forward. Annie recognized Lou Pirelli's stocky, muscular build. He moved fast, gun in hand, weaving to avoid providing an easy target. He thudded across the drive, hunkered behind the magnolia tree. "Police. Hands up. Out from behind that fern. Now."

Hyla Harrison, gun in hand, covered Lou. She held the gun with both hands, the barrel aimed at the quivering fronds. A swarm of officers fanned out to form a backup perimeter. Billy Cameron's old sedan pulled up behind the police cars. Billy swung out of the car, strode forward, big, strong, imposing.

Marian's VW nosed past the Lamborghini, jolted to a stop. The driver's door was flung open. Marian popped out, lean in a navy turtleneck sweater and black jeans.

One of the officers — he was young with short brown hair and an unlined face — yelled, "Take cover. Active shooter at large."

Marian ran to the far side of her car, knelt, but she had the Leica in her hands, ready to take a series of photographs.

Annie reached for the door handle.

Max grabbed her arm. "Wait."

"I don't see Jane anywhere." Annie's voice shook.

"Maybe she's in the house. Maybe she's all right." Max gave her arm a reassuring squeeze.

Lou Pirelli's voice was deep, harsh. "We have you covered. Come out from behind that fern, hands up." He left his cover, eased toward the flower bed, alert, ready to fire.

The fern fronds quivered again, parted. Jane Wilson was on her hands and knees, crawling forward. In the glare of Maglites, she was pale, hair tousled, a purplish bruise on the left side her face, her velveteen jacket snagged. She pushed herself up, stood, looked small in the glare of the lights. "Don't shoot. Please." Her voice was high and shaky. She held out empty hands half raised, eyes blinking against the glare of the flashlights. "Someone shot at me."

Lou Pirelli came out of his crouch, stared.

"Janey? Janey Wilson?"

She squinted to see. Her face changed. "Is it Lou? Angie's big brother?"

He hurried to her, putting his gun in his holster. "Yeah. I'm Lou."

Billy Cameron was directing officers. "Sweep the area. Be careful not to mess up any footprints. The call came in twelve minutes ago. It looks like the shooter got away."

Annie opened the car door, jumped out. Max was right behind her as they crossed the street. She stopped on the sidewalk.

"Lou." Jane wavered unsteadily.

Without fanfare, as if it were the most natural thing in the world, he spread an arm around her shoulders. "You're safe now."

A barefoot man in a Braves sweatshirt and gym shorts stood on the opposite curb. "Somebody shot a gun. Eight past nine. I called 911. I looked out and didn't see anybody."

Billy joined Jane and Lou, spoke to her quietly. "Are you hurt?"

"I tried to duck and fell. I hit my face on something." She began to shake, perhaps a delayed reaction to shock, lifted a trembling hand to the bruised portion of her face.

Lou tightened his grasp. "Don't worry. We're here. I'll take care of you. What hap-

263

pened?"

She looked up at him. "I was late getting home. I usually get home before dark. But I owed some hours at the store so I stayed late."

Billy was encouraging. "You arrived here a few minutes after nine. What happened?"

Her blue eyes were huge. She took a deep breath, tried to stop trembling.

Maglites swung back and forth across the yard, around the house, into the woods. Officers moved cautiously, shouting, "Police. Come out with your hands up. Police."

The neighbor joined Annie and Max and Marian on the sidewalk. "I thought she was a goner after I heard the shots. I knew they were across the street. Had to be her house. The Jenkinses" — he jerked a thumb to his left — "are out of town, and" — he pointed to his right — "that house is empty."

"How many shots?" Marian held her pen over a sheaf of folded copy paper.

His red face was pugnacious. "Three. Three for sure. After I called 911, I got my gun out. But when I snuck out on the porch, I didn't see a soul. Not anywhere."

Jane's voice was thin but steady. "It happened so fast. I parked in the drive and got out. I walked across the yard and started up the steps, and all of a sudden there were shots. I knew what they were. I tried to get out of the way, and that's when I fell." She reached down, touched an ankle. "I twisted my ankle and my head hit something. There's a wisteria bush next to the fern with knobby branches and that's how I hurt my face. I stayed really still and burrowed down behind the fern. I was afraid whoever shot at me would come and find me."

"Did you hear anything?"

She looked at Billy blankly. "The shots."

"After the shots."

She clasped her hands tightly together. "I don't know."

The neighbor took a couple of steps forward. "Hey, Billy. Joe Mackey here. I heard the shots, came out right after I called 911. I didn't see anybody. I didn't hear a car. I was on the porch soon enough to hear a motor and see taillights."

An engine gunned and a rusted black pickup squealed to a stop. The cab door opened and Tim Holt was out and running toward the house. "What the hell's going on here?" He hurtled toward Jane and Lou, glaring at Lou. "Get your damn hands off her. What the hell do you think you're doing?"

"Tim." Jane slipped free of Lou's support, stepped forward, one hand outstretched in front of Lou. "Someone shot at me a little while ago and they came to help."

Tim checked himself midstride, looked like he'd been body slammed. "Shot at you?"

Billy Cameron moved closer. "Miss Wilson is unharmed. She sustained a bruise when she took cover behind a fern. She's safe now."

Tim's face twisted in fury. "I told everybody she could be in danger. Like the others are. I called you this afternoon, told you people you needed to get this thing solved. So now somebody's shot at her. No thanks to you she isn't dead." His head swung around. "Where is he? I'll kill the —"

Billy's tone was sharp. "The shooter escaped before we arrived. You are impeding our investigation."

" 'Impeding our investigation.' " Tim's voice was heavy with sarcasm. "What investigation? Now they say somebody pushed poor old Fred off the pier and Ves Roundtree's dead somewhere and Mr. Nash is on a slab. What investigation?"

"Tim, hush." Jane was angry. "It doesn't help to come here and act ugly. Please be quiet." She turned back to Billy. "I didn't hear a car. I didn't hear anything but the shots."

On the front steps, Hyla Harrison aimed a Maglite at the clapboard siding to the right of the front door. "Bullet holes here, Chief. Estimate six feet from the ground. If I stand on the second step, it looks like the shots were just above and to the right of the target. Maybe not a real good shot. Or shot from a pistol, not a rifle."

Billy nodded. "Get photos. Mavis can remove the slugs after you've measured." He turned back to Jane. "Would you like for a paramedic to check you?" He gestured at the flashing light of an ambulance that had pulled up behind the police cars.

Jane touched the bruise. "I'm not really hurt."

Only hurt emotionally, Annie thought. Jane could no longer go in or come out without a flicker of fear. To know another person deliberately aimed a gun at you, intended to take away your life, was as devastating as solid earth turning to quicksand beneath your feet, sucking you to oblivion.

"We will complete our search. You may wish to go inside."

Jane's eyes slid toward the door, where Hyla was photographing the evidence of metal tearing into wood.

Tim bulled forward. "No two ways about

it. Thank God I decided to check on you. I'll go get my gear."

Annie saw the recoil in her eyes. Jane didn't want him to stay all night. She'd promised her mom. Jane wanted love, if that's what they had, to bloom in happy times, not when death lurked. Annie rushed forward. "Come home with us." She looked at Billy. "She will be much safer. No one can get at her at our house."

Annie reached sleepily for the phone on her bedside table. "Hello."

"Annie, my dear. Still in bed." Laurel's husky voice faintly accusing. "On such a troubled Friday morning. But that suggests all is well. Or as well as it can be. I just heard about the shots at Jane Wilson. We need to rally round to keep her safe. I've texted Emma and Henny. Both are quite bright and shining in the morning."

Annie decided it would not be a good start to her day to take umbrage at the implication that she and Max were derelict as adults to still be in bed at, she squinted at the clock, six A.M. She swung her legs over the side of the bed. "Good for them." She managed to sound cheery.

Max rolled up on one elbow, hair mussed, expression muzzy.

268

She mouthed, "Your mother. Worried about Jane."

Laurel's tone was a shade stiff. "To think of that young woman all alone."

Annie said quickly, "She's here. We brought her home with us."

"Splendid. That's the very best solution. I'll let Henny and Emma know all is well. Call us if there is anything we can offer, though it does seem now that Billy is best equipped to discover what happened." The call ended.

Annie knocked gently on the guest room door, spoke loud enough to be heard. "Breakfast will be ready in half an hour. Come down whenever you wish." Max was already downstairs, cleaning strawberries.

The door opened. Jane looked out shyly. "I hope I'm not a huge bother." Although Jane had taken only a few minutes last night to pack a bag, she was certainly lovely this morning in a beige Windsor plaid sheath dress and double strap bronze heels. A necklace with several strands of amber, black, and crystal beads sparkled.

Annie smiled. "You're no bother. Max loves to cook and he especially loves to cook for guests. He's already in the kitchen."

Annie led the way downstairs and they

settled at the kitchen table.

Max brought coffee and orange juice, served bowls with freshly sliced strawberries. "The quiche will be ready in a moment." He turned back to the stove.

Annie offered sour cream and brown sugar to Jane, who chose sour cream.

As they ate, Annie carefully avoided any reference to murder and gunshots, talked brightly about the latest Hannah Dennison book. "Her characters are fabulous. I love" — she took a bite of a succulent strawberry, savored the sprinkle of brown sugar — "the way a really good book could only have been written by that particular author. Good books are never copycat." She chattered on as Max brought them each a plate with a generous slice of quiche. She wished she could do something to erase the dark smudges beneath Jane's eyes, restore an eager bloom to her rounded face, remove the memory of shots in the darkness.

As Max replenished their coffee cups, a knock sounded at the back door.

He looked surprised, walked to the door, opened it. "Hey, Lou. Come in."

Jane twisted a little in her chair. She looked pleased, surprised, uncertain.

Lou Pirelli stepped into the kitchen, looked immediately toward the table.

"Morning." His gaze settled on Jane. "I wanted to check in with you. I'll be going to work with you. We thought it would be a good idea for someone to be on hand for a while." Lou spoke with the easy drawl of a native islander. He wasn't in uniform today. He wore a soft blue polo and khaki slacks and tasseled loafers. A uniform tended to create a sameness in appearance. In civvies, Lou's curly dark hair, handsome face, and athletic build made him distinctive. "If you don't mind."

Annie saw relief in Jane's rounded face. And pleasure. How nice for Jane. She looked at Lou. Oh. And oh.

Annie felt restless, popping up and down every few minutes to check her e-mails, to place orders, to make phone calls for a committee meeting for Friends of the Library. When the radio news announcer led the top of the hour with a breathless description of a shooting on Bluefish Road, she switched to a cool jazz station.

Agatha watched with glowing green eyes and a tail that flicked irritably.

Annie returned to the table determined to focus on the chapbooks. She picked up Laurel's *Merry Musings*. She smiled in agreement as she read: *If an elephant's in the way, find another path.* Excellent advice. Her present elephant was her inability to immerse herself in the ordinary life of the store and her job and committees and volunteering and tennis and —

"Happy Days Are Here Again" rang.

Annie answered. "Is everything okay?" So much had not been okay in recent days.

Marian spoke in a staccato rush. "Heads-up. Bob Farley just thumped into the station, told Mavis he was turning himself in. I was there, checking the overnights, everything from the shooting on Bluefish Road to a stolen chicken coop out on Bidwell Lane. The TV reporter from Savannah was refreshing her makeup, waiting to see Billy. I swung around to be sure I'd heard right. It was Bob Farley. Not the man he once was, too thin now, but impressive, thick sandy hair, chiseled features, would still look good on a *GQ* cover even though he's too gaunt. There's an air about Bob. He was dressed like a *GQ* guy, blue blazer, a triple-stripe dress shirt, no tie, chinos, loafers. I guess you dress up to go to jail. He said, 'I killed Fred Butler, Ves Roundtree, and Adam Nash. I tried to kill Jane Wilson.' He was composed, but his face had an empty look. I whipped out my Leica. The TV blonde moved like a tigress, motioning her camera guy to whir. I was shooting photos of Bob. The door to the offices opened and Billy walked out. Mavis must have buzzed him the minute Bob started talking. The TV gal yelled at Bob, pushed a mic in his face. 'Statement for the press.' Bob ignored her. Billy came up to the counter. Bob said it all again, same words, nothing more, nothing less. The TV gal's mic was right in his face. Bob wasn't emotional. His voice was kind of tired. Billy never changed expression. The TV gal's yelling like a banshee at this point. 'Are the murders solved? Three crimes? Bob what? What's your last name?' Bob half turned, said formally, 'Robert J. Farley,' turned back to Billy. Billy said, 'Come this way,' and held the gate open. I called out, 'Where's Ves Roundtree's body?' No answer. Billy yanked open the door to the back. They started down the corridor and the door shut. I was going nuts. I kept pestering Mavis. I wanted a statement. Finally the printer started clacking. She went over to check, picked up a sheet, handed one copy to me, one to the TV reporter, who moved so the light was better, and started talking as her cameraman filmed. 'A reign of terror ended shockingly this morning on Broward's Rock, a sleepy resort island off the coast of South Carolina, when . . .' "

Marian took a breath. "Probably been picked up coast to coast at this point. Murder with your morning coffee. Here's the statement: *Broward's Rock police announced that Robert J. Farley is a person of interest in the deaths of Fred Butler and Adam Nash and in the disappearance of Vesta Roundtree. Farley was taken into custody when he claimed to be responsible for the crimes. He's being held on suspicion of murder.* That's it. Nada mas. Nothing about an arraignment."

Marian cleared her throat. "Talk about dancing on the head of a pin. I don't get what Billy's doing. Why wasn't Bob arrested for murder, plain and simple? If murder is ever plain and simple. Anyway, I used my cell to record Bob's repeat. TV will run with the film, which also got him admitting to the murders. I know Billy doesn't like to show his hand but this time I don't see where he's going. I wrote the story, pulled up the stuff on all the deaths. But I had a couple of hours before my deadline. I knew what I had to do. I went out to the studio. Katherine was working on a watercolor. When I walked in, she turned and smiled. She's truly beautiful, that sleek dark hair and classic features. Or maybe I should say she would be beautiful if she didn't sag like she'd been pressed through a wringer. She looks haunted. Not even the smile hid her stress. I know her fairly well because she teaches classes at the Haven. David's taken oil painting from her and she's encouraged him."

Marian's son was gifted, loved art, planned to be an artist.

"Anyway, Katherine gave me a sweet smile, asked, 'How's my favorite young painter?'

"I said, 'He's doing fine and working hard.' I felt like a rat dripping slime. I walked up, stopped a foot away from the easel. She looked at me and knew I had bad news. Her face went blank. I saw terror in her eyes. I said, 'Billy Cameron issued a statement announcing Bob is a person of interest in three murders. Bob's being held on suspicion of murder.' It was like watching a hurricane surge destroy dunes. One minute everything is beautiful. The next, the sea oats are a memory and the dune isn't there. She gave a low moan and she was running past me, the brush flung on the floor, still wearing her painting smock. The door slammed and she was gone." A pause. "I'd imagine she's at the station."

Annie drove too fast, made it to the station

in just under four minutes. She slammed out of her car, yanked out her cell phone. Max was likely on the back nine. He'd insisted today was a day to enjoy living, and he lived to golf. She texted: *At police station. Bob Farley confessed, arrested. Will try to help Katherine.*

Annie hurried up the path, stopped by a young palmetto palm a half dozen yards from the station. Katherine Farley stood next to the trunk with its jagged thatched covering, the remnants of dead fronds. The wind rippled her paint-spattered smock. Her face was white as alabaster. A faint tracery of veins was apparent on one temple. Katherine held out a hand. "You heard?" Her voice was dull, defeated. Agonized.

"Marian called. She thought" — it had not been said but Annie knew it was so — "you needed someone."

"I need Bob." Katherine shivered. "Bob didn't kill anyone." She spoke with the intonation of a child repeating words she doesn't understand. "They were nice to me. Billy took me into his office and he told me what Bob said. I told him it couldn't be true, wasn't true, Bob would never hurt any living thing. He wouldn't." Her luminous brown eyes brimmed with tears. "Billy was nice to me. He said he was sorry. I told him

I had to talk to Bob. He said he'd go see. It seemed to me he was gone such a long time, and when he came back inside the office, he stood with his back to the door and I knew he didn't want to tell me." Tears trickled down her cheeks. "Bob won't see me. But I know Bob was at home that Thursday when someone tried to kill Ves. I was gone then. I told Bob I was delivering a watercolor across the island. When I got home, his car was exactly where it was when I left." She spoke emphatically, trying to convince Annie. "I know that's so because there was a huge pinecone by the back right wheel when I left. The pinecone was lying in the same place when I got home. It would have been smashed if he'd gone anywhere."

Annie said nothing, but her face must have revealed her thought.

"You think he wouldn't confess to murders he didn't commit. But he did. He lied. I know why." Now her eyes were dry, her face drawn. "He's lying to protect me. Bob thinks I killed them."

The sea breeze was picking up. Katherine's smock billowed. She brushed back a dark tangle of curls, stirred by the wind from the harbor. "I told him I was delivering a watercolor I'd just finished, an alligator on the bank. But he came down to the studio and saw the painting was still there. I knew he was puzzled. He looked at the watercolor, then at me. I started talking about something else. He didn't ask me. But he was right. I didn't make a delivery that Thursday. I went to Ves's house." She took a deep breath. "I have to tell Billy. Will you come with me?"

12

Annie loved the view of the harbor from Billy's office window. February offered days that hinted of spring to come, shining blue sky, puffy white clouds, silvery porpoises leaping as if for joy. A brisk onshore breeze trimmed jade green water with whitecaps. A shrimp boat moved steadily past. An iceberg-white yacht glided south.

Annie turned her gaze to Billy, sitting stolidly behind his shiny yellow oak desk. His stepson Kevin had made the desk. The varnish was sticky and there was a slight list to Billy's right. Billy's face was expressionless, but his eyes were intent.

Katherine leaned forward. She looked insubstantial in the smock, but her voice was clipped and urgent. "I want you to understand why I was upset. Bob, oh God, he went to Gurney Point and I think he would have jumped into the water if your officer hadn't followed him. I tried to thank her and she was matter-of-fact, said, 'Ma'am, it's my job to see that people are safe.' " Katherine's voice quivered. She pressed her lips together for an instant, managed to keep going. "That's what I was carrying with me. I talked to Bob. I told him" — the planes of her face sharpened — "I can't live without you. Oh, I'd live. But it wouldn't be life. There wouldn't be joy or meaning, only one dead dull day after another. I told him he must never never never think he's a burden. That's what I was dealing with the next day, the Thursday that someone set the trap for Ves."

Katherine looked out the window at the harbor, but Annie knew she didn't see blue skies or puffy white clouds.

"Bob went to Gurney Point Wednesday. The next day was the Thursday Ves fell." Billy spoke quietly.

Katherine faced him. A pulse fluttered in her slender throat. "All day I tried to think what I could do. There isn't much money now. I can't earn what Bob did. And" — her tone was fierce — "I won't sell his paintings. He'll never paint again. I can't sell his paintings. I decided to go see Ves." She brushed back a swoop of dark hair. "I thought she'd help me. She's —" A breath. "She was kind. I was going to tell her how

I'd nearly lost Bob. I was going to ask her for twenty thousand, tell her somehow to subtract it from whatever we'd get someday, and I would promise never to tell any of the others. They all wanted money from her. I could see why she felt like she was surrounded by crabs with their claws grasping. But this was Bob's life." She stared at Billy, her eyes huge. "I drove to her house."

Billy held up his hand. He opened a drawer, lifted out a recorder, placed it on the desk, turned it on. He looked at Katherine and recited the Miranda warning.

She stared for an instant, gave a strangled laugh. "I don't care. I'm trying to tell you what happened."

Billy nodded. "Police Chief Billy Cameron. Friday, February twenty-sixth, interrogating Katherine Farley, a possible person of interest in the murders of Fred Butler and Adam Nash and the disappearance of Vesta Roundtree. Now —"

Annie heard Billy's words, was puzzled. Billy talked about Ves's disappearance, but Bob admitted he'd murdered her.

"— Mrs. Farley, what time did you arrive at Ves Roundtree's house on Thursday, February eleventh?"

Katherine pleated her fingers together. "About twenty after five."

"Did you see any cars?"

For an instant, she looked surprised. "No. I suppose that should have told me she wasn't there. I didn't think about it. I wanted to see her. I thought she'd put her car in the garage. I pulled up on the drive. I started to walk back to the front of the house, but as I came even with the porch I saw the back door was open. I veered that way, went up the back steps. I was right, the back door was open."

"Ajar or fully open?"

"Wide open. I hurried up the back steps, came to the door, knocked on the jamb." For the first time, the rush of words slowed. "I pulled open the screen, stepped into the back hallway."

"Could you see the stairs?"

Katherine's nod was impatient. "The hallway extends from the front door to the back door. The stairs were to my left. I would have had to go to the front of the hall to go up the stairs. Or to look up the stairs."

"Did you?"

"No." Her voice was flat.

"What did you do?"

"I stopped inside the screen door and called out. There was no answer." Now her words came slowly. "I don't know if I can

282

make you understand, but suddenly I was afraid. It was quiet. Terribly quiet. The back door open. Calling for Ves and no answer. I started backing up and then I was at the door and outside and running for my car. I don't know why I ran. But I did. I slammed in the car and got out of there as fast as I could."

Billy's gaze was considering.

Annie wondered if Billy felt he was hearing the truth, a woman who likely had entered a house where a killer lurked and interrupted the cleaning of a slick step or a woman spinning a tale to divert an investigator. Had she walked into the hallway and the sound of the door and her call sent a killer scurrying upstairs and out of sight?

"Did you tell anyone of this experience?"

"No."

"Why are you telling me now?"

Her shoulders tightened. "The next week on Wednesday we went to Ves's house."

Billy nodded. "That was the day Ms. Roundtree told you how she'd been hurt, the day Fred Butler died."

She nodded. "That night, after we got home, Bob went to his room." For an instant she looked defensive. "He has his own room now. He sleeps poorly and he doesn't want to keep me awake."

Annie heard more than the halting explanation, wondered if Bob Farley resisted closeness because he was no longer able to make love to his wife.

"I was restless. I couldn't seem to read. I decided to go to the studio. I didn't come back to the house until a little after midnight. Bob was in the living room. I told him I'd been working."

"Did you meet Fred Butler?"

"No." A steady gaze. "I did not meet Fred. I had nothing to do with Ves's disappearance on Monday or Adam's death on Tuesday." A pause. "I was working in the studio Monday night. I delivered the alligator painting Tuesday afternoon." She looked defiant. She had good explanations for her whereabouts at all the critical times, but that didn't change the fact she had the opportunity to have been on the pier or at Ves's house or in Adam's office.

"Did you go to Adam's office?"

"I did not."

"Did you shoot him?"

"No."

"Your husband's gun was gone when I came to your house Wednesday. I called you on the extension. When you joined us, you claimed you had no idea where the gun was. Is that true?"

284

Her shoulders bowed. "I took the gun from the bedside table the day after Bob tried to jump into the water. Bob was in his shower. I slipped downstairs and put the gun in my trunk. I was afraid to keep it where he could get it."

"What did you do with the gun?"

"I went to Blackbeard Beach and threw the gun as far as I could."

Billy made a notation. "Convenient that you claim to have disposed of the gun long before Adam Nash was killed or shots were fired at Jane Wilson."

"Not convenient. True." Katherine's stare was straight. "I wasn't home last night when someone shot at Jane. I was working in the studio. I'm trying to finish a commission. We need the money. I didn't come back to the house until ten or so. This morning we had the radio on and heard that shots were fired at Jane last night. Bob looked upset. I told him I thought it was awful. She's so young and so nice. I thought he looked at me strangely, but everything has been so odd. I asked him if he wanted to do anything this morning and he shook his head, said he was tired, thought he'd read, so I went to the studio. I heard Bob's car leave." She looked defiant. "I'd fixed it where I can track his cell on GPS. If he'd started for somewhere solitary, I would have followed. He parked downtown so I didn't worry."

"He came here. He confessed."

"He's lying." There was pain in her voice. "He thinks he's saving me. He knows I could have killed them. I was out at the times the paper said they died. Worst of all, he knew the gun was gone, and I was the only person who could have taken it."

Billy said smoothly, "Unless you were as surprised as you seemed when I was at your house and Bob took the gun, used it, hid it or threw it away."

"Not Bob." It was a cry of despair. Her mouth twisted. "You think I'm lying to protect him. I would lie for him. But I'm not. He's lying for me, and I didn't kill them. Neither of us killed them. Don't you see, Bob knew I lied about the delivery. He wouldn't understand why I'd tell a lie unless I had something to hide. I did have something to hide. I didn't want to admit I'd gone to Ves's house, especially not after she told us someone tried to kill her. Bob knew I was out at all the times that mattered. This morning, after I went to the studio, he thought about the times and my lies and decided I'd tried to kill Ves, and Fred saw me so I had to kill him. He knew the only reason I would hurt anyone would be for him, so he came here, claimed he'd killed them." Katherine's face was no longer defiant or hopeful or anxious. She looked like a woman driven to despair. "Please tell Bob I didn't shoot anyone. Tell him everything is all right. Let him go."

Billy's face furrowed. "I told your husband he could call, arrange for a lawyer to come. He insisted he did not want a lawyer."

Katherine was adamant. "He must have a lawyer."

"I agree. He confessed to a series of crimes. I have taken him into custody." Billy's expression was odd, part exasperation, part dismay. "Normally I wouldn't disclose his response, but you are his wife. As I locked the cell, I told him again that he could remain silent and call a lawyer. He hooked one hand around a bar and said, 'I don't want a lawyer. I have nothing to say. Not to a lawyer. Not to you. Not to anybody. I'm keeping it for the judge. When I go to court, I'll tell the judge I'm guilty. End of story. Until then, I intend to relax.' He turned his back on me and limped to the cot."

"He lied about the murders." Katherine's voice was shrill. "He thinks he's protecting me. Tell him I'm here and that I've told you everything. Tell him I will get a lawyer. Tell him" — her voice shook — "I want to see him."

"I will tell him." Billy's face was expressionless.

Annie thought his voice was uncommonly gentle.

When the door closed behind him, Katherine turned to Annie. "He has to see me."

Annie wanted to reassure Katherine, but she could hear Billy's voice, stolid and uninflected as he quoted Bob Farley: "I'll tell the judge I'm guilty. End of story." "Perhaps tomorrow he'll talk to you."

Katherine spoke rapidly. "I'll get a lawyer. Jed Lowery handles things for us. The minute I get out of here, I'll go straight to his office."

Annie knew Jed, who wrote wills and handled probates and real estate law. He was pleasant, intelligent, and had likely handled criminal matters only if appointed by the court. "There's a wonderful defense attorney in Savannah. Handler Jones."

Katherine came to her feet, paced to the window. She whirled to look at Annie. "How can it be such a beautiful day and my whole life is falling part?"

The door opened. Billy stepped inside, closed the door behind him, remained standing. He was an imposing figure, tall,

288

solid, powerfully built. Slowly he shook his head. Annie saw sadness in his eyes, sadness at bringing hurtful news to a woman desperately afraid for the man she loved.

Annie watched Katherine's car bolt out of the police lot. She felt empty and sad. How did lives get so tangled? Bob and Katherine. Before his accident, they'd been a golden couple, the envy of many, physically attractive, full of charm and life, gifted, busy, successful. Now Bob was in a cell and Katherine was frantically trying to save him. What was the truth? Was Bob lying to protect her? Or was he quite certain that Katherine went to Ves's house, made the step slick, and when threatened by Fred's knowledge met him on the pier and pushed him to his death? Fred would not have been afraid for his safety with a woman. She could have convinced him that she wanted to talk, that they could reach an understanding. After that, perhaps it seemed easy to go see Ves, perhaps force her to leave the house at gunpoint. Had Ves died in the woods or was her body somewhere in the sea? As for Adam, was his murder simply to increase the size of the pot or had he become a danger?

The fact that Bob was in a cell meant

either he was guilty or Katherine was guilty. No matter how much Katherine loved him, admitting her guilt would not help him. He would obviously claim she was making it up to protect him.

Katherine had the opportunity to commit the crimes.

Bob or Katherine? Katherine or Bob?

Annie looked out at the harbor. She didn't know when the water had ever seemed more beautiful, its color a rich jade green and above, a bright sky full of promise. A yacht neared shore, its hull a gleaming white. A man and woman stood near the prow. They looked young and happy, coming to the island for a holiday.

It was unsettling to juxtapose her memory of Katherine's face and the beauty of the day. Her cell phone rang, the tune for Max. As always, she felt a surge of happiness.

Hyla Harrison, crisp as always in her french blue uniform, pointed at the chair Katherine had occupied.

Billy nodded. "Pick up what prints you can. Check them against the unidentified prints on the screen door at the Roundtree house."

Hyla's green eyes were alert. "She can claim she touched the door when she came to dinner there or the night that Ms. Round-tree called them there to warn them."

"The prints may be among the most recent, overlaying other prints. It's been several days since she was there as a guest. And" — his blue eyes were grim — "her husband may use a cane, but I imagine I can prove he customarily opened doors for her."

Hyla's gaze was admiring.

Annie hurried along the sidewalk toward You Want It, We Have It, the secondhand store where Jane Wilson worked. Max's call to arrange lunch at Parotti's had given her some perspective. It was up to Billy to decide whether Bob or Katherine was guilty. But Bob in jail likely meant the danger was over. If Katherine was the murderer, she would not attack anyone now. Jane Wilson no longer needed to be afraid. Annie was eager to bring her that good news. The bell sang a cheerful song as she opened the shop door. She stepped into the center aisle, looked about.

Jane came hurrying up the aisle, her bronze heels making a sharp tattoo as she hurried forward. Close behind her loomed Lou, broad face easing into a warm smile. "Hey, Annie."

Annie smiled in return. What a handsome

couple they made, sturdy muscular Lou, sweet-faced Jane with her cloud of soft brown hair. That sheath dress set off her willowy figure quite perfectly.

Lou was in charge. He made a high five. "Have you heard the news? Bob Farley's in jail."

Annie knew neither Lou nor Jane was thinking of what that reality meant to Bob and Katherine. Understandably, they were elated that Jane was safe from attack.

Jane's sweet face was suddenly somber. "It's dreadful for Katherine to know that Bob did such terrible things."

"Katherine says he's innocent."

Lou was sardonic. "What else is she going to say?" His face brightened. "Hey, Annie, put in a good word for me. I'm trying to persuade Jane to close down the shop, come out on my boat with me."

Jane gave him a cheerful smile. "I can go with you Sunday. I can't close down. I owe too many hours anyway."

"I'll get my sister Maggie to take over." He was determined. "She used to work at Walmart in Hilton Head. She knows how to handle a cash register." He pulled out his cell. "I'll call her right now."

Annie was surprised. Obviously the station would alert him that he no longer needed to protect Jane, but didn't he need to get back to work? She blurted out, "Don't you have to work, too, Lou?"

He gave her an impish grin. "The chief was going to have a patrol keep an eye on the shop today, but I was due a few days off so I decided to take them. Jane and my sis Angie were really good friends in high school. The least I could do."

Jane's cheeks were pink. "Isn't that sweet of Lou?"

"So" — his tone was teasing — "you owe me. I don't want to waste my time off, and boating alone is no fun. I'll get Maggie over here ASAP." He pulled his cell phone out of his pocket. "I'll step outside," he said, and he hurried toward the front door.

Annie suspected he intended to tell Maggie she had to help him out, it was big-time important.

The door closed behind him. Annie turned to Jane. "I know it's a huge relief. You can tell Tim he can relax."

For an instant, her face was still. "Oh. I suppose I should call Tim." The front door began to open. "But not right now."

Hyla Harrison reported in her usual crisp fashion. "I checked the prints we made on the screen door Tuesday. Several correspond with those left on the chair by Katherine Farley. However, they are overlain by prints from Ves Roundtree."

Billy Cameron asked quickly. "Are any Farley prints on top of other prints?"

"No, sir. I picked up fragments of her prints below Ms. Roundtree's prints."

"Are any of the prints on the screen door smudged?"

Hyla's eyes narrowed. "I would not describe them as 'smudged.' Portions of prints overlay prints but there is no indication, for example, that a gloved hand gripped the panel."

"Good work, Officer."

As the door closed behind Hyla, he faced an unpalatable truth. He had a perilous course to navigate. A buzz. He flicked on the intercom.

Mavis's voice was uninflected, but he knew she was stressed. "The mayor called again. Demands that you return his call. Now."

"Thanks." He clicked off, glanced at the clock. A quarter to five. His smile was humorless. What if he told the mayor it was quitting time and he had the weekend off and he'd get back to him on Monday? Sometimes he thought it would be nice to have a workday that started at nine, ended at five. He'd had an offer last year from an island boat builder to join his crew. For a millisecond he imagined the smell of sawdust, cutting a plank of Douglas fir to the right specifications, ending up with a hull that was seaworthy and fine. He picked up the phone, called.

There was no salutation. "You missed the press conference. I spoke with reporters an hour ago. They're here from all over. One TV crew helicoptered in from Atlanta. It would have been helpful if you'd been here. *Triple Murderer Confesses.* I told them you were busy wrapping up the case. I guess you were, though what you have to do escapes me since Farley's confessed. None of that matters now. We'll make the five o'clock news big. Very big. The message will be loud and clear. The murders were the work of one possibly deranged individual, and Broward's Rock, the loveliest sea island off the coast of South Carolina, is safe. Absolutely safe. Revelers welcome. Old ladies. Kids. Honeymooners. The arrest didn't happen a minute too soon. The PGA tournament is here next month, and for sure we don't want nationwide coverage of Murder Island. That would kill the tourist trade. You should have called and filled me in. My secretary saw the feed about Farley on TV and ran in to tell me. I'm sure you intended to keep me informed. I had to wing it from what I picked up on TV." Mayor Cosgrove's voice wasn't the mellifluous tenor known to island residents. It was clipped and sharp edged.

In the privacy of his office, Billy's face was hard, but he kept his tone pleasant. "This is a complex investigation —"

The mayor interrupted. "What investigation? The man confessed."

"People confess. Sometimes they're lying —"

The mayor broke in again, and now his voice was rough. "Don't screw this up, Cameron. The murders are solved. Period. I've already talked to the circuit solicitor. I told him you'd be in Beaufort for the arraignment Monday. Ten A.M. Be there." The phone was slammed in the cradle.

Murder Island. A reporter or newscaster must have used the phrase, and it rankled Mayor Cosgrove. His main focus was bringing visitors to the island. The more tourists, the more money in local coffers, and Cosgrove liked spending money. Billy was all for art, but he thought the town could have found a better use for money paid a local artist — young, sexy, and voluptuous — for a series of red-and-purple rectangles that now graced the harbor front and, according to the artist, represented eons past, present, and future. There had been rumors that the married mayor and the artist had a "close" relationship.

Billy yanked his mind back to business. To be fair, the mayor had a point. Bob Farley had confessed. Presto. Case solved. Island's resort reputation shiny again. The majestic reach of the law reassuringly restored.

Billy knew what the mayor expected. Wrap up the case. Get the evidence to the circuit solicitor. There was enough evidence for a charge, likely enough for conviction. Brice Willard Posey, the overbearing ham-faced posturing circuit solicitor, would love leading the charge. Lots of newspaper attention. Maybe even make the cable news. Farley might be guilty, but his car with the hitch for a wheelchair was distinctive, and careful inquiry found no witness who saw that car or a man with a cane near Adam Nash's office late Tuesday afternoon. Still, it was a gray February day, not many out and about. By Monday he needed to bring a murder charge or free Bob.

Billy leaned back in his chair. He had to find out the truth about Bob Farley.

Annie heard the ping of her cell phone, picked it up. A message to her, Max, Henny, and Laurel from Emma.

Emma: *TV running a feed on Bob: Triple Murderer Confesses. Crime spree ended. Arraignment scheduled Monday.*

Laurel: *Katherine's arranged for Handler Jones to come to the island tomorrow.*

Henny: *Fred's killer needed the strength to heave his body off the pier. Bob?*

Annie didn't chime in. What was left to say? Instead, she looked again at Laurel's text. Kind Laurel had obviously gone to the Farley house or studio, found Katherine, offered support, and was glad to learn Katherine had hired wonderful Handler Jones. Annie pushed away the memory of the night she'd entered the jail, using the code for the entry pad courtesy of Billy, and whispered in darkness to Max in his cell. Dark days. The dead days of summer. She had come so near to losing Max, because appearances can deceive and lies can endanger the innocent.

Bob Farley confessed.

Katherine claimed innocence.

Who was telling the truth?

13

Max added a new log. The fire crackled, sparks flying. Annie glanced at the flames, then at Max as he settled back on the leather sofa. He felt her glance, looked her way, smiled, then picked up his book, a new Brad Meltzer novel. Dorothy L curled beside him. He stroked her soft white fur. A contented purr rumbled loud enough for Annie to hear.

Annie had a sudden chill vision of Katherine Farley's studio. Likely it was dark now. Annie looked at the clock. A little after eight. Velvet night pressed against the windows. They hadn't drawn the curtains because they had no near neighbors. In a moment, she'd get up, put her book aside, an Alafair Tucker title by Donis Casey, and pull the cords, make the serene room even more cozy.

A distant rattle, a knock at the back door, brought Max's head up. "I'll go see."

Friends often came to the back door instead of the front. He pushed up from the sofa. Dorothy L jumped down and padded after him.

"Hey, good cat."

Annie recognized Billy Cameron's voice, came to her feet.

Billy walked to the fireplace, turned, stood with his back to the warmth. "Sorry to bother you tonight." He looked weary. His posture was straight as always, but lines grooved in his face.

Annie hurried to speak. "You are never a bother." Her voice was firm and her gaze said more. *You are our friend. We will always owe you. You know you can call on me or Max. Anytime. Anywhere.*

He understood, nodded gravely. He walked to the sofa, sat beside Max. He spoke quietly. "I find Bob Farley's confession suspicious. I may be wrong. Maybe he killed the three of them. But I've never dealt with a confessed murderer who didn't talk and talk and talk. Bob says he killed them, but that's all he'll say. No details. What time did he meet Fred on the pier? Did he hit him with his cane, stun him? How did he get him over the railing? Or did he pull the body to the opening for the ladder down to the side dock. If so, how did he have the strength to shove him past the platform? Where is Ves's body? How did she die? What time did he go to Adam's office? Why kill Adam? Why shoot at Jane Wilson? How did he miss? I checked: Bob's a sharpshooter. We estimate the bullets traveled about thirty yards before they slammed into the house. Bob Farley shouldn't miss at thirty yards. What does Bob say? Monotone: 'I killed Fred Butler, Ves Roundtree, and Adam Nash.' Period."

Max looked at him steadily. "You think he's lying."

"I do. I've done everything I can to encourage him to talk. I have one last hope." He turned to Annie. "Will you help me?"

Annie's breath caught when she reached the back steps of the station. She'd been this way only once before, the night Billy gave her the entry pad code so that she could talk to Max, alone in a cell, accused of the murder of a beautiful young woman he'd never known. As she tapped the numbers, she was grateful for the chill breeze from the harbor. It would be too much to bear if the air had been hot and heavy and sultry as it had been on the August night her life crumbled around her.

She pulled open the door, stepped into

the quiet corridor of the cell block. The ceiling inset lights were muted. She stepped inside. The door closed behind her. She walked forward.

A dimly seen figure came up to the bars of the third cell. Most visible was the blob that was Bob's white face.

Annie came even with the cell, uncertain how to begin, what to say. The words came slowly. "Katherine wants you to know she's innocent."

"How did you get in?" His head turned as he peered up and down the cement corridor.

"I know a way." If she told him Billy had given her the code, he would say nothing. Yet she was speaking truth, even if not all the truth. "When Max was arrested, a friend gave me the code to the entry pad at the back door." Billy was her friend. "I'm here because Katherine knows you are innocent."

Thin hands gripped the bars, but his face was a pale blob in the shadowy cell. "She knows I'm innocent." There was no joy in his response. Instead, there was grimness.

Annie hurried to offset the implicit assumption that Katherine's knowledge was based on her guilt. "Katherine is innocent, too. She went to Ves's house that Thursday but Ves wasn't there. Katherine went in the house and found no one there. She suddenly felt afraid and she rushed outside. She didn't know about Ves's fall until the following Wednesday."

His fingers locked tighter around the steel rods. "She told me she was making a delivery. She lied."

"She didn't tell you where she was going because you would have wanted to know why she planned to see Ves. She didn't want to tell you that she was going to ask for money. She thought Ves would help, that Ves was kind."

"Katherine wanted money for me, didn't she? Katherine never cared about money. She wanted to make things better for me. Take the cripple here and there, pretty things to see." His tone was bitter.

Annie didn't think he was bitter with Katherine. He was bitter with the fact of his injuries, his incapacity.

"Katherine loves you." Annie spoke with all her heart.

"Yes." The single word was bleak.

"She knows you're innocent. She swears she's innocent. You don't need to lie to protect her."

He spoke at a rapid clip. "The police know — or they'll find out — she was in her studio the night Fred was killed and the

303

afternoon Adam was shot. She was alone. She was in the studio when shots were fired at Jane."

"There are others who don't have alibis." Annie was sure this was a fact.

"The gun is gone." There was a note of finality in his voice.

"She threw the gun in the ocean after you went to Gurney Point."

Silence.

Annie put her heart into her voice. "Tell Billy you made a mistake."

Bob's voice was harsh. "He'll arrest Katherine."

Annie was startled. Perhaps Bob was right. Perhaps Billy believed Katherine committed the murders. Billy had a passion for justice. Would he use Annie to save Bob and then charge Katherine? Billy was tough.

"That's how it is." Bob's voice was grim. "Tell Katherine —" His hands dropped from the bars. He was tall and thin, too thin, a shadowy figure. "— I love her." He turned away, limped to the cot.

Billy always drove the speed limit. The headlights did little to pierce the pall of darkness that swathed the island at night.

Annie described the conversation. Her voice broke as she quoted Bob's final words:

304

"Tell Katherine I love her."

Billy loomed big and solid in the driver's seat. He slowed for a deer bounding across the road, picked up speed. "Bob knows Katherine. Until my dying day I'll carry with me the certainty that he's lying to save her. I don't like for perps to walk. But if she's guilty, she's built her own hell. The only thing that matters to her in life is Bob. She would live and die for him. I think she killed for him. I know murderers. They come in all stripes. People kill because of pride, fear, anger, greed, passion. Most of all, greed or passion. Some people want money or power enough to destroy any obstacle in the way. Katherine's driven by passion. She will do whatever she has to do to make Bob's life better. Now he'll go to prison. Or be executed."

Billy sat cross-legged on the floor, his little blond daughter next to him. She moved her piece and gave a shrill whoop. He threw up his hands in surrender. "You did it!" She hopped up, ran toward the kitchen. "Mommy, I won, I won!"

He folded the Chutes and Ladders board and reached for the box. He was still smiling as his cell phone rang. He glanced at caller ID, stiffened. What the hell? He swiped. "Billy Cameron."

The jacket of Billy's Windbreaker sagged from the weight of his gun. He rarely carried a gun. There shouldn't be danger. Not if the hurried words were true. Anger was hot deep inside. Billy knew the back of his neck was reddening. He drove at his usual pace, the headlight beams no match for the pool of darkness beneath overhanging tree limbs. Why Gurney Point? But the remote far north end of the island at half past nine should be inhabited only by owls, foxes, deer, raccoons. He came around the last twist in the road, glimpsed wind-bent pines but no car in the turnaround space at the end of the road. He cut the lights, glided to a stop, another twenty feet. No reason to make himself an easy target. The windows were rolled down. He listened intently, heard the soughing of tree limbs in a stiff breeze, the whoo of an owl, and, distantly, the rush of water at the base of the bluff.

He was ready to ease out through the window when he heard his name called.

"Billy, I'm over here." A flashlight flickered on, was turned up, revealing a face he knew, then the beam swept over his car.

Billy opened the door, moving fast, his hand firm on the butt of his gun.

Annie thought Billy Cameron looked tired as he held the door of his office open. Of course, he didn't usually work on Saturdays, though the police station was always in operation. This morning his shirt was crisp, his brown slacks creased, his loafers well shined, but his face was weary. Bluish shadows marked the hollows below his eyes, and there was a small spot of tape on his chin where he'd likely nicked himself shaving.

Annie moved ahead of Max, took the chair nearest the window that overlooked the bay. She glanced outside at puffy white clouds in a robin's-egg blue sky, lacy whitecaps on pea green water, and outriggers with the nets lowered on a passing shrimp trawler. Max sat in the chair next to her.

Billy closed the door, moved behind his desk.

Max was curious. "It looks like you're stuck with Bob. Will the arraignment be Monday?"

Billy settled behind his desk. "There have been some further developments. There may be an arraignment Monday. I would like to arrange a meeting at Ves Roundtree's house under your auspices, Max."

Max looked surprised. "My auspices?"

Billy spoke matter-of-factly, but his dark blue eyes stared intently at Max. "Ves contacted you, asked you to assist her the evening she invited the Farleys, Curt and Gretchen Roundtree, Jane Wilson and Tim Holt, Adam Nash, and Fred Butler to her house to inform them of her fall and to warn one of them that she had a gun and didn't intend to die."

Max nodded. "Ves wanted me there as a witness, although I wasn't the only one who helped her. She first talked to Annie. Annie drew me in and then my mom and Henny Brawley and Emma Clyde. We were all involved."

"But as far as the guests are concerned, you were there as Ves's agent."

"That's right."

"That gives you the status" — Billy sounded pleased — "to contact those with an interest in the investigation on behalf of Ves Roundtree."

Max looked bewildered, but he heard his cue. "I will be glad to do anything I can on behalf of Ves."

Billy gazed at them without expression, spoke as if thinking aloud. "Obviously, this won't be your usual Saturday evening. But I

certainly understand that you feel an obliga-
tion to Ves and have decided to contact
everyone involved and invite them to come
to Ves's home at seven o'clock tonight. Since
Ves sought your help before she disappeared, you know she would want everyone informed about the arrest and scheduled arraignment. The police are glad to
cooperate and relinquished the house key to
you as Ves's agent. You spoke with the chief
and he agreed to come and present the
facts."

Annie blurted, "What about Bob Farley?"

"He'll be there." He pushed back his chair
and stood. "The department is always eager
to work with the community."

Annie had a pen-and-ink sketch of a
champion seal point Siamese. She thought
Billy's face was similarly inscrutable. Apparently he'd told them as much as he intended
to reveal.

As they rose, he said casually, as if in
afterthought, "It might be as well to invite
Emma, Henny, and Laurel since they as-
sisted you earlier. Ask them to be there at
seven and tell them they should direct their
complete attention to the person with whom
they spoke. Let me see" — a pause as if
recalling names — "Emma spoke to Katherine Farley, Henny to Bob Farley, Laurel

to Tim Holt, Max to Curt Roundtree, and Annie to Gretchen Roundtree." His face was bland. "At a quarter after seven, I want each one of you to watch that particular individual." On that pronouncement, he moved to the door, held it open for them to step in the hall, closed it firmly.

As the Lamborghini picked up speed, Annie twisted to look back at the station. "Billy's up to something. Did you notice when he talked about watching people he left out Jane Wilson?"

"I noticed. Maybe Billy feels she's innocent because someone shot at her. But that doesn't give us any idea why he wants anyone watched. He said the arraignment is on for Monday. What's the point of getting everyone together tonight?" He shrugged. "Anyway, it's up to us to persuade people who don't want to have anything to do with the police to show up. I'll call them. You can text the Incredible Trio and invite them over for shrimp creole at six. That gives us plenty of time to explain. Not that we can explain much. Henny will have a dozen questions about our assignment to watch a particular person. Emma will probably quote from either Marigold or Inspector Houlihan. And Ma, who knows" — a quick smile — "what she will think. Or say. Anyway, we'll follow Billy's script, pretend the gathering is my idea."

Annie perched on the edge of Max's desk. It was odd to be there on a Saturday morning. Death on Demand, of course, was usually open. She'd hung the Back Soon sign in the window. It would be wonderful to have Ingrid Webb, the world's best clerk, back from her vacation Monday. Max looked comfortable in his large leather chair, holding a legal pad, making notations. He scanned what he'd written, gave her a thumbs-up, put the pad on his desk. She glanced at the index card in her hand as he punched a number, then speakerphone. She liked lists. This one was short if not sweet — Jane Wilson and Tim Holt, Gretchen Roundtree, Curt Roundtree, Katherine and Bob Farley. Not that she needed a list to remember these names. One of her favorite lines from *Casablanca* was Captain Renault's bland directive on the airport tarmac: "Round up the usual suspects."

"Don't miss our special on eyeliner today." Gretchen's voice as she answered the phone was as smooth as honey. "How may I help you?"

Max was equally smooth. "Gretchen, Max

Darling. I'm calling a meeting at seven tonight at Ves Roundtree's to bring everyone up to date on the investigations into the deaths of Fred Butler, Ves Roundtree, and Adam Nash."

"Why?" Her tone was flat, almost hostile.

Max was unruffled. "There's been a lot of loose speculation about the status of the case and some errors in television reports. However, the police have reached a conclusion and Chief Cameron has agreed to share that information."

"Do you mean we can get this all behind us? Get our lives back?"

Annie thought about three lives lost. Fred, Ves, and Adam wouldn't get their lives back.

"That's my understanding. I look forward to seeing you at seven."

"I'll be there." Gretchen's voice still held a note of anger.

Max clicked off, looked thoughtful. "She sounds innocent. I'd still put my money on her as the killer. Though" — his expression was wry — "if she was going in for homicide as well as jewel thefts, you'd think she'd take out her blackmailer." He punched a number.

"Sea Side Inn. How may I direct your call?"

"Curt Roundtree, please."

As the room telephone rang, Max lounged back in his chair. "I doubt we'll find sonny boy hunkered in his room —"

"Hello." Curt's voice was wary.

"Max Darling call—"

"Not int—"

Before he could finish, Max interrupted. "You'll be interested. The murder case will be closed tonight and the disposition of your father's estate discussed. Seven o'clock. Ves Roundtree's house." Max punched Off. "I don't much like sonny boy. And" — a huge smile — "since the call came through the switchboard, he can't call back. I doubt he has any idea about Confidential Commissions. Stew, baby, stew." Max punched a number.

"You Want It, We Have It." Jane's voice was cheerful.

"Hi, Jane. Max Darling."

"What's happened?" Now her voice was thin.

Annie understood that visceral response.

"Everything's fine. I wanted to let you know I've called a meeting of everyone who was at Ves's house that Wednesday." There was no need to explain which Wednesday. Jane would well remember the last time she saw Fred Butler. "Chief Cameron has agreed to give a final report on the crimes."

"It's over, then." Her voice was odd. "Bob Farley killed them?"

"It's over." Max said nothing about Bob.

"Ves's house? I don't know if I can bear to be there again. I'll remember Ves at her shop, those frizzy red curls and the way she had so much energy. I don't know if I can bear it."

"Please come. She'd want you to be there. Ask Tim Holt to come with you."

There was a pause. "Tim? I haven't seen him for a day or so. I told him I needed some quiet time. You can call him." She rattled off a number. "Do they know what happened to Ves?"

"I believe the chief will answer all questions."

"She was kind to my mother. I'll come."

"Seven o'clock."

"Seven o'clock." Her voice was heavy as she repeated the time.

"We'll see you then." Max clicked Off. He gave Annie a quick look. "You have a soft spot for birds who fall out of nests, even for baby alligators. I'm glad Jane's innocent." He was already punching the number.

"Tim Holt." His voice was strong and pleasant.

"Max Darling." He repeated the by-now-familiar pitch.

"I saw on TV that Bob Farley's in jail. Why meet?" He sounded puzzled and not particularly interested. Old news was old news.

"There will be some information that hasn't been released to the press."

"Yeah? Well, I'd just as soon forget about the whole thing. And Jane's sick of it."

"She's coming."

"Oh. If she said she's coming, I'll bring her."

"Thanks. We'll see you then." He clicked Off.

Annie shook her head. "I don't think Jane wants to deal with Tim." Had she told Tim she wanted some space because she was reeling from murders and Ves's disappearance and gunshots in the night? Annie remembered the sound of her voice when she answered the phone. Full of cheer. Annie had a clear picture of that moment in their kitchen when Lou looked at Jane.

But Max was staring at the phone. "One more call. This one's tough."

Annie understood. His bland come-over-to-Ves's-for-the-latest-on-the-murders spiel was a nonstarter with Katherine Farley.

"Hello." Katherine's voice was deep, brusque.

"Max Darling. As you know, I tried to help Ves when she said she was in danger.

I've arranged for the police to provide the latest information about the crimes. Everyone is coming to Ves's house at seven, and Billy Cameron will describe the results of the investigation."

"What investigation? There's no investigation. Billy's jailed an innocent man, a man obviously disturbed. But that's the easy way out, isn't it? An arrest makes the police look good. Three murders solved. Billy Cameron accepted a confession he knows is fake. He'll put Bob on trial, kill him." Her voice shook with rage. "And you want me to be there? Hear all about that dangerous killer, Bob Farley, who can barely walk with a cane, who doesn't have the strength to lift a bag of groceries. Go to hell." The connection ended.

Annie was already heading for the door. "I'll talk to her."

Max was on his feet. "Billy said for Emma to watch Katherine tonight. She may have killed all of them. I'm coming with you."

Annie stood in the doorway. "She won't see you. You're an enemy now. I'll go." She had a sudden sense of certainty. "I'll be safe."

Sometimes men made things too complicated. Annie held tight to that thought as she walked up the steps to Katherine's studio. She turned the old-fashioned brass doorknob, stepped inside. She wasn't sure why she chose the studio rather than the Farley house on its stilts with a view of the lagoon. When she was inside in the entry area, now unlit, she looked past easels and tables littered with paints and brushes and jars. Light streamed through the skylight, illuminating a cream leather sofa where Katherine sat, holding a small painting.

Annie's shoes made a hollow sound as she crossed the old wooden floor.

Katherine turned a pale, hard face. "Leave me alone."

"Bob will be at Ves's house tonight."

For an instant, Katherine sat rigid, the painting clutched in her hands. "Bob will be there?"

Annie came nearer, sat down on the sofa. "Billy doesn't think Bob is guilty. Last night he let me into the jail and I talked to Bob. I don't think he's guilty either."

Katherine's burning stare into Annie's eyes never wavered. "Billy thinks he's innocent?" There was a rising note of hope. "Why did he arrest him?"

"He hasn't actually arrested him yet. He's holding him for investigation, and he had no choice after Bob said he killed them. I told Bob you were innocent."

"Did he believe you?"

Annie wasn't sure. But she would never make that admission. "Yes, but he's afraid Billy will arrest you because you were at Ves's house that Thursday and you were out the other times. And the gun is gone."

Katherine rested the painting on her lap and pressed her hands hard against her cheeks. "Oh God, I wish I hadn't thrown it away. But I did. I threw it away before Adam was killed or someone shot at Jane. But I can't prove that's what I did."

Annie glanced down at the painting. Bob had often painted vivid splashes of color with the vigor of a carnival or swirling dancers or pulsing rhythm. This painting, an eight by twelve, was muted, the faint violet of sunrise, a hint of the ocean below, the promise of new beginning.

Katherine once again held tight to the frame as if a lifeline. "Bob's afraid for me. But he knows I'm innocent." Tears slid down her cheeks. "We have to tell Billy."

"He knows. It's Billy who wants everyone to be at Ves's house tonight. He asked Max to arrange the evening, make it look like Max was in charge. Billy has something planned. I'm sure of it. He believes Bob is innocent."

"That's all that matters." Katherine's face was still haggard but now there was hope. "Bob will be there. I'll come."

Annie hoped deep inside that she hadn't held out a hand to pull Katherine aboard a tumbrel to her destruction.

Emma sipped espresso. "Damn good. I'll have another macaroon. You're a dandy cook, Max." Emma's emerald green caftan and sandals matched the glow of the massive stone in a ring on her right hand.

"Chef," Laurel corrected. Laurel's beige cable sweater and chocolate brown slacks emphasized the golden sheen of her hair and the Nordic blue of her eyes. She took a dainty nibble of a raspberry truffle.

"Whatever." Emma waved a stubby hand, and the emerald flashed.

Henny used a spoon to retrieve the maraschino cherry from the mound of whipped cream on her cappuccino. "We are grateful to Max for a wonderful dinner and to Annie for a great dessert selection. We have dutifully refrained from talk of murder but" — she glanced at the clock — "we leave here soon to go to Ves Roundtree's house. As I understand our instructions, at precisely a quarter after seven I fasten my eyes on Bob Farley, Emma observes Katherine Farley,

Max watches Curt Roundtree, Laurel stares at Tim Holt, and Annie gazes at Gretchen Roundtree. May I ask what we are looking for?"

Max turned his hands over, palms up. "My guess is that Billy will announce something, and he wants a witness who can testify about a particular person's response."

Emma nodded sagely. "As Marigold says, *Even a clever criminal isn't always on guard.*"

Laurel put down her piece of candy, half eaten. Her dark blue eyes were grave. "I don't feel comfortable about this evening." She quoted from her chapbook, *"In rattlesnake country, watch where you step."*

Henny looked from one to another. "I share Laurel's uneasiness." She rose. "It reminds me of *Rebecca.* Foreboding, uncertainty, suspicion, a sense that life is a quicksand, insubstantial and treacherous. Perhaps tonight nothing will be what it seems to be."

14

Annie loved dancing at the country club on Saturday evenings. The music was different each Saturday night. She'd circled this date because Max loved the latest in pop, and the band was sure to play "Happy" and "Walking on a Dream." Annie wished they were on their way to dance. Instead, Max followed the now familiar route to Sunshine Lane, turned into the drive to Ves Round-tree's house.

The Lamborghini's headlights didn't dispel the gloom of the tree-shrouded drive. He pulled up behind Ves's van. Annie felt cold. The van was precisely where it had been parked when she and Billy came looking for Ves. The house was dark. Max turned off the headlights. There wasn't a glimmer of light until he opened the driver's door. He pulled a small laser flashlight from the pocket of his blazer, turned it on. He held the light until Annie stepped out and came around the car to join him.

She put a hand on his arm. "I don't like this."

The little laser beam illuminated the flagstones to the back porch, emphasized the surrounding dark, the unlit looming house. "We'll light the place up." His tone was easy.

Annie understood she was reacting to Ves's disappearance, to a sense that evil lurked. She hurried to keep up with Max. He thudded up the back steps, opened the screen door, tried several keys, found the one that fit. The door opened. More darkness. Max flipped switches, and light, wonderful, warm, glowing light, shone on the porch and in the hallway and living room and dining room. The house smelled stale. Dust dulled the surface of the marble-topped hallway table and the tall mahogany grandfather clock. Max stepped to the thermostat near the clock, tapped. The fan whirred into action.

Annie checked the time. Last spring Ves's house was included in a tour of old homes. Ves proudly recited the provenance of the antique, a Roxbury tall clock made by Simon Willard in 1795. That lovely day Ves was at her most energetic, talking fast, her reddish curls quivering as she gestured.

Now the clock was dusty and it was ten minutes before seven.

The clock chimed seven o'clock as Jane Wilson and Tim Holt, the first to arrive, came through the front door. They stopped uncertainly in the archway to the living room.

Max gestured to the far side of the room. "Sit anywhere you like."

Jane touched the scarf at the throat of a white silk blouse. The scarf, a gorgeous floral weave azure paisley, matched the blue of slim-legged wool slacks accented by white leather ankle boots. "I wish I hadn't come." Her voice wobbled.

"Hey, Jane." Tim was hearty. "We'll see what the cop has to say, then go to Whistler's for a drink."

"I don't want a drink." Her voice was still tremulous. "I want to go home."

Annie moved nearer. "Thanks for coming. We know everyone is concerned about what's happened, and now we can find out what's true and what isn't true."

Tim shrugged. "I thought everything was already definite. That crippled guy confessed. What else is there to say?" His face darkened. "I don't care if he is a cripple, I'd punch him if I had a chance." He grabbed Jane's hand. "Scared the hell out of me that night. I turned into your street and there's cop cars everywhere and somebody shot at you." He looked at her with his brows drawn, his face jutting. "But you're okay, and I won't ever let anyone hurt you. And now we can plan our wedding."

Jane gave him a quick glance. "Shh. Not in front of everybody. And you're hurting my hand."

He loosed his grip. "I get mad whenever I think about him shooting at you. He's lucky I won't be able to get my hands on him. Where is everybody? We" — he took Jane's arm again — "want to get out of here as soon as we can, do something fun." He led her to an Empire-style carved mahogany sofa, the bolstered ends upholstered in red satin with a gold medallion pattern. Jane slid close to one end, pressed against the pillows. Tim plopped next to her, bent near to murmur something. She shook her head, made no response. For an instant, his face was hard, then he again began to talk softly. The sound of his voice was warm, entreating. Her posture remained rigid and she never took her eyes away from the opening to the hall.

A rattle as someone knocked. Max pulled the front door open. Katherine stepped inside, hurried to the archway, looking quickly around the room. She whirled toward Max. "Where's Bob?"

"Billy's bringing him."

Annie felt a twist inside. So much was the same, sleek black hair in a chignon, aristocratic features, but now Katherine's face was tight and hard and her thin shoulders hunched. She wore unrelieved black — black silk blouse, black wool trousers, black leather ballet flats. No jewelry. Perhaps a dash of makeup. She surveyed the room again, her gaze cold and hostile, acknowledged no one, strode to a small settee with room for two.

Another knock, voices, steps in the hallway. Gretchen Roundtree brought with her a faint exotic scent. Her blond hair glistened and her smooth face looked confident. A pearl necklace glowed softly against a pale rose cashmere sweater. Her cream skirt was short and stylish. Curt was casual in a blue-and-yellow plaid cotton shirt, khaki slacks, and sneakers. He glanced around the room. "Where are the gendarmes?"

Max was pleasant. "Chief Cameron will be here soon."

Curt looked combative, ready for a quarrel. "I'll give him five minutes, then I'm out of here. I'm damn tired of the island, this house, and everybody here." He dropped into a wicker chair, stuck his legs out straight, bored and resentful. Gretchen shot her son an irritated glance, then her face was once again smooth. She sat in a chair near the fireplace. Her gaze moved to Katherine. Gretchen's smooth face altered for an instant. The lacquer of self-absorption was pierced by Katherine's despair. She took a tiny breath, was once again self-possessed.

The back door opened. Heavier steps sounded. And the faint tap of a cane.

Katherine came to her feet, eyes wide, lips trembling.

Billy Cameron, big and powerfully built, reached the archway. Bob Farley came up beside him. He looked frail and tired.

Annie wasn't surprised to see Billy wearing a white shirt and gray trousers and loafers, but Bob wasn't dressed in the orange jail coveralls. She remembered Marian's description as Bob came into the police station. Tonight he was wearing the blue blazer, triple-stripe dress shirt without a tie, chinos, and loafers he'd worn Friday when he confessed. Bob's hands were not manacled.

Katherine was running across the room. "Bob, oh, Bob." She wrapped her arms around him. Bob stood stiffly for a moment, then a hand lifted to gently smooth her sleek hair. He bent to rest his face against her head.

Billy watched them, his face expressionless. He cleared his throat. "If you'll take your seats now."

Katherine lifted a tear-stained face, looked into Bob's eyes. "I was afraid I'd never have you near again. Bob, please tell them the truth."

Bob pulled away. He looked around the room. "I didn't know we were coming here." He glared at Billy. "What's the point? Take me back to that damn cell. I told you I killed them."

"Bob." Katherine's cry was anguished.

There was a flash of pity in Billy's eyes.

Annie saw that look, quickly gone. She was afraid she knew what was going to happen. Billy brought Bob here, a Bob not in prisoner's clothes, a Bob without handcuffs, but Billy intended to leave with a murderer. And he felt sorry for Bob.

Katherine tugged at Bob's arm. "Bob, come with me. We'll sit over here." She pulled and slowly he moved. She held tight, pressed against his shoulder when they were seated. She paid no attention to the others, ignored the sounds from the hallway, her every sense attuned to the man beside her.

A flurry of steps in the hallway.

Max nodded a welcome as Emma, Henny, and Laurel crowded into the archway. "Good of you to come."

Emma's bellow was stentorian. "I see everyone is here. All of us are eager to find out what happened to Ves. We appreciate being included since we tried to give her a hand after her fall."

Annie noted varying looks of surprise on the faces of the assembled guests, but perhaps there was a lessening of tension. The evening was taking on the aspect of a civic meeting.

Max said quickly, "We're a little short of chairs. I'll get some from the dining room."

Emma's light blue eyes scanned the room. Henny's expression was bland, an island leader attending a public gathering, ready to contribute if called upon. Laurel's quite stunningly lovely face was dreamy, as if she might soon follow a Tibetan path to a remote hut.

Max placed dining room chairs, two on one side of the archway, two on the other. The action seemed unstudied, unplanned, simply a man making provision for more guests than a room could comfortably seat. The fact that the chairs faced the earlier arrivals seemed unremarkable.

Emma walked majestically, a sturdy block

of emerald green, to the far chair on the right of the archway. Henny slipped into the chair next to her, turned her face to speak quietly to Emma. Laurel moved as if she walked on clouds, sank into the far chair on the left and smiled at Annie as she settled beside her. Annie wondered how her mother-in-law could appear so utterly otherworldly, as if at any moment she might consult with a nightingale in flight. Max remained in the archway, Billy a little behind him.

Annie glanced at her watch. Five after seven.

"My hope tonight" — Max's tone was pleasant — "is to represent Ves Roundtree. Monday night Ves realized that Fred Butler was killed because he saw someone he knew at her house the Thursday afternoon she fell. For several Thursdays, Fred left work early, claiming a dental appointment. Instead, he came here to dig for pirate gold. He was here the afternoon the step was waxed on the staircase. Fred melted away into the woods, since he was trespassing. Fred was unaware of Ves's fall until she called a gathering here. That Wednesday was the night Fred drowned. His death was murder."

Billy cleared his throat, stepped forward.

"I'd like to take a moment here to clear up some confusion." He looked at Max. "If I may?"

"Of course." Max was agreeable.

Billy said briskly, "We want to give the circuit solicitor as much information as possible about Fred Butler, and we realized we don't have an account of his actions as he left this house the night he drowned." He turned to Max. "Who was the first person to go outside that evening?"

Annie glanced at her watch. Ten after seven.

Max shook his head. "The guests went out together. I stayed behind to ask Ves if she wanted me to spend the night, but she said she was fine as long as she had her gun."

Billy looked around the room. "Can anyone help us out here?"

Gretchen's breathy voice was disdainful. "We escaped like a herd of gazelles running from a leopard. Have you ever had anyone accuse you of trying to kill them? Good luck on who saw Fred. Who cared about Fred?" Gretchen was imperious in a Queen Anne chair near the fireplace. One hand toyed with a sapphire pendant. Her fingers were long and bony, the nails painted a deep raspberry. "It took forever to get out of here.

The drive is narrow, so we were parked behind each other. Curt and I arrived first so we had to wait until the other cars left."

"This scarcely seems worth talking about." Katherine's voice was sharp. "Fred didn't drown here. I hate talking about that night. What difference does it make when we left this hideous place? If you care, Adam stormed out first and Fred was right behind him. Jane and Tim were in front of us. We went straight to Bob's car. I think Fred was standing by his car. The shadows were pretty dark. Headlights were on but it was a black night. Once we got outside, you couldn't make out where anyone was."

"Fred's headlights were on?" Billy asked pleasantly.

"Everyone had their headlights on."

Annie's watch read thirteen after seven.

Gretchen bristled. "It took longer than it should have. Fred's car was the last in the drive. I think he was behind Adam. I almost honked."

Curt gave his mother a sly look. "You sure did. I caught your hand, reminded you there was a nutcase with a .45 in the house and to simmer down."

"Anyway" — her voice held remembered pique — "it took Fred forever."

Billy looked at Katherine. "You thought

Fred was standing by his car. Mrs. Round-tree says Fred's headlights were on. So" — Billy's tone was casual — "someone else must have been standing at Fred's window, talking to him. Who —"

The grandfather clock chimed the quarter hour. Steps sounded in the hallway.

Billy half turned toward the archway, but Max gazed into the living room to watch Curt Roundtree. Annie stared at Gretchen.

The steps stopped. Annie felt a presence in the archway, but she kept her gaze fastened on Gretchen.

Gretchen's eyes widened. Her lips parted. "Oh my God." There was shock in the suddenly slack muscles of that perfectly made-up face.

There was a melee of sound, the tone ranging from incredulity to amazement.

Ves Roundtree stepped into the living room. She might have been arriving for a chamber of commerce luncheon, a bronze turtleneck sweater, a checked wool skirt with a gather at the waist that created a cascade to one side, her signature high heels. But her face was hard and implacable.

Annie retained an indelible impression of Gretchen's initial response, utter and total amazement. Now she scanned the others.

Curt Roundtree gave a whoop. "I wish I'd

known. I'd have taken bets. Is she dead or not?"

Jane Wilson came to her feet, her face a vision of happiness. "Ves, how wonderful. You're alive." Jane began to cry.

Tim Holt looked stolid, unmoved, broad hands planted on the knees of his jeans. Katherine stood, too, hands clenched, her narrow face eager, eyes burning with light and happiness. "This proves Bob was lying. This proves he's innocent. Let him go."

Bob gripped his cane, his fingers curled on the handle. He looked up at his wife. "I was frightened for you. The gun was gone. I thought . . . I guess I was nuts. I went from thinking you'd done awful things for me to knowing you were innocent. But I was afraid they'd charge you. Because of the gun."

"I threw the gun in the water." She sank down beside him. "Don't ever leave me." He drew her close, his good arm tight around her shoulders.

Ves moved forward. She stopped a scant foot from the red Victorian sofa, looked down. "You weren't surprised when I came through the archway. Everyone was shocked. Except you. You watched me without any reaction. You knew I was alive."

Laurel was at her elbow. "No reaction at

all." Her blue eyes were stern.

Ves's voice was harsh. "You killed Fred and Adam, shot at Jane —"

A cry came from Jane.

"— but you knew you didn't kill me."

Tim Holt slowly rose, stood in front of Ves, muscular and powerful. His handsome face was amused. "I said you were nuts. That's what I told everybody. Nutcase deluxe. I don't get any of this. Asking everybody over here for what? So you can come in and accuse somebody, I guess. I'm the guy without any connections, so dump on me. I don't think so. You say I killed some people because I'm not surprised to see you. I don't give a damn where you are or if you are. You can do whatever whenever. I've had enough of this —"

Billy broke in. "Fred's cell phone had no calls that evening. His home phone had no calls. Fred took his car to the pier, met someone. How was that meeting arranged? Katherine saw someone at the window of Fred's car. It was here that he heard about the trap set for Ves. He was in the backyard, saw someone come. The night he died he looked across this room at you —"

Tim was sardonic. "Sure. Pick me. But it won't do you any good. He could have looked at anyone. Or maybe he already had a date for the pier before he came here. You can't hang this on me."

Billy continued, his voice heavy. "— and you understood that somehow Fred knew you'd been here. You didn't know Fred was looking for treasure in Ves's backyard on Thursdays. But you made up your mind to kill Fred." Billy turned to Jane, his voice deep, demanding. "Who stood by Fred's car window?"

Jane pressed her fingertips against her cheeks. Her face was tallow colored. Her blue eyes held horror and despair and sickening understanding. Shots in the night and Tim pressuring her to marry him immediately. Ves's money at the end of a dark rainbow.

Tim turned toward her. "I was with you. I didn't go up to the old geezer's car. Why would I?"

Jane slowly backed away from him, blue eyes huge in her young stricken face. Steps sounded from the hall, and Lou Pirelli was beside her, one strong arm around her shoulders. She turned, clung to Lou.

Ves's voice carried, clear, accusing, definite. *"Ecce signum."*

Annie glanced at Max and he mouthed, "Behold the proof."

Annie saw Jane's shoulders shaking. Jane

knew. Jane was in Tim's truck. Jane saw him at the window of Fred's car. Tim may have been reassuring. *Hey, Fred, you and I need to talk. I didn't wax anybody's step. I went up to the door and knocked. No answer. I left. But you and I are kind of on the spot. Let's meet on the pier. Say half an hour. We can work out our times and go to the cops. We may be able to help them.* It wouldn't have taken long to say, then return to the truck, climb up into the cab.

Jane's voice was choked. "Tim said the old geezer, he meant Fred, dropped something and he'd hurry and pick it up and take it to him. When he came back, Tim told me people were sure funny. Fred dropped a rabbit's foot and was real glad to get it back. Said it was a good luck piece."

Tim's face turned an ugly red. "Jane, they've planned this. It's a setup." He started to walk toward the archway. "I'm out of here. I'm not going to be anybody's fall guy."

Billy, big, burly, immovable, blocked him. Billy shot a quick glance at Lou, who gave an emphatic nod. There was a satisfied look on Billy's face. He spoke in a measured tone. "Timothy Holt, I am arresting you on suspicion of murder." He gave the Miranda warning, gripped Tim's arm.

Tim turned a venomous glare on Ves. "They don't have anything on me. I'll sue you. You can't get away with this."

The confident look on Billy's face assured Annie that Billy was sure he had a case, could build a case, that Tim Holt was a murderer who would face trial and Ves was safe. Billy spoke to Ves. "You did the right thing to come out of hiding."

Ves spoke slowly. "I was frightened. Annie said you'd listen, but I didn't think you would believe me when I claimed someone killed Fred. That's why I left that night. I worked it all out. I have loads of frozen food. I packed up everything I needed and took it to Rufus's house. The electricity stays on year-round because we have occasional winter renters. Next I went to the shop. I was almost well from the fall, well enough to ride an electric scooter. I got a scooter at the shop, came home, and" — a flush stained her cheeks — "I made it look like something had happened to me, the chair knocked over and blood on the doorframe." Her lips twisted. "It's easy to bleed when you're afraid you're going to die. I jabbed an earlobe. I left the door open, the lights on. I used a flashlight and took a bike path on the scooter to Rufus's house. I never turned on any lights. I used my

337

flashlight at night. I watched on the TV in the den. After Adam was shot, I felt paralyzed by fear. Then I started to wonder. Why shoot Adam? Everyone thought it was to increase the survivors' share of Rufus's estate. But I wasn't dead. I wondered if somehow Adam knew who Fred met on the pier. And I was right. Adam was in the car in front of Fred. He looked in his rearview mirror, saw Tim talk to Fred."

Tim folded his arms, his face defiant, his posture cocky. "Prove it."

Billy clicked handcuffs on Tim's wrists. "We know more than you think."

Ves had the last word. "I came back because I had to choose. *Aut vincere aut mori.*"

Max murmured to Annie, "Either to conquer or to die."

15

The place settings of hand-painted china made the dining room table elegant. Fresh gardenias in the centerpiece provided a sweet scent. Ves stood at one end of the table. "Thank you for being my friends when I needed friends."

Annie felt a glow. Ves's ivory silk dress emphasized the brightness of her red curls. Everyone looked festive, Laurel a vision of loveliness in a pale blue dress, Emma sturdy and commanding in an orange caftan reminiscent of a South Seas sunrise, and Henny regal in a high-necked velvet dress the same shade as the iris on the hand-painted china.

"I also wanted you to know that I spoke with the trustee. I can do what I wish with the corpus of the estate so long as it is distributed to some or more of the heirs who are alive during my lifetime. I thought about Rufus and those he wanted to share in his wealth. For that reason, I have provided a substantial sum to Bob and Katherine, Jane, and my nephew, Curt. All of us suffered because of Tim's greed. Money can't solve everything, but sometimes it smooths a path. And I used some of the income to reimburse the town for the search for me. And now, I'll serve —"

Emma cleared her throat. "Along that line, I wanted to say" — and her blue eyes were icy — "I don't like blackmailers." Emma's strong square face was as tough as any cowboy's boot. "Sometimes I have a soft spot for the reckless. Raffles was a good sort."

Annie pictured E. W. Hornung's famed safecracker A. J. Raffles, who smoked expensive cigarettes and wrote poetry when he wasn't stealing from the rich.

"I was thinking about Raffles the other day and happened to drop by the Perfumerie —"

Annie had difficulty imagining Emma in that haven of scent and unguents.

"— and it turned out Gretchen was most interested when I told her about my idea for a book about a blackmailer. The victim calls the blackmailer and engages in a back-and-forth about money and what will happen if a payment isn't made. The victim is recording the call. When it is concluded, the victim prints out the conversation. There is a neat technology that can do that. The victim calls again, points out possession of a recording of the incriminating call, and suggests they both walk away — unless the blackmailer is willing to go to prison." A satisfied smile.

"Reprehensible," Laurel chided, but she smiled.

Henny nodded. "I hope the recipient of your wisdom forgoes future thefts."

Ves laughed out loud. "Emma, if I ever take to a life of crime, I will consult with you first."

Helium balloons, red, yellow, and blue, bobbed on a line tethered to the coffee bar to celebrate the publication of three distinctive chapbooks. In Annie's private estimation, the three literary efforts could also be described as amazing and she would say so with a very straight face, especially in her mother-in-law's presence.

"Beer Barrel Polka" blared from the sound system in deference to Emma's new title, set at a Czech festival. Death on Demand was jammed, blue-haired ladies from book clubs, bright-eyed retired professors, male and female, island gentry, island shopkeepers, some of the regulars from Parotti's, the

Friends of the Library in full force. Of course, Emma's birthday cake, a triple decker chocolate cake with raspberry icing, had its own table.

Ingrid Webb, aided by husband Duane, manned the front cash desk. Annie and Max worked behind the coffee bar. Lines stretched from three tables set up beneath the watercolors. As Annie finished an orange slush, added a cherry to the top, she was grateful for small favors. She had seated the three authors honored tonight in alphabetical order, Henny Brawley, Emma Clyde, and Laurel Roethke. Emma *always* expected to be queen of the hill and took the center table as in the natural order of things. Henny was unpretentious and undemanding. Laurel was . . . Laurel.

Dark blue eyes perhaps spacier than usual, Laurel charmed customers, often taking a moment to gaze deeply into a buyer's eyes then speaking as if they shared a secret rapport. Annie overheard, "You remind me of a stag at sunset." The male recipient of this observation straightened his shoulders, pulled in his paunch, and swaggered away from the table with a half dozen chapbooks. To a sour-faced forty-year-old, she trilled, "I see you as a little girl. Serious but with such an impish sense of fun. Now, that is a great gift." And a miracle occurred and the sour look was replaced by a shy smile.

Emma, majestic in a swirling silver caftan and spiky hair silver as well, sported a beaded headband with a centerpiece of turquoise. The author was most amiable as she received awed tributes from adoring readers. A gruff chuckle as she modestly proclaimed, "Perhaps saying I'm better than Tey is an exaggeration. It's such a shame she wrote only eight mysteries." The implication: Poor dear can't match my one hundred and twenty. And counting.

Henny was elegant in a brown suede jacket and tan trousers and boots. She clapped her hands together in delight. "You've read Henry Calvin, too? *It's Different Abroad* is simply splendid."

Annie fixed two cappuccinos, held them out to Ben Parotti.

Ben nodded approval. "Could you shave an extra bit of that dark chocolate on top of this one?" He held a mug forward. "Miss Jolene loves your chocolate. She says she's sure it's Belgian."

Marian Kenyon slid onto a stool. "You look frazzled. Frazzled but happy. Quite a crowd. Make yourself a frappé and cool off and then I'll order."

Annie gave her an appreciative smile. "A

touch of liqueur, even over ice, and I'd curl up like Agatha and not move. Agatha's in the storeroom, draped over my computer keyboard. That's how she makes a statement. I told her wall-to-wall pays for cat food. She wasn't impressed. But I'll take a minute and fix myself a limeade."

"That sounds good. Make four for us. I hate to tell you, but it's sweat town in here tonight. That's what you get when you jam in more people than the fire code allows. I estimate almost two hundred."

Annie poured seltzer over fresh squeezed lime, added a dash of strawberry syrup, took a huge swallow.

"Great covers." Marian held up three distinctive pamphlets.

Annie agreed though there had been big changes in cover format from her original plan of shooting stars for Laurel's *Merry Musings* and titles like spokes around a wheel for Henny's *Classic Crimes*. Only the huge magnifying glass for Emma's *Detecting Wisdom* had survived. Now the warm glow of a Tiffany lamp next to a stack of books added color to a rich mahogany desk in *Classic Crimes*. *Detecting Wisdom* featured scarlet letters against a gray background and a magnifying glass tilted over a footprint. The blue letters of *Merry Musings* floated in a swirl of pink. Annie was reminded of cotton candy but immediately banished the thought as Laurel had an uncanny way of reading Annie's mind. She looked toward the third table, saw herself regarded by a mildly inquiring gaze. *Not cotton candy. NOT cotton candy.* An abstract of a flamingo. That was it. *Flamingo, Laurel, flamingo.*

"Annie?"

She looked at Marian.

"I lost you there for a minute. Take several deep breaths. Gulp some more sugar and take your time to make our limeades. I'll bring you up to date on the jerk." Marian now referred to Tim Holt in all contexts, except in print, as the jerk. As she'd told Annie, outrage lifting her voice, "What kind of creep shoots at a girl, even if he misses, to bully her into marriage? Not because he cared about her. All he cared about was her portion of Rufus's estate." Marian's dark eyes glittered with malice. "Cocky is as cocky does. That's what Billy always says about perps. Would you believe they found the murder gun, the slugs match the ones in Adam's body, hidden in Holt's truck? They did. Damn near had to take it apart but they found it. And with fingerprints, no less. That was announced this morning. And" — she chortled — "I love it that the gun was found by Lou Pirelli. He's a truck nut. Has an old one he tinkers on all the time. He knew where to look and how to look." As Annie made limeades, Marian's restless gaze roved among the crowd. "Speaking of. There's Lou with Jane. Lou's got a good head. He won't press her. He'll take his time, make life fun for her again, and one of these days, they'll be Mr. and Mrs. Lou Pirelli. They're looking at the paintings. Here they come."

Annie put the last limeade on the counter.

Jane wormed through the crowd, Lou close behind her. She lifted her voice. "This is such a wonderful evening. I was looking at the watercolors."

"She knows all of them." Lou spoke with pride. "Her mom loved those books."

Jane's blue eyes held happy memories. "*The Man in the Brown Suit* by Agatha Christie, *The Black Goatee* by Constance and Gwenyth Little, *Murder's Little Sister* by Pamela Branch, *The Affair at Royalties* by George Baxt, and *The Shanghai Union of Industrial Mystics* by Nury Vittachi."

CHAPBOOKS

Classic Crime by Henny Brawley
The Circular Staircase (1908) **by Mary Roberts Rinehart, 1876–1958**

Mary Roberts Rinehart was among the earliest mystery authors to include humor and a female protagonist. Her books reflect their times. Women wore hats. An unchaperoned single woman spending the night with a man was unthinkable. Rinehart was at one time the highest paid author in America. She was the first woman war correspondent to reach No Man's Land in France in WWI. She loved America's West and championed Indian tribes then in desperate straits.

The Thirty-Nine Steps (1915) **by John Buchan, 1875–1940**

Buchan's hero Richard Hannay is a gentleman adventurer — brave, stalwart, always understated in the finest British tradition. Buchan, 1st Baron Tweedsmuir, was once described as a man of unintimidating gay alacrity and a warmth of companionable charm. One of his sons said a few years after his death: "Everything at home sprang into cheerful new life the moment my father entered the front door."

The House Without a Key (1925) **by Earl Derr Biggers, 1884–1933**

Debut of Honolulu detective Charlie Chan, a wise and philosophical man with a gift for insightful comments. A fascinating return to the Hawaii of the '20s and a fine introduction to Chan's understanding of the nuances of Eastern and Western attitudes. Chan is a fully realized character in the novels, unlike his depiction in movies.

The Murder of Roger Ackroyd (1926) **by Agatha Christie, 1890–1976**

Christie delighted in taking advantage of unconscious assumptions made by readers. She employs this technique as well in *Crooked House* and *Death on the Nile.* Discover her humor and charm in the autobiographical *Come, Tell Me How You*

Live, a lively account of the daily routine on one of her husband Max Mallowan's archaeological digs.

Gaudy Night (1935) by Dorothy L Sayers, 1893–1957

An elegant exploration of the balance between love and independence, and a fascinating portrait of university life, its passions, prejudices, and sometimes, pain. Sayers was a remarkable woman for her time or any time, brilliant, clever, inventive, and fiercely independent.

Ming Yellow (1935) by John P. Marquand, 1893–1960

Marquand's literary novels explored the world of wealth and status. He received a Pulitzer for *The Late George Apley.* In a different vein entirely were the Mr. Moto novels, where the wily Japanese agent's efforts involved American adventurers. The early titles provide an understanding of China and Japan in the 1930s, and they are great fun.

Fer-De-Lance (1934) by Rex Stout, 1886–1975

The first Nero Wolfe and an introduction to the famous fictional brownstone on West 35th Street. While testing commercial beers, and to his amazement finding one acceptable, Wolfe says: ". . . a pessimist gets nothing but pleasant surprises, an optimist nothing but unpleasant." Wolfe and his assistant, Archie Goodwin, the narrator, unfailingly provide superb entertainment.

The Case Is Closed (1937) by Patricia Wentworth, 1878–1961

When all hope is lost, call on London's most unusual private enquiry agent, Miss Maud Silver. A man is accused of murder, convicted, and is now in prison, but his wife and her cousin believe in his innocence. Only Miss Silver can use her perception and guile to save him. Miss Silver often knits bootees for babies and is likely to quote Alfred, Lord Tennyson: "And trust me not at all or all in all."

Cause for Alarm (1938) by Eric Ambler, 1909–1998

A preview of the clash of fascism and democracy in WWII. Ambler revealed the dark heart of fascism in several of his 1930s thrillers. After the war Ambler became a successful screenwriter as well as a novelist. He had a talent for comedy, and *The Light of Day* (1962) chronicles a hapless rogue hero in desperate trouble in Greece and Germany. It was made into a movie entitled *Topkapi*.

Rebecca (1938) by Daphne Du Maurier, 1907–1989

One of the great opening lines in fiction: "Last night I dreamt I went to Manderley again." The tone captures the foreboding and unease that permeate the story of a second wife who lives in the dead Rebecca's shadow. Brilliant. A haunting novel about love and jealousy and cruelty. The author said of her work: "a sinister tale about a woman who marries a widower." Du Maurier's novels were often tinged with a horror that lingers in a reader's mind.

Above Suspicion (1941) by Helen Mac-Innes, 1907–1985

The adventures of a husband and wife team of amateur spies looking for an anti-Nazi spy in pre-WWII Europe. The background is based on MacInnes's journal entries while on her honeymoon in Bavaria and the darkening cloud of war that was fast approaching. Her husband, scholar Gilbert Highet, served in British intelligence in WWII.

The Norths Meet Murder (1940) by Frances and Richard Lockridge. Frances, 1896–1963. Richard, 1898–1982.

Frances and Richard Lockridge used their skills as reporters to create the Pam and Jerry North series, distinguished by Pam's intuitive leaps and Jerry's steadying influence. The Norths are among the early cool couples in mysteries, and the martini-bright style was influenced by sketches Richard wrote for the *New Yorker.*

Drink to Yesterday (1940) by Manning Coles, Pseudonym of Cyril Henry Coles, 1899–1965, and Adelaide Manning, 1891–1959

The first of the Tommy Hambledon British agent novels. Coles served in British intelligence in WWI and WWII, and Manning worked in the War Office in WWII. They also created four entertaining ghost novels, including *Brief Candles* and *Happy Returns,* about two cousins, one American and one British, who died in the Franco-Prussian War and return to help a modern-day descendant.

The Fog Comes (1941) by Mary Collins, 1908–1979

Murder in an upper-class family in fog-shrouded Northern California. Collins wrote six mysteries in the 1940s with intelligent, independent women protagonists. Each is a stand-alone and all are absorbing. Her last novel was *Dog Eat Dog* in 1949.

The Hollow Chest (1941) by Phoebe Atwood Taylor Writing as Alice Tilton, 1909–1976

Taylor was famous for her Codfish Sherlock, Asey Mayo, but under the Tilton name she wrote comic mysteries about professorial Leonidas Witherall. The spitting image of Shakespeare, he was known to friends as Bill. *The Hollow Chest* is a rollicking read with unexpected twists on every page. Tilton's books during the war years, such as *File for Record* (1943), depict the home front during WWII, from gas rationing to air raid sirens to junk drives.

Great Black Kanba (1944) by Australian Sisters Constance and Gwenyth Little. Constance, 1889–1980. Gwenyth 1903–1985.

Their only mystery set in Australia, a murder-struck journey across Australia by train. All but one of their books included *Black* in the title. The Little books were wacky tales with macabre twists and a laugh a page. Another favorite is *The Black Goatee* (1947). In the postwar housing crunch, desperate house hunters steal silently into the unused wing of a home to find homicide instead of comfort.

The Franchise Affair (1949) by Josephine Tey, 1897–1952

A chilling tale that shows how easy it is to enmesh the innocent with false accusations. The village turns against a mother and daughter accused of kidnaping a teenager, but the lawyer they seek believes in them. Tey's novels were imaginative and unusual.

The Chinese Chop (1949) by Juanita Sheridan, 1906–1974

The first novel to star writer Janice Cameron and her soon-to-be friend and champion Lily Wu. Three subsequent novels are set in 1950s Hawaii, when much of old Hawaii still existed. Juanita Sheridan was as adventurous as any of her fictional heroines. She wed often, traveled far, and claimed that her maternal grandfather was killed by Pancho Villa.

Man Running (1948) by **Selwyn Jepson, 1899–1989**

The first Eve Gill novel. During WWII, Jepson was a recruiting agent for SOE in Britain. He believed, despite his superiors' objections, that women made excellent agents, because the strong ones possessed a cool courage and could work alone. Winston Churchill gave him the authority to recruit women. Jepson's respect for women is reflected in his creation after the war of supercool Eve Gill as a protagonist in six imaginative tales.

Murder's Little Sister (1958) by **Pamela Branch, 1920–1967**

Disheveled, irascible *You* editor Sam Egan implores his staff: ". . . as a team let's have a stab at Misadventure, mm? If some swine's found a clue, we gradually introduce Suicide. Soft pedal it. Nothing of interest to a lurking journalist. Nothing definite, nothing chatty, nothing squalid. Remember, we don't want suicide and I absolutely refuse to have Murder." Pamela Branch entertains from the first page to the last. There are a great many clever mysteries, but few reach the heights of creativity and nonsense spun by Branch.

Killer's Wedge (1959) by Ed McBain, 1926–2005

The first in his magnificent 87th Precinct novels, the finest police procedurals ever penned. Police work is rendered accurately, with characters as real as the cop next door. In this superb book, life and death hang in the balance and tension ratchets to a tumultuous finale.

My Brother Michael (1959, 1960) by Mary Stewart, 1916–2014

The first sentence: "Nothing ever happens to me." An intelligent, intriguing woman is drawn into an adventure set against a background delineated with grace and precision. Mary Stewart is deservedly compared to the Brontës. Stewart's prose shines with erudition and charm.

Dance Hall of the Dead (1973) by Tony Hillerman, 1925–2008

Tony Hillerman grew up in Sacred Heart, Oklahoma, and attended an Indian boarding school for eight years, his introduction to a different culture. Warm, kind, and wise, Hillerman's mysteries, set in the Four Corners, depict the consciousness of Navajo and Zuni tribes. Hillerman titled his autobiography *Seldom Disappointed* (2001) in a tribute to his mother's dictum: "Blessed are those who expect little. They are seldom disappointed."

Crocodile on the Sandbank (1975) by Elizabeth Peters, 1927–2013

Mystery author JoAnna Carl takes a copy of *Crocodile on the Sandbank* to hospitalized friends, saying if that didn't make them feel better, nothing would. This first in the series featuring Amelia Peabody, a Victorian archaeologist in Egypt, entertains, educates, and delights. Elizabeth Peters (archaeology-trained Barbara Mertz) also wrote as Barbara Michaels.

Death in Zanzibar (1983; Originally Published in 1959 as the *House of Shade*) by M. M. Kaye, 1908–2004

Kaye's military husband was posted to various exotic locales, which she used as backgrounds for many of her suspense novels. Her most famous novel is *The Far Pavilions* (1978), an epic novel of British-Indian history. Kaye was born in India and educated in England, but her ties to India were deep and lasting.

DETECTING WISDOM
BY EMMA CLYDE

Observations by sleuth Marigold Rembrandt and Inspector Houlihan:

MARIGOLD: A scared rat has sharp fangs.

MARIGOLD: If a woman thinks all she has is her body, life will treat her that way.

INSPECTOR HOULIHAN: Sex or money. Money or sex. If it's money and sex, all hell breaks loose.

INSPECTOR HOULIHAN: Don't hesitate to be tough.

MARIGOLD: Avoid mean streets. If you can't, be prepared.

MARIGOLD: Casual conversation has been the undoing of many.

MARIGOLD: How sweet it is when the good guy has more firepower than the perp.

MARIGOLD: If you have a secret, keep it.

INSPECTOR HOULIHAN: A good cop always has your back.

MARIGOLD: Pride is the serpent inside you.

INSPECTOR HOULIHAN: Everybody lies. It's up to us to figure out which lies matter.

MARIGOLD: In a tight spot, stare down your accuser.

MARIGOLD: A bad dream is your subconscious knocking on the door of a closed mind.

INSPECTOR HOULIHAN: Never take anything for granted.

MARIGOLD: Charm often disguises a weak character.

INSPECTOR HOULIHAN: Sex can make a man into a damn fool. Ditto for a woman.

MARIGOLD: Even a clever criminal isn't always on guard.

MARIGOLD: Watch out for wide eyes, a charlatan counterfeiting sincerity.

INSPECTOR HOULIHAN: Accepting a favor is the first step to corruption.

MARIGOLD: A man who cheats on his wife or a woman who cheats on her husband will cheat you, too.

MARIGOLD: When a perp panics, anything can happen.

INSPECTOR HOULIHAN: Listen for words that aren't spoken.

MARIGOLD: Self-absorption is the armor of the wicked.

MARIGOLD: The imps of hell clap their

hands in delight when you e-mail in
haste.

INSPECTOR HOULIHAN: Let people talk.

MARIGOLD: There are many different ways
to tell the truth.

MERRY MUSINGS, MODEST MAXIMS FOR HAPPINESS

BY LAUREL DARLING ROETHKE

Happiness comes from giving, not taking.

Catch a falling star before it knocks you
flat.

Indulge a friend's weakness for trite
pronouncements.

Sufficiency for one is deprivation for
another.

A cheater never knows the satisfaction of
earning a win.

The prize isn't power, wealth, or privilege.
The prize is love, which can't be forced,
bought, or inherited.

A dog loves you because you are you.

Laughter lifts hearts.

It never hurts to ask.

Life is a cancan so kick as high as you can.

Everyone is important or no one is
important.

Be kind.

In rattlesnake country, watch where you
step.

Each person has a story.

A faraway train whistle tugs at our hearts.

A cat on politics: Nonsense will only be tolerated if seasoned with catnip.

A dog on politics: Will vote for bone.

Life is hard for everyone.

Is it true? Is it fair? Is it honest?

Listen for the distant laughter of angels.

Look for the saints among us.

God's gifts to us: a sunrise, the scent of the sea, snowflakes, a smile.

On a cold, gray day, imagine a July afternoon and the feel of sand beneath your feet as you walk on the beach.

Always wonder why.

If an elephant's in the way, find another path.

Of course there are unicorns.

A seashell is like a memory. The life is gone. The beauty remains.

Smile first.

ABOUT THE AUTHOR

Carolyn Hart is the *New York Times* best-selling author of more than fifty novels of mystery and suspense, including the Death on Demand mysteries and the Bailey Ruth Ghost mysteries. Her books have won multiple Agatha, Anthony, and Macavity awards. She's also been honored with the Amelia Award for significant contributions to the traditional mystery from Malice Domestic, and was named a Grand Master by the Mystery Writers of America. One of the founders of Sisters in Crime, Hart lives in Oklahoma City, where she enjoys mysteries, walking in the park, and cats. She and her husband, Phil, serve as staff — cat owners will understand — to brother and sister brown tabbies.

The employees of Thorndike Press hope you have enjoyed this Large Print book. All our Thorndike, Wheeler, and Kennebec Large Print titles are designed for easy reading, and all our books are made to last. Other Thorndike Press Large Print books are available at your library, through selected bookstores, or directly from us.

For information about titles, please call:
(800) 223-1244

or visit our website at:
gale.com/thorndike

To share your comments, please write:
Publisher
Thorndike Press
10 Water St., Suite 310
Waterville, ME 04901